THE BALM OF GILEAD TREE

ALSO BY ROBERT MORGAN

FICTION

The Blue Valleys

The Mountains Won't Remember Us

The Hinterlands

The Truest Pleasure

Gap Creek

POETRY

Zirconia Poems

Red Owl

Land Diving

Trunk & Thicket

Groundwork

Bronze Age

At the Edge of the Orchard Country

Sigodlin

Green River: New and Selected Poems

Wild Peavines

NONFICTION

Good Measure: Essays, Interviews, and Notes on Poetry

The Balm
of Gilead Tree

NEW AND SELECTED STORIES

Robert Morgan

GNOMON

The author would like to thank the following publications where most of the stories first appeared: "Little Willie" in *Above Ground,* Xavier University Press, edited by Thomas Bonner, Jr. and Robert E. Skinner; "Sleepy Gap" in *Carolina Quarterly;* "The Balm of Gilead Tree," "The Ratchet," and "A Taxpayer & A Citizen" in *Epoch;* "Murals" in *Greensboro Review;* "Kuykendall's Gold" in *South Carolina Review;* "Dark Corner" and "The Tracks of Chief de Soto" in *South Dakota Review;* "The Welcome" in *War, Literature and the Arts.*

"A Brightness New & Welcoming," "1916 Flood," "Pisgah," and "Tail-gunner" first appeared in *The Blue Valleys* (1989); "The Bullnoser," "Death Crown," and "Poinsett's Bridge," first appeared in *The Mountains Won't Remember Us* (1992). Reprinted by kind permission of Peachtree Publishers, Ltd.

"Poinsett's Bridge" was reprinted in *New Stories from the South,* 1991; "Death Crown" was reprinted in *New Stories from the South,* 1992; "Dark Corner" was reprinted in *New Stories from the South,* 1994; "The Balm of Gilead Tree" was reprinted in *New Stories from the South,* 1996 and in *Prize Stories: The O. Henry Awards,* 1997.

I have been privileged to work with four splendid editors: Susan Thurman, Ellen Wright, Shannon Ravenel, and Duncan Murrell. Special thanks to Michael Koch, Lamar Herrin, Jonathan Greene, and Robert West for their enduring support.

Cover illustration: "Balsam Poplar" from *A Natural History of Trees of Eastern and Central North America* by Donald Culross Peattie. Illustration copyright © 1950 by Paul Landacre, renewed 1977 by Joseph M. Landacre. Reprinted by arrangement with Houghton Mifflin Company. All rights reserved. *Balm of Gilead* is one of this tree's common names. Special thanks to Jeffery Beam for finding the cover illustration.

LCCN 99-73466

ISBN 0-917788-73-7

PUBLISHED BY GNOMON PRESS, P.O. BOX 475,
FRANKFORT, KY 40602-0475

CONTENTS

The Tracks of Chief de Soto

POV   1st person, Native American girl
Flat, emotionless tone

THE YEAR THE HAIR-FACES came to our village we heard
about them long before they reached our valley. Runners
from Saluda and Pumpkintown, who carried the word to the
council house, and hunters coming back from battles with the
Catawbas, brought the news of a strange tribe marching
across the flat lands. No one believed the stories, for no one
believed men would travel so far without women. The chief of
the hair-faces rode on a large dog, they said, and wore a shirt
that shone like water. The hair-faces did not have women,
they said, but used men from tribes they had conquered as
women, to bear their tents and supplies. We wondered if the
hair-faces had parts like other men, or were different under
their shining clothes.

According to the stories, the hair-faces did not hunt deer or
other game, but drove with them through the woods a vast
herd of bears that squealed and grunted. Each day they killed
another bear for their meals.

It was the moon of new leaves. The leaves on the oaks were
the size of squirrel ears. The frost was gone from the valley,
though higher on the ridge the dew froze white as feathers in
the night. We always planted first in the Blood Soil Field near
the valley's head because that ground was hidden by trees and
the mountain from cold wind. I liked that field the most

because it was the first we seeded each year. I was tired of the long winter, of eating old corn and half-dried squash.

First we burned the stalks and brush from last year, like singeing the pin feathers from a plucked turkey. I brought a flaming stick from the lodge and set the dry stalks ablaze. It was a clear cool day, and fire leaped and crackled from brush to brush, popping and hissing as it touched wet roots. The stalks said the death chant of the old year, my mother said. And the smoke blessed the new season. The stalks smoked their peace and friendship with the next crop.

The flames leapt almost high as the trees, talking to the cool sky in chants and stories of past summers. It was just past the time of the full moon, and the smoke rose up at evening with the moon. Corn planted on the full moon would grow tree-high, all stalk and little ear. Corn planted on the dark of the moon would be all root and leaves. The waning half-moon was the perfect time, when the moon was shaped more like a seed of corn.

After the field was burned, the dirt was powdered with ashes and soot. I took my stone hoe and raked the soil fresh. I raked away the rocks and broke the crust that had set from winter rains. I raked hills round as baskets. I hoed the dirt until it was smooth as corn meal and crumbled like maple sugar. The top of each hill I made level as a ball-playing ground. I knew the soil would bless the corn if I scratched and caressed it. I took away each stick and pebble.

"You don't have to make the soil pretty," my mother said. But she knew I liked to get the hills smooth as a deerskin before planting. "How the soil looks won't matter to the corn," she said.

"It matters to the earth," I said. "And the earth will bless the corn."

For planting we had saved the best ears from the baskets

2

and bins. The longest and straightest ears were wrapped in deerskin and put aside after harvest.

"Each ear is a little man," my friend Cricket said, and held up a long bright ear.

"Or a very big man," I said, and laughed. We shelled the corn into baskets by rubbing the ears together. The seeds flashed like little flames in the sun.

In the Blood Soil Field the ground heats up by afternoon, even at planting time. Out of the wind there, you can warm up and drowse. I sat in the dirt punching seeds into the hills. I stuck my finger into the red soil to bury each seed we dropped. I could feel the sun on my back and in my hair. I took down my dress and let the sun warm my shoulders and breasts. It had been a long cold winter.

"You will need to hurry," my mother said.

The sun warmed the back of my head and made me float. I wanted to sit still and dream. The sun behind my head pulsed and grew purple as twilight.

But the ground was cold just under the surface. When I pushed the seeds in, my fingers got cold at the tip. I put my hands on my knees to warm them. We wanted to get the corn planted that day before the moon waned further. Corn planted too late got buried in weeds and grass by mid-summer. Early corn outgrew the weeds and reached up in the sun ahead of everything. A little hoeing around the hills to keep away morning glories was all that would be needed.

I had heard a many-voices bird calling from the oak trees. I listened for its songs, but some boys were climbing trees at the lower end of the field. They played war all day and shouted warnings and threats from the trees, so we didn't notice at first. They climbed up the trees like scouts who watch for the Iroquois or Creeks approaching.

"They're coming," we heard Blue Stone's son yell again

and again. We ignored them until a boy ran along the edge of the field. No male is supposed to touch the ground at planting time, or the blessing on the field will be canceled.

"They're coming," the boy said.

"Get away," my mother said. "You'll bring bad medicine."

"They're coming," the boy cried.

Chief Flying Squirrel and the men had left to hunt in the east and fight the Catawabas before the full moon. They would not be back for at least another day, and only women and children were left in the village.

I looked down the valley, and there was a man, taller than any man I had ever seen, walking up the trail. Then I saw he was tall because he sat on a large dog. He wore a shining hat shaped like a snail. A long knife was tied to his waist, and he carried a pole with a colored skin flapping at the end. Just as the stories had said, he had hair on his face, long, black and curling hair.

Behind him came a line of other hair-faces, riding on big dogs. And behind them still more walked and carried long sticks. Some wore hides and some wore pieces of shining cloth. Their clothes were torn from walking through briars and thickets.

"Let's run into the woods," I said.

"No, we'll see if they plunder our town," my mother said.

Behind the men with poles walked men in black gowns, as many as the fingers on one hand. They carried beads and held black leather boxes in their hands. They all came marching right up the trail and through the edge of Blood Soil Field. The big dogs stepped on our hills of corn.

And then we saw behind the men in black a woman with the hair-cut of a Creek. Her hands were tied together and she carried a carved chest. A hair-face led her by a rope tied to her neck. She ignored us as she passed. From the white doeskin and beadwork she wore, we knew she was a chief's daughter. Her feather cape was made with orange and red and blue feathers.

Behind the princess walked a line of men bound with bright collars round their necks. They carried leather packs on their backs. Though most were naked, some still wore the paint and cloth of Appalachees. All stooped under their heavy burdens. That was the strangest sight of all, to watch the Appalachee men do women's work while bound in ropes.

And behind the bearers came the herd of bears we'd been told about. Their fur was thin and stiff as an oppossum's, and their noses flat at the end. There must have been more than the fingers on both hands times the fingers on both hands. They had large drops of sweat on their noses. They pushed each other and pawed the dirt and stuck their noses into weeds. Hair-faces with long sticks ran along beside the bears and whipped their backs. The bears smelled different from other bears.

Pigs?

They drove the bears right through the Blood Soil Field, trampling our rows. "Look at the seeds," I said, running to one of the hair-faces and pointing to the hills we had planted. He swung his stick and stung me with the leather string at the tip. I pulled my dress up over my shoulders. I had forgotten I had taken it down in the warm sun.

We followed the procession to the village, curious to see what the hair-faces did. I thought again of running away into the woods. But I had to see what the strange men wanted.

When we got to the village center the first man stepped down from the big dog. He stood on the mound in front of the council house, and the Creek woman stood beside him. Her hands were still bound, and she held the little carved chest.

The tall hair-face addressed us. He took off his shining hat, and as he spoke the Creek woman said his meaning in the words of ordinary people. "I am Chief de Soto," he began. "I have been sent by a greater chief over the water to make friends with your chief. I come in peace."

The hair-face waited for the Creek woman to change his words into human language. He looked around the square of the village. The men in black dresses stood beside him.

"I claim all these mountains for my great chief," he said.

One of the men in black dresses opened his leather box and turned the white leaves inside. As he looked at the white leaves he said other words the Creek woman did not repeat. Then he looked up at us and moved his hand up and down and level with the horizon.

"I am looking for the bright rocks," the chief hair-face said. He took a stone out of a pouch and held it up to glitter in the sun. "I have been told there is a city of bright rocks in these mountains," he said. "You will show me where the city is, and you will show me where to dig for more shining rocks."

He stopped and looked inside the council house, and up and down the length of the village. Even the dogs and children had gathered to listen to him.

"Where is your chief?" he said.

No one spoke. No one knew what to say to the hair-faces. No one had the authority to speak for Chief Flying Squirrel to the great Chief de Soto. Since the hair-faces did not understand ordinary words we would have to speak to the Creek woman.

"You don't have to talk," Chief de Soto said. "But you will have to work. You can work with the Appalachees. You will dig for the bright rocks."

The Creek woman spoke without looking at us. It seemed she was the wife of the Chief de Soto. She held the carved chest, and Chief de Soto opened it. Inside were pearls, huge shining pearls. Each pearl was worth a chief's price. The Chief de Soto held up a large shining pearl. "If you help me find the bright rocks," he said. "I will give you each a pearl."

A gasp ran through the crowd. We gathered closer to the Creek woman to ask questions. We had never seen so much wealth as the little carved chest held. My mother asked her where the pearls came from. The Creek woman said her name was Ocala, and that she was captured by the Chief de Soto near the big water. She had brought the chest of pearls to him as a peace offering when he came to her village. But he captured her and made her his wife and prisoner, and his word-cook in the places they marched to. That was the story she told us.

Each hair-face took a woman for his wife. Some took two or three, and some kept trading to get the woman that suited them. I was claimed that evening by an older hair-face. I was little more than a skinny girl myself, and he had gray hair both on his face and head. But he was bigger than the other hair-faces, and some kind of chief himself. He saw me standing in the square and came and put his hand on me. I stepped back but my mother pushed me forward. At that time I had only counted the moons of blood on the fingers of both hands.

We brought the hair-faces squash and turkey meat, and bread made of chestnuts. They sat in the council house, where the sacred flame burned, and on the mound in front of the council house. If they were gods they still ate like men. They ate like we ate on feast days. They ate until they belched and broke wind.

They brought into the council house a great pot of wood, and drank bowls of red water from the vessel. It was not like water sweetened with maple sugar, and it was not water flavored with sweet nuts. The woman named Ocala said it was the juice of berries changed into medicine. The hair-faces drank from the great pot every day, and the red water made them happy and lazy.

The hair-face who claimed me made me stand behind him in the council house and serve him bread and turkey. I tried to say that women were not allowed in the council house on ordinary days, but he ignored me. The Creek woman told me his name was Menendez. He was a chief, but not the great chief. He served the great Chief de Soto.

"Purple Grass," I told her I was called. I was named for the purple mark under my breast which was shaped like a blade of purple branch grass. "Purple Grass," I told her to tell Menendez, but I'm not sure he understood.

After the hair-faces ate they drank more from the big pot. The pot was like a round wooden basket. They sang and got in quarrels, and the black dressed men stood up and spoke. The Creek woman told us they spoke about the Chief Spirit who loved us and had sent them to us with a message. I listened to learn what the message was. I never was sure, except that we were supposed to love the Chief Spirit and do what the black dressed men wanted.

The hair-face named Menendez would not let me leave him. After it was dark, and after he had eaten and sung, he led me out into the night. I guessed he wanted to go to our living house to sleep, or to his tent at the edge of the village. I showed him the way to our lodge, but in the dark he did not see me point. He pulled me into the first lodge we came to, which belonged to Blue Stone. Blue Stone was away hunting with the other men, and his wife was at the square. Blue Stone's children ran out into the night as we came in.

When he took off his shining coat and long leather moccasins I saw the hair-face was built as other men. He had hair not only on his face, but on his chest and even on his back. He had much curly hair around his private parts. I almost laughed when I saw the curly hair down there like the hair of a dog.

I believe the hair-face had not had a woman for many sleeps. He trembled like a buck when I took off my dress. His eyes glittered in the firelight of Blue Stone's lodge. He seemed hot as though sick with a fever. He did not mate with me from behind, but made me lie down and rolled on top of me. The hair on his face scratched my ear and neck.

Emotional detachment

While I lay under the hair-face I thought of the corn that was still unplanted. Two more days and it would be too late for the half moon. The Blood Soil Field would be bare, and would then grow up in weeds. And next winter the grain bins would be empty. It seemed stranger than I can tell to be lying with a hair-face in the night, giving and receiving pleasure. But I ached because the cornfield was unplanted. The Blood Soil Field would lose its blessing. And the soil would take revenge for our neglect. Next day I would tell the hair-face we must plant the corn before the moon waned further.

But the next morning the hair-face Menendez slept late, and I was afraid to leave him and go to the field. I should have been working by the time the sun rose. But I stayed in Blue Stone's lodge. The hair-face had thrown his cloak over me, and I was afraid to slip away. I thought of the field unsmoothed, unseeded, and watched the hair-face sleep.

But we did not go to the Blood Soil Field later that day. When all the hair-faces woke they gathered the women and children in front of the council house. The Appalachee men stood in ropes beside the men in black dresses. The great Chief de Soto held up a shining rock and said we must look for more. The Creek woman said we must show the hair-faces where to dig for more shining stones. We must dig out baskets and pots full of the stones. She said the great Chief de Soto

9

had been told by the Appalachees there was a city of shining stones in the mountains. He had taken the warriors hostage until he found that city. So far he had only found villages like our village. He would take us hostage unless we told him where the city of shining stones was.

My mother told the Creek woman to tell the great Chief de Soto he should go across the mountains to Birdtown or Foxtown. Maybe he would find the town of shining stones there on the west-washing river. Ocala told the great Chief de Soto, but he laughed and said he'd heard the shining stones were in our town. Unless we showed him where the shining rocks came from he would kill us all. But if we showed him many baskets and pots of shining rocks he would give us each a pearl from the chest.

When we found a shining stone it was always in Shooting Arrow Branch, up near the head of our valley. My mother pointed up the valley and said that's where the shining rocks were found. But they were found in the streambed, not by digging. They were the tears of the sun, dropped in grief when the sun went dark in the middle of the day. The shining rocks could sometimes be found in rattlesnake dens, she said. But our agreement with the rattlesnake forbade us to dig into their dens. Long ago our people made a pact with the rattlesnake, agreeing to never dig into their dens or kill them as long as they gave us fair warning with their tails before they bit. The rattlesnakes especially liked the tears of the sun.

When the Creek woman told the great Chief de Soto my mother's words he laughed again. He said he was not afraid of any snake. He said it was the duty of men to kill all snakes, since snakes were bearers of evil spirits.

The hair-faces gathered us together and marched us all up the valley to Shooting Arrow Branch. As we marched I thought of Blood Soil Field lying empty in the warm sunlight.

The top of the burned and raked ground would harden into a crust in a few days. And before another moon weeds would darken every spot of the field. And when it rained the soil would bleed away like the life inside an unmarried woman.

When we got to Shooting Arrow Branch the sun was just warming the deep valley. The hair-faces asked my mother where the shining rocks had been found. The Creek woman asked at what place they should dig to find more shining rocks. But my mother said there was no one place the stones could be found. The stones might be anywhere in the stream, in the gravel, on the bottom, in mud along the side.

"If you don't tell us where the shining rocks are," the great Chief de Soto said, "we will kill one of your people."

When the Creek woman told her those words my mother looked back at the rest of us, and then she marched along the bank of Shooting Arrow Branch. She walked under the poplar trees and past some laurel thickets. The woman named Ocala followed her, and the hair-faces followed them. The Appalachee men and all the rest of us followed too.

My mother pushed the laurel bushes aside and stopped right at the edge of the branch. She pointed to a shoal where water came over rocks in a lip of white foam. White sand glittered at the end of the pool below. "There," my mother said, "There is where the shining rocks are found."

The hair-faces gathered like men about to kill a bear or panther. They brought their shining tools, their platters and pots, and raked through the gravel of Shooting Arrow Branch. Minnows swam this way and that way in the pools. My husband Menendez waded into the water in his leather moccasins and scooped up a plate of gravel. He shook the plate as though he was sifting cornmeal, and then held up a shining rock the size of a robin's egg. The tear of the sun glittered, dripping in his hand. He gave a shout, and the other hair-faces ran to look at his find, as though it was a pearl or perfect arrowhead. The hair-faces were like boys who have caught a hummingbird.

They began scooping up the bed of the stream and turned Shooting Arrow Branch muddy. They made the Appalachee men chop down trees with shining tools, and they made the women dig the banks with sticks and heavy spoons. All the valley was confusion. Soon the banks and stream were nothing but mud.

Some of us women dug up the soil and loose rock of the banks, and others carried it in baskets to the stream where the hair-faces washed and sorted the dirt. Other women dumped the remaining mud and gravel further down the stream. Soon we were all smeared with mud and clay. We dug into the banks until we were up to our knees. We dug until our hands were cold and blistered by the grit. The holes we dug soon filled up with water, and we dug standing in cold puddles. Our dresses, our skin, even our hair, got covered with mud.

Every time a hair-face found a shining stone he shouted for the others to come see it. The great Chief de Soto had a leather bag in which he placed the shining stones. He made the Creek woman walk behind him carrying the pouch.

"Why do the hair-faces want the shining stones?" we asked Ocala.

"Because in their country the shining stones are the most powerful medicine," she said. "More powerful than shells or feathers, more dear than red pipestone."

"But the shining stone is too soft to be used for hatchets or arrow points," we said.

"Whoever has the most shining rocks in their country can be a great chief," the Creek woman said.

We worked in the muddy holes until our backs were sore. My feet wrinkled from standing in the water. We worked all day with nothing to eat. The hair-faces whipped those who stopped working. They tied them to pine trees and whipped them with cords until their backs bled.

At sundown we marched back to the village. Tired as I was I thought how we would starve next winter because the fields had not been planted. Those left alive by the hair-faces would have to hunt every day for turkeys and squirrels. The women and the children would starve.

When we got back to the village we washed in the stream. Our dresses were ruined with mud, and we scrubbed them on the rocks and left them by the fire to dry. I saw that each day we dug we'd ruin more clothes. We'd have to go naked to the diggings if we were to have any dresses left.

After we washed, and served stewed turkey to the hair-faces, and they drank from the great pot of red water and sang, the black robed men stood up at the council house and spoke to us. They held their beads and opened the leather boxes. The Creek woman cooked their words for us to digest.

"Besides the Great Father across the water, there is an even greater father in the sky," the black robed man said. He pointed to the stars just coming out. "The father in the sky has sent a message to you. You are his children, and he loves his children as all fathers do."

The Creek woman said the father in the sky spoke to us through the hair-faces and through the leather boxes. My mother asked how the leather boxes could speak, for she did not hear their voices. The hair-faces laughed. *Bibles*

"The Great Father in the sky speaks from the leaves of the leather box," the black robed man said. "The leaves in the box talk. They talk through marks on them the way tracks in the sand tell where a bear walked, or paint on the face tells it is the time of war." *writing*

Of all the mysteries about the hair-faces, the talking leaves were the strangest. The black robed men carried around the voice of the Great Father in the sky in their leather boxes. I watched the leather boxes to see if they made a sound, if there was fire or lightning inside them.

"The Great Father has sent a son, and also a sacred ghost," the Creek woman said. "The ghost is here now with you."

We looked above the air of the village and saw only the stars. But the stars did not whisper as they did in winter. It was the moon of first leaves, and the stars were silent.

After the black dressed men spoke, and we had cleared away the scraps, my husband Menendez followed me back to our living house. My mother was there with the hair-face who had chosen her. Tired as we were the hair-faces kept us awake with mating. Never had we seen men so hard to satisfy. My mother's new husband wanted to trade women, but Menendez would not agree. He put his hand on his long knife. My mother was older and more experienced at lovemaking than I was, but my husband Menendez would not agree to trade. Finally we slept.

~ · ~ · ~

By the third day we waited for the men of our village to return and free us from the hair-faces. The men should have returned from the hunt the second day. All day as we worked in the pits we wondered when the men would appear. We expected them to be watching, and attack from the woods. Or we thought they might wait until night and kill the hair-faces while they slept, after they had drunk much red water from the big pot.

All day, the third day, I listened for sounds from the woods. Our people could make the call of the turkey, or the chatter of a squirrel, or the bark of a fox, in such a way only we knew it was them calling. Only those listening for a sign could tell it was not the animal. This was done by calling too many times, or waiting a little too long between calls.

On the morning of the third day I heard an owl, but the cry only came once from the pine woods on the ridge. And later, as we worked in the mud by Shooting Arrow Branch, I heard a turkey in the poplars above. But the noise of the tools ringing on the rock and feet splashing in the branch confused all other sounds. All day I glanced at the woods for a sign of our men. I knew if they did not return that day they had been killed in battle, or they had seen the hair-faces in our village and run away. I heard the songs of the many-voices bird, and the echoes of the hair-faces shouting from the mountainside, but I did not hear a call from our men.

That day the Appalachee prisoners were made to dig into the hill above the branch. The Creek woman said the great Chief de Soto thought the shining rocks were coming from the womb of the hill. He thought that by digging into the hill all the shining rocks could be found at once. The hair-faces did not believe the shining rocks were tears of the sun. My mother tried again to tell the great Chief de Soto where the shining rocks came from, and that the sun would not bury his tears, but a hair-face by the pit stung her with his leather cord.

The hair-faces had gathered a bag of shining rocks, but were angry we had not found more. They blamed us for digging too slowly. They whipped the Appalachee men to frighten them, and pointed into the hill where they must dig.

The Appalachee men carved out a hole like a cave in the side of the ridge. They carried the dirt out in baskets, and the women carried the baskets further down the hill and dumped them by Shooting Arrow Branch. The stream was all pits and piles of dirt, muddy rocks, and slashed trees. Never had I seen so much dirt moved, except when the mound under the council

[Handwritten margin note: The language of the land is being drowned out]

house was made. The clearing smelled like mud and sweat and raw dirt.

The afternoon of the third day the Appalachee men ran out of the cave they had dug. The hair-faces pointed their fire sticks at them. The Appalachee men coiled their arms and stuck their fingers up and shook them. My husband Menendez whipped the Appalachees with his cord, but still they would not go back into the cave.

When the Creek woman was brought up the hill she told the hair-faces the Appalachee men had found a nest of rattlesnakes in a crevice of rocks. The snakes sleep in winter deep in the ground in great balls knotted together. There were many times the fingers on both hands, and the snakes had been awakened by the digging and were untying themselves from the ball and shaking their rattles. The Appalachee men were scared they had offended the rattlesnakes by disturbing their sleep.

When my husband Menendez heard them he went into the cave and fired his firestick. The great Chief de Soto directed all the hair-faces to go into the cave to make their firesticks spit flames. Smoke with a special stink drifted out of the cave. We women watched as the hair-faces brought burning sticks and threw them into the cave. As fire and smoke began to boil from the entrance rattlesnakes crawled out into the light. More than the fingers on both hands times the fingers on both hands crawled slowly into the daylight. The hair-faces killed them with digging sticks and their long knives. The snakes were just waking up, and were sluggish and easily killed.

Finally the snakes quit coming from the cave, and the smoke died down. There were piles of rattlesnakes in the mud, like limbs chopped off trees. The hair-faces stooped inside and raked out many more snakes with the burned sticks. The great Chief de Soto went inside the cave and came back out into the sunlight. He spoke to the Creek woman.

"Where are the jewels and shining rocks in the snake den?" he said. "You said the rattlesnakes guard great treasures, but there is nothing inside the hole but dirt and snake droppings. Is that what you call jewels?"

The hair-faces then told the Appalachee men to return to work in the cave. But the men refused. They sat down on the dirt, among the dead snakes, and looked ahead. The hair-faces shouted and whipped them with their leather cords, but the Appalachee men would not respond. They would not offend the rattlesnake spirits by working in the cave.

"You will return to work or one of you will die," the great Chief de Soto said. The Creek woman said his words to them.

The ropes were brought, and each of the Appalachees was bound. They sat among the dead snakes and ignored their bonds. Their indifference made the great Chief de Soto more angry.

"Which of you will die?" the great chief said. He pointed to one of the Appalachees and my husband Menendez and another hair-face lifted the man up and led him to an oak tree. They threw a rope over a limb of the oak tree and tied the end around the Appalachee's neck. They pulled the end tight over the limb so the Appalachee had to stand on tiptoes to keep from choking.

Then they brought two more Appalachees over to the oak and made them lift the other on their shoulders. They tied the other end of the rope to a laurel bush. My husband Menendez kicked the two Appalachees away from the oak tree so the third was left hanging by his neck. For a long time he choked and jerked, his eyes bulging as we watched. Finally he quit twitching, and my husband Menendez cut him down.

Each of the Appalachee men was tied to a tree and whipped until his back bled. But afterward they still would not return to the cave. The great Chief de Soto walked among them, and cut several with his long knife, but none would return to dig in the cave. By then it was almost dark.

~ . ~ . ~

That night the Creek woman disappeared. I don't know at what time during the night she slipped away. But the next morning she was gone. The great Chief de Soto looked in every lodge and living house in the village for Ocala. He shouted to the other hair-faces, and they looked also in the laurel thickets and grain bins, and in the holes where we kept squash and pumpkins.

Without the Creek woman to speak, we did not know what the hair-faces were saying. But we watched them search for her again and again. They looked under every basket and skin, and every pot. And then we saw they were looking not only for the Creek woman but also for the chest of pearls. She had taken the carved chest and all its gleaming treasure.

We learned later that Ocala had also taken the bag of shining rocks when she escaped. And one of the Appalachee men had escaped with her. In the night she had freed him from the ropes and they had fled into the woods. By daylight they had run so far away the hair-faces could find no trace of them. It was assumed they had gone to the south, but no one knew by which trail. Ocala must have married the Appalachee and offered him the chest of pearls, and the bag of shining rocks.

The great Chief de Soto walked back and forth in our village. After looking again in every living house and lodge he stood in front of the council house and shouted to his men. He had lost his wife and the pearls and the bag of shining rocks, as well as his word-cook. I had learned a few words of the hair-face tongue from my husband Menendez, but he did not know it. The great Chief de Soto gave orders, and then changed them. He asked that his riding dog be saddled, and then he decided not to ride.

When my husband Menendez brought him the rope Ocala had cut from the Appalachee man the great chief flung the rope away and slapped Menendez. He walked to the west end of the village and looked toward the further mountains. Then he walked to the south gate and looked through the gap in the palings down the trail. The great Chief de Soto carried his long knife in his hand. Once he slashed at another hair-face and cut him on the arm. One of the black dressed men ran beside the great chief and spoke in a quiet voice.

Smoke blew from the council house. The women had been careful to keep the fire there after the hair-faces had arrived. The flames in the council house must not die, or the village would have to be moved to another site. The sacred fire had not gone out since my mother was a little girl. The fire was named Foxtail, and as long as the fire talked and barked the village would be safe. The fire had been blessed by the medicine man Little Finger more moons ago than anyone could remember.

The great Chief de Soto stood by the fire and a black robed man brought him a cup of red water. The great chief drank and threw the cup into the flames. The fire hissed and then sprang up again. We watched, fearing the flames would be doused. But the tattered fire rose higher than before.

The great Chief de Soto walked from one side of the council house to the other. Then he called for the great pot of red water to be brought out and he signed for each of the hair-faces to get a cup full. Then he gestured for each of the women to get a cup. We brought bowls and pots, and some drank from their cupped hands.

After that morning we called the red water laughing water, because we laughed more that day than ever before. The great

Chief de Soto had his men kill one of the grunting bears, and they roasted the carcass over a great bonfire in the square. All day we drank the laughing water and ate the sweet white flesh of the bear.

That day my mother brought out the sacred drum, and we beat the drum before the council house. We women laughed like little girls because of the laughing water, and we took our dresses down to our waists and danced before the council house. The hair-faces sang and danced, though they did not laugh as much as the women. We sang and beat the drum, and played games like children running among the houses and lodges. We were like players of the ball-game who get excited with the play and cannot stop. Women danced with hair-faces other than their husbands, and mated in the thickets and in the daylight with others. After mating and dancing they returned to the council house and drank more of the laughing water and ate more white bear meat. The women talked and sang, and the hair-faces talked and sang. Except for a few words, no one knew what the others were saying. Only the black robed men did not sing and dance, though they each drank some of the laughing water.

The great Chief de Soto put his long knife back in its skin and danced with the women. He drank several cups of laughing water, and then he danced with me. I found I was dancing with my hips, and with my breasts, in a way I never had before. He looked into my eyes, and I danced and laughed without knowing why. I danced in ways I had not planned. I felt warmed by the laughing water, and lifted, as though in a foaming pool. I felt the wind rushing in my head, roaring past my ears and pushing me high into the sky.

His eyes glittering, the great Chief de Soto danced close to me. He looked into my eyes as the drum beat and then he reached for me. Without knowing why I jerked backward, and he followed. I danced back, and he followed again. We danced to the edge of the council house, and when I got near the laurel bushes I turned and ran, laughing over my shoulder. The great chief followed, laughing also.

When I reached the bank under the persimmon trees the great chief fell on me and we rolled in the leaves. The handle of his long knife hurt my side, but I ignored it. I laughed because it hurt but did not hurt. I felt I was there and I was not there, and I rolled in the leaves laughing. Never had mating been so sweet to me. I laughed and wanted the lovemaking to go on longer and longer.

But after the great Chief de Soto and I mated, I lay there in the leaves looking up at the blue sky and wondered if Chief Flying Squirrel and our men were watching from the mountains. I wondered if our men would attack the hair-faces while they were dancing and mating with us, or if our men would return at all.

The great Chief de Soto slept against me in the leaves until it was almost dark. When he woke the stars were coming out and it was cold on the ground. He awoke confused as any man that rises from a troubled sleep. He had dropped his cup in the chase through the laurel bushes, and he gestured for me to go find it.

I had to look on my knees in the shadows before touching the vessel. Dirt and leaves stuck to the rim and it was empty of laughing water. I wiped it carefully with the back of my hand before giving the cup to the great chief. He took it without a word, and we walked back to the square where the great fire was still burning. The women and the hair-faces were still eating the white flesh of the bear and drinking the laughing water, but they were no longer beating the drum or dancing.

~ · ~ · ~

Next morning the hair-faces left our village. They took all the corn and baskets, squash and pumpkins they could find in our bins and holes, and loaded them on the backs of the Appalachees. The Appalachees still bled from the whippings, but the hair-faces loaded even more tools and deer hides on their backs.

I thought the great Chief de Soto planned to burn our village. In the early morning he carried a torch from the bonfire, looked into every house and lodge. He turned over pots and baskets, and cut loose hides stretched on pegs. Perhaps he was still looking for the bag of shining rocks. Perhaps he thought we had hidden other treasures from him.

My husband Menendez kissed me in the square before the council house, and fondled my breasts. Then he climbed on his large dog and rode with the great Chief de Soto out of the village. The Appalachee men and the grunting bears were driven behind the hair-faces through the gap in the palings and down the trail. They left by the western gate, taking the Oconee trail. The women and children gathered at the gate to watch them leave. The hair-faces disappeared into the valley just as the sun was rising over Panther Mountain.

It was silent in the village. Our men were gone, and the hair-faces were gone. All our corn and squash and pumpkins were gone. It would be two months before any peas or corn could be harvested. We would have to live on greens plucked beside the branch, and fish trapped in the creek. I was thinking of taking my hoe to the Blood Soil Field when I heard my mother scream. I ran to the council house.

My mother stood beside the place of the sacred fire. While drinking the laughing water and dancing with the hair-faces we had forgotten to feed the flames. For more than a lifetime the fire had not gone out. We stood in the silent council house and looked at the pile of ashes. I turned to my mother, and she looked at the other women. The fire could only be started by a medicine chief. It must be started by rubbing dogwood sticks over dried deer moss and fungus, until the spark from the wood caught the tinder. The medicine chief made a special prayer that no one else knew, to bless the flames.

"We'll have to move the village," Blue Stone's wife said. She was from Birdtown, and had never liked our village up high near the headwaters.

"No," my mother said. "We'll make a new village here, and when the men return they can start a new fire in our new place."

My mother took a basket and a flat rock, and began to scrape the surface of the ground in front of the council house. "We'll scrape away the tracks of the old village," she said. "All the tracks of the hair-faces and other tracks will be gone. Then we'll sprinkle new soil on the ground and the village will be new."

All morning we crawled on our knees over the village and scraped every spot of ground around the houses. We carried the old dirt to the mound of the council house and piled it higher, so it also looked new. With flat rocks from the stream we smoothed the dirt and carried away all ashes and trash. Then we carried sand from the branch and sprinkled the whole village with new soil. The ground shone white in the midday sun by the time we had finished. The sand was so white and clean you didn't want to step on it. Tiny rocks in the sand glittered like eyes. The village looked completely changed. The living houses seemed to have been set down on new ground.

"When the men come back they can light a new sacred flame," my mother said.

"They may not come back," the wife of Blue Stone said.

"When they know the hair-faces are gone they will return," my mother said.

After we finished sprinkling the ground it was past midday. I had a pain in my head, and all the women were tired from the night of dancing and drinking laughing water. I walked to the spring for a long drink. But the cold water did not stop the hurt in my head.

I took my hoe and what seeds I could find in the bins and hurried to the Blood Soil Field. I was afraid weeds had already sprouted in the fresh raked hills. The ache behind my eyes was like a shadow that would not pass away. The pain swam in my head like a fish in a jar.

"The signs are not favorable," my mother said, when she saw me walking toward the Blood Soil Field. "The moon has waned too far for corn planting. It will be the next half moon before another likely time."

"Now that we have a new village," I said, "perhaps we can plant by new signs."

I had only one basket of seeds. There were too few to put four to the hill. And they were not the seeds we had set aside for planting. The hair-faces had taken our baskets of fine seed corn. I had only loose grains picked up from the bins. Before pushing each seed into the dirt I would have to make sure its heart had not been eaten out by mice or worms.

Only the tiniest weeds had broken through the crust of the Blood Soil Field. I got on my knees and raked the dirt fresh again on each hill. I brushed away the crumbs and thin crust that had dried since the hair-faces came. It was like flesh that enjoys being touched. I counted out my seeds carefully, one to each hill. If I was fortunate I might have enough to plant the whole field, or most of it. I would have to look in all the houses and bins and baskets for seeds to plant the other fields.

The women had gone to sleep after sprinkling the sand over the village. I was alone in the field except for a cloud just over my head, and a many-voices bird singing in a dogwood at the edge of the woods. Children played in the trees further down the creek. As I sweated, the hurt in my head seemed to fade away. But there were red spots like tracks down my Disease arms. I shivered and counted the seeds and pushed them into the softest dirt I could find on the hills. When I raked the dirt smooth over each seed it was the newest, brightest soil under the sky.

Poinsett's Bridge

SON, IT WAS THE most money I'd ever had, one ten dollar gold piece and twenty-three silver dollars. The gold piece I put in my dinner bucket so it wouldn't get worn away by the heavy silver. The dollars clinked and weighed in my pocket like a pistol. I soon wished they was a pistol.

"What you men have done here this year will not be forgotten," Senator Pineset said before he cut the ribbon across the bridge. "The coming generations will see your work and honor you. You have opened the mountains to the world, and the world to the mountains."

And he shook hands with every one of us. I still had my dirty work clothes on, but I had washed my face and hands in the river before the ceremony. The senator was as fine a looking man as you're ever likely to see. He wore a striped silk cravat and he had the kind of slightly red face that makes you think of spirit and health.

The senator and all the other dignitaries and fine ladies got in their carriages and crossed the bridge and started up the turnpike. There was to be a banquet at the King House in Flat Rock that evening to celebrate the road and the bridge. I shook hands with the foreman Delosier and started up the road myself for home.

Everything seemed so quiet after the ceremony. The warm fall woods was just going on about their business, with no interest in human pomp and projects. I carried my dinner bucket and my light mason's hammer, and I thought it was time to get home and do a little squirrel hunting. I hadn't spent a weekday at home since work started on the bridge in March. Suddenly two big rough-looking boys jumped out from behind a rock above the road and ran down into the turnpike in front of me.

"Scared you?" one said. And then he laughed like he had told a joke.

"No," I said.

"We'll just help you carry things up the mountain," the other said. "You got anything heavy?" He looked at my pocket bulging with the silver dollars. I had my buckeye in there too, but it didn't make any sound.

"Yeah, we'll help out," the first one said, and laughed again.

~ · ~ · ~

Now I had built chimneys ever since I was a boy. Back yonder people would fix up on their own a little cabin and make a fireplace of rock, then the chimney they just built of plastered mud and sticks. Nobody had the time or skill for masonry. Way back yonder after the Indians was first gone and people moved into these hollers a wagonload at a time coming to grab the cheap land, they'd live in any little old shack or hole in the ground with a roof over it. The first Jones that come here they said lived in a hollow tree for a year. And I knowed other families that hid theirselves in caves and lean-tos below cliffs. You just did the best you could.

My grandpa fit the British at King's Mountain and at Cowpens, and then he come up here and threw together a little cabin right on the pasture hill over there. You can see the cellar

27

hole there still. And where we lived when I was a boy the chimney would catch fire on a cold night, or if pieces of mud fell off the sticks, and we'd have to get up on the roof and pour water down. You talk about cold and wet, with the house full of smoke. That was what give Grandpa pneumonia.

That was when I promised myself to build a chimney. Nobody on the creek knew rockwork then, except to lay a rough kind of fireplace. Only masons in the county was the Germans in town, the Doxtaters, Bumgarners, and the Corns, and they worked on mansions in Flat Rock, and the home of the judge, and the courthouse and such. I would have gone to learn from them but I was too scared of foreigners to go off on my own. People here was raised so far back in the woods we was afraid to go out to work. So I had to learn myself. I'd seen chimneys in Greenville when Pa and me carried to market there, and I'd marveled at the old college building north of Greenville. "Rockwork's for rich folks," Pa said, but I didn't let that stop me.

After the tops was cut and the fodder pulled one year I set myself to the job. First thing that was needed was the rocks, but they was harder to get at than it might seem at first. They was rocks in the fields and pastures. Did you just pry them up with a pole and sled them to the house? And the creek was full of rocks, but they was rounded by the water and would have to be cut flat. That was the hardest work I'd ever done, believe me, getting rocks out of the creek. It was already getting cold, and I'd have to go out there in the water, finding the right size, and tote them up the bank, prying some loose from the mud, and scrape away the moss and slick.

They was a kind of quarry over on the hill where the Indians must have got their flint and quartz for arrowheads. The whole slope was covered with fragments of milk quartz and I hauled in some of those to put in the fireplace where the crystals could shine in the light.

I asked Old Man Davis over at the line what could be used for mortar and he said a bucket of lime mixed with sand and water would do the trick. And even branch clay would serve, though it never set itself hard except where heated by a fire.

Took me most of the fall, way up into hog-killing time, to get my stuff assembled. I just had a hammer and one cold chisel to dress the rock. Nobody ever taught me how to cut stone, or how to measure and lay out. I just learned myself as I made mistakes and went along.

Son, I remember looking at that pile of rocks I'd carried into the yard and wondering how I'd ever put them together in a firebox and chimney. My brother Joe had already started to play with the rocks and scatter them around. Leaves from the poplars had drifted on my heap and already it looked half-buried. I waited until Ma and Pa and the other younguns had gone over to Fletcher to Cousin Charlie's. In those times people would visit each other for a week at a time once the crops was in. I stayed home to look after the stock. One morning at daylight I lit in and tore the old mud chimney down. I knocked most of it down with an ax, it was so shackly, and then I knocked the firebox apart with a sledgehammer.

Well there it was, the cabin with a hole in the side and winter just a few short weeks away. That was when I liked to have lost my nerve. The yard was a mess of blackened mud and sticks, and my heaps of rocks. I thought of just heading west and never coming back, of taking the horse and going. I stood there froze you might say with fear.

But then I seen in my pile a rock that was perfect for a cornerstone, and another that would fit against it in a line with just a little chipping. So I shoveled out and leveled the foundation and mixed up a bucket of mortar. I put the cornerstone in place, and slapped on some wet clay, then fitted the next rock to it. It was like solving a puzzle, finding rocks that would join together with just a little mud, maybe a little chipping here and there to smooth a point or corner. But best of all was the way you could rough out a line, running a string or a rule along the edge to see how it would line up, so when you backed away you saw the wall was straight in spite of gaps and bulges. I worked so hard selecting and rejecting rocks from my pile, mixing more clay and water, setting stone against stone, that I never stopped for dinner. By dark I had the hole covered with the fireplace, so the coons couldn't get inside. I liked the way I made the firebox slope in toward the chimney to a place where I could put a damper. And I set between the rocks the hook from which Ma's pot would hang.

It wasn't until I was milking the cow by lantern light I seen how rough my hands had wore. The skin at the ends of my fingers and in my palms was fuzzy from handling the rock. The cow liked to kicked me, they rasped her tits so bad.

By the time Ma and Pa had come home from Cousin Charlie's I had made them a chimney. I made my scaffold out of hickory poles and hoisted every rock up the ladder myself and set it into place. It was not the kind of chimney I'd a built later, but you can see the work over there at the old place still, kind of rough and taking too much mortar, but still in plumb and holding together after more than sixty years. I knowed you had to go above the roof to make a chimney draw, and I got it up to maybe six inches above the comb. Later I learned any good chimney goes six feet above the ridgepole. It's the height of a chimney makes it draw, that makes the flow of smoke go strong up the chimney into the cooler air. The higher she goes the harder she pulls.

People started asking me to build chimneys, and I made enough so I started using fieldstone, and breaking the rocks to get flat edges that would fit so you don't hardly have to use any mortar. They just stay together where they're laid. And people asked me to steen their wells and wall in springs and cellars. It was hard and heavy work, taking rocks out of the ground and placing them back in order, finding the new and just arrangement so they would stay. I had all the work I could do in good weather, after laying-by time.

Then I heard about the bridge old Senator Pineset was building down in South Carolina. Clara — we was married by then — read about it in the Greenville paper which come once a week. The senator was building a turnpike from Charleston to the mountains, to open up the Dark Corner of the state for commerce he said. But everybody knowed it was for him and his Low Country kind to bring their carriages to the cool mountains for the summer. They found out what a fine place this was and they started buying up the land around Flat Rock. But there wasn't hardly a road up Saluda Mountain and through the Gap except the little wagon trace down through Gap Creek. That's the way we hauled our hams and apples down to Greenville and Augusta in the fall. That same newspaper said the state of North Carolina was building a turnpike all the way from Tennessee to the line at Saluda Gap.

The paper said they was building this stone bridge across the North Fork of the Saluda River. It was to be fifty feet high and more than a hundred feet long, "the greatest work of masonry and engineering in upper Carolina," the paper said. And I knowed I had to work on that bridge. It was the first turnpike into the mountains and I had to go help out. The paper said they was importing masons from Philadelphia and even a master mason from England. I knowed I had to go and learn what I could.

Senator Pineset had his own ideas about the turnpike and the bridge, but we knowed there'd be thousands of cattle and hogs and sheep drove out of the mountains and across from Tennessee as well as the rich folks driving in their coaches. That highway would put us in touch with every place in the country you might want to go to.

I felt some dread, going off like that not knowing if they would hire me or not. I had no way of proving I was a mason. What would that fancy Englishman think of my laying skill? And even if he took me on it was a nine mile walk each way to the bridge site. I knowed the place all right, where the North Fork goes through a narrow valley too steep to get a wagon down and across.

There's something about the things a man really wants to do that scares him. He's got to go on nerve a lot of the time. And nobody else is looking or cares when you make your choices. That's the way it has to be. But it was a kind of fate too, and even Clara didn't try to stop me. She complained, as a woman will, that I'd be gone from sunup to sundown and no telling how long it would take to finish the bridge through the summer and into the fall. And she wouldn't have no help around the place except the kids. "They may not do any more hiring," she said. But I knowed better. I knowed masons and stone-cutters of any kind was hard to come by in the upcountry, and there would be thousands of rocks to cut for such a bridge. And when I set off she give me a buckeye to put in my pocket for luck. She didn't normally hold to such things, but I guess she was worried as I was.

Sometimes you get a vision of what's ahead for you. And even if it's what you most want to do you see all the work it is. It's like foreseeing an endless journey of climbing over logs and crossing creeks, looking for footholds in mud and swamp-land. And every little step and detail is real and has to be worked out. But it's what you are going to do, what you have been give to do. It will be your life to get through it.

That's the way I seen this work. Every one of that thousand rocks, some weighing a ton I guessed, had to be dressed, had to be measured and cut out of the mountainside, and then joined to one another. And every rock would take hundreds, maybe thousands, of hammer and chisel licks, each lick leading to another, swing by swing, chip by chip, every rock different and yet cut to fit with the rest. Every rock has its own flavor, so to speak, its own grain and hardness. No two rocks are exactly alike, but they have to be put together, supporting each other, locked into place. It was like I was behind a mountain of hammer blows, of chips and dust, and the only way out was through them. It was my life's work to get through them. And when I got through them my life would be over. It's like everybody has to earn their own death. We all want to reach the peacefulness and rest of death, but we have to work our way through a million little jobs to get there, and everybody has to do it in their own way.

∾ · ∾ · ∾

The Englishman was Barnes, and he wore a top hat and silk tie, though he had a kind of apron on. "Have you been a mason long?" he said.

"Since I was a boy," I said.

"Have you ever made an arch?"

"Yes sir, over a fireplace," I said.

"Ours will be a little bigger," he said and looked me up and down.

"Let me see your hands," he said. He glanced at the calluses the trowel had made and sent me to the clerk, who he called "the clark."

I was signed on as a mason's helper, which hurt my pride some, I'll admit.

All morning I thought of heading back up the trail for

33

home, and letting the fine Englishman and crew build whatever bridge they wanted.

And if I thought about leaving when the clerk signed me on
as an assistant, I thought about it twice when Barnes sent me
away from the bridge site up the road to the quarry. It was
about a mile where they had picked a granite face on the side
of the mountain to blast away. One crew was drilling holes
for the black powder, and another was put to dressing the
rock that had already been blasted loose.

I had brought my light mason's hammer and trowel, but I
was give a heavy hammer and some big cold chisels and told
to cut a regular block, eighteen inches thick, two feet wide,
and three feet long. The whole area was powdered with rock
dust from the blasting and chipping.

"Surely you don't want all the blocks the same size?" I said
to Delosier, the foreman from Charleston.

"The corner stones and arch stones will be cut on the site,"
he said. "In the meantime we need more than five hundred
regular blocks, for the body of the bridge." He showed me an
architect's plan where every single block was already drawed
in, separate and numbered.

"You're cutting block one aught three," he said.

Some of the men had put handkerchiefs over their noses to
keep out the rock dust. They looked like a gang of outlaws
hammering at the rocks, but there was nothing to protect
their eyes. I squatted down to the rough block Delosier had
assigned me. After the first few licks I felt even more like going
home. It would take all day to cut the piece to the size Barnes
required. I wasn't used to working on rocks that size and
shape.

After a few more licks I saw where the smell in the quarry
come from. I thought it was just burned black powder, but it
was also the sparks from where the granite was hit by the

chisels. Every time the steel eat into the granite it smoked and
stunk a little. With a dozen people chipping the whole place
filled up with dust and smell.

But I kept at it. I had no choice but to keep working
because I would never have another chance like that. And
even then I knew that if you don't feel like working in the
morning it will get better if you just keep at it. You start out
feeling awful and if you work up a sweat the job will begin
taking over itself. You just follow the work, stick to the job, and
the work will take care of you. I put my handkerchief over my
nose and started hammering along the line I'd measured and
scratched on the side of the block. I was already behind if I
was going to finish that block in one day.

"You want a drink, boss?" The slave held a dipper from
the bucket of water he'd just carried from the spring on the
mountainside.

I pushed down the handkerchief and wiped the dust from my
lips. The cold water surprised me. I had been concentrating so
hard on work I'd forgotten I was thirsty. And I wasn't used to
being waited on by no slave or called boss.

When we stopped for dinner everybody washed their hands
in the creek and we set in the shade and opened our lard
buckets. Clara had packed me some shoulder meat and biscuits.
My arm was a little sore from the steady hammering. My
block was cut on only one side. Delosier inspected my work
and spat without commenting. I had made a clean face, but
I'd have to speed up to finish that evening.

The slave that carried water had a harmonica in his pocket
which he began playing. There was a slave boy named Charlie that carried tools and messages between the quarry and
bridge. "Hey Charlie," somebody was always calling, "Hey
Charlie, get this bit sharpened."

Charlie started dancing right there in the clearing to the

harmonica music. He started to move the toes on one foot, and then the foot itself. You could see the music traveling up his leg, up to his waist, and then travel out one shoulder and around till he had his hand dancing. You never saw such a sight as when he started dancing all over. The harmonica played faster, and the boy started dancing around in circles and the first thing you know he was doing somersaults all over the clearing.

Then the harmonica player moved back in the shade and slowed down and the boy slowed down too. He danced backwards getting slower, like he was winding down, slower and slower, until he stopped and the music went down one arm and through his body and down a leg until only the foot was moving, and then the toes. And he stood still all over when the music stopped.

Now the funny thing was Delosier had been watching and enjoying the dancing as much as any of us. But as soon as the music stopped he said, "That's enough of that. You're wasting energy on my time. You boys can play and dance on your own time."

I didn't see no call for what he said, since it was dinner hour. But we all put our dinner buckets down to go to work, and the boy, sweating something awful from the dancing, run to sharpen more chisels. I hunkered down over my block.

∽ · ∽ · ∽

"Never mind what our names are," the older boy said.

"No, I won't mind," I said.

"We'll just walk along with you a little ways, to keep you out of trouble."

I tried to remember if I'd seen them anywhere before. Chestnut Springs even then had a lot of rough people, liquor people and all. Names like Howard or Morgan kept coming to mind, but I couldn't place them. Our folks had come from South Carolina and I knowed a lot of people from Landrum and Tigerville, but I couldn't place them.

"You just got paid down at the bridge," the older boy said.

"I worked on the bridge," I said. I could have said I walked this road every morning and evening for nearly five months, and I'd never seen them.

"You wouldn't fool us," the younger one said. "We watched all them big shots from up on the mountain. And we seen all of you'uns standing around before they cut the ribbon."

"You should have come down and had some punch, and some sweetbread," I said. "One of the carriages from Greenville brought a basket of sweetbread and a keg of punch, along with a big bottle of champagne for the dignitaries."

"We got our own bottle," the older boy said.

"Can't we help you carry something," the younger brother said. He lifted a side of his vest and I seen the pistol in his belt.

"I'm doing fine," I said.

"Ain't you got something just a little too heavy for you to carry," the older one said. I noticed he had a knife about eighteen inches long stuck in his belt.

If only another carriage would come along, or if we'd meet a wagon coming back from mill, I could ask for a ride. I prayed that somebody I knowed would be walking down the mountain. But there was nothing ahead but the road through the holler, built while we was building the bridge, winding up toward Saluda Gap.

"What you got in there, Boss?" the older brother said, and prodded my pocket with the pistol.

"You got something a-ringing a regular tune," the younger one said.

"You wouldn't lie to us?" the other one said.

I stepped back, and just then I seen the rock in the younger one's hand.

≈ . ≈ . ≈

After the first day I was almost too tired to walk back up the mountain. And the next day I was nearly too sore to lift a hammer. But I made myself keep going, and after a while I worked the soreness out. It took about a week for me to learn to cut a block a day, getting surer and ever closer to the measurements. It took ten men to slide one of those blocks up on an ox cart to carry to the bridge site. Delosier showed us how to do things with rollers and skids and pulleys you never would have dreamed of. I had never handled big stuff like that before. It looks like there ain't nothing a man can't do if he just takes time to study it out.

I got a little bit of a cough from breathing the rock dust, but after seven or eight weeks we had most of the blocks cut and moved down to the bridge itself. They had put up a frame of poles and timbers to build the arches on, and I looked close to see exactly how Barnes and Delosier done it. If a giant could pick up all the rocks of an arch and drop them into place at once you wouldn't need a frame underneath. But with regular men moving in a rock at a time there was no other way. Delosier built a big A-frame with pulleys to hoist the stones into place. It was something to watch.

They had a spot right down by the river where we did the final dressing of blocks before they was lifted into place above. Once the arches was built we could roll everything out onto the bridge as we went, but the arches had to be put in place first. It was convenient, and cooler by the water. We wet the drills and rocks to keep down the dust.

"Everything will be fine unless there's a flash," I said to Delosier.

"What do you mean a flash?"

"A flash flood," I said. "On ground this steep it can come up a flash tide pretty quick."

"It's not the season for flash floods," Mr. Barnes, who had overheard me, said.

"A flash can come anytime," I said. "All you need is a cloudburst on the slope above."

"You mountain folk are so superstitious," Mr. Barnes said. "All you ever do is worry about lightning, panthers, snakes, floods, winds, and landslides."

I knew there was truth in what he said, but it was like he was saying that I, as an assistant mason, didn't have a right to an opinion either. But I let it go and went back to work.

But along in July it come up the awfullest lightning storm you ever seen. You know how it can thunder in South Carolina, there at the foot of the mountain, after a hot day. It was like the air was full of black powder going off. We got under the trees, until we saw a big poplar on the ridge above turn to fire and explode. Splinters several feet long got flung all over the woods. We got under the first arch then, knowing the rock wouldn't draw the lightning.

"When the Lord talks, he talks big," Furman, another mason's assistant said.

The slaves got in under the cover of the arch saying nothing. Lightning struck up on the ridge again, and it was like the air had jolted you.

"The Lord must have a lot on his mind," the harmonica player said.

"Maybe telling us how sick of us he is," another slave said.

The storm passed over for a minute and then come back, the way a big storm will. Lightning was dropping all around on the ridges above. It was so close you could hear the snap, like whips cracking, before there was any thunder. Snap-boom, snap-boom. The air smelled like scorched trees and burned air.

"This old earth getting a whipping," the harmonica player said.

After about twenty minutes the worst of it passed, and we could hear the thunder booming and rattling on the further mountains. While it was still raining a little we got out and stood in the drizzle and the drip from the trees.

"What is that roar?" Delosier said.

"Just wind on the mountain, boss."

"No, it's coming closer."

It did sound like wind on a mountainside of trees, and my first thought was we was having a little twister. They don't come often to the mountains, but they have been known to bore down out of the sky twisting up the trees.

And just then it hit me there was a flash tide coming down the valley. "It's the creek," I hollered, but no one seemed to notice.

"It's the river," I hollered again. "Let's get the tools." Must have been a dozen hammers and chisels, several T-squares and rulers, levels and trowels under the bridge. And there was an extra set of block and tackle. Only Charlie and the harmonica player seemed to hear me. They run down and got five or six of the sledgehammers, and I got one end of the big block and tackle and started to drag it up the bank.

Then everybody all at once saw the water coming. It was gold colored from the red clay and frothy as lather. The river was just swollen a little bit, as was normal after a hard rain as nearby runoff spilled into the stream. But somewhere higher up a valley had been drenched all at once with the cloud's insides dropping into a narrow branch holler. It was not like a wall of water exactly. It was more like a stampede of furry paws rolling over each other slanted down to a frothy front that swerved and found its way through trees and bends.

Besides the foam you could see sticks and leaves and all kinds of trash tossed up and tumbled around.

Everybody pulled back from the banks at once and I had to wrap the big block and tackle around a tree. Then I run back up the hill with the rest.

That big cowcatcher of water come through the narrow valley tearing saplings loose and bending trees over till they pulled out by the roots. There was a wind with it too, a cold breeze swept down with the tide. I thought at first the bridge was going to go, the frames we had put up for the arches. But I guess there was enough weight on them now to hold them down. The bridge was far enough along to stay intact.

"The Lord have mercy," the harmonica player kept saying.

"Oh blast, oh blast it all," Mr. Barnes said, and took off his hat as he watched the charge of water swirl through his frames and pilings and suck through the arches.

"Oh blast it all," he said.

"Everybody safe?" Delosier called.

We looked around and everybody seemed to be there, wet from the rain and white-faced with shock. The body of a mule shot by in the current, and then a chicken coop. A cart that had been used at the quarry come down. And a big black snake passed, spun around as it tried to swim.

"The Lord almighty."

The water rose to the groin of the biggest arch, and slapped at the stones a while. But once the high mark was reached the flood begun to recede, pulling back from the banks, drawing most of the debris with it, letting go of roots and stumps. As fast as it had come the flash shrunk back to the river bed, leaving sticks and trash caught in the tops of bushes and the banks scoured. You could tell how high it went because the ground there was bare as a plucked chicken. Roots and rocks was exposed in the dripping slope.

Many tools had been washed away, and some of the blocks we was cutting had been carried down by the tide. Several logs and saplings had been lodged against the pillars of the bridge.

"Why look at that," Charlie said, and pointed to what looked like a seed box. "Boss, I don't want to look at that," he said to Delosier. It was not a seed box, but a pine casket, half rotted away. Everybody crowded to the box, but there was nothing in it except some rotten rags and bones.

"Don't that beat all," Delosier said.

Mr. Barnes directed four men to carry the box up the hill and bury it above the road.

"Shouldn't we find out who it was and return it to the family?" Delosier said.

"And how do you propose to do that, sir?" Mr. Barnes said. "This could have come from anywhere up stream, and we have work to do."

As soon as they had started up the hill Mr. Barnes turned his glare on me. "Jones," he said, "You could have warned us."

"I told you it might flood," I said.

"Jones, you might have warned us effectively," he said. "From what you said I understood there was only the remotest chance of a flood, and that after days of rain."

"A flash can come up quick," I said.

"So I notice," he said. "You folk never know how to say what you mean."

The other time I saw Mr. Barnes lose his temper at me was when I put on the hoist a block that had been overchipped. The rock was already cracked a little and when I tried to smooth it up a chunk two inches wide come off. But in a big block that didn't seem to matter. We could turn it inside and no one would know. I didn't see Mr. Barnes come up behind me as I was fixing the ropes.

"You know *perfectly* well that won't do," he said. He tapped the rock with his cane.

"We can turn that side in," I said.

"Jones," he said, "I'm disappointed in you. Hiding shoddy work. Very disappointed."

I was taken by surprise. Nobody had talked to me like that since I was a little boy. It was not what he said but the tone of his voice that was so shocking and humiliating. I had heard him scold others but it was different when he turned his scorn on me.

"Jones, if you can't meet our standards you can go back to your chimneys," he said. "Go back to your stick and mud. No one requires your presence here."

"I'm sorry, sir," I said. And immediately I was more humiliated to have apologized. It was as though his manner and his rage had pulled the apology out of me with no decision on my part, as if I had been hypnotized by his glare and his anger and had no choice.

"Well then," he said. "You'll get rid of that block and go back and cut another."

It was after he strode away that the anger and hate began rising in me, pushing aside the surprise and embarrassment. He has no right to talk to me that way, I kept saying to myself. Everybody on the job, including the slaves, heard him tell me off for almost nothing. It was like a public whipping. And not only had I felt helpless to defend myself, I had actually apologized to that limey lord-over-creation. That's why my grandpappy fit the Revolution, to get rid of such strutting peacocks, I said to myself.

"Massa Barnes sho like to have his say," the harmonica player said as we carried the hammers and chisels back to the quarry to cut the new block.

He's going to tell off one man too many, I thought to

myself, and end up with a hammer in his brain. All that morning while I was chipping at the new block, measuring and marking, sweating with the excitement of my anger as well as the work, I kept running through my mind plans for revenge. The thing I wanted most was to sink my hammer through his top hat into his skull. I saw the silk collapse and blood spurt as the bones crumbled. I chuckled with pleasure at the image.

And then I saw myself doing it all with my hands, fighting fair.

"A fist in the gut and a knee in the face when they double over," my cousin Nary liked to say. While chipping that extra block I must have kneed Barnes in the face a thousand times and seen the blood gush from his nose. I hammered until my eyes were filled with sweat and my breath was coming short. I hammered like it was Barnes's head I was cutting down to size.

Of course what some fellows would do was just walk away from a job where they talked to you that bad, then come back with their gun and shoot the rawhiding foreman. And I saw myself coming back with my shotgun and filling Barnes's belly with buckshot. It would take him days to die of peritonitis as he swelled up and screamed with the pain.

I worked so hard I was plumb exhausted by dinner time when I had to walk back down to the bridge to get my dinner bucket. And as I walked I thought I was so mad because I didn't know how to talk back to Barnes. He had took me by surprise and the cat got my tongue. And it was only words. Sticks and stones, I kept saying, sticks and stones. His hardness was what made Barnes such a good builder. I had learned a lot about masonry and also how to run a job, how you demand that everybody meet the standards. By the time I got to the bridge I was feeling better about the whole thing. I took my dinner bucket from the spring and set down on the bank with Delosier and the other masons. It was midsummer, and the jarflies was loud in the trees all around.

"They do sound like rattlesnakes," somebody said.

"Except a rattlesnake's not up in an oak tree."

"You can't always tell where a sound's coming from in the woods, especially if they's a big rock nearby."

Barnes come out of the little shed he used for an office. The men lived in tents, but he boarded in the Lindsay house down the river. He kept all his plans and instruments in the little office.

"Jones," he said. "We won't need that extra block after all. We've already used the block you chipped on the inside." Then he strolled away toward the spring. It was so hot he had taken his jacket off, and his armpits was wet.

I was instantly mad all over again, that he had made me waste a morning's work on that extra block. I imagined sinking an ax into his spine as he walked away.

"I never knowed him to change his mind before," Furman said.

"He could have changed it before I wasted a morning's work," I said.

"Don't get riled up again," Delosier said. "That's the closest I've ever seen Mr. Barnes come to an apology."

That evening I went back to dressing blocks before they was hoisted into place, and was more careful than ever not to overchip a corner or side. But I didn't like Barnes anymore, and I wished the job was already over.

$$\sim \cdot \sim \cdot \sim$$

When I woke up on the turnpike my head hurt like thunder. My pockets was empty. I looked around for my dinner bucket. They had throwed it down the bank, and my ten dollar gold piece was nowhere in sight. I set back down where I had crawled to and held my head, which throbbed like it was in a vise. After a whole spring and summer's work I had nothing to show. Clara had put the corn in pretty much by herself, with a little help from the kids and from my brother Joe. She was now drying peaches and apples on the rooftop, and on sheets spread out on the bank behind the house. The stock would have less fodder for the winter, and there was no money for shoes or coffee. I'd have to find another job building a chimney or springhouse wall. I had wasted half a year and all I had to show for it was a bloody knot on my head.

"You seen the big ceremony," Clara would say, "And the rich folks going up to Flat Rock for their banquet. I guess that's your pay. You can tell everybody that."

I was just going to set awhile, to catch my breath and stop my head from swimming. They was tracks all around me in the dirt, but I knowed I could never identify them big rough brothers from their tracks, which could have been made by anybody's big brogans.

My head hurt so bad I thought it must be cracked. And I felt thirsty. There was a spring in the bend about a mile ahead. I'd have to stumble up there if I was to have a drink. I was about to gather my strength and try to stand when I heard somebody holler.

The mountainside was steep there and it was hard to tell where the sound come from. But while I was looking and holding the back of my head this cow come around the bend ahead, this big red cow, and then another, and two more, and three or four others, and still more behind them. Boys with switches run along beside them. They just kept coming down the turnpike like a flash flood of beef, hooking and slobbering.

"Stand aside," one of the boys called. "Hey mister, stand aside."

I stumbled to my feet and backed over the edge of the road and stood in the leaves as they trotted past. There was men behind popping their whips and the boys with hickories run alongside hollering "Aye, aye" when one of the animals slowed or started to turn aside.

You never seen so many cattle. They must have passed for twenty minutes, raising the dust and bawling, lifting their tails and spraying the ruts. Finally along come the end of it, a wagon loaded with cooking gear and blankets.

"Where you coming from?" I asked the driver.

"Why friend, we've driv these cattle all the way from Tennessee," the man said.

"Where you going?" I said.

"Wherever they buy cattle," he said. "Augusta, maybe Atlanta."

Then they was gone and the dust settling in the late summer light coming through the trees.

Son, I stepped back into the road and started up the mountain, but hadn't took more than ten steps when somebody hollered behind me, "Step aside, sir. Step aside."

I looked back and there was the prettiest carriage you ever seen with a black driver all in livery carrying his long stiff whip. They was lanterns of polished brass and glass on the corners and shiny black fenders. You never seen people dressed up like them inside, ladies with parasols and dresses so low you could nearly see the nipples on their bosoms, and men in top hats and silk cravats. And behind that carriage was other carriages, and buggies and a whole bunch of wagons carrying supplies and servants. It was some big party from the Low Country coming up for a picnic in the mountains. I've heard Fremont, the general and governor of California, was in that party. He was just a boy then. I stood back and let them pass, and they ignored me just like I was air.

Then when I did get started up the turnpike finally, stepping around cowpiles and horse apples, my strength coming
back a little at a time, I met more drovers coming down the
mountain. It was like they had opened a flood gate and flocks
of sheep came along, baaing and pushing and jumping over
each other, churning the road to powder. And then a drove of
hogs came, nosing and grunting, squealing when prodded by
boys with sticks. I thought I had seen it all, but just then
around the bend come a flock of turkeys, all gobbling and
squawking. And behind them a bigger flock of geese come
waddling, driven by more boys and followed by an old
woman who carried a sack on her back.

"We's come all the way from Kentucky," she said.

Finally I thought I had the road to myself. I knowed I'd have
to hurry if I was to get home by milking time. Clara was going
to be mad, but there was no point in putting off the bad news.

"Watch out, watch out, sir," somebody called behind me.

It was a man in a buggy pulled by a shiny mare that just
clipped along. He had a sack on the seat beside him. And I
recognized Sam the peddler from Spartanburg. He used to
come around with a pack on his back, and we almost always
bought cloth and buttons and such from him and asked him
to stay for dinner. And now he was driving a fine buggy with
a carriage horse.

After he passed it seemed late in the evening. The road was
already nearly in shadow. They was a buckeye laying in the
tracks, but I couldn't tell if it was mine. It had been stepped
on by a cow and I let it go. But I seen something shiny in the
dirt ahead. It was my light mason's hammer. Them big rough
boys had dropped it there as they run away. They didn't have
no use for a mason's hammer, and thought it was too heavy
to carry. I picked it up and wiped the grit off the handle and
head before starting again for home.

Kuykendall's Gold

Mr. KUYKENDALL must have heard me scream for he turned around and looked toward me. He was both startled and confused. I knowed he couldn't hardly see, and I run through the laurel bushes to him.

"You ain't supposed to be here," he said.

"Look out!" I said, pointing toward the rattler. But he ignored me. He didn't see the snake and he thought I had followed to spy on him.

"Get away from here," he said, and raised his cane like he was going to hit me. I seen the rage on his face. He was wore out and sick and in pain, and he had been startled just as he reached his goal. I tried to grab his arm and pull him away, but he swung the walking stick and hit my right ear. It hurt like a jar had been broke on my head.

"You old fool," I said, and pointed to the rattler. The woods seemed to be whirling around and the light was sickening.

"Get back to the house," he said. Just then the rattlesnake struck like it was attaching itself to Mr. Kuykendall's leg. I seen the big jaws bite down on his bandaged calf. But I don't think Mr. Kuykendall knowed what happened. His legs was so sore he may have thought he had broke open one of the wounds. He looked at me with fury, gasping for his breath.

49

I thought he was going to hit me again with the cane, and backed away.

Finally he seen where I was pointing. The big snake was still clamped to his leg. He kicked and it jerked away, coiling up again. He hit the snake with his stick and flung it back a few feet. Then he stumbled toward me. From the look in his eyes I seen the world was turning upside down for him. The light had gone crooked, and was crumbling.

∽ · ∽ · ∽

I never understood why people want to call a girl bad just because she's young and lively, and pretty. It's like the badness is on their minds and they see it wherever they look. If God has give a girl certain gifts what is she supposed to do? Go around mourning and hide herself? And if you enjoy life, and enjoy looking good, what are you going to do, make yourself miserable just to please miserable people?

If you're a pretty girl but ain't got no money they want to see you in misery. If you ain't got no position they want to see you humble. Well I never was humble, even when we didn't have nothing, long before I met Mr. Kuykendall or before I seen Flat Rock. And if I can help it I'll never be miserable again neither.

We come walking up the mountains from Rutherfordton way back then. And it's true, we didn't have nothing to our name. Ma had died the summer before of the fever and Pa caught the fever and couldn't do no work for Mr. Burns, and we got throwed off our land. Me and my four brothers had fever too, but we didn't have it bad as Ma and Pa did. Except for little Lucius that died and was buried in the churchyard beside Ma.

I wasn't quite sixteen, but I was already full grown, you could say, and every man in the county had his eye on me. I had that blond full-bosomed look that older men are especially took by. Mr. Burns called me into his big fine house. I'd never been in there except when they give play parties at Christmas and Fourth of July. They was high ceilings and wall paper like shiny cloth and all these sparkling lamps.

Mr. Burns was setting by the fire with his foot propped up cause he had the gout. He smelled like snuff and some kind of toilet water.

"Falby," he said to me. "I know you all has had a hard time."

"Yes sir," I said, "we have."

"The fever is no respecter of persons," he said. "But I can't keep tenants that don't work the land."

"No sir," I said.

"But *you're* welcome to stay," he said. "You can stay right here in the house with me and Mrs. Burns. And you won't have to do no work."

He looked at me steady. He was looking at my ninnies under my dress.

"I'll have to ask Pa," I said.

"I done asked your Pa," he said. "And your Pa agreed you was to stay here with us."

That took me by surprise. But I found out later he paid Pa fifty dollars to leave me there. I found out because I seen the money in Pa's boot and they wasn't nowhere else he could have got it. Fifty dollars was a fortune back then, and Pa didn't have nothing else.

Looked like I didn't have no choice, so I got my things and moved into the big house. And Mrs. Burns showed me to this room on the second floor that was real nice. It had a polished lamp and a cherry wood table and a window that looked out over the tobacco fields where we used to work all the way down to the river. I had seen that window many a time from down in the fields.

Mrs. Burns give me a fine new dress, and I set around trying to be a lady all that day. I washed my hands real good and at dinner I watched what knives and forks everybody used and tried to follow them. Nobody drunk their tea out of their saucer and I didn't neither. The younguns kicked and pinched under the table, but Mrs. Burns didn't say nothing. I guess everybody spoils their grandchildren.

That evening Mrs. Burns said she would teach me to play the spinet. When she looked at my hands she said I'd have to brush under my nails and put lotion on my hands. Mr. Burns set by the fire reading his paper from Charlotte and didn't pay no attention to me. I wished somebody would say something funny so we could laugh.

After I took a candle and went up to my room I set there thinking what it was going to be like to do nothing but set around and learn to play the spinet. The servants had started a fire in my fireplace and the room was warm as July. It was getting into November and the nights was chilly. I was going to ask Mrs. Burns for some material to sew with the next day.

Long after the house was quiet and everybody seemed gone to bed my door opened real slow and there was Mr. Burns. He had on his nightcap and nightgown. I was not entirely surprised to see him. It was like I had knowed why I was there without knowing it. I stood up and he put his fingers to his lips. He limped because of the gout.

I won't tell you no more of that night except I done what he wanted me to do. I seen I didn't have no choice. I knowed old men was grateful to a young girl. It was like Mr. Burns had a terrible need, for he was near about beside hisself when he took off my dress and put his hands on my ninnies. The rest was easy I guess.

Mr. Burns stayed more than half the night in my room, and

then he got up and limped back down the hall. I laid there wondering about my situation and thinking about what I could do. I tried to think about what would happen to me. Wouldn't nobody marry me if I lived there like some handmaiden or concubine out of the Bible. Mr. Burns already had a wife, and he had children that would heir the place. I didn't see how I could end up as anything but a servant myself. And Mrs. Burns could throw me out on the road anytime she wanted to, just like Mr. Burns was throwing Pa out of his house and off the land. I burned with shame that Pa had took money for me. I wasn't no bad girl, and never was no bad girl. It was just that men hankered after me, and women called me bad.

I stayed in the house four days, and every night it was the same. I thought Mr. Burns might get tired and stay away one night, but he didn't. It was like the gout fevered him and kept him stirred up, though he was over fifty.

And I seen how Mrs. Burns resented me. She was polite and proper, but of course she despised me. Why she agreed to take me in was for her own reasons. She had some agreement with Mr. Burns I never did know nothing about. He give her something if he could have me, or give her some special power over him long as I was around. It was something between them I never figured out. But I seen she hated me and would get around to doing me dirt when she got the chance. I worried what I was going to do.

On the fourth day I seen Pa and the boys going along the road carrying everything we owned in tow sacks. Pa didn't have no horse or livestock. He didn't have no furniture that was his own, and hardly more than the clothes on his back. We had worked Mr. Burns's land for near fourteen years, and didn't have a thing to show for it. It near broke my heart to see them walking up the road toward the west without me.

You could see the blue mountains way up the road. I knowed that's where they was going, into the dark wilderness where they was free land, and where nobody knowed who Pa was.

All day I thought of Pa and my brothers walking up that road with sacks on their backs. They was my only kinfolks, and I wouldn't never see them again. Wasn't no good staying at the Burns's. They could throw me out on the road myself whenever it suited them.

After supper that night I went back to my room and put everything I had in a pillowcase. I didn't have no heavy shoes or heavy coat, but I took the fine quilt off the bed. When I slipped out the side door of the house I figured it would be an hour before Mr. Burns found I was gone. Even then he might not raise a fuss, knowing he'd have to wake the whole house up and explain how he found out I was gone.

I knowed exactly the road Pa and my brothers had took. All I had to do was foller it with my bundle to catch up with them. It was hard walking in the dark, stumbling on ruts and stepping in mud puddles. Dogs come out from houses and barked, and when I heard a rider I stepped into the bushes until he went by.

I had walked about ten miles. It must have been after midnight when I seen this dying campfire by a creek. I didn't want to cross the creek in the dark, so I skirted along the bank to where I could look closer at the fire. I thought it might be fox hunters. They was four figures sleeping with their feet to the flames and their heads resting on sacks. It was Pa and my brothers. Pa didn't seem at all surprised to see me. But he wouldn't say much neither. I knowed what he had done, and he didn't want to talk about what had happened at Mr. Burns's house.

The only bedding I had was the quilt I'd brought, so I put that down on the ground on the other side of the fire. Ain't nothing rough as sleeping on the ground when you're not used to it. Every rock and root sticks into your back, and any slant makes you feel like you're going to roll away. I looked up at the stars thinking things can't get no worse than this. And I wondered what was going to happen to me now. But I was sore and tired out from the long walk, and next thing I knowed it was daylight and I was looking up at all the sycamore trees along the creek.

We started walking into the foothills that day. The road was just a track of red dirt. We didn't have nothing to eat, and we didn't have no money except the fifty dollars Pa had in his boot he didn't think I knowed about. Pa had brought a little corn meal but he didn't have no gun to kill a squirrel or rabbit. He just had one pot and a frying pan. My brother Peter tried to steal some taters from somebody's tater hole but almost got bit by a cur dog. Pa kept looking for a whiskey still as we walked along.

But we did keep meeting herds of cattle and sheep. They was drove by men with long poles and whips. They had come across the mountains they said all the way from Tennessee and Virginia and they was going toward Charleston. We met herds of horses and droves of hogs and even flocks of geese. They filled up the road and we had to stand in the weeds and leaves to let them pass.

They was this big flock of geese drove partly by little boys, and when nobody was looking Pa grabbed a goose and run off into the thicket. They was such a racket I don't reckon nobody could hear it squawking. By the time the goose drovers was passed and we had found Pa back in the pine thicket, he had already wrung the goose's neck and started a fire. We roasted that goose and eat it in the middle of the evening like we had never eat nothing before.

But that was the last thing we had to eat for two and a half days. They wasn't many houses once we got into the hills, and the places we seen was mostly way back in the hollers. The mountain people had big dogs in their yards. I got so hungry I kept stopping at springs to drink and fill myself up. Way back up on the mountains you'd see men clearing new ground and burning logs.

"Where we going, Pa?" my brother James said.

But Pa never answered. I knowed he was looking for some place with a liquor still and some free land. Maybe he was looking for a new wife too.

The hills got higher and the valleys deeper. The ground was cold to my bare feet, and I was sore all over from walking so far and sleeping on the ground. The mountains rose blue and rumpled way ahead. We walked up this long narrow valley and climbed through a steep gap. The road wasn't nothing more than a track. At the top we seen this long level land ahead, like it was flat country on top of the mountains. I was near give out. We kept meeting herds of hogs and sheep and the road was almost too filthy to walk on. I seen I was going to have to do something. Pa didn't seem to have no plans except to keep walking.

I hollered to one of the stock drovers, "What is the next place we're coming to?"

"Kuykendall's tavern," he hollered back. "You're almost to Flat Rock."

"Who runs it?" I said.

"Old Man Kuykendall," he said, "that keeps a still and a stand."

I told Pa to stop and I went into the laurel thicket and put on my best dress, the one Mrs. Burns had give me. I put on my shoes too, and I stood over a pool in the branch and combed my hair. And then I washed my face so it was all fresh and pink.

My brothers looked at me when I come out of the woods like I was a stranger. Pa didn't say nothing.

Another four or five miles we come to Kuykendall's stand. It was a great big log building with all kinds of pens and barns and cribs behind it. That's where drovers kept their stock overnight while they stayed in the tavern. Somebody was killing hogs out back, and you could smell the distillery. I knowed I had walked as far as I wanted to.

It was dark inside the tavern. They was a counter and two long tables with benches. Each end of the room had a big fireplace with bear skins and painter hides stretched on the walls. They was all kinds of jugs and bottles and kegs behind the counter. And this old man who looked to be eighty stood at the bar counting coins into a till box.

"Howdy do," I said. I walked up to the counter and set down on a stool.

"How do," he said. I seen that though he was an old man he noticed me. The dress Mrs. Burns had give me was low cut, and I had pushed it down far as I could. I turned a little, this way and that way, on the stool. Ain't no man so old but he cares about a pretty girl.

"May I be of help to you?" he said. He stood straight for an old man, and still had wide shoulders. He had on good plain clothes. The coins he was counting was just pennies and half pennies, with a few shillings and bits mixed in.

"I might be of help to you," I said.

He looked at me in the dim light from the window. I stared at the kegs behind him like I was studying something. I knowed it wouldn't do to look him in the eye that moment. I wanted him to be studying me and not be thinking about anything else. I looked out the window where men was hoisting hogs up on a pole to butcher them.

"Do you know how to draw a pint?" Mr. Kuykendall said.

"I know how to do whatever is needed," I said.

"Then draw us each a mug of cider," he said.

~ · ~ · ~

I don't care what anybody says. I made Mr. Kuykendall a good wife. And I worked hard as the ugliest kitchen maid. If I liked pretty things it was partly because Mr. Kuykendall enjoyed giving me fine things and seeing me wear them. It cheered him up to have a wife that wore ribbons and jewelry. He run a store on the other side of the tavern, and he give me anything I wanted. And it pleasured him to do it.

Every time a peddler come through with a necklace or locket Mr. Kuykendall bought it for me. He said I had the prettiest neck he'd ever seen, and he liked to see pearls around it. I had lockets that hung down between my ninnies, and he liked for me to wear jewelry at night. I wore jewelry that nobody else but him could see. I had a belt made of gold links and amethysts that I wore around my waist, and I had a jeweled garter and anklets. And sometimes I put a ruby in my navel.

But Mr. Kuykendall was stingy with everything else. He liked his pleasure, but he was mostly a tightwad. He counted every penny and every half penny in his till. And when his grown-up younguns come asking for money to buy land or a horse he often as not said no, or offered to loan them money at interest. Of course they blamed me. They said I spent all the old man's money on silks and jewelry and they wouldn't be nothing left for them. People rumored it that I wore a diamond ring on my toe, but it wasn't true.

Mr. Kuykendall had fought in the Revolution was how come the government give him a big tract of land in Flat Rock. But he also got first choice on buying other parcels of land from the state. Most of it was mountain land way back in the valleys. That's what his younguns wanted him to give them, that and money for horses and gambling debts.

After me and Mr. Kuykendall had been married a month he give my Pa a hundred dollars and Pa and my brothers moved on further west. They was my only kin, but Mr. Kuykendall didn't want them living with us. I told my brothers they could come back and stay with us anytime. I slipped and told them that. But that was when I started thinking. I wondered where Mr. Kuykendall had got the hundred dollars, because I never did see more than small change around the tavern. They was a strong box in our room, but I had looked in the strong box, and wasn't more than thirty or forty dollars inside. I knowed people looked up to Mr. Kuykendall like he had a lot of money, and his younguns asked like they knowed he had a lot of money, but I never did see where he kept it.

I started counting money in the till, and in the strong box, and I seen that whenever the amount of money growed beyond about thirty dollars the extra amount disappeared. Yet when a peddler come back with cloth or new supplies Mr. Kuykendall always had money to pay him. I knowed the distillery was doing business all the time, selling jugs and barrels of brandy and liquor, as well as bottles and jars.

"Where do you keep your money?" I said to Mr. Kuykendall. "I need to know if you're not here and I have to pay for a load of corn or a steer."

"Ain't got no money," he said.

"But what if I needed money?" I said as I took off my dress.

"You won't need no money, Falba," he said. He always said "Falba," like it was spelled.

"But what if I did?" I said. He took my ninnies in his hands. I had on a ruby pendant that hung down between them.

59

"Long as I'm alive you won't never need money," he said.

I couldn't say no more because that would sound like I was thinking about him dying. I didn't want to make him mad, or overreach my hand, and us just married a few weeks. But I got to studying about where his money was, in case something did happen to him. It was a mystery.

Every night Mr. Kuykendall counted his coins in the till and then put them in the strong box. And then the next day he would take some coins back to the tavern to make change. Yet the amount of money in the strong box never growed. Every time I looked they was still about thirty dollars there, in silver dollars and one or two gold pieces. No matter how many gold pieces he took in from the distillery or tavern or in rents from his land, the amount never growed in the strong box.

I didn't have no clue where the extra gold pieces went until one day I was looking around our room and I lifted Mr. Kuykendall's shot pouch from the wall. He had his guns on pegs and his powder horn and shot bag hanging beside them. But he was too old to hunt much. I never did see him go off in the woods with a gun. But that shot bag seemed awful heavy and full. I took it down off the peg and looked in it. The leather was wore slick and didn't have no dust on it, like it had been used not too long ago.

I lifted the flap and looked in, and seen the lead balls. But I stuck my fingers into the pouch and felt something flat and colder than lead. They was gold pieces under the shot. Five and ten and twenty dollar gold pieces. My heart liked to jumped out of my chest. Mr. Kuykendall's treasury was right in the room. I put the shot pouch back on the peg and after that I kept my eye on it. The bag seemed to get a little heavier each week. I didn't say nothing to Mr. Kuykendall and I didn't take nothing from the hoard except once when a peddler come that had an opal ring. I took twenty dollars from the bag, but I was going to tell Mr. Kuykendall and show him the ring when something else happened that made me forget it.

It was way up in the middle of the night. It was almost a year after I had come to Flat Rock. I had a headache and took some drops to help me sleep. I woke up in the dark for some reason, feeling plumb drunk from the drops and from my cold. Mr. Kuykendall was not in bed, but I heard him moving in the room. It was like he was getting dressed. I laid there and didn't make a sound.

He was putting his boots on, and then he put on his coat. I heard the creak of leather, and wondered what he was doing. Then I thought he must have took the shot bag from the wall. That woke me up for sure. Before that I felt I might be dreaming. I laid there completely still until he left the room. When I was sure he wasn't coming back I got up quick and throwed on a shawl and got my shoes.

Somebody was moving around in the tavern, and then I heard a door close. I looked out the window and seen this lantern go across the yard by the stock pens. It was Mr. Kuykendall all right, and they was somebody with him. It looked like it was Theo, Mr. Kuykendall's biggest slave. Theo stooped down, and Mr. Kuykendall tied something around his head. It was a scarf he wrapped right over Theo's eyes. And I seen Theo was holding the shot bag in one hand and a shovel in the other. Mr. Kuykendall picked up the lantern, and placed the strap of the shot bag over Theo's shoulder. He put Theo's hand on his own shoulder, and they started off into the dark. By the time I got out the door I seen the lantern going into the woods. I run past the stock pens full of cows and hogs. I kept stumbling on things in the dark and stepping in mud. By the time I got to the woods I could see the lantern way off through the trees. They wasn't follering no trail.

It was shivery cold, and I didn't have nothing on but the shawl. I kept running into limbs and getting slapped in the face by brush. I knowed my face would be all scratched up if I didn't slow down. I put out my arms, hoping they wasn't no thorns or briars. I stubbed my toes on rocks and logs. The lantern kept bobbing up and down ahead like it was floating on a river.

I tried not to make no noise stepping on sticks and rattling leaves. Everything was wet with dew, and that made it easier, though my feet was already cold. Mr. Kuykendall couldn't hear too good, but Theo might hear me follering. I was hoping they made so much noise theirselves they wouldn't notice me.

The woods north of the tavern was divided by Pheasant Branch. I'd walked up there a few times to get away from the noise and smoke of the stock drovers and the mean looks of women from the church. It made me feel better to get out in the laurels sometimes and listen to the birds and look for periwinkles and pretty rocks in the branch. Green grass growed along the branch when everything else was gray and brown. I always did like to be around a stream. I liked the mystery sounds of water, the shiny sands and the minners going this way and that way in a pool. They was always something to get your attention, where a clay bank is exposed or a crawfish hides in the rocks. But I'd never gone more than half a mile up the branch, and I didn't know the woods beyond that.

The woods is so different at night it might as well be another world. The stars and the limbs and the shine from the creek get all tangled up. The lantern crossed the branch and I got my feet soaked in the water before I knowed it. Mr. Kuykendall led Theo right up the branch like it was a trail, and then he climbed up on the west bank and went that way for a while. We was going through pines, for the needles scratched my face and I felt the rough bark.

I didn't know where we was. We zigzagged back and forth across the branch half a dozen times, and I wasn't even sure what direction was which anymore. I knowed Theo must be lost with the blindfold on. I thought we could be halfway to Asheville, or down in South Carolina. My feet and legs was all covered with mud.

Then I seen the lantern had stopped moving, and I stopped and listened. Mr. Kuykendall was talking to Theo, but I couldn't tell what he was saying. His voice way out there in the dark made me shudder. It was like they was praying or performing some witch's service. A tiny step at a time I edged up closer and got in behind some laurel bushes.

They was standing under this big maple tree on the bank above the branch. Mr. Kuykendall hung the lantern on a limb and in its light the tree looked chalky white, like it was underground and had lime or mold on it. Mr. Kuykendall took the blindfold off Theo.

"I don't see nothing at all," Theo said, looking at the ground all around.

"You ain't supposed to see nothing," Mr. Kuykendall said. He pointed to a spot under the big tree. I couldn't see a thing there but sticks and leaves. "Clear it off," he said.

Theo set the shot bag down and begun clearing away trash and dirt with the shovel. The blade rung on a rock, and after he had cleaned away a place he bent down and lifted this big rock.

"Don't get no dirt in the pot," Mr. Kuykendall said.

I stretched far as I could without coming out of the laurel bushes, but I still couldn't see what was in the hole. I could see the dirt cleared away, and the big flat rock Theo had lifted aside. But the rest was just darkness.

"Go stand in the dark," Mr. Kuykendall said. The slave walked to the edge of the circle of lantern light and looked into the dark.

"You don't see nothing," Mr. Kuykendall said.

"I don't see nothing, Marse Kuykendall."

While Theo was looking out into the darkness, Mr. Kuyk-endall knelt on the ground and opened the shot bag. He brought the lantern down close and counted coins out of the pouch into the hole. The money tinkled and rung on other money. It sounded like they was a great heap in the hole. But I couldn't see a thing below the level of the dirt. All I could see was Mr. Kuykendall's face and its look of delight as he counted out the gold pieces. It was a look that compared with his face when he put his hands on my ninnies and when I pleasured him the most. It was the counting out that was part of the pleasure, like the work of love. It was like his whole long life was caught and changed into the gold, from his fight-ing in the war for independence to his rich old age.

As a wife I didn't know whether to feel jealous or pleased. He had left me out and fooled me. It was like I was a little girl he played with but didn't trust. Men don't want women to know what's going on with their business. They want women to look pretty and cook for them and be there to please them. But at the same time I was glad the money cheered him up so. And I was glad he had all that money. I had wondered where his wealth was. I felt like I knowed him for the first time.

He counted the coins slower and slower. I could see he was enjoying it so much he didn't want it to be over. It was like he was tasting every gold piece with his fingers. I could almost feel the coolness and sweetness in each coin he touched. The money flashed in the lantern light like little faces and wings.

Finally he finished and seemed tired out by it all. "Cover it up," he said to Theo.

I knowed I had to start back. I had to be back at the house before they got there. I had to be in bed by the time Mr. Kuykendall got back, and to seem warm and asleep. I was going to have to find the way all by myself.

I tried to fix in my mind the way the big tree looked so I would know it when I seen it again. It was wide as a door and had a fat crooked limb that leaned over the branch. The money hole was about six feet out from the trunk, not quite halfway around from the branch side.

Soon as Theo's shovel rung on the rock, as he scraped the dirt back on, I started backing away. And when I got a little distance off I started running. I run with my arms out to protect my face. I run in the direction I thought was the tavern. As I run I thought it was good Mr. Kuykendall was old and would walk back slow, leading Theo in the blindfold. I wished I had knowed Mr. Kuykendall when he was young and strong. I'd seen how smart and strong he was as an old man, but I wished I'd knowed him back when he was a soldier in the Revolution. But if I had I'd be an old woman myself, I thought, or dead like his other two wives.

I didn't know where I was until I heard some cows bawling. They was off to my left and I knowed they must be in the stock pens. I had gone about half a mile out of the way. I hurried to the house and washed my feet at the spring and slipped in bed. It was near daylight before Mr. Kuykendall returned, but I was warm by then and pretended to be asleep.

∽ · ∽ · ∽

If people think you are bad they will say everything you do is bad, no matter what happens. If you like to enjoy yourself, and you're pretty, they'll say you're a bad woman. A rumor gets started and next thing you hear is that you're a road whore, a hussy, a bad influence.

I admit I liked to talk to the drovers when they come into

the tavern and I was working behind the counter. They come in tired after a long day of walking or riding. It made them feel good to see somebody pretty, after looking at the rear ends of cows all day as they crossed the mountains. They liked to hear a woman's voice after all them nights camping by creeks and days of walking through dust and mud. I served them cider and ale and corn liquor or brandy from the still, and they got to feeling better quick. And you know how it is: after a few minutes they're already falling in love and flirting and trying to get you to notice them.

But I was helping Mr. Kuykendall out. I was working hard as the next woman. And men started stopping at the tavern more than ever cause I was there. They liked for me to talk to them, and joke with them. I acted like I didn't care. Most wives is so hard and disapproving, men like to see a woman that enjoys herself. That's why women around Flat Rock didn't like me. The few times I went to church they didn't even speak to me. They said I didn't have no faith and love for Jesus. And I didn't see no use to go to meeting if they was going to high hat me. Many's the time I've give the preacher a dollar, or five dollars.

People don't think of anybody else's feelings. They'll say things to hurt a person and not even care. There I was, a young girl that married Mr. Kuykendall and made him happy and helped out in his tavern. I was young and in good health and wanted a family same as anybody. But I was working every day, up to my elbows in dust and dishwater, and selling cloth in the store, and even writing things down in the ledger. But I was married to an eighty-year-old man. Did they ever think about that? Did they even care what that meant?

I noticed Homer Hoppas first time he come to the tavern. I thought he was one of the drovers from up in Tennessee. But he wasn't. He had been out squirrel hunting and got thirsty on the way home from Glassy Mountain. He leaned his gun on the table and had squirrel tails sticking out of his pockets. He was a big feller with black hair and fair skin.

I thought he was the handsomest feller I'd ever seen, but I didn't treat him any different from anybody else. It was like some little thing changed in me when I seen him. It was so small it was nothing, but I felt it. It was an echo way back somewheres that I heard.

"What can I bring you?" I said.

"What you got?" he said, and looked at me for just a second longer than was usual.

"Ale or cider?" I said.

Nothing happened then except that I remembered him. And I knowed he'd be back. I thought about him at odd times of the day and night and it made me feel good. It was like this little thing had turned over inside me.

I noticed every day, but he didn't come back for a week. I wondered if I was wrong. Every day I wiped the bar and joked with the drovers same as before, but I watched the door. I acted even better to Mr. Kuykendall, and I worked longer every day. I dressed a little more careful, and put more ribbons in my hair.

After about ten days I was pulling a glass of brandy from the keg, with my back toward the smokey room, and I felt the light change. It was a Friday night and the place was loud and full of stock men and neighbors. It was getting up toward election time and men was arguing over candidates and accusing each other. You know how it is when men get to arguing politics while they're drinking. Some was for President Adams, but most called him a hide-bound, tight-fisted, tory old maid of a leader. They was lots of red faces.

I turned around and through all the smoke and noise I seen him. He already had his blue eyes on me. I waited till I had served three others before I went over to him. I didn't want to look too interested. But I couldn't think of nothing else.

Let me ask you to consider my position. Here I was, a young girl that had been sold twice to old men. And I had done my best to look after Mr. Kuykendall and please him and help out with his business in every way. But I was still young, with the needs and feelings of a young girl, and a heart that had never been touched. Ask any woman. It was like they was a place in my heart that had never been reached before. Ask any woman, and she will tell you what that means.

I didn't do nothing quick, and I didn't rush nothing with Homer Hoppas. We just talked a little every week or so when he come to the tavern. We both knowed what we was feeling. We didn't need to say nothing about it. And I didn't even know he was married until it was too late. Beyond a certain point a woman can't help herself, don't want to help herself. They was men every day with their eyes all over me. Big strong men, red faced men. Men with long black beards and fine horses. I wore my low cut dresses. Men would put out a hand and I would push them away and swing out of their reach.

But it was Homer I thought about. It was like my blood had been touched with a yeast. I worked harder but my mind was never on what I was doing. Things must have gone on that way for a month, till one night Homer come in and set down near the door. Mr. Kuykendall was standing by the till, the way he always done. And Priscilla, the maid, was helping me out. I was hot and sweaty and went out onto the back porch to wipe my neck and bosoms and get a drink of water.

I was standing by the bucket with the dipper in my hand when I seen Homer step out of the shadows. He had gone around by the outhouse. He didn't say nothing as he approached me. It was like somebody had throwed powder in my blood and I was half asleep and half trembling when he

touched me. He pushed me into the shadows against the wall.
I don't remember a thing except how I couldn't do nothing. I
wouldn't have cared if Mr. Kuykendall and all the ladies from
the church had come out to watch us. It was like my blood was
chasing after itself to every place he touched me. I couldn't
have stopped him if I'd knowed it would cost me a million years
in hell.

Homer never said a thing. He lifted me right up on hisself.
He pushed me up against the wall, and his feet was jerking the
way a dog's will when he mounts a bitch. It was like neither of
us was controlling what we done. It was like I was swimming
and swimming backwards in a deep sweet pool. When he was
finished we practically fell over. I was so weak I had to hold
onto him and the wall for a minute or two, before I could feel
my feet on the ground.

After a few more minutes I pushed my dress back down
and patted it in place. Then I splashed water on my face and
neck and wiped them dry before going back into the tavern.
Mr. Kuykendall was still standing by the till.

$\sim \cdot \sim \cdot \sim$

It wasn't too much longer after that that Mr. Kuykendall's
health begun to fail. He was a strong old man, and he had
always been the stoutest kind of man. But once he started to
fail it went quicker and quicker. The doctor said it was his
heart. But I think it was just old age, because everything started
to go wrong at once.

Some people blamed me. They said I had broke his heart
and worried him sick with my doings. They said I spent all his
money on dresses and jewelry and that caused him to get sick
in his mind. And other people said I didn't take care of him
after I started seeing Homer.

They's people will tell you just having a young wife will kill

69

an old man. They'll say the excitement of having a young woman around all the time will wear an old man out. Trying to satisfy a young woman is the death of any old feller, they'll say. They mean that any young woman that marries an old man does it to kill him and take his money. She does it, they say, to wear him out in a few months and then be free.

But wasn't none of it true. Mr. Kuykendall was an old man when I married him, and I pleasured him when I could. And I made him happy. He could be manly as any man when he felt like it, when he was feeling good. But he had all the things any old man has: rheumatism, shortness of breath, a bad stomach and wind.

The first I noticed he was failing was when I woke up and he was setting by the bed trying to get his breath.

"Are you sick, Mr. Kuykendall?" I said.

"I'll be all right," he said. "Soon as I can catch my breath."

But he wasn't all right. He set there trying to breathe for hours. He had me open a window to let in fresh air. "They ain't no air in here," he said. "Open that window."

"It is open," I said.

Once it got daylight he felt better. It was the dark smothered him. He seemed afraid of the dark like a little child will. He was afraid of the night and he was afraid to lay down anymore. He said it smothered him to lay back in bed. He was afraid he would die if he laid back in the dark.

That was the way it went for the next few weeks. Some days he would feel better and could get his breath. But mostly he felt worser. It made him mad that he couldn't walk around like he was used to doing. He had always worked and done what he wanted to. He had been a soldier and a strong man. It made him so mad to be weak he would knock things around and holler at me or the maid when we tried to wait on him.

Men don't bear up well in sickness the way women does.

Men is used to having their way. But a woman's used to being patient and making do with disappointments. She will accept pain and weakness. But a man just gets mad and frets and cusses and tries to hurt people's feelings. He tries to punish his loved ones because he's sick and can't no longer do what he wants to.

But I found I could take care of Mr. Kuykendall in his bad shape. The worser he got the better I was at it. I never thought I could be a nurse, but there I was, looking after him day and night almost. Theo helped him get up and the maid brought him things. But every time he got bad he hollered for me. It was like he come to depend on me for comfort, the way a little kid will depend on his mama.

I would be out in the tavern and I would have to come running when he hollered out. Or I would be trading in the store and buying furs or selling cloth. And I could hear Mr. Kuykendall hollering across the house. The worst was when I was trying to sleep and he would be setting by the window and start groaning until I woke up. I couldn't get no sleep for all them weeks. He was like a little child that has to be fussed over and petted. He was afraid of the dark, and he was afraid he would lose his breath and couldn't get it back. I think he was terrible afraid he was going to die. I done what I could. I brought him soup and fed it to him, and hot tea, and molasses and honey.

It was like we had a new kind of marriage. I had to stay with him, and I found I was a nurse whether I liked it or not. He couldn't stand for me to be out of his sight. It was like he was depending on my strength for him to live. When he was feeling better he held my hand, and he couldn't hardly take his eyes off me. Sometimes at night I would take my dress down to my waist and hold the candle up so he could see me. It cheered him up to see my ninnies more than anything else.

71

They was young and round and big. I would stand there and let him enjoy me. Sometimes I took my ninnies in my hands and rubbed them. That seemed to delight him most of all.

But when he took another spell he couldn't think of nothing but trying to get his breath. He coughed and heaved half the night. His eyes stared at nothing, as he tried to get more air. "Leave in some fresh air," he said. "I'll be fine if I can just breathe."

I learned not to tell him the window was already open. I'd go to the window like I was follering his orders, and sometimes that would make him feel better. The room would get cool and he would feel stronger.

But after a few weeks nothing would make him feel better. When his sons come by to talk about the property he wouldn't hardly pay no attention to them. He acted like he couldn't hear them. I knowed they was afraid he would die and they wouldn't know where his money was kept. They told me to leave while they talked to him. But it didn't do them no good. If I started to leave Mr. Kuykendall would holler out, "Falba, get back here." And then he would cough for a while. He would set in his chair and cough; he wouldn't go to bed.

I done things I never thought I would do. I washed him every morning with a rag and a pan of warm water. His old man arms and legs begun to look wasted, and they hadn't before. I washed every part of him and he felt better then. And I brought him soup, and I held his forehead while he coughed. "Falba," he hollered, if I stayed away from him for a few minutes. I seen Homer in the tavern, but I couldn't get alone with him for more than a few minutes. It was like Homer belonged to another world. After staying up all night with Mr. Kuykendall it was like Homer was somebody I had dreamed about.

After about a month of his setting by the window Mr. Kuykendall's legs started going bad. The right leg was worser than the left, but they was both in sorry shape. The skin turned kind of purple and got dry and scaly. But the worst thing was the sores come on the backs of his legs. They started out like little places that wouldn't heal and every day they got bigger. The doctor said it was because he set in the chair all the time. He said the only thing that would help would be to lay down on the bed all night. But Mr. Kuykendall wouldn't lay down at all.

I done things I never thought I could. Every morning I washed off the legs and rubbed them with camphor. And right around the sores I put some salve. And I put oil on the bandages before I wrapped the ulcers up. It was hard to look at them legs going black and purple and the sores breaking through the skin. But I found out I could do it.

Every morning I unwound the old dirty bandages and cut the cloth away from where it had stuck to the sores. Mostly it was blood that was dried. They wasn't no scabs forming on those wounds. You could see the tendons under the blood. I found the only thing to do was look right at the ugliness of it. I snipped away the bindings and got warm water and washed the wounds. It was like you could make things a little better just by putting clean bandages and salve on the sores. I don't think it really helped. But it made Mr. Kuykendall feel better to be clean, and it made me feel better to do something for him, something that took a long time.

The sickness touched Mr. Kuykendall's mind worse and worse. If you feel bad long enough it makes you think wrong. I would see him looking at me as I went about my work. He was scared I would leave him alone, especially at night. It was like he was a baby and I was his mama and he was afraid of the dark. His eyes was follering me wherever I went. His eyes had gone bad, and he couldn't see in dim light.

73

"Where you going?" he would say.

"I'm gonna get some more water," I'd say.

"Don't go," he'd say.

"I've got to get some clean water." I was just a young girl and here I was doing all this stuff for the old man. People never mentioned that when they talked about me. I done everything for Mr. Kuykendall, including the things you're not supposed to mention. Me and Theo had to lift him on and off the pot. And I had to clean him up just like I was a servant.

But the more I done for Mr. Kuykendall the more I wanted to do. That's what surprised me. Maybe I wanted to prove that people was wrong about me. Maybe I wanted to show the doctor and all the people who come to the tavern what a good wife I was. Or maybe I just wanted to show myself what I could do. I couldn't hardly believe how hard I worked. I hadn't been married to Mr. Kuykendall that long, and here I was nursing him.

One time Homer come to the tavern at night and I slipped out into the pine woods with him. And though it was a great relief to get out of the sickroom for a few minutes I didn't enjoy it much as I expected to. It was like my mind couldn't get entirely away from poor old Mr. Kuykendall where he gasped for breath and coughed by the window. I wished I could stay out all night in the dark with Homer, and yet I had to go back in and do what needed to be done.

"Where you been?" Mr. Kuykendall hissed when I come back to the room.

"I've been out in the tavern," I said.

"No you ain't." Mr. Kuykendall started coughing. His face turned red and he heaved in his chair. He would start a word and then cough through it before he could say it. I patted him on the back like I was pounding dough.

"Have some syrup," I said. I got the bottle of soothing syrup. It had both liquor and drops mixed with the honey in it.

"Theo said you was gone," he said.

"I was gone," I said, "to the outhouse."

But he didn't believe me. It was like he knowed where I had been. In his sickness he had the kind of cunning drunks sometimes have. His mind come back at times, though his body was giving out.

"I'm gonna give you something," he said the next day. And I understood what he meant. He was going to pay me for all I had done for him. He was going to give me a present to make me stay with him.

"Gonna give me a pretty?" I said, playing along with him.

"Something real pretty," he said.

"Don't need to do that, Mr. Kuykendall," I said. But he seen I understood him. I didn't understand how his mind was working most of the time, but I understood him then. I could have asked him about the pot of gold in the woods, and I could have asked about his will and all his property and the stand and distillery. But I didn't. People can accuse me of every kind of selfishness and stealing, but I didn't even mention his will when he was sick. Whatever he done with that he done before he got sick.

I seen he had something on his mind. They was something he was thinking about no matter how bad he felt. All through the night he coughed and fretted. Sometimes his legs started to hurt him, and he set there and cried like a little baby. He hollered and I put my hand on his forehead and my arm around his shoulders. He felt so bad he didn't hardly know what he was doing. But that night he didn't cry none. He just set there studying on something and breathing heavy. He looked little and stooped over, compared to the big strong man he had been.

75

"Don't ever leave me," he would say.

"I ain't gonna leave you," I would say. "Where would I go, Mr. Kuykendall? My daddy's done gone and my mama's dead."

But he didn't believe me. Every few minutes he'd say it again. It was a long night. I didn't hardly get no sleep. Every time I laid down he'd holler again and I'd have to get the syrup, or a drink of water, or help him to the pot.

Just as it begun to get daylight he told me to bring his shoes.

"You ain't strong enough to walk," I said.

"Get my damn shoes," he said.

I got his shoes and tried to put them on. But they wouldn't fit at all. His feet had swole up, and I couldn't much more than get the toes in the shoes. "Ain't gonna fit, Mr. Kuykendall," I said.

He grabbed a shoe out of my hand and threw it across the room.

"Shame on you," I said. "Ain't gonna do no good to get mad."

He kicked out at me. I don't know if he meant to hurt me or just lost control of hisself. "Bring my slippers," he said. He had these sheepskin slippers he wore in winter. They was thick and warm and had a rawhide string that tied them on. But it was early summer and he hadn't wore them in months.

"You're in no shape to go out," I said. But I brought him the slippers. He didn't say nothing else. He put his mind to getting the slippers on over his bandages. Then he reached for his cane and stood up.

"Mr. Kuykendall," I said.

"You stay here," he said. He was unsteady as a drunk man. I thought he was going to trip before he got to the door.

"Mr. Kuykendall, you're too weak to walk," I said.

He turned in the door and looked at me. "You stay right

here," he said. "I'm going to get something for you." He hobbled down the hall dragging his slippers on the puncheons and went out the back door.

As soon as he was outside I run to the door and watched him. It was early summer and they was a heavy dew on the grass and weeds. Wasn't nobody else up, and it would be an hour before the sun was out. It was around the time of the longest day of the year.

I watched Mr. Kuykendall limping right toward the pine woods. He was leaning on his cane, and it must have been painful to walk with all those sores on his legs. His breath was short but he just kept going steady into the trees.

I run back to the bedroom and throwed on a dress and put on my shoes. I didn't have time to get a bonnet. When I run through the grass it swished, the dew was so heavy. By the time I got to the edge of the woods I could just see Mr. Kuykendall's white head as it bobbed through the limbs. He was going north, and I knowed where he must be heading.

It was dark inside the trees. On an early summer morning it's like the air is full of dew or mist. Every limb I touched wet me a little. I couldn't see to walk in the shadows, and first a pine limb scratched me, and then I run into a spider web. I didn't see the spider, but the web stuck across my face like a veil and got all tangled up in my hair and eyelashes. By the time I tore away the cobweb I could just barely see Mr. Kuykendall way off through the trees.

I knowed I should watch out for snakes, for copperheads and rattlers was crawling that time of year. But it was too dark underfoot, and they wasn't time. To keep Mr. Kuykendall in sight I had to fight with limbs and split my way through briars and undergrowth. My feet broke sticks and rattled leaves, but I didn't reckon it mattered. Mr. Kuykendall was too hard of hearing to notice.

77

Suddenly I seen he had stopped. He was standing in the oaks leaning both hands on his walking stick. It was like he was holding onto the stick for strength. I knowed he was having one of his dizzy spells. When he got short of breath he couldn't see nothing or think about nothing. He might have forgot where he was. I wondered should I go up to him. It would make him mad if he seen I had follered him, and might make his attack worse. It like to broke my heart to see him standing there all bent over like he was lost in the woods and too weak to go any direction. I stood still and watched him. If he fell down I'd run to him, and then go back to the house for help. They wasn't anything else I could do.

This bird started singing in the tree above him. I don't know what kind of bird it was. But it had a loud song, like it was calling Mr. Kuykendall. Its voice filled up the woods with a whirling sound like something going round and round. It sounded like it was saying, "Wake up, wake up, you're still alive."

And Mr. Kuykendall seemed to hear the bird calling and woke from his spell. He looked around like he remembered where he was and what he was doing. He started walking, but not in exactly the same direction as before. He cut to the left, toward the branch. I follered him maybe fifty feet behind.

When he got to the branch he just stepped through it and across. He didn't foller it the way I expected him to. I wondered if he remembered the way to where he was going. He crossed the branch and climbed through the laurels on the other side. He slipped once and had to grab hold of a bush. I don't think his sheepskin slippers give him much footing on the leaves. The slippers was wet with dew and didn't have no heels. I was glad I had follered him. He was sure to fall and need some help getting back. I just hoped he didn't break a hip the way so many old people did.

Something exploded in the brush off to the left. I froze with fear, thinking somebody had fired a shot. It was like a hole had been knocked in the air. The pain of shock hurt through my bones to the soles of my feet. And just then I seen the pheasant that rose through the undergrowth and flew out through the trees. Mr. Kuykendall stopped and looked around. I just had time to drop in the brush as he looked my way. He had heard the pheasant flush and was trying to see what it was. I didn't think he could see well enough to notice me.

"Who is it?" Mr. Kuykendall hollered. He thought it was somebody that made the noise. "Who's out there?" he said. "This is my property." He looked around trying to see who had startled him.

I felt so sorry for the old man I wished I could go to him and lead him back to the tavern. But I knowed he'd just be mad. It might kill him if he got too angry.

"Come on out," he hollered. "Show yourself."

You could see light in the tops of the trees by then. It was a still summer morning, after the pheasant flew away. Mr. Kuykendall's voice echoed through the woods. He turned around looking for whoever had disturbed him. A squirrel run out a limb above him, and further away I could hear a woodpecker tapping.

Finally Mr. Kuykendall give up trying to get an answer and started walking again. But this time he bore to the right, back toward the branch. I wondered if he had any idea where he was going, or if he was lost. They wasn't no path nor markings on the trees. I felt strange out in the woods in the early morning follering that old man. If he died out there what would people say about me? Would they accuse me of not looking after him? of letting him wander off by hisself? I'd have to try my best to bring him back to the tavern.

When he got to the branch he turned and walked right into the water. The sheepskin slippers made a sucking noise as he stepped on mossy rocks and mud. I stayed on the bank and walked along beside him in the bushes. I had to duck under laurels and part brush to see where I was going. I started to sweat even though it was still cool.

"Get out of my way," Mr. Kuykendall said. "Get back out of my way." It was like he was talking to the limbs and bushes. He seen people around him that wasn't there. "Get back," he hollered, "or I'll run my sword through you." I stood and listened. He must have thought he was back fighting in the Revolution.

Then I seen this limb moving near his head. It looked like the limb was untwisting itself, like a big screw turning. And I almost hollered out, for I seen it was a long snake that come unwinding itself off the limb where it had been sleeping. It dropped into the water with a splash and Mr. Kuykendall turned around to see what it was. But I don't think he ever did catch sight of the snake. It was a big long water snake that swum to the bank and disappeared into a hole. I shivered.

"Come out and show yourself," Mr. Kuykendall said. I thought for a second he had seen me or heard me. But he turned away. He was still seeing ghosts in the air.

I wondered how much further he would go. He was so weak, and stumbling on rocks and pools in the branch. But he was a determined man. He still had the spirit and will of the old soldier. He stumbled on, and I follered him in the bushes. He mumbled to hisself, and suddenly I realized he was talking about me.

"Oh Falba," he was saying, "I'll buy you the prettiest necklace you ever seen."

I stopped dead still. He panted for a moment, trying to catch his breath.

"I'll buy you a string of rubies to hang over your bosoms," he said.

I found my eyes wet, just listening to the old man and his imaginings. Didn't seem fair to let him get loster in the woods, but I didn't know what else to do. He started walking again in the water, grabbing hold of limbs and feeling with his stick the way ahead.

After what must have been another half mile he stopped and looked up. They was a maple tree on the bank, reaching its gray limbs out everwhich way. Its bark looked like it had been dusted with chalk. Mr. Kuykendall squinted his eyes and searched around.

And then I seen it was the same tree where Theo and Mr. Kuykendall had come to. I couldn't see no rock under it, but of course the big rock had been covered over with leaves and trash. They was weeds and briars around the tree, now it was summer. Mr. Kuykendall seemed to be trying to decide if he had found the right place. He must have had sweat in his eyes for he kept wiping his brow with his sleeve. And I guess he just couldn't see, and he was feeling dizzy besides. And maybe he was looking around to see if anybody was follering him.

A blue jay was squawking in the tree, way up in the top. It was like the jay was guarding the tree and warning us. It was ordering us away. I don't think Mr. Kuykendall could even hear the blue jay. He was trying to get his bearings. He looked around, and then stood leaning on his stick to catch his breath.

Finally he seemed to decide he was in the right place. The bank was too steep for him to climb directly. He stepped out of the water and started easing up it sideways. He had to stop and rest several times before he got up to the level ground. I seen he was trembling and sweating.

But he knowed where the rock was. When he got his breath he walked right to the spot under the big maple. I moved up close as I could in the bushes. I didn't see how he could lift the big rock anyhow.

Mr. Kuykendall reached down to rake the leaves away. And just then I seen the rattler. It was the same color as the leaves and trash and I wouldn't have seen it except for its tail. The snake coiled up and its tail blurred. I don't think Mr. Kuykendall seen it at all. When he reached down again I hollered out.

~ · ~ · ~

I grabbed up a rock and throwed at the big snake and it crawled off into the brush. Much as I wanted to kill it I had to let it go. Mr. Kuykendall was bent over like he couldn't get his breath, and he couldn't see where he was. I'd heard rattlesnake venom will make you numb and stop your heart.

"You better set down," I said to Mr. Kuykendall.

"You had no right to foller me," he said. It was like he couldn't think about the fix he was in. All he could remember was he had told me not to foller him.

"Set down and I will look at the bite," I said.

"Get away from me," he hollered. He swung the stick and I backed away. My ear was still throbbing from the lick before. He started walking down the bank toward the branch. He was so unsteady I knowed he was going to fall.

"Set down and I will go for help," I said.

"Damn your help," he said. He seemed to blame me for everything that had gone wrong, which is the way of men. I wondered what my duty was. I had tried my best to look after him. But I didn't want to be hit no more. I wondered if I should just push him down and go for help. But I was afraid he would break a hip if he fell.

"Set down, old man," I hollered. I had not talked to him like that before.

82

"Damn woman," he said. "Ain't gonna buy you no more pretties."

"You've got to set down," I said. "I'll help you."

He swung the stick again, but I flung up my arm and just got hit on the elbow. He wasn't hisself no more. He was like a wounded animal that snarls and is too weak to fight back except to bite the helping hand. He couldn't hardly get his breath, and I don't think he knowed where he was. I reckon his head was swimming as it did when he had his spells.

He stumbled down into the branch and started walking, taking one short step at a time. I follered along the bank, pushing limbs aside and getting scratched by briars. Every few feet he stopped and rested on his walking stick. The water sucked around his slippers every time he moved. I don't know where he thought he was going. He may have thought he was going back to the tavern, though he was walking in the opposite direction. Or maybe he thought he was back in the war and marching.

"Mr. Kuykendall," I called. But he ignored me. He might not have even heard me. When he stopped I could hear him panting, and the crows making a fuss in the pines overhead. "Mr. Kuykendall," I hollered. He looked around like he had heard me, but couldn't see nothing. He seemed to lean back to look up, then caught hisself, and pitched forward into the branch with a big splash.

I run down through the dripping bushes and tried to turn him over. He was a big heavy man and he had fell in the shallow water. I couldn't hardly move him. His face was right in the little pool and I lifted his head up to keep him from drowning. I raised his head high as I could, and the water dripped off his nose and eyebrows. But his eyes was open and set. He must have been dead before he hit the water.

I set down on the bank trying to think what to do. He was

way too heavy for me to drag out of the branch. I thought I should turn him over so the crawfish and worms couldn't eat into his eyes. But even if I did turn him over his face would dry and begin to rot in the hot summer air. I figured it was better to leave him in the cool water.

For an hour I must have set there in the leaves and pine needles trying to think what to do. The crows was calling in the trees, and Mr. Kuykendall just laid there like he was taking a long drink from the branch, or sleeping in the cold water. After all his long life and the pain of the past few weeks, it looked comforting just to lay there in the cool water. Mr. Kuykendall had fell in a little open place, and the sun was starting to touch the tops of the trees.

But what was I to do? What was I to tell people? They was rumors about Mr. Kuykendall's pot of gold. All Theo knowed was it was under a big maple tree. Theo was an old man who couldn't see too well hisself.

Mr. Kuykendall had stumbled maybe six hundred feet from the place his gold was buried. But it was deep thicket all around. Even if people guessed what he was doing it would take them a long time to find the tree and the wash pot full of gold. I seen what I had to do. I stood up and started running toward the tavern. I would tell everybody the truth, up to a point. I would say I had gone looking for Mr. Kuykendall and found him dead in the branch.

As I run around sourwoods, tearing my dress on briars and catching cobwebs on my hair, I thought how people would say these woods was haunted in the future. They would say they seen Mr. Kuykendall's ghost looking for his gold along Pheasant Branch. They would say they seen spooks and haints for years to come. And they would dig all over the miles of pine woods and all along the branch looking for the wash pot. But Theo would never tell, for he would be hoping to look for it hisself. They would dig up hundreds of holes, but never find it under the rock.

I was almost out of breath before I got to the clearing. My clothes was wet with sweat and stuck with bark soot and leaves and spiderwebs. The dogs begun barking as I got close to the edge of the yard. As I started calling for help, I thought maybe I wouldn't dig up the gold for a while. It would be my secret, and I'd decide later what to do with it. Let people say whatever they wanted to.

"Help me," I hollered, as I run out into the sunlight.

Little Willie

Nᴏᴛʜɪɴɢ ᴇᴠᴇʀ ᴅɪᴅ hurt me no worse. You would have thought he was my own flesh and blood. When they brought that little body back and I seen what had been done to it, it like to broke my heart. It ever did startle me to see red blood coming through black skin, just as red as yours or mine. On the dark skin it looked even brighter. And it stung to think it was my own fault, it was all my doing. If I hadn't made him a little blue jacket for his birthday nothing would have happened.

I looked at that little body and seen it was twisted wrong. The back wasn't right, and it made me sick to see blood on the back of his head where something heavy had hit him. A woman is always scared for younguns, because they can't look out for theirselves and it's up to you to get them raised. And no matter what you're doing you worry about where the children are and what might happen to them. I had got my children growed up and didn't think I would have that responsibility no more. And then we got Little Willie.

"Put him down there on the table," I said to Judd and Steven. "Put him right there." He was bleeding so you wouldn't think a little body would have that much blood in it. I was thinking we would call the doctor and he would operate on the table and set some of the bones. But I could see Little

86

Willie's eyes was open and he wasn't breathing. I catched him in my arms and listened to his heart and they wasn't no sound but my own breathing. I thought, if I have to lay him out we'll keep him on the kitchen table and wash the blood and dirt off him and straighten his body. I don't know what I was thinking.

I pushed the salt cellar and pepper shaker out of the way so they could lay him down. And then I thought how hard that wooden table was under his little head.

"No, put him on the bed," I said. I didn't want him to lay on that hard cold table that still had crumbs on it from breakfast.

"It won't do no good, Celia," Judd said.

"He'll just get blood on your covers," Steven said.

"Don't care nothing about blood," I said. "Put him on the big bed." I meant our big bed in the front room. It was the softest bed.

"You'll get blood on the featherbed," Steven said.

"Put him on the trundle bed," Judd said.

"Put him on the big bed," I said.

They had laid little Willie on the table and was looking at me. They had blood all down their fronts from carrying him. It was fall weather and everybody bleeds worse when it's colder. I reckon blood can't clot if there's a chill.

"Celia, you're not hardly at yourself," Judd said. He had sawdust stuck to his pants and his clothes give off cold air.

"I'll get out the trundle bed," Steven said.

"I'm plenty at myself," I said. "It wasn't me that done it." I was ever one to get mad when I was grieved. That's the way some folks show their grief; they want to lash out and hurt somebody.

Steven pulled the trundle bed out and they lifted the body off the table. They was two big wet spots on the wood.

I was going to protest the trundle bed was too low on the

floor. Didn't seem right to put him down that low. But they had already done it. Willie looked bigger down on that little bed. A youngun always looks longer laying in bed.

"We better close his eyes," Judd said.

"No," I said. I guess I thought if we didn't close his eyes he might still see out of them.

"Celia, he's dead," Judd said.

But I couldn't believe it. It seemed to me like they was something we was supposed to do. If we only knowed what it was.

"Mama, you stay over here; you go over here and set down," Steven said. He led me back toward the kitchen. Nothing in the kitchen but that cold table with the blood on it. That's when I seen I had to get hold of myself. It wouldn't do to let myself go.

"Let me be," I said to Steven. "I'm going to wash him off and lay him out."

"I can do it myself," Steven said.

"I'll do what I have to do," I said. They seen I meant it and they stood back. I've laid out half the people in the community, and I wasn't going to shirk my duty. Judd had already put pennies on Willie's eyes. I was careful not to knock them off. I took a rag and tied it under his chin and across the top of his head. You don't do that the mouth stretches open and looks awful and won't close after the body gets stiff.

I unbuttoned his clothes like I was trying not to disturb him asleep. It's a kind of reverence you feel for the dead, like you don't want to bother them. People will whisper around a corpse and walk on tiptoe, even though they know the dead don't hear nothing.

I heated water in the kittle on the fireplace and I washed Willie best I could like it was Saturday night, or like he had been sick with the fever. I scrubbed off the dried blood and dirt and pieces of bark and leaves stuck to him. I tried to straighten the body out, but the back kept its awful twist. To straighten him out I'd have to break something else, and I didn't want to.

Judd and Steven made a pine box out at the woodshed. All the time I was washing Willie and putting fresh clothes on him I heard them sawing and hammering. They come in a couple of times to measure his length. "Where is his jacket?" I said.

They didn't say nothing.

"Where is the blue jacket I made him?" I said.

"Still under the tree," Judd said.

"I want to bury him in it," I said.

"It's got blood on it," Judd said.

"I'll go get it," Steven said.

            ∾ · ∾ · ∾

Back then they was always rumors about runaways. You'd read in the paper that a slave had escaped from Georgia or down in South Carolina and was thought to be hiding in the mountains. Or they would be a rumor about somebody living in a cave at the head of the river or seeing an Indian with curly hair back in the Flat Woods. But I never had actually seen no runaways. Didn't seem like nothing ever happened in this valley but working and going to meeting. We lived here year after year and things just trifled and creaked along.

But we heard about this bunch of slaves that had run away from Georgia, a family of them, and word was they was headed for the high mountains to join up with the Indians or going over to Tennessee to live with the Melungeons. I reckon they is lost tribes everywhere, and these escaped slaves was looking for one of them. Maybe they just wanted to rest a while in the mountains till they could get away to the north. The Cherokees had plenty of slaves of their own, as I've heard tell.

89

They was a kind of handbill passed around at the store down on the Turnpike. It said to be on the lookout for dangerous runaway slaves. It said that anybody with news of their whereabouts should send a telegram to this place in Georgia. "Caution is urged," the handbill said. "These fugitives may be armed and dangerous."

But I didn't think nothing about it. My younguns was raised and only Steven was still at home. We had enough cleared land and enough stock to keep us going as we got on in years, and we had Steven to look out for us. Even after we divided up the old place we still had plenty of land, except Judd wanted to clear a patch on the ridge above the spring for another peach orchard. You can't put peaches in the valley or they will bloom early and get killed.

It was along in early spring about tater planting time that the handbills was passed around. Judd and Steven had been burning brush down by the creek and at supper time they come in tired and smelling like smoke. I always loved the spring because you feel like starting over and doing things right. I put out a pone of hot cornbread and a bowl of creesy greens with fatback.

"What have you done with the buttermilk?" Steven said. He knowed I always put a cupful in the bread.

"Ain't done nothing with the buttermilk," I said.

"The buttermilk is all gone," he said. He had been up to the springhouse to get butter and sweet milk for supper.

"Was too dark to see," Judd said.

"The buttermilk was gone," Steven said. He was tired and irritated. His eyes was red and itching from the smoke.

"You got smoke in your eyes as well as a sunburn," I said.

"I think we burned some poison ash," Steven said.

"Had you got in the smoke of poison ash you'd be covered

now with blisters," Judd said. He sounded short-tempered too. A sunburn and a windburn will make you feel contrary.

That's when we heard this racket out at the chicken house. It sounded like a fox or weasel had got into the roost. Hens was cackling and flustering and the rooster was crowing.

"I'm going to get me a fox," Steven said, and grabbed his rifle. His face was red from the windburn.

"Might be a painter," Judd said. "They're starving this time of year."

"Too early for a painter," Steven said.

He run out into the dark. I knowed he'd circle around and try to catch the fox as it come out the back of the chicken house. I went to the door and listened, but I couldn't hear nothing for all the fuss the hens was making. I knowed they wouldn't lay no eggs the next day, after being stirred up so bad.

Judd lit the lantern and come out on the back porch with me. We waited to hear a shot, but the chickens kept cackling.

"Get out here," Steven hollered. It seemed strange he would be hollering at a fox or painter. "Get out here," he shouted again.

We strained our eyes at the dark but couldn't see a thing except shadows around the chicken house. Judd held up the lantern and walked out in the yard past the woodpile. I was afraid we might see some of our neighbors caught stealing chickens.

"All of you, get over here or I'll shoot," Steven hollered again.

And then we seen them coming out of the dark. At first it looked like nobody was there. We seen the light shining on Steven's rifle, and we seen Steven's face. Next thing we seen was their eyes. You never saw such scared people. As they come out into the lantern light we seen they was wearing rags and they looked plumb starved and wore out. They looked like they had been running for days and days through briar thickets. Their hair stood out in the lantern light.

It looked like they was three men in overalls, and a little boy come out of the dark behind them. But when they stepped into the light better I seen one was a woman dressed in a man's overalls. Nobody knowed what to say. Their faces looked black as the night. One of the men was holding a big red hen and he put it down on the ground. With a cackle the hen run away into the dark.

The truth was I was scared. I didn't know if they had guns or razors on them. The handbill said to watch out for armed and dangerous slaves. Steven had the rifle on them and Judd and me just stood there too surprised to say nothing. They looked too tired to do much of anything.

"Don't need to steal no chickens," I said. "I'll give you something to eat."

Judd held the lantern and they come up on the porch.

"Let them stay outside," Steven said.

"Can't stay outside," I said. "It's cold and dark." I figured it was better to have them in the light where we could see them. Steven followed them into the kitchen and held the rifle on them.

"You all better behave yourselves," Steven said.

I was scared and I was mad they had intruded on us. But I was pitying for their awful condition. They looked like they had run all the way from Georgia without eating a bite. One of the men had a cut on his face like a limb had near jabbed him in the eye. I handed a piece of cornbread to each of them, and they started eating without a word. It was a pitiful sight.

"You all set down," I said, and pointed to the floor. Wasn't but three chairs around the kitchen table. I started mixing up some meal to make mush. We had nigh finished the creesy greens and wasn't nothing else on the table. I got down a jar of red cherry jam off the shelf and started boiling water for coffee. I figured coffee would do them more good than anything else. They needed strength to run on into the night.

While I worked I tried not to look at the little group setting on the floor. Steven stood there with his rifle in his hands and Judd leaned against the doorpost watching them. The slaves looked around the room as they eat cornbread like they expected to be shot, but they was too tired and too hungry to care much anymore. Their shoes was all broke and wore out and you could see blood on the woman's feet. I reckon they had been running so long their feet had blistered and then started bleeding when the blisters broke.

I told Judd to get the pitcher of sweet milk Steven had brought from the springhouse and give them each a cup of milk. They drunk the milk like they was terrible thirsty. I hadn't never seen nobody starved like that before.

"Here Willie," the woman said, holding a cup to the boy's lips. But the boy was half asleep. He looked like he had been drugged and couldn't hardly hold his head up. His eyes had a glassy look like he had a fever. The boy leaned up against the woman and went to sleep.

It come to me that not only did we have to worry about the runaways stealing from us, or killing us — though they didn't look much dangerous setting there on the floor eating corn-bread — but that we was breaking the law by aiding them. According to the law they was criminals. We could be put in jail ourselves for feeding them and not turning them in to the sheriff. I seen we couldn't let them stay the night. That was too dangerous.

"You all got to eat this and get," I said, serving them hot mush in bowls with sugar and milk in it. I poured their coffee in pewter mugs. The boy was sound asleep leaning on the woman.

"You all got to eat and get on," Steven said. I seen he had been thinking just what I had. We was already criminals for feeding the runaways. First we had been stole from, then we had been scared nigh to death, and then we broke the law. But looking at them wore-out people hunkered down you couldn't have done nothing else. It wouldn't have been Christian not to feed them, law or no law. I seen we was in trouble one way or another.

Just when they was eating the mush we heard the dogs way off. I would have thought it was somebody fox hunting or coon hunting except for the way the slaves jerked up. They heard it before I did and stopped eating.

"Wake up," the woman said to the boy and shook him.

We all listened for a second and heard the baying again. It was different from a bluetick or redbone bellering. It was the baying of a bloodhound. Sounded like it was across the creek. They was coming down the mountain on the other side.

"Wake up," the woman said to the boy and smacked him. He opened his eyes groggy like somebody sick with the croup.

"You all going to have to get," Steven said, and motioned for them to stand up. But they was already stumbling to their feet. They put the bowls of mush on the table and was ready to run. Except the little boy wouldn't hardly wake up. The woman stood him up and he just leaned against her.

"Willie!" she hollered, and shook him. He opened his eyes again and looked around like he couldn't remember where he was.

"Willie!" she hollered again. She smacked him on both cheeks, the way you would somebody that fainted. The two men was already out the door in the yard.

"Ma'am," the woman said, looking at the door and back at me, "Willie can't go no furder." Then she looked at me in the eyes. It was one mother speaking to another.

94

"Willie ain't gone make it," she said.

"Leave him here," I heard myself say. "We'll hide him."

"We come back for him," she said. She pushed him to me and then she was out the door and into the night. I didn't see which way the slaves run. Judd and Steven said they run north toward Mount Olivet, said they run toward the spring branch so they could stay in the water and not leave no tracks for the bloodhound to smell. I didn't have time to think. I had too much to do, and the sounds of the dogs was getting closer.

First thing I done was pick the little boy up. He was already asleep again, and too sick or tired to notice all the fuss. I called Judd to carry the lamp and I toted the boy up the steps to the loft. I had strings of onions and red peppers hanging up there. I laid him down right in the eave of the loft and covered him with onions and dried peppers. I figured that would cover up his smell. We had some tobacco hanging up there, and I laid some of them leaves over him too.

Then I hurried back down the steps and started cleaning up the bowls and mugs. I cleaned them out in the slop bucket and washed each bowl and cup fast as I could and put them on the shelf. The table was still set with the leftovers from supper for the three of us.

"Steven," I called, and handed him a can of powdered red pepper. "Sprinkle this around the yard and chicken house."

The hounds had crossed the river and was coming up through the bottom land it sounded like. You could hear men hollering and little dogs barking, and then the sound of the big hounds.

"I don't want to break the law," Steven said. He was still holding his rifle.

"You've already broke the law," I said. "Put that down and sprinkle this in the yard or we'll all be arrested." As soon as he was gone I took a bottle of turpentine and spilled some on the floor where the slaves had set. Then I took my mop and scrubbed the kitchen floor and the porch. By the time the dogs and men on horses come panting and bellering into the yard Judd and me and Steven had set down at the table like we was finishing our supper. We got up and went to the door when somebody knocked on the porch with his rifle. Dogs was running all over the yard baying and barking. I was so scared my hands shook when I opened the door.

"Have you seen the slaves, Ma'am?" the man on a horse said.

"Ain't seen nobody," I said.

"The dogs followed them right here," the man said.

"You're scaring my chickens," I said. The hens was making a bigger racket than before.

Steven and me and Judd stepped out on the porch. The men that held the dogs each carried a lantern. The big hounds bellered and the little dogs yipped and whined. They was a bulldog in the pack that didn't make no sound at all.

"It's a crime to aid a fugitive slave," the man on the horse said. He had on a long coat like some kind of raincoat that hung down almost to his feet in the stirrups. His horse was wet, either with sweat or from crossing the creek.

"Ain't seen nobody," I said.

"Ma'am, the dogs followed the trail right to your place."

"We heard something scaring the chickens," Steven said.

A big bloodhound come right up to the steps and circled around the yard like it was nervous and confused. I hoped Steven had sprinkled the pepper all over the yard like I told him to.

"Harboring runaways is a serious crime," the man said. He shifted his rifle from one arm to the other.

"We ain't harboring nobody," I said.

But he never believed me. The dogs kept circling and hollering in the dark. The men looked in the barn, and they looked in the woodshed and chicken house, making the hens set up an even worser fuss. I knowed I wouldn't get no eggs for two or three days. They went around the house two or three more times and finally they come back to their boss on the horse.

"We're going to search your house," the boss said.

"We ain't got nothing to hide," I said.

Two of the men come in with their lanterns and they looked in the closet and in the trunk. They went down to the basement, and they climbed up to the attic. While they was up there I thought my heart was going to jump through my ribs. I seen Steven looking at his rifle in the corner, but I was glad he didn't try nothing.

They ain't nothing as humiliating as having people search through your things. It's like you're naked and they can look over your body poking and prodding. It's like you're already declared guilty without ever having a chance to defend yourself. If people can tear through your house you don't have no rights. You might as well be a slave yourself.

I didn't look at Judd, for I knowed he was taking it hard. He was always one that didn't like to be bothered on his own place. He didn't say nothing, but most times he didn't when he was mad. I hoped he wouldn't grab up a gun and shoot the men going through our things. If he shot one of them he would get shot, or they would hang him and take everything we had for harboring a runaway. Judd ever did have a bad temper when he was riled. I just hoped he seen we didn't have no choice.

The two men come back down the steps with their lanterns. I don't reckon they had found nothing. I seen later where they had throwed the tobacco leaves around, but they didn't suspicion nothing under the onions and peppers. Willie

97

was so sound asleep he didn't know nothing about it. It's hard to see things in an attic anyway. Because of the tilt of the roof and the fact you're stooping it's hard to judge distances. I guess in that hot close air the men didn't try too hard to search. It was the growed-up slaves they was looking for anyway.

When they come back outside and the man on the horse seen they hadn't found nothing, he looked around the yard like he was trying to decide what to do. The dogs was hollering and whimpering, maybe from the pepper that burned their noses.

"What is your name?" the boss said to me.

"Celia," I said.

"I mean what is your family name?" the man said, turning to Judd. Men never do like to talk to a woman.

"I'm Judson Jones," Judd said.

"And who are you?" the man said to Steven.

"None of your damn business," Steven said.

The boss man shook his head and looked at Steven. "I'm going to write you all's names down," he said. "And if we don't find them slaves we're coming back here."

To tell the truth that man made me feel guilty, even when I was riled at him. These flatlanders always talk like they are in charge and used to telling people what to do. He talked like he was the law, judge and jury, and we was just trash and criminals.

"Ain't seen no slaves," I said and spit in the yard.

"I hope you ain't," he said.

And then he called to the men with dogs, and told them to circle around the place further out, and then go further out still. They scared the horse in the barn and we heard him whinny and kick his stall. The lanterns was jerking around in the dark like big lightning bugs.

"Here they went," somebody yelled. I reckon the dogs had got out beyond the pepper and picked up the trail going north. Everybody run up toward the springhouse going in the right direction. The man on the horse didn't say nothing else. He just rode away toward the springhouse and the pasture hill.

I don't know how far the running slaves had got by then. We heard the dogs and hollering men go up the branch and across the hill. They got further away and quieter, then after they crossed the hill we couldn't hear them no more, except for the wail of the bloodhounds from time to time. Other dogs in the valley had heard them and started barking at one place after another. We stood on the porch listening until we couldn't hear nothing anymore, except the spring peepers down by the branch and sometimes a hen that was still upset and would cackle in her sleep.

∼ · ∼ · ∼

We never did hear what happened to the runaways. We looked in the paper and we listened for news in the gossip that went around. Everybody talked about the fugitives and the posse of men that come through following them. Some people claimed to have seen the slaves, or had milk and chickens stole. If everything was stole that people said was stole it would have took an army of slaves just to carry it. People want to have something exciting to tell, so if one chicken is stole the next thing you know it's a hundred. Maybe the slaves got caught, or maybe they got over the mountains to Virginia and on up north. We never did hear. One thing I know is they never come back for Little Willie.

But we had to figure out what to do with Willie. If people knowed he was one of the runaways somebody would tell and send the law after him. I don't mean *all* my neighbors would do that. But they is always somebody that will tattle and backbite. It was too dangerous to risk it.

So we had to come up with a plan. It was Judd that thought of it first. And then me and Steven figured out how it ought to be done. They's a difference between thinking of something and then seeing how to actually do it. What we planned out was this: to keep Little Willie hid for a few days in the attic, or in the closet, when we seen somebody coming. Since we lived down by the creek and off the road not that many people come that way unless we was having a cornshucking or a quilting party. If we just kept him out of sight we might get by with it, him being a little kid about two or three years old. We kept him hid and it worked.

When a few weeks had passed Judd and Steven loaded up the wagon with a ham or two and some jugs of molasses, like they was driving down to Greenville to trade. They told people they needed a new grubbing hoe and some new seeds. It wasn't the regular time of year for going to Greenville. They put some quilts in the back and told Willie to lay still under them all the way down the mountain. That little feller was fidgety and I reckon it was hard for him to lay still anytime except when he was asleep. But he was scared too, and could remember running all them days from Georgia with the dogs following them. So he stayed in the closet when I told him to, and he laid under the quilts until they got way down in Greenville County.

The plan worked except for one time. They left early, just after sunup, and then got down to North Fork about the middle of the morning. It was getting warm in May, and they stopped for a drink at a spring just below Brown's Tavern. Judd got a drink and Steven got a drink, and they was thinking of some way to give Little Willie a drink under the hot quilts when this old drunk sees them and comes down from the tavern porch.

I reckon he was one of them Morgans or Gosnells that lives down that way. He must have been sleeping in the sun on the porch and they woke him up.

"What you got there?" he said, looking in the wagon.

"Just a few hams and some syrup," Judd said.

"Ain't much of a load," the drunk said.

"We're going to Greenville to buy seed and a new grubbing hoe," Steven said.

"Maybe you're going to Greenville to get some government liquor," the man said. Just then Willie moved under the quilts. I guess he was hot and nervous, listening to the man talk right above him.

"I seen something move," the drunk said. "Right under them quilts."

"Ain't nothing there," Judd said.

"I seen it with my own eyes," the man said. They was in a pickle, for no telling what a drunk will do or say. They was still too close to home for anybody to see Willie. Gossip has a way of traveling like the fever.

"Don't touch that quilt," Steven said.

"What you hiding?" the drunk said.

"We got a rattler in there," Steven said, "a living rattler."

"Then you better kill it," the man said. "I'll get my gun."

"We're going to sell it," Judd said. "They's a judge in Greenville will pay ten dollars for a big rattler, but it's got to be alive."

The drunk took his hand off the wagon and they climbed up on the seat and drove on. Before they got to Greenville they took Willie out from under the quilts and let him set up on the seat between them. He was streaming with sweat and near burned up.

They done some trading in Greenville and they bought some seeds and got a big grubbing hoe from a blacksmith.

They bought me a roll of cloth and they got some fishhooks and a little poke of mint candy for Willie. About dinner time they started back to the mountains with their load, and they drove into the valley just before milking time with Little Willie setting big as you please in the wagon.

We narrated it around that we had bought the boy to help out on the place. It was the only way to protect him. I told it that Judd was getting old and Steven needed somebody to help around the house and yard. We was going to raise Little Willie to help us in our old age. I think some people had their suspicions but they didn't say nothing.

Not many in the mountains ever had slaves. Only a few big families down in the valleys that kept stands on the Turnpike could afford to buy one. Mountain folks was too poor, and they didn't grow much cotton. We was above what they call the cotton line.

"I never thought I'd see you buy a slave," my friend Iris said.

"We're getting old," I said.

"Where did you get the money?" my sister Maureen said.

"We saved it up a little bit at a time," I said. "A youngun that you have to raise don't cost too much."

Little Willie was the liveliest youngun you ever seen. He run all over the place. We cautioned him to stay near the house, not to go to the river or up to the road. But it wasn't long until he knowed ever inch of the pasture and gullies, the ditch alongside the field, and the spring branch. He built little dams on the branch as boys will, and he caught minnows and put them in the ponds where the water swelled up.

Wasn't long till he was helping me out some. He fetched water from the springhouse, and he carried butter out there to be chilled. Sometimes he churned and sometimes he helped hull strawberries. I was joyed to have a child in the house again. Me and Judd spoilt him. He was so black his skin shined, but it didn't make no difference to us. When they was nobody to see us we spoilt him.

I worried some that if the law ever asked for his papers we didn't have none. I kept thinking about making some up, a bill of sale that said we had bought him. But my hand wasn't good enough to make documents and I didn't know who I could trust to do it. I figured things would take care of theirselves in time. I didn't know but what his mama would come back for him sometime. I thought before we died Judd and me could make out a document saying Willie was free. Of course we knowed Steven would do the right thing by him. But what if Steven got married and his wife wanted to sell Willie, or send him back to Georgia? I worried about it, but didn't know what to do. We didn't have no legal right to Willie and the law could take him anytime. But I thought that as time passed things would work theirselves out. The way to get things done would become clear.

We never did know Willie's age exactly. But we made the day he come to us his birthday, the day after April Fools' Day. We decided he was three when he come, and every year we celebrated his birthday. When he was six I made him a little blue jacket out of store cloth. It was bright blue, a kind of royal blue, and he was so proud of the jacket he wore it all the time, even to bed. And in the summer he would sometimes carry it with him even though it was too hot to wear.

I had thought about teaching him some letters. But everybody knowed slaves didn't learn letters, and I thought it might raise suspicions. I was still scared people might connect Willie with the runaways, and turn him in to the law.

It was the fall of the year when Judd and Steven was cutting timber up on the ridge above the spring, clearing a patch for a peach orchard. Little Willie went with them. Sometimes he would take one end of the crosscut saw for a few minutes, and sometimes he would carry a dipper of water for them up from the spring. He was the kind of youngun that always had to be doing something. He'd be looking for bird nests, or ground squirrel holes. Sometimes he'd start running just for the fun of it, and run and run and run along the ridge and pasture he felt so good.

It was the kind of fall day where it's frosty in the morning and then warms up in the sunshine. They got hot pulling that saw and along in midmorning Willie took his jacket off and laid it in the leaves. He shouldn't have even wore his good jacket into the timber, but like I said he took it everywhere with him.

They was chopping and sawing, and they started cutting the biggest poplar tree on the slope. We used to have yellow poplars bigger than what you've got now. They growed all over the ridge above the spring. Judd said wherever you've got a lot of poplars will make a good orchard. Willie had laid his little blue jacket in the leaves while he was helping to pull the crosscut through that big tree.

I've always been glad I'm just an ordinary person that stumbles along. I think people that knows too much has a hard time, and people that thinks too much and asks too many questions wear theirselves out. But it's the best people, the most religious type people, that have the hardest time of all. They get so set to follow their conscience they can't enjoy nothing, and their expectations are too high. People that live only for spiritual things get too jarred and tore by the roughness of the world. Most of us just get along, and try to give the world as good as it gives us. People that expect too much pay an awful price, and are unforgiving to theirselves. I'm glad to be just common folks, otherwise I don't think I could stand things that happen.

Yellow poplar is soft wood and it don't take too long to cut even a big tree. Judd chopped out a scarf on the side he wanted it to fall. They wanted to fell the tree not straight down the slope as it would naturally go, but out along the ridge so it would be easier to saw up. They kept on sawing and the tree started popping at the stump. A poplar sounds like fire crackling when it begins to break the last solid wood as it starts to lean.

"Get back," Judd said. He had always told Little Willie to run back from a tree when it starts to fall. You see which way it's leaning and you go the other way. You have plenty of time for it takes a big tree a second or two to gather speed. And then it won't kick back off the stump until the limbs hit and bounce.

Little Willie jumped back like he was supposed to. He was a smart youngun and always learned quick how to do things. But just as he started to run he seen his blue jacket in the leaves right where the tree was going to fall. I don't believe he even thought about it. Or if he did he thought he could get the jacket and run before the big tree come down. It was such a tall poplar it was turning like a big spoke toward the hill. He just knowed he had to get the jacket and they was time.

"Don't," Judd hollered, and tried to grab him. But Willie was too quick for Judd. Steven was standing up on the ridge with the ax and couldn't reach him. "Get back," Judd hollered.

Willie reached down and got the jacket and was turning to jump back, and I think he would have made it too except his foot slipped in the leaves. You know how damp the ground is in the woods. They was slick rotten leaves under the new leaves, and under that, mold and mud. And the ground was steep. His foot slid and down he went clutching the jacket. It all happened so fast Judd didn't have time to do nothing but watch. The tree was leaning and Willie could still have rolled out of the way except he was off balance and holding the jacket instead of pushing hisself away. The tree hit him on the head, and bounced up off the stump kicking back, and hit him again. I think he was killed by the first lick. They had to saw the log in two places to get it off him.

When something terrible happens it's like you can't see it all at once. You take in a little bit, and then a little bit more. Judd and Steven carried Little Willie into the house and I told myself he was just hurt and needed a doctor. I seen his back was turned funny and the head was wrong. "Go get the doctor," I said to Steven.

"Ain't no use to get a doctor," Steven said.

I knowed he was right, but it was like I couldn't hear it. We put Willie on the kitchen table cause I was thinking that's where the doctor would operate to make the back straight. I stood there looking at the little body all broke up, and thought how human life didn't amount to nothing at all. You was here one second and then gone the next like it didn't matter. It was wrong of me to think that, but it kept coming to my mind human life didn't mean a thing.

∼ · ∼ · ∼

After I washed his body and laid it out in fresh clothes, I washed the jacket Steven had fetched from the ridge. I sponged out the stains and ironed the blue cloth so it looked new. I kept Willie's jaws tied up in a rag, to keep the mouth from setting open, and I soaked a cloth in camphor and put it on his face. To see a little body with a handkerchief on its face was one of the saddest sights.

I sent Judd up to see the preacher the next day, and the preacher come to see us. He said he wouldn't preach the funeral of no slave in church, but he would preach the service right here in the house. So that was what we done. Funerals at home ever did seem more sacred anyway. Folks should be honored and talked over right where they lived.

A few neighbors come and offered their sympathy. I reckon their feelings was for our loss of property, for most thought we had bought him for hundreds of dollars. Nobody brought things to eat, as they usually do after funerals, since Willie wasn't a member of the family.

After the preacher finished up we sung "Amazing Grace," which was a song that Willie always liked, and then we put the pine box in the wagon, along with a pick and shovel, and drove up to the cemetery. It was quiet up there on the hill, and the sun was bright and hot. They was still orange and yellow leaves on the maples, and that purple look some oaks get before they shed their leaves. It didn't seem like a day for a funeral.

"Where do you want to put him?" Steven said. We didn't have no slave burial ground in our graveyard.

"Right here," I said, and pointed to a place near the end of our family row but off to the side a little, next to the edge of the woods. You can see the place there now where I put a fieldstone marker. We have kept the weeds mowed off and one of these days I'm going to get a cut stone with Willie's name carved on it, though we never did find out what his last name was.

A Brightness New & Welcoming

H ERE JOHNNY, have a swallow."

The two South Carolinians held the wooden bucket between them, and the orderly drew out a dipper full and held it to his lips. John took as much into his mouth as he could, hoping the quantity would cover the muddy taste. The only water in the camp came from a well in the corner of the yard, a hole not more than twelve feet deep and covered over with boards. The wagon coming from town brought a keg of water for the guards and officers, but the prisoners had to drink from the well.

"Better drink it up, Reb; all you'll get for a while."

The Sandlappers moved on with the heavy leaking bucket. John couldn't tell if the taste of the water was worse than the smell of the camp. He held the wetness on his tongue a few more seconds and forced himself to swallow, then lay back on the cot. The canvas above was completely still. There was no sun, but no wind either in the hazy heat. It was so humid the lake itself seemed to have risen and filled the air with a viscous stench. How could it be so hot this far north?

"Better drink it up, Reb," the orderly said two or three tents away.

It was the spring he thought of most often, of the trail down into the hollow, and the rocks he had put at the lip of the pool. The water boiled out from under the root of the great poplar. For that high on the ridge it was a bold spring. When he found it, when he was looking for land to buy across the line in North Carolina, there was a muck of leaves and sand collected around the head. And he dug it all out, dug a channel for the overflow to move the runoff quickly so the little swamp hardened and grew grass. And he shoveled out the basin back to the roots of the poplar and the pores from the mountainside. There were at least three fountains coming together, and as the basin cleared he saw the sand dance above the inlets. He gathered a pail of the whitest sand from the branch and spread it on the floor of the pool, and rimmed the edges with rocks. On the hottest days of July the water was cold when he came down from the cornfield. It tasted of quartz rock deep under the mountain. Sometimes when he found a specially brilliant crystal he would place it in the spring to sparkle for all to see. Spring water was touched by all the mineral wealth it had passed through, the gold and rubies, silver and emeralds in the deep veins. The water was a cold rainbow on the tongue.

And he built for Louise a washstand in the meadow just below the spring, a puncheon table where she could place her tub and washboard, and wring out pieces before spreading them on bushes to dry. He brought the cauldron up from North Fork in the wagon and placed it on three rocks high enough to keep the fire underneath.

"You put that thing close to the spring," she said. "I ain't breaking my back carrying water to wash for you men."

"There's only one man here."

"There will be more. I'm thinking ahead."

He cleared out the brush on the side of the hollow and leveled out a bench for the washstand. He'd seen women use stumps for the washing or bend over tubs set on the ground. But

Louise was already showing her condition. It was easy to chop the young poplars on the south side, and to grub up the woods floor. Within a year they had worn a regular path to the spring, and to the wash pot. And the ironweed and goldenrod and Queen Anne's lace sorted themselves out in the meadow he had cleared.

On a hot day, coming into the hollow from the bright field, you couldn't see much in the shade at first. A few mosquitoes and deerflies in June and July made the air seem needled, and the rocks wet the knees of your pants when you knelt to drink. As you put your lips to the surface of the pool and sipped, or scooped the gourd into the scattered reflections, your eyes adjusted, and you could see the sand and quartz on the bottom like beacons on a plain. Tiny spring lizards gripped the deepest floor, and the pores under the root were ebullient and busy as ever. It was like watching an hourglass that never ran out of grains, a source feeding tirelessly as time, the flow running long before he ever saw or bought the acres and long after he left them. Nothing made him feel the vastness of time as much as the spring. It seemed the dial of some instrument. He looked into its depths and at the reflections on the surface. He stayed so long looking into the cold lens he had to mask his embarrassment when Louise came up behind and said, "Don't you ever get enough to drink?" and he had to turn back to the blinding sunlight and work.

But he had lost track of his memories. Sometimes he thought he was back home after the war, and at other times he thought he had deserted again and was hiding out at the spring. In the cool mornings he watched the mist on the creek valley below as he walked out to milk in the wet grass and stopped between the gap and the spring to listen to the bobwhites call.

~ . ~ . ~

They were coming around with a bucket of oatmeal. The same two Sandlappers carried it and the orderly ladled out the porridge in cups. At least they called it oatmeal, though there were husks mixed in, and shells of bugs and fly wings, all hard to tell apart. And the mess was watery and unsweetened. It seemed to make his dysentery worse.

"This one stinks so bad I hate to go by him," he heard one of the Sandlappers whisper.

"Tarheel can't help his stink," the other said. "Besides, he won't eat."

John could no longer smell himself. When the fever first struck he could sniff his heated skin; the flesh seemed to be cooking on the bones and the outer layers dying. His hands smelled like meat that had been half boiled and was sweet with first decay. But all the sweating, all the diarrhea, the vomiting, left no scent in his nostrils. The nerves in his nose had been burned out. If only somebody would wash him.

But he had no money, and the orderlies left him alone except for the drink of water twice a day, and the cup of oatmeal or soup.

"Hey Powell, what time is it?"

It was Woodruff in the next tent. They had emptied out his own tent except for him, but Woodruff was still in his, only six or seven muddy yards away. Before he got too weak he and Woodruff had talked across the space. Only Woodruff knew he had the watch still. They had an agreement. If the orderlies knew about the gold timepiece it would long ago have been gone. It was all he had left.

He reached under the cot where the watch was tucked into the rags. He would have to think of a new hiding place because they might clean up the rags there any day. The metal was cooler than his hand. He listened again. The Sandlappers with their bucket were four tents away. He brought the dial close to his face and called, "Eleven-thirty."

Woodruff didn't really care about the time; he just wanted to talk, wanted to know if he was still conscious. The doctor came around only once every day or two now, which meant they had given up on him. The doctors attended those who might recover. All they really knew how to do was amputate. The saw was their favorite instrument. They had taken Woodruff's arm, and now he was getting stronger. But he had seen other cases, both on the field and in the camp, where some boy begged them not to cut, screamed he'd rather die than be a cripple. And they held him on the table and poured the morphine down him. And when the boy woke he cried for days and said he still felt his leg rotting out in the ditch where they had thrown it.

There were things he wanted to tell Woodruff again, about how you reached Mountain Page by the Buncombe Turnpike and Saluda Gap, about the trail up to his place by the Red Old Field. He wanted to tell him again about the spring. He couldn't remember how much he had told him before. Maybe he had told him everything already, or maybe he had just thought about it and was remembering the intention. All this had happened before, and he had thought about it before. He was too weak to talk now.

A bell rang somewhere. And there were shouts and a whistle. He concentrated hard to remember where he was, to visualize the tents of the hospital section of the camp. He was number four on the seventh row. There was nothing but mud and rotting canvas. And beyond the sick area was the yard where all the others lived, with puddles here and there full of urine and excrement, rotting rags. Most of the refuse had been thrown there when the yard was frozen over, and when thaw came the depressions filled and turned putrid. No one would wade in to clean them out. The camp was so level there was nowhere for the water to run, without ditches to the lake. And the prisoners were too weak to work or care. When they arrived in early winter they hoped for rest and warmth and regular rations, after the long train ride north, after the starvation of the battlefield. The cattle cars got colder as they crossed Kentucky and Ohio, Indiana, Illinois, each night more freezing than the last.

When they stopped to exercise in a field, around a bonfire, he was too stiff to take a step, and the guard prodded him to circle the fire with the rest.

"Johnny too lazy to walk," he joked.

There must have been five thousand in the camp. In the early months they gathered for prayer meetings and singings on the frozen ground, and clapped and stamped the ice to keep warm. The wind off the lake could knock you down. They sometimes crawled to the well, and had the water blown out of the bucket before they returned to the tents.

$$\sim \cdot \sim \cdot \sim$$

"Enlist now and receive a bonus," the handbills in Flat Rock said. He told Louise he would take the bonus and serve his term. Everybody said the fight would be over in six months, at most a year. And the bonus would buy the fifty acres of adjoining land which the Nixes were willing to sell.

He walked to Hendersonville and signed on, at the tent in front of the courthouse. And Louise cut his uniform from homespun and dyed the material with butternut in the pot behind the house. He had his picture made in Hendersonville, holding the Bible over his heart.

"I'll be back in time to put in crops next year," he told her, when she stood with hoe in hand by the young corn.

"You'll have to carry through this year but I'll be back in the spring."

And he walked down the trail and up the road in his new uniform, carrying a duffel and a blanket, and biscuits with sidemeat for his lunch.

And for the next six months he walked and drilled, he rode on trains. He waited in the sun, and slept on grass, in tents, in cold wind. He ate the hardtack and potato gruel with bits of meat floating, and he cursed the mud and march up the Valley of Virginia, and down the Valley of Virginia. Across the Rapidan and the James, along the Potomac, he marched and waited. Once the men said they could see the dome of the Capitol in the distance, but all he could see was a wisp of cloud to the east.

The letter from Louise began, "Dere husbun John, it raned all thrue the fall, but I saeved most of the corn. The babye wannt come till March." By then the fighting looked different. It seemed the Yankees would not give in no matter how hard General Jackson whipped them. By Christmas he was studying on his foolishness for enlisting. While lying on the frozen ground, or shivering on sentry in the long star-covered night, he thought of his cabin up the branch beyond Mountain Page and Louise by herself milking and carrying a sack to mill. Her people lived just over at Saluda Gap, but her brothers had all joined. He'd seen her brother Mem once after a battle and they were so happy they danced and slapped each other's shoulders before the marching took them apart.

Through Christmas and New Year's he studied, and knew it was dangerous to think so much of what he'd left. It was no good to hanker. It made him careless on sentry and careful in battle to stay behind others if possible, loading and reloading.

He would not have thought it could be so cold in Virginia. He had seen men shot for stealing a ham from a smokehouse they passed, and others hanged from trees along the road for deserting to go home at Christmas. They were an example, the general said.

Through the long days of February, the long days by the sour fire, the nights in the pitiful tent, he studied on his bed at home, and Louise there by the fire waiting for the baby. He was trapped, he was helpless to escape, this far from home and without money. He didn't even have a map for getting back to Carolina, and it was too dangerous to confide plans, to ask for directions.

A warm day in March decided him. A breeze crept out of the south smelling of new grass and fresh plowed ground. He thought of Louise with a baby and unable to break the fields and put in a crop. He had promised them the one year. That night when he went out to stand guard and was relieved he just kept on walking. By dawn he was forty miles to the west. He walked up the Valley of Virginia, past burnt-out farms, up the James River, sleeping in cowsheds, shooting squirrels until his powder gave out.

And walked into the yard one evening at milking time and knocked. Louise was feeding the baby and looked up in terror, pulling her shawl down over her shoulder as he stepped in. For the country lived in fear of the outlaw gangs. And she didn't recognize him behind the beard, the shrunken features.

"I thought you was an outlier," she said. "I prayed you would come, now that it's corn planting time.

$\sim \cdot \sim \cdot \sim$

Never had he been so happy and so scared at once. Though the place was back up the hollow a mile from any road, he still feared working in the fields in daytime. No telling who might pass and report him. Only family could be trusted, and sooner or later the Home Guard would come looking.

The horse was startled the first morning he hitched her up for plowing while it was still dark. There was frost on the grass, and the faintest light in the east. The stars were still out as he creaked with the turning plow down to the potato patch. There was a heavy stubble because Louise had not cleared the fields of stalks in the fall, and he did not want to burn the acres and call attention with the smoke. As he broke the ground he had to keep clearing away the stalks that gathered on the plow's tongue and shaft. Whoaing and starting again he turned perhaps a third of an acre before the sun came up over Callahan. He ran a couple more furrows before unhitching the plow and heading for the shed. He'd leave the horse in harness and perhaps Louise could plow a little after breakfast to cover his work in case it was noticed.

But because they had no money and would have nothing from the garden until July, and because he knew he'd have to leave sometime for the army or prison, he started cutting tanbark. The tanning yard in Tryon was still working and the sap was just now in the chestnut oaks. His oaks were on the highest land on the ridge, and every day he took the ax, after plowing and planting before dawn, and vanished into the woods. If the Guard came looking what could they find, his pipe, his clothes, his baby? Let them search.

Tanbark was a one-time crop because the trees had to be cut to be peeled. Once the trunk had been felled a skilled peeler could ring the bark with the ax every three or four feet and shuck off sleeves and curling strips of the skin. The inner bark was sopping wet with sap. That was the part the tanners wanted. When they got a wagon load of bark they crushed it in their mill and then soaked the pulp to leach out the tanning acids. It was that steeped water they bathed the leather in for months, sometimes half a year.

John worked quickly, knowing he had only a few days

before the sap had lost its prime and the first leaves came out. He was still weak from the long walk back from Virginia, and his hands blistered from the ax. Sometimes his fingers cramped so he could not let go the handle after chopping and flensing off the bark for hours. When he had to rest he sat down in the leaves, listening to the silence of the woods, a crow calling from somewhere in the hollow, a robin in the cucumber trees. He thought of his unit still fighting in Virginia. He lived every day as though this would be his last summer on the place.

At night he dreamed he was still in the army, and was hoping there would be bread and grease in the morning. He wished he were closer to the fire. And woke with Louise beside him, and the cabin warm, and knew it was time to hitch up the horse.

Already things were getting scarce in the stores. The price of salt had risen a hundred-fold. People were digging up the floors of their smokehouses and boiling the dirt to get the salt drippings, then boiling down the water for a cup of the dirty salt. Salt would soon be more valuable than its weight in gold, it was said. The price of leather had quadrupled, and with most shoemakers away in the army boots were no longer to be had. John wore his infantry boots until they cracked, and he patched them crudely with a piece of cowhide. Soon he would be going barefoot.

Louise continued to attend church, carrying the baby so no one would be suspicious. Once she hitched up the wagon and drove all the way to North Fork Church, to tell his daddy and Mama he was home. It was at North Fork he had first seen her, when she walked with her sister down from their place at Saluda Gap on Sunday. And Mama invited them to stay for dinner. That afternoon he walked back up the long hollow through Chestnut Springs, seeing them home. By the time they got to the old Poinsett Bridge they were holding hands. At the place where the road started winding up the mountain face below the Gap, they kissed in the shade of honey locusts. And before they walked into the clearing at the top of the mountain and were greeted by the Ward hounds they agreed to be married.

The next Sunday Mama and Daddy drove up to visit, bringing a bushel of potatoes and several moulds of butter. But their arrival must have aroused suspicion, for no sooner had they sat down to eat than four members of the Guard rode up into the yard.

"Here, Johnny, can you take a drink of this?" It was a large woman dressed in black bending over him. He raised his head slightly, and she poured from a bottle into a spoon and held it to his lips. The thick blackberry syrup felt sweet and hot going down his throat. Already flies were touching his lips to get the stickiness.

The big woman looked like his aunt Icy Mae. Suddenly he remembered who she was, Mrs. Atkins, "The Angel of Death" the prisoners called her, because she wore black and visited only those thought to be dying. Her husband had been killed in Virginia, and in her weeds she visited the camp each week to bring orange juice and syrup, sometimes candy and cakes, to those in the worst condition. Her visit to him meant the doctors had put him on the most critical list.

"May the Lord bless you," she said, screwing the lid back on the bottle. "All you need now is to rest. You have nothing to fear. Where are you from, Johnny?"

"North Carolina."

"I'm sure your family in North Carolina think of you often. You are ever in the care of God. Have you had a letter from them?"

"No."

"Next week when I come I'll bring pen and paper and write to your family. Are you married?"

Before she left she asked if his soul was right with God, and he nodded.

"God bless you, dear Johnny," she said, and moved on to another tent. The flies buzzed to his sweetened lips, but he was too weak to lick the last of the syrup away.

"Could you give Powell some morphine?" he heard Woodruff ask the doctor when he came around later.

"No, he's resting now, and there's no morphine to spare."

$\sim \cdot \sim \cdot \sim$

When he was saved at the revival John felt a terrible shame and conviction as he walked up to the altar, along the aisle lit by lanterns. The planks he put his face against were cold, and he prayed to be forgiven, to be accepted into the flock. But it was the way his tears wet the pine wood and made it smell of resin he was thinking of when Pastor Howard touched him on the shoulder and asked if he accepted Jesus as his personal savior. When he nodded the preacher took his hand and raised it and said, "Thank you Lord. We have a new brother."

When he stood he felt the relief flooding him, the faces of the Amen Corner and the choir accepting him. He felt lighter than he ever had, and assumed it was the burden of sin that had been lifted from inside him. And all that night, as everyone shook hands, and as he walked back home swinging the lantern, and as he lay in the loft listening to the katydids, he was at peace, and in a brightness new and welcoming.

But weeks later, and months later, when the brightness had faded, he wondered how it was he had changed. He was the same, thinking the same temptations, fearing and doubting the human way. "Once saved always saved," the Baptist preachers said. Had he really not been saved? He was the same John as ever except that he was now a member of the church and had been baptized in the pool at the bend. Was he an imposter? Had it merely been the approval of his mother, of the preacher and the congregation, he had sought?

The sergeant of the Guard was a Ballard from the Macedonia Church. Through the window John saw him dismount and walk toward the door. John put a finger to his lips, looked at Louise and Mama and Daddy, and climbed the rungs to the loft. He pressed himself against the cobwebbed chimney at the far end of the house by the time Ballard knocked at the door.

"Ma'am, we're looking for your husband. We've heard he's been hiding out."

Louise stepped back and the sergeant walked into the room, looked at the table with its extra plate, and inspected the corners. He climbed the ladder and looked around the dark attic from the top rung, as John pushed himself closer into the clay and rock of the chimney. Then Ballard lowered himself back to the puncheon floor.

"You tell John if you see him," he said to Louise, "You tell him the Law will go easy if he gives himself in. Otherwise he can be shot on sight by any member of the Guard as a deserter. You tell him, hear?"

"You folks want to stay for a bite of Sunday dinner?" Louise said.

"No Ma'am, we got duties," the sergeant said. "But we might just take a piece of chicken to nibble."

"Then I'll get a box."

"Won't be necessary," he said, and took the platter of fried chicken up and emptied the pieces into his hat.

"Do you want a napkin?"

"This will do just fine."

When he was gone they all sat around the table, Louise and

his mama and daddy and little Emma, looking at the empty platter and the bowls of beans and rice, corn and okra. They were still sitting there without reaching a fork when John climbed back down the ladder.

~ · ~ · ~

There was a clump of laurel on the slope above the spring. After Ballard's visit he was afraid to stay in the house in the daytime. And after the leaves had come out on the chestnut oaks there was no more bark to be peeled. When he finished his early morning work in the corn he retired to the little opening in the laurels he had made and furnished with a cot and blanket. There he sat most of the day, looking down on the spring, at Louise working over the wash table, little Emma asleep on a quilt. He sipped from his water jug and hoped it wouldn't rain.

And later, when the Guard came again, and again, and searched the loft, he retreated further up the mountain by day, and then met Louise at the spring at dark where she gave him a basket of bread and bacon, fresh corn. Sometimes they used the cot in the laurels, in the early evening, with katydids loud in the woods around and stars prickling through the canopy above. As they lay in the dark he knew he would turn himself in, as soon as the tops were cut and the fodder pulled.

~ · ~ · ~

"Woodruff," he was calling when he woke. "Woodruff!" But something was wrong. The last thing he remembered was the two Sandlappers and the orderly coming round with the pot of soup. But he had been too weak to touch a spoon or cup to his lips. He no longer felt the heat. It had turned cool while he slept, and the flies were gone. He could no longer smell the stench of the camp, the mudholes and privies, and the sewage from Chicago floating in the lake. He shivered and wished he had a blanket tight around him, over the scraps of dirty cotton. He wished he was by a fire. He could smell only his own fever and heated nostrils. It was a ripe cooking smell, as though he were baked and getting tender.

Something was wrong. They were in battle again and shells were going off, worse than the night he surrendered. Then the air was full of lead bees and the hiss of grapeshot. It seemed impossible that anyone could survive the air full of lead. When the Yankees appeared with their bayonets he raised his arms.

But it was wrong now, the shooting and bombardment. The air was lit, the filthy canvas, with red and green and yellow flashes. All seemed reflected on water, and on the hazy sky. One blast followed another. Maybe the Southerns had broken through in Tennessee or Virginia and run the Yankees all the way to Illinois, pushed them back into Lake Michigan, driving them to Canada where they belonged. Maybe the Federals were blowing up the city and its arsenals and powder magazines to prevent their being seized. Maybe they were blowing up the prison. He didn't care about the war anymore.

The charges were getting bigger and brighter. He heard a bomb hiss in the water and then go off. It was so cold he jerked and thought he must be remembering the last battle. It was winter and he had been asleep a long time since the awful July heat and stench. A soldier was screaming somewhere as they sawed off his leg, and then one of his arms, and cauterized the stubs with red-hot irons that hissed and scorched as they touched the flesh.

He was so cold it must be December, and the war had reached such a desperate stage they were killing the prisoners by firing on the prison from gunboats. If he had to die it was better to die in battle. The flames and blasts were many-colored.

He must be hallucinating with hunger as he heard men did. It was only a matter of time before his tent was hit. Would the fire warm him? Would he be warmed by the flames of hell, in the lake of fire?

He didn't know what it meant. He had never known what it meant. Grownups and preachers and teachers and politicians acted like they knew what everything meant. He kept thinking as he grew up he would learn too. And he thought once he joined the church it would be clear to him. But nothing was revealed, and he just kept waiting. And everything happened as it did, and he was still waiting for the explanation. He had forgotten the reason for all the men in mud and rags and dying, and the women at home digging up the smokehouse dirt for salt. And the questions from when he was young, of what he was doing alive anyway, and why he was himself and not someone else in another country and time, got pushed to the side, but were left hanging, like jobs still to be done.

Something was wrong, and he was tired and cold. And things had been wrong a long time, since he woke up and the firing was going on. Since he got sick and could no longer catch rats and birds for meat. Since he turned himself in after the fodder was pulled. Since he joined the Confederate army. It traced all the way back. Something had always been wrong. Something was wrong at the beginning of creation he guessed. It was in the nature of things that they were wrong. On the night before he left for the army he listened to the oaks muttering outside the window and the hush of the distant waterfall, and knew things were wrong.

"Woodruff," he called out again. And this time in the flame light from the shells Woodruff loomed above him and bent down closer.

"Woodruff, who's firing?"

"Speak louder Powell. Can you speak?"

And with every cell concentrating its energy he shouted, "Who's firing?"

"It's the Fourth of July, Powell. They're having fireworks in the city. And I heard a guard say they're celebrating the fall of Vicksburg and a Yankee victory at Gettysburg, in Pennsylvania. I stood out by the fence and watched the show."

He wanted to tell Woodruff how cold he was, and where the watch was in the cot. But he couldn't tell if he was speaking or not. He heard himself say the words. Maybe he had already said them and was remembering what he had said. Or maybe it was just the memory of his intention to speak that he recalled. It was the timing that confused him.

That's the way it was on the train coming north, after he surrendered. It was cold and windy in Tennessee, but colder in the mountains of Kentucky. They huddled in their rags in the cattle car. There was no room to lie down. He sat on the stinking straw and the car lurched and rattled and light sliced through the cracks stabbing his eyes. He leaned on one buttock till it got sore, and then the other. And his bones ached. It must be the ache of fever, or the hurt of the cold.

No one sang in the railroad car as they kept jerking and shaking north. Somewhere in Kentucky snow began to sift through the cracks and wet the straw under them. He was sure the cold in his nose and throat would become pneumonia. There was already a weakness in his breath.

As he drowsed and slept and woke through those long nights on the train, he began to be confused about what had already happened, and what he had merely thought about. He dreamed he had gone to the prison camp and was being returned at the end of the war. He thought of Louise and talked with her, and then remembered he was on the train. He thought they had arrived and were assigned quarters, and then he woke on the train, a white winter sun shredded through the cracks. He asked the man he leaned against if they were still in Ohio and the man said, "You asked me that two minutes ago, friend."

Every twelve hours they stopped the train and all were ordered out to stand beside the tracks and relieve themselves in the weeds. He decided he would stay inside at the next stop and lie down on the straw. He was constipated anyway with fever and low rations. And then he couldn't remember if he had stayed inside at the last stop or just planned to at the next. Act and intention and memory were mixed up. In one dream he went into the weeds during a stop and ran off into the dark snowy woods looking for a lighted cabin where they would let him in. He even saw the inside of the cabin, the hearth where stew was steaming, the bucket of water in the corner. "Any child of God is a friend," the woman said when she opened the door. She held a nursing child. She was shorter than Louise. She fed him stew and he ate and drowsed until the guards knocked on the door and jerked him back into the cold. He wasn't sure but what it had happened and he had been pushed back onto the prisoner train. He licked his lips for some residue of the stew, and tasted nothing but his chapped skin and soot.

The cot shook and shivered and Woodruff hovered nearby. "Powell, can you hear me? Are you awake?" The cot trembled like the floor of the cattle car. Maybe it was him who was shaking. He must give the watch to Woodruff. It was down there somewhere. It was solid and cold in his hand. Long ago Woodruff had said there was a letter from Louise that said she was fine except the outliers took all the corn he had grown and ran their horses over what they couldn't carry, grinding it into the mud. And there was a new baby named John. And it was too dangerous to live at the place before he got back, so she had returned to her family at Saluda Gap. But that was a long time ago. Or maybe in the future, or in a dream, when Woodruff read it to him as he leaned down close as he was now.

"Look what I brung you now," he said.

And in the bright light he saw the little bottle brought to his lips. The spiritous liquid chilled his tongue and warmed his throat as Woodruff poured in drop after drop. The drops soaked right through his tongue and skin and rose like vapor into his sinuses, and through his brain with an ether-like breath, like salve on a burn.

And then the drops seeped down his spine and throughout his veins. Until the day was very bright and dark at once. He kept thinking of the row of sunflowers he had planted along the fence, and they were huge and bright, though he remembered them as black—bright and black. Woodruff was still talking even though he had stopped talking.

$$\sim \cdot \sim \cdot \sim$$

When he got off the train in Greenville he saw the station was still standing, but the building had been stripped of every bit of decoration and furnishings. The windows were broken in places, and some panes seemed to have been removed intact, for what purpose he couldn't guess. Many stores nearby were boarded up, and blue soldiers patrolled at every intersection. Little groups of soldiers stood around fires at each corner. It was cold in the April dawn.

Greenville did not seem to be the town he remembered. But then he had never spent any time there, usually driving through with a wagonload of produce for the Augusta river market. He and his daddy made the trip every December when the hams were cured. There was a stillness, a deadness, about the town. But it was still early. A few people were out besides the soldiers. A negro chopped wood on a side street as he passed. It was all so quiet, so empty. The dogs he saw were showing their ribs.

"Hey, Johnny," a soldier called after him, but he kept on walking.

He was glad to reach the countryside and follow the red clay road north through green banks and new weeds in ditches. There were almost no horses or cows in the pastures, but many of the patches had been broken up.

In his soreness and weakness from the long train ride the road seemed to stretch out forever ahead, getting longer with each step. He hoped somebody would come along with a buggy or wagon and offer him a lift. He wished he had some money and could stop at a large house and ask for something to eat. They would give it to him for nothing, but he could not ask if he had no money in his pocket. He wished he had a uniform, and not the rags from the prison camp. He wished he had shoes, for the rocky road bit into his feet.

When he increased his pace, the soreness in his lungs returned. The least stretching hurt. The pain had stayed with him long after the pneumonia that came in the long spring rains. For a week the lake water had lapped right into the camp and spread into the tent and under the cot. He stopped to cough, and rest on the bank.

A mockingbird seemed to be following him. He had heard it running through a medley of voices and saw its gray form and cocked tail in an apple tree above the road. And then it was sitting on a fence post ahead as he approached. And later it was off in the oaks as he wound through the woods. It kept repeating a three-note theme, along with its other quotes and variations, following him for miles. Was it trying to tell him something?

By noon he reached the peach country at the edge of the hills. And though it was late for blossoms a few trees still shone and shivered above the red clods. They seemed like pools of sparkling water at a distance. He stopped several times to watch the petals in the breeze and rest his lungs.

Because he had gotten off the train so early he had gone eighteen or twenty miles. Should he ask the man plowing with a mule if he could stop and stay at his house? The tightness in his lungs was slowing him. Should he stop at the dust-covered house ahead and tell them who he was, hoping they'd invite him in? A cur with hackles raised greeted him at the side of the road, its eyes fixed on his. He walked on, stooping to give himself a slight advantage with his weight.

The road turned into the hills, and he saw the blue mountains above. They rose like smoke in the haze of the northern sky. I am rising a step at a time, he thought. Continuing like this, one foot after another, I could step into the sky, into heaven. A step at a time he could reach any height, and deep into the future. The thought gave him strength. The higher he got the newer were the leaves on the trees. On the mountain the grass was green but shorter. He was climbing back into early spring. The slopes were many shades of yellow and gold and faint greens. All sharps and flats, he thought. Women bent over washtubs by branches. Smoke from the cauldron fires rose above the trees. He saw apple trees blooming in the little hollows, protected from frost, and dogwoods further up the slope. And further still redbud and sarvis stood out like puffs of coral cloud on the higher ridges. A cowbell tinkled out of a cove, the music carried by a downdraft. He passed a smokehouse with a pile of dirt in front where the floor had been dug up. Once he smelled the scent of mash blown up a mountainside and realized someone had enough corn for making whiskey. The church at Mountain Page needed new shingles. Somebody had torn the door off the schoolhouse in the Old Field above the road.

It was late in the day but not dark when he turned into the trail. Some of the poplars were in leaf but the maples were just budding. It had been a late winter, and he could tell by the packed-down leaves in the woods there had been a lot of snow. The sweet-shrubs were just beginning to bud, but would not bloom for another month. He could look far down over the piedmont he had crossed, but the roads and hills were indistinct with distance. It was cool this high.

He stopped by the spring, fearing to see it was clogged with sticks and rotting leaves. But the pool had been kept clean, and the clear water thrust up from under the poplar roots and dimpled the surface like wrinkled silk. He took the gourd from its stick and drank slowly. The tart cold taste seemed to come from the deepest part of the mountain, from the beginning of the world. He had forgotten the living poplar taste and the quartz taste of mountain water. On the path by the washstand he wiped the drops from his beard.

The yard in front of the house had been swept with a willow broom, and geraniums in boxes were blooming along the porch. There was a box of cabbage slips that had been wet down by the door. He felt the gold watch in his pocket as he knocked. A baby cried inside. The door was opened by a young woman whose hair had come down over her cheeks and neck. She held a baby on her hip. He bowed to her slightly, and pulling the watch from his pocket held it out to her. "My name is Woodruff," he said. "And I have brought you this."

Pisgah

WHEN THE BELL rang inside the one room school, children emerged from both front doors at once, clutching their lunch buckets and shoving each other into the sun. It was the first day of the spring session, and the recent rains had left the playground goose pimpled, darkened here and there by puddles.

"Let's see where they go to eat," Carlton, the biggest boy, said to his friend James. Their eyes followed the new boy and girl who had moved to the side of the group. Most children sat on the steps in the sun, or walked down to the spring to open their lard buckets and eat lunch. The new boy and girl looked around them, as though hoping no one was watching, and hurried to the pines at the edge of the clearing.

"We'll follow them," James said.

"No, wait till they get their buckets open," Carlton said. "Then we can see what they've got."

Several of the others were watching Carlton now, while pretending to go about the business of eating. Having new students in the school was an important event, and they knew Carlton would not let the chance pass without some response.

The new boy and girl had gotten behind a pine tree before opening their pails. Carlton and James shuffled over to the edge of the clearing.

"What you all got to eat there?" Carlton said, stopping a few feet from where the younger children sat on the pine needles.

"My name is Nelse," the boy said. He turned slightly away from his interrogator. Both he and his sister had stopped eating.

"What is your name?" Carlton said to the girl.

"Mossy Bell," the girl said without looking up.

"You look like a mossy bell," Carlton said.

He and James laughed and moved closer.

"I can't tell what you're eating," Carlton said.

The boy on the ground did not say anything.

Carlton glanced back at the schoolhouse. During the lunch hour the teacher always sat at her desk eating from a brown paper bag and correcting assignments. Then at the end of the hour she came outside to the outhouse before ringing the bell again. She was not in sight, and several of the other children had moved over to the edge of the woods to observe.

"What do you think they are eating, James, lard or mush?" he said.

Carlton leaned over to look into the little girl's lunch pail.

"Where you people from?" James said.

But neither the boy nor the girl answered. They looked at the ground.

"They're trash from up on Pisgah I bet," Carlton said.

Sun on the pine needles raised a sweet resiny scent. There was something sickening in the smell and the fresh breeze.

"They must be eating grits right out of the bucket with their fingers," James said. "Just sopping them up."

"Can't you all afford bread?" Carlton said.

A tear bulged in the little girl's eye.

The other children gathered closer, looking from time to time back toward the schoolhouse. Those who had gone to the spring returned, wiping their mouths on sleeves, and came over to see what was happening. The blue Pisgah mountains reared far above them.

"What kind of clothes is them?" Carlton said and pointed. The girl's black stockings had holes in them. The boy wore a coat that was too big and too heavy for the season.

"Is that your daddy's coat?" James said.

"Maybe it's his mama's coat," Carlton said.

"Maybe they ain't got no mama or daddy," Ulyss said, but Carlton looked at him, and he said nothing further.

"I bet they're Indians from up there on the mountain," James said.

"Hey, are you a big brave Cherokee?" Carlton said, and patted his lips in a war call. He danced around a few steps. There was snickering in the group.

"Can't we see what you got in them buckets?" Carlton said. "We're awful curious about what Indians eat."

Both the boy and the girl had put their hands over the pails. Neither would look up.

"I think they're eating cold mush," James said.

"No, it's just a dab of grease on bran," Carlton said. "Here, let's put some salt in it. It needs some seasoning." He began to kick dirt toward the buckets.

"And it needs some pepper too," James said, and he kicked dirt and pine needles toward the children.

Laughter ran through the group. Someone threw an acorn that landed on the boy's head.

"I'll bet they eat itch-rag stew," James said.

The girl began crying, her face in her hands over the bucket.

"Ain't you done enough?" Ulyss said.

Carlton turned and shoved Ulyss backwards, and then pushed him again. While the others watched to see if there would be a fight the boy and girl stood up and ran off into the pines, leaving a bucket lid on the ground.

"Hey, you forgot your dinner plate," Carlton called, picking up the lid and sailing it after them.

"Let's follow them," James said. But just then the teacher rang the bell.

∼ · ∼ · ∼

"Nelse, we ain't got a bit of coffee," Mama said. "We ain't got coffee, and no money neither."

He was still in bed on the pallet in the loft above the fireplace. The quilt was wrapped tight around his shoulders, but the chimney was warming from the fire Mama had started below. He sat up and listened to the roof just above his head. The rain had stopped and the shingles were quiet.

"Is it snowing?" he said.

"No, it ain't snowing," Mama said. She bent over the fireplace stirring oatmeal. At least there would be something hot for breakfast. Nelse buttoned on his pants and climbed down the ladder. Mossy Bell was sleepy at the table, wrapped in one of Mama's shawls.

"George never would have let things come to such a pass," Mama said. "We never was out of coffee or money long as he was alive."

Daddy had gone off to the Confederate War and never returned. Nelse could not remember him, though he came back on furlough when Nelse was three.

"It's a pretty fix we've come to," Mama said, as she spooned out the oatmeal on the plates. Two things Mama lived for were tobacco for her pipe, and coffee. She had been out of tobacco for more than a week, and now the coffee beans were all gone. The hog meat had been used up by February, and most of the potatoes in the cellar. From now until garden time they would live on the oatmeal left, and grits and bread, and greens pulled on the banks of the branch.

133

"There's nothing on the place to trade," Mama said, as she sprinkled a pinch of maple sugar from the gourd on the oatmeal. She was indulging them with sugar because there was no coffee. All the chickens had been eaten or sold except two setting hens and the rooster. The cow was dry and due to freshen in a month.

Mossy Bell looked down at her plate and stirred the sugar into her porridge. She had talked less and less since they quit going to school.

"She'll talk when she's good and ready," Mama liked to say.

Nelse ate fast, burning his tongue a little on the smoking spoonfuls. This morning Mama was glaring at everything and he wanted to get outside as soon as possible. Bright sunlight sliced through the cracks around the door.

"It must have cleared," he said.

"You go on down to the store and see if Old Salem will give us something," Mama said.

"He said last time there wouldn't be any more until we paid," Nelse said.

"Well, you'll just have to pester him," Mama said. "Tell him we ain't got a bit of coffee."

As soon as he scraped the last of the oatmeal from the plate Nelse stood up to go. After the days of rain he wanted to get outside the house. And he did not like the way Mama glared at him this morning, as though she blamed him because the coffee was gone. The coffee had been getting weaker for several days, as the March rains continued.

He unlatched the door and stood in the blinding rush of early sun.

"Here, take this," Mama said. It was her silver thimble, the one Aunt Josey had given her before the war, when she married. "If Old Salem won't trade any other way get what you can for this."

"What will you sew with?" he said.

"I'll do," she said.

He ran out onto the cold wet ground. The rain had left puddles in the path down past the stable. A few weeds were just beginning to show green around the edges of the clearing where he had burned off the stubble last month. The cow was restless in her stall and he threw her a handful of tops before going on. Mossy Bell or Mama could bring corn and water to the hens and rooster.

The trail wound down to the spring and then on toward the cove. The air was so clear he could see through the bare oaks and hickories down valley where poplars and locusts were already budding green. Spring arrived weeks later up there than in the valley. People said no one should live this high above the creek, but Daddy had cleared his patch up here, and built the cabin, and Mama said that's where they would stay.

At a glance Nelse scanned the valley from the green at the lower end up to the lavender of the bare slopes and on up to the black of the balsam covered peaks. There was not another house in sight until the very end of the cove, halfway to Brevard.

How could he get Old Salem to give them any more credit? He felt the thimble in his pocket and shuddered with the morning chill and the wet ground between his toes. At least he was out of the house and the rain had stopped. He ran down the trail, banking on the turns and sometimes hopping from shoulder to shoulder over the worn track. A blue jay squawked. Where the trail passed a little ramp meadow he thought he saw something flash into the undergrowth, and stopped to look closer. Great beads of water flashed wherever sun touched the wild onions.

Spots of sunlight mottled the leaves under the bushes of

sweet shrub, and the leaves themselves were many-colored shades of tan and brown, bleached and pressed by the winter snow. Shadows and black rotting pieces of bark dotted the woods floor, and spoons of water standing in the few curled leaves. But something was there; he had seen it move.

Nelse stepped closer to the edge of the undergrowth. It was the eyes he saw first, the big wet agates between lashes, and then the fawn emerged from the dapple of the leaves and brush, so delicate and tiny it must be almost a newborn. Its legs were thin as his fingers, and it stood only a little taller than a cat. Its spots blended with the leaves.

He breathed out slowly. He must have been holding his breath for a minute. There were sweet shrubs behind it. Maybe if he edged up very slowly he could catch it.

As he eased closer the fawn did not move. Yet he imagined it was about to tremble in the cold morning air. Was the doe somewhere nearby watching him? Had the doe been killed or died when the fawn was born? A stick broke under his foot and the fawn blinked, but did not run. If he could get near enough he could leap and hold it in his arms. The bushes behind would prevent it from running in that direction. He paused, not daring to breathe. Another blue jay squawked above, and he waited for it to stop.

The fawn seemed to disappear and reappear as he watched. It seemed possible it might vanish into the forest floor like some vision, something he had dreamed. When he was a body length away he sprang, crushing a little sweet shrub in front as he went down. Only at the last instant did the fawn start, and almost jump over his left arm. But he caught the little neck and pulled the body to him. His chest hurt where the bush had gouged into him, but he ignored the pain and stood up, pressing the fragile body under his chin.

The fawn made leaping motions, and trembled in his

hands, its heart fluttering against the tiny ribs. He felt something hot and wet down his shirt, and saw that it was a boy fawn.

Clutching the body to his dampened shirt Nelse ran on down the trail. He was warm now and sweating as he threaded the footlog and climbed a rise. He was concentrating so on the fawn in his hands he was almost at the schoolhouse before he noticed the cries of the children at recess.

Quickly he slipped off the trail and swung through the pine woods, staying behind the brush and trees. He made an even wider circuit around the outhouse, hoping no one had gone farther into the woods. It had been almost a year since he and Mossy Bell attended. After that one day Mama said they might as well stay home and work, if the big boys was going to kick dirt in their dinners. If Daddy was alive he could teach them to read the Bible for themselves. It was too far down to walk off the mountain anyway.

At only one place could Nelse see the children in the schoolyard. They were kicking a ball and chasing each other from end to end of the clearing. It looked as though James and Ulyss were pushing each other, and just as they were about to fight Carlton walked up and placed his finger between their faces. "Best man spits over my hand," he said. They both began spitting and hitting, but just then the teacher came to one of the doors and rang the bell. James and Ulyss reluctantly followed the others back into the building, still shoving and trying to trip each other.

Crouching behind the brush Nelse watched the playground empty. The trees where he and Mossy Bell had sat down to eat were just in front of him. The pine needles were still pressed neatly by the winter rains, showing no sign of last year's kicking and scuffle.

It was only another mile to the Brevard road. Nelse dreaded

the road because it was all muddy ruts, and there would be traffic on it. But it was the only way he knew to get to the store. People would ask him about the fawn as soon as they saw him.

He had no sooner reached the road, and was skipping along the shoulder trying to stay out of the cold puddles and thick-lipped ruts, when he met a mule and wagon. The driver had several sacks in the bed; he must be coming from the mill.

"Got yourself a pretty," the driver called. "Looks like he's anointed you already." And the man laughed as he creaked and lurched on.

Nelse had to walk on rocks across the creek, and then another wagon caught up with him.

"You want to ride, boy," the driver called, slowing his two horses.

"No sir," Nelse said, and hurried on along the bank.

"You the Searcy boy from on the mountain?" the driver called as he passed. "The one that don't go to school."

"Yes sir."

"I knowed your pa," the man said.

"Yes sir." Nelse slowed down, hoping the wagon would go on.

"They's a doe probably looking for her little un," the man said. "But's a pretty little thing." He drove on past.

It must have been another two miles to the store. Nelse's feet were sore from the cold gritty mud.

❧ · ❧ · ❧

He had not been to the store since Christmas when he brought a basket of eggs and half a pound of ginseng to trade for cloth and shoes. That's when Old Salem said there would be no more credit. The road was dry and dusty then, with dirt like soot on all the weeds and nearby bushes. The store sat on its pillars back from the creek, but now the water swirled right up to the platform of logs in front of the door. The spate from the rains made the creek look fast and dangerous. Horses were tied to the railing of the platform, and there were several wagon teams tethered to trees in the yard. A shiny salesman's buggy was tied to the post beside the pump. Nelse climbed the log steps into the dark store.

"Well look at this little feller," someone said. The speaker smelled of whiskey and wore a gray soldier's uniform ragged at the elbows. Nelse could not see much more in the dim light.

"Somebody robbed the cradle," another man said.

"You can't bring animals in here," the storekeeper said behind the counter. Old Salem looked bigger than Nelse remembered. He could feel the thimble in his pocket.

"But ain't he a pretty little thing," the man in the uniform said.

"Looks like he forgot hisself on you," the well-dressed salesman said.

The fawn, which had quieted down on the walk, was startled by all the talking. It trembled in his arms and wet him again.

"You're going to need to wash in the creek," the man in the uniform said.

"You'll have to get that thing out of here," Old Salem said. "I can't have it fouling my store."

"Aw, it's just wetting him. Ain't hurting a thing else," the salesman said. "Can I hold him?"

"He might jump," Nelse said.

"I'll hold him real good, boy," the salesman said.

"He'll wet your suit," someone said.

"Naw, I'll put a sack around him," the salesman said, picking up a feed sack. The salesman took the fawn in his large hands and held it out like a kitten or puppy. "Ain't he a cute bugger," he said.

Now that his eyes were adjusting to the dimness Nelse could see the men gathered along the counter and around the big pot-bellied stove. There was the driver who had passed him, and several men in boots and overalls, the loggers who had been cutting on the mountain and drove their logs down with the spring freshet. They must have got their money and were drinking some of it up in celebration.

"Your maw got anything to pay on her account?" Old Salem said, leaning across the counter.

"She'll pay," Nelse said.

"What'll you take for this little thing?" the salesman said. "I'll bet my kids would love it."

"Hadn't thought to sell it," Nelse said.

"I'll give you a dollar for it, boy," the salesman said.

"Aw, he's an orphan boy," the man in the uniform said.

"Like as not he stole it hisself," the salesman said.

"He caught it and it's hissun," the man in the uniform said.

"I'll give you five dollars for him," the salesman said. "It's not worth it, but he's such a cute little thing."

Nelse was going to say yes, but one of the loggers lurched over to the salesman and said, "This here boy caught that deer all by hisself, which is more than any of you could do."

"Yeah," another said, "All by hisself."

"Alright, make it seven," the salesman said. "Make it seven."

While the man in the uniform held the fawn wrapped in the sack the salesman counted out seven silver dollars into Nelse's hand.

"Now you can pay what your Maw owes," Old Salem said, "And have some left over besides."

"How much?"

"You'll have almost four dollars left."

"You treat him square, Salem," one of the loggers said.

Nelse stood at the counter as he had seen Mama do and

140

ordered a bag of coffee beans, a bag of sugar, a dozen fish-hooks, a poke of powder, a primer and speller for him and Mossy Bell, and a big piece of gingham cloth for Mama.

"That's all I can give you for the four," Old Salem said.

"I need a pocketknife," Nelse said.

"The four dollars is spended," Old Salem said.

"Give him a damn knife, you skinflint," one of the loggers said.

Old Salem handed him a Buck knife with two blades, and wrapped the other goods in brown paper, and tied string around the bundle.

"I'm buying a round all around," the salesman said, holding the fawn in the crook of his arm. There was cheering, and while the men were toasting the salesman Nelse slipped out the door with his package.

The sunlight blinded him for a moment, but the mud of the road was warmer now, and he noticed how the leaves were already out on the sycamores along the creek. It would be weeks before they saw leaves that big on the mountain that loomed blue in the distance above. The big trout would be in the headcreeks by now. He could feel the thimble still in his pocket. The package in his arms was light, even though he held it away from his still-damp shirt. He was careful to leave the trail before he got to the schoolhouse.

Dark Corner

I WOULD DIE IF ANYBODY around here knowed I was one of the Branch girls that walked through this country back then. I don't think a soul here realizes that was me and my sisters. I sure haven't told them. If people had any hint of such a story it would spread faster than flu germs, narrated around in every baby shower and phone call.

If people knowed I was one of that big family that stopped here like beggars way back yonder I couldn't have married and lived on this creek. Not that these kind of people ever accept anybody that ain't their kinfolks even if they marry kin and live here forty years. I guess I was always meant to be a foreigner, but at least they wasn't no scandal. Nobody had dirt on me. I was lucky that way.

You take the people at the church. Somebody will whisper a person stole something from the building fund, or so and so was stepping out on her husband while he worked at the Dupont plant, and next thing you know it's gone from one end of the valley to the other as fact. It don't pay to trust nothing you hear, unless you see it with your own eyes. And even then you can't always be sure.

❧ · ❧ · ❧

We had got off the train at Greenville. I say got off, but it was more like they threwed us off, Mama and Daddy and me and my five sisters. Daddy had bought us tickets far as Atlanta, and we had come all the way from Brownsville, Texas. I don't know where he got the money for the tickets, except from selling what little we had. And maybe he sold some things we still owed money on. He had done it before.

Our tickets give out in Atlanta, and we was still two hundred miles from Uncle Dave's house west of Asheville. It was a great big train station and we stood around with our cardboard boxes tied up with string and Mama's trunk of clothes with a few pots and pans.

"Let's get on the train," Daddy said.

"We ain't got no tickets," I said.

"You hear what I say, get on the train," Daddy said.

Crowds was pressing all around us, and my sisters was trying to look unconcerned, like tourists coming back from a month in Florida or a visit to St. Louis.

"They'll put us in jail," I said. I was always the one to argue with Daddy when he concocted his schemes. Not that it ever done any good except to get him riled. Nobody else would face up to him, and it just got me in trouble.

"We'll ride until they throw us off," Daddy said. "And then we'll have to walk."

"You mean they'll throw us off the train while it's moving?" I said.

"Do what your daddy says," Mama said. She was always telling me not to argue. The more she told me the worse I was for arguing. I feared something terrible was about to happen. We'd had hard times in Texas, but we never had been throwed off no train.

"Every mile we ride is one less we have to walk," Daddy said.

We got our things on that train just before it pulled out of the station. I was so worried I couldn't enjoy a minute of the ride. We had craved to get back from Texas to North Carolina. I was homesick to see the mountains, and our kinfolks at Asheville. But I didn't hardly notice the mountain we passed outside Atlanta and the hills and red clay fields. It was beginning to look like home, but all I could think of was what was going to happen.

Daddy told us what to do, and we got further than we ever hoped we would. I don't know if the conductor was just lazy, or we was lucky. It was a crowded train, and we moved around from one car to another. Once when we seen the conductor coming my sisters and me hid in the washroom till he had gone to the next car. Daddy and Mama slipped back into the baggage car once. Daddy had rode the railroads a lot, after the Confederate War, and he knowed all kinds of tricks.

I was sick with worry, and it seemed like the longest train ride I ever took. We made it past one stop in the Georgia hills, and then all the way across the Georgia line. My sisters and me held our boxes tight so we wouldn't lose them when we got caught and throwed off. The train rumbled and lurched along, and we moved from seat to seat and car to car. I felt like I was taking a headache and wanted to throw up.

We crossed a river into South Carolina, and though the hills was no higher the countryside seemed more familiar. The trees looked the way trees was supposed to, not like they did in Texas and Mississippi. It even seemed like the air was different. My hands was sweating so they stuck to the box I was carrying.

"Let's try to get to the back," I said to my oldest sister Katie. When we come out of the washroom the conductor was nowhere in sight. I was looking for Mama and Daddy. Daddy had said we should not stay all together, but I didn't want us to get thrown off the train at different places. I was trying to look down the length of the car when somebody tapped me on the shoulder. I jerked around so quick I dropped my box. It was the conductor. "Come with me," he said.

I felt my whole body go hot with embarrassment. When I bent over to pick up the box my face got even redder. As we followed the conductor through the cars to the front everybody watched us. Shirley, my littlest sister, begun to cry. I took her hand.

The conductor led us to the front of the first car. That surprised me, for I thought they would throw us off from the back, from the porch of the caboose. But Mama and Daddy was standing by the door of the first car. Daddy looked out the window at the passing fields. He didn't look at me.

"The law allows us to put you off at the next stop," the conductor said. "That's all we can do to deadbeats and white trash."

Daddy turned to the conductor, then looked away.

"You low-down trash are lucky today," the conductor said. "The next stop is normally Anderson, but this train only slows down there to throw off the mail. You've got a free ride all the way to Greenville. Of course, when we get there I'll have the police arrest you."

Shirley started crying again, and I held her by the shoulders. We had had some bad times in Texas, but we had never been arrested. The sheriff did come to our house and carry all our things out into the road. They made us leave the house, and they dumped all our clothes and furniture out in the sand on the side of the road. That was painful, let me tell you.

And while we was standing there trying to decide what to do, and Daddy was talking about going to borrow a wagon, and to look for accommodations, to telegraph back to Asheville for money, the wind come up. The wind in Texas will hit like a pillow in your face and knock you back with surprise. It will come up out of nowhere and lift everything loose and snatch it away.

Before we knowed it our clothes and Mama's bolt of cloth, her box of patterns and all our magazines and papers got jerked off the pile and flung away. We all grabbed something, but the rest got whipped away. It was like trying to stop a flood with a poker.

"Catch my hatbox," Mama said. But the hatbox tumbled off the pile and went rolling along the dusty road. It broke open and all Mama's scarves and handkerchiefs went flying over the weeds. The wind jerked things out of our hands and sent them swirling up in the air. It wasn't a twister exactly, but it was like a twister.

As our things scattered and went flying Daddy run around trying to catch this and that. But everything he touched got pulled away. Finally he stopped and started laughing. His hat got blowed away and he faced into the wind, his hair pushed back, and he laughed. It was a bad laugh. It was a laugh like a curse. He looked at us holding our boxes and dresses like he expected us to laugh too.

And then when the wind died down a little he started stomping and kicking the furniture that was left. He kicked a chair until he broke one of the legs, and then he picked up the chair and beat the other chairs. Mama had a dark green vase she had brought from North Carolina and he banged that till it broke. Everything that was little he stomped on.

When he stopped laughing and kicking we didn't have nothing left except what we held in our hands. In the weeds along the edge of the road we picked up a few stockings and clothes. They was still Mama's trunk left, and one little table we could sell to a second-hand store.

～ · ～ · ～

The rest of the way to Greenville we stood up on the train. It was like we didn't have a right to a seat now that we was found out. The conductor didn't say we couldn't set down, but we didn't just the same. I guess we was afraid he would tell us to get back up. Mama stood looking at the floor and Daddy watched out the windows. Shirley quit crying, and then Ella Mae started. I held them both, one on each side of me. Callie and Katie and Rita didn't say nothing.

It must have took another hour to get to the station in Greenville. I didn't hardly notice the little shacks with the rows of collards behind them outside town. We rolled by warehouses and cotton gins, coal yards and water towers. It was beginning to rain.

The conductor made us stand on the train until everybody else had got off. The other passengers looked at us as they went by and whispered.

"Are they going to put us in jail?" Ella Mae whispered.

"Hush up," Mama said.

Shirley begun to cry again.

"Look what you've brung us to," Mama said to Daddy.

"At least you didn't have to walk all the way from Atlanta to Greenville," Daddy said.

Finally the conductor led us into the station. He took us to this little office where a policeman was waiting. Daddy carried Mama's trunk on his shoulder and set it down by the door.

"These are the people," the conductor said.

"Is the railroad preferring charges?" the policeman said.

"They are thieves," the conductor said.

It was musty in the office. The rainy air made the smell more noticeable. It was raining hard outside now, and you could hear horses and wagons splashing in the street. The conductor left because the train was ready to pull out.

The policeman didn't say nothing to us for a long time. He looked at us like we was stray cats they had picked up. I seen he enjoyed lording it over us, making us feel worser.

"You're hoping I will arrest you," he said finally. "So you'll get to spend a night in jail and get a free meal."

"We just want to be," Mama said.

"Trash like you are hard to break," the policeman said. "To put you in jail would waste the taxpayers' money."

"We didn't hurt nobody," Daddy said. "The train would have come to Greenville anyway, where we was on it or not."

"Shut up," the policeman hollered. He leaned his face about three inches from Daddy's. "You should be horse-whipped."

He made us stand there feeling awful for about half an hour. He called us trash and scum and deadbeats, then told us to get out of his sight and out of town. He said he wouldn't waste a penny of the taxpayers' money feeding us.

We carried our boxes and Daddy carried the trunk to the door of the station. It was raining hard, and we stepped to the side of the entrance under the overhang. The policeman followed us to the door. "Get on away from here," he said.

We started walking out into the rain. We held the boxes over our heads to protect us a little. We didn't even have newspapers to use for umbrellas. It was raining harder than ever. Once Daddy stopped and looked back, but the policeman was still standing at the door and he hollered, "Go on now, get!" like we was stray dogs he was chasing away.

I didn't know what we was going to do. It was pouring cold rain and the wet was beginning to sink in under our arms. It had been spring in Texas, but it was late winter here. I just had a little old jacket, and it was already soaked.

Greenville was bigger than it seemed at first. At least it stretched out farther. I figured if we could get out in the country we could stand under a pine tree or maybe crawl into a hayloft. Maybe somebody would let us set on their porch until the rain slacked off.

They was nothing but stores along the street far as I could see. Puddles stood on the bricks, and in places the sidewalk was only mud. My teeth was chattering, and my feet squished inside my shoes.

"Where we going?" Rita said. "I got rain in my face."

"Hush up," Mama said.

People hurried past us on the street, stepping out of our way. Horse apples stained puddles.

"I'm stopping here," Daddy said. He had to set the trunk down to open the door. It was a dark little store with "Kalin and Son" wrote on the window. Daddy carried the trunk inside and we followed him. It was so dark I couldn't see nothing at first, and it wasn't much warmer inside than it was out. But at least it was dry. A little man with glasses stood behind a counter, and they was a kind of cage around him. The place had a funny smell, like silver polish, and brass and bronze things.

"Don't touch anything," the little man said. He watched us crowding into the dark store, and dripping on the floor.

"I want to sell this," Daddy said, and pointed to the trunk.

"What's inside?" the man said.

"Just some clothes, and pots and pans," Daddy said.

"You want to sell the clothes?"

"I'll sell anything you will take," Daddy said.

"Don't drip on the furniture," the man hollered at Katie. She was standing close to a stuffed chair. Maybe she had started to set down in it. Everything in the store was used. I realized it was a pawnshop. "Let's see what you've got," the man said.

Daddy took out the blouses and stockings, the extra pair of pants, a frying pan and a saucepan, and laid them on the counter. He took out Mama's scissors and thimble, some knitting needles, and the family Bible.

"That's not for sale," Mama said.

"It's worth nothing to me," the man said. Daddy set the Bible aside. Then he lifted the leather trunk up on the counter, and the man looked inside.

"I'll give you two dollars," he said.

"For the trunk?" Daddy said.

"For all of it."

Daddy looked at Mama and back at the pawnbroker. "The scarves are worth five dollars," Mama said.

"Two dollars it is," the man said.

"I'll keep the pants," Daddy said.

"Keep the pants," the man said. "They're worn out anyway."

The man give Daddy two silver dollars and a box to put the Bible and pants in.

It seemed to be raining even harder when we stepped back into the street. It was like the sky was tearing to pieces and falling on us. The rain seemed cold and greasy. We walked past the rest of the stores and we walked past rows of houses that didn't have no paint on them. Wagons went by and splashed us, and we tried to stand aside out of their way. My dress got splattered with mud.

It was such a relief to get out of town finally, into the country where they wasn't somebody watching us every step. We stopped at a store the first crossroads we come to. They was men playing checkers by the stove inside and they looked around at us like we had come from the moon. But the warm air felt mighty good.

Daddy bought a box of soda crackers and a can of sardines

for each of us. We hadn't had nothing to eat since before Atlanta.

"Where is you all from?" the man at the counter said, looking at our wet dresses and dripping hair. Our boxes was wet and soft.

"We're from Asheville," Daddy said. The men around the stove had quit talking. Daddy walked over and held out his hands to the stove door. They shifted their chairs around to make room for him, and the rest of us moved closer to the stove.

We stood in the dark store and eat our sardines. I tried not to get juice on my dress or spill none on the floor. But I was so hungry I didn't care too much. When I finished the sardines I wiped my hands on the soda crackers before I eat them.

"Where is you all going?" the man at the counter said.

"We're going back to Asheville," Daddy said. "We've done been to Texas."

$\approx \cdot \approx \cdot \approx$

When Daddy sold our house near Asheville he said he could buy a thousand acres in Texas with the money. He said we would raise cattle in the sunshine, and not have to do no more hardscrabble farming. He wanted to get away from the fussing and backbiting in the Baptist church. He wanted to live in open country, and not in the shadow of a mountain. We went to Brownsville, because that is where Great-grandpappy had been give a square mile of land by the Republic of Texas for fighting in the war against Mexico. That was way back before the Confederate War even. Great-grandpappy had gone out there and fought against Santa Anna, but instead of taking his tract of land he come back to the mountains. The family had talked for years of going out there to Brownsville, and claiming that land.

"I'll bet they's a thousand head of cattle on that property," Uncle Dave would say at Christmas dinner.

"They might be gold on it," Daddy would say. "It's close to Mexico and they's gold in Mexico."

But when we got to Texas, after riding on the train for almost a week, Daddy went to the courthouse in Brownsville, and they said they didn't have no record of Great-grandpappy ever owning any land grant. They asked him if he had any receipt for taxes paid on the land. Daddy didn't have no records at all except what he had been told by Grandpappy. They asked if he had any deed, or any charter from the Lone Star Republic.

So Daddy give up trying to claim the square mile of land and tried to buy a place. We had spent some of the money going out to Texas, but he still had about eight hundred dollars. We lived in a boarding house, and every day we went out looking for property to buy. But we found all the good ranch land and all the farm land wasn't for sale. Most of the places for sale wasn't fit for nothing. It was the poorest soil you ever seen. Wasn't nothing but a little brush growing on it. And it was too dry, even by the river, to do any real farming. People growed little gardens, but they had to carry water to them in buckets.

The place Daddy finally bought wasn't neither a farm nor a ranch. It was about a hundred acres outside town. Somebody had tried to grow cotton on it at one time. Daddy was going to try to raise cotton and some wheat. He bought an old horse and he put all us girls to hoeing cotton and carrying water for the garden. The water there tasted awful. We drawed it from a well and carried it in buckets to sprinkle on the peas and corn and potatoes.

It was like that ground had no life in it. The soil was dead, and had no grease at all. It was flat and starved of water. In

Carolina you put a seed in the ground and it springs right up. In the hot bare soil at Brownsville, the seeds went to sleep, and when they did sprout they made the sorriest corn you ever seen. I doubt we got five bushels to the acre.

Daddy kept spending his money and couldn't get none back. Times got leaner and leaner. We lived on cornbread, and we lived on taters. We lived on whatever we had. We run plumb out of money. They wasn't no money in Brownsville, except what the big cattlemen brought in, the people with big ranches. They wasn't no jobs, and what they was was took by Mexicans. Mama and me done sewing, but they wasn't much of that to take in.

Every week they was less to eat. Daddy sold off his shotgun, and he sold off his horse, and he sold off his tools. We lived on grits, and then one week we lived on tomatoes because we had a few bushes that come in. It was always hot and dusty, or cold and wet, in Brownsville. They wasn't no in-between times. Maybe we was so hungry and worried we didn't enjoy the pretty weather when it come. I just remember mud, and I remember dust.

When you fall off your dresses don't fit no more. They hang on you like sacks. You wonder how you ever filled up your clothes. And when you're worried you get weak and lazy. You sleep late in the morning and you go to bed early at night. You fall asleep in the afternoon. You want to sleep and forget how bad things is. If you close your eyes and fall asleep maybe you will dream things is better. You get to where you don't want to go any place or do anything. It all winds down, like you want to stop living, to stop the worry of living. I dreamed the world was a breast we sucked from, and sometimes the breast went dry.

Daddy tried to borrow money, and he tried to find work. He worked a few days for a blacksmith helping to shoe horses.

But mostly they hired Mexicans because they didn't have to pay them nothing.

"The Lord is punishing us for leaving Asheville," Mama said.

Finally the sheriff come and throwed all our things out of the house.

$\sim \cdot \sim \cdot \sim$

When we left the store it was beginning to get dark. I felt some better after eating the sardines and soda crackers. But I hated to leave the warm stove and go back out in the rain. My box was so wet it was about to crumble.

"Where we going to sleep?" Katie said.

"Hush up," Mama said. "We'll find a place."

The road beyond the store was nothing but mud, and we walked along the edge in weeds and grass. The grass was getting green, but they wasn't nothing else putting out in upper South Carolina. We met a man in a wagon coming back from mill. He had several meal sacks in the bed behind the wagon seat. He looked at all us girls like we was something from a circus.

"How do," he said.

"How do," Daddy said.

They wasn't any houses that seemed friendly. Most was set way back from the road, and big dogs barked in the yards. You'd see a lantern or a lamp around some. Others was dark but had smoke coming out the chimney. I knowed Daddy was looking for an empty house. We was too many to stop and ask for hospitality. Or maybe we was too wet and discouraged to stop and ask anybody to take us in. If we'd had plenty of money we'd have stopped at the biggest house and asked for room and board, and they would have took us in. And when we offered to pay they like as not wouldn't have took our money. It's all a matter of how you're feeling, and what people think of you. We was too wet and wore out to have any pride, or confidence.

Daddy had coughed in the store two or three times. I thought he must have got a cracker crumb caught in his throat, or the smoke from the stove was bothering him. But he coughed again several times while we was walking up the road.

It was almost dark when we seen the churchhouse ahead. They was tombstones in the yard, some of them leaning ever-which way like they was drunk. The church was just a little building, all dark and set back in the woods. They was a damp smell of wet leaves and oak trees all around.

"Let's stop here," Daddy said.

"This is a graveyard," Ella Mae said.

"Hush up," Mama said.

The meeting house door was unlocked, and we all climbed the board steps and slipped inside. It was so dark we couldn't see a thing.

"Smells musty," Rita said.

"It's colder than outside," Callie said, her teeth chattering.

Daddy searched through his pockets and then struck a match. The churchhouse wasn't no bigger than a regular living room. It had benches and a platform up front for an altar. They was a barn lantern hanging from a rafter. The little stove at the side didn't look no bigger than a coal bucket with a pipe coming out of the top. They was a pile of cobs and kindling beside the stove.

"I'll start us a fire," Daddy said, and begun coughing again.

"I ain't sleeping in no church," Rita said. "Not with all the graves outside."

"Me neither," Shirley said.

"Hush up," Mama said.

155

"The Lord said he would provide," Daddy said. "And what he has provided is his own house."

"You can't sleep in a church," Callie said. "It would be a sin."

"Ain't no sin," Mama said.

The churchhouse was so cold we was all shivering and chattering our teeth. It seemed twice as cold inside as out in the rain. Daddy put some kindling and cobs in the stove and lit them. We crowded close to the light of the fire.

"Ain't we going to light the lantern?" Katie said.

"A light might attract attention," Daddy said. None of us argued, because none of us wanted anybody to see us in the church. We might not be doing anything wrong, but we didn't want anybody to catch us there either.

Daddy left the door on the little stove open, and as the fire caught it begun to throw out light and warmth. We moved two of the benches up to the stove and set down. We had been standing up and walking since Atlanta. It felt sweet in my bones to set down and hold my hands out to the fire.

Daddy started coughing again. I guess the dampness had sunk into his chest.

"You need something hot to drink," Mama said.

"Be alright," Daddy said. "Once I warm up."

Mama untied the box she had been carrying and tilted it toward the firelight. She looked through the combs and brushes and packets of needles and took out a crumpled paper sack. "This is the last of our coffee," she said. "I ground it before we left."

I could smell the coffee. It had been ground for three days, but still smelled good. Mama got up and started looking around the meeting house. She felt her way among the benches and around the edge of the church. Behind the altar she found a bucket and dipper. It was for the preacher to drink from when he got all hot and sweaty preaching. The bucket was about half full of water. Mama set the bucket on the stove and poured the coffee in.

"I hope that water's clean," Daddy said, and coughed again.

"It smells fresh," Mama said. "It was brought in on Sunday I reckon."

As the water begun to simmer and the bucket rattled on the stove it filled the church house with the smell of coffee. The water started to boil and Mama stirred the coffee with the dipper. It was like the fumes theirselves made us feel better. My face begun to tingle from getting warmed up after being cold and wet so long. My fingers started itching as I held them out to the stove.

After the coffee had boiled about five minutes Mama set the bucket off the stove. We didn't have nothing to drink out of but the dipper. We'd have to drink the coffee scalding hot. Of course Daddy always drunk his coffee that way anyway. Mama dipped out about a third of a dipper full and handed it to Daddy. "Sorry I don't have any cream," she said.

"And no sugar neither," Daddy said.

"And no crumpets at all," Mama said. She laughed, and Daddy laughed. We all started laughing. It felt so good to get warm, and to be setting down in the privacy of the church, we all felt a little light-headed.

"Would you like some coffee, Ma'am?" Mama said to me, after Daddy had drunk from the dipper.

"After you, Ma'am," I said and giggled. We all laughed again. That's the way we drunk the coffee, passing the dipper around with exaggerated politeness.

"Coffee, Ma'am?" I said to Rita.

"Please," she said, and took the dipper.

The coffee made us feel happy and silly. It warmed the mud

inside our bones, and the soil in our blood. We laughed and drunk coffee, and then Daddy started coughing again.

"You need some pneumony salve," Mama said.

"I just need some sleep, and a day in the sunshine," Daddy said.

After we finished the coffee we pushed eight benches close as we could to the stove, and we laid down on them to sleep. I was so tired I must have dropped off, bang. As I slept I heard Daddy coughing, and I dreamed it was raining. I dreamed again the world was a great breast from which we sucked milk and coffee and time. Everybody sucked all they could, and sometimes the breast went dry. It was a long hard dream, like I was walking and working. When I woke the fire had died down in the stove and Daddy was still coughing.

We didn't have nothing to eat in the morning, and we didn't have no more coffee. And all the wood and cobs by the stove had been burned up too. We didn't even need to get dressed since we had slept in our clothes. Daddy said we had best get out of the church before it got completely light. "The Lord has shared his house with us," he said. "But some of the deacons may not be as kind."

Daddy was coughing bad, and his face was flushed like he had a fever.

"You ain't in no shape to walk," Mama said to him.

"I'm in better shape to walk than to set here and freeze to death," he said.

It had quit raining in the night, but it was wet outside, and they was a fog over everything. You couldn't even see the road from the church door. I was so stiff from sleeping on the bench, and so sore from walking the day before, it felt like I had to walk sideways. I needed to stretch and rest, and I needed to wash my face. But they wasn't nothing to do but start walking.

"I never thought I would sleep in a church," Rita said as we stepped onto the wet grass.

"It's bad luck to sleep near a graveyard," Callie said.

"Hush up," Mama said. "We've got a long way to walk and you might as well save your breath."

We walked through the fog up the muddy road. Daddy's coughing made dogs bark from houses we couldn't see. He would cough and we could hear echoes. We tried to surround the puddles and walk on the grass when we could. Men on horses passed us, and wagons passed us. But nobody offered us a ride. They was too many of us.

My feet was sore and my shoes was still wet from the day before. My right shoe had broke open down where the lace started. I had to favor that foot or I'd get more mud in the shoe. It was the grit in the mud that hurt. The grains of sand cut into my toe making a blister.

But we couldn't walk fast anyway. Daddy had always walked ahead and the rest of us had to keep up with him. But that morning he walked slow, and he took little steps. Sometimes he coughed so hard he had to bend over holding to his knees.

By the middle of the morning it begun to clear up. The fog opened in places and you could see the sun. And then the fog just seemed to melt into itself and disappear. It was a clear morning, with everything wet and shining. You could see the blue mountains ahead. At first I thought they was clouds, but they went all the way across the world to the north. The fields everywhere was plowed and red and the pastures and yards dark green. You could see buds on the maples and oak trees looking red and light green.

As we kept walking Daddy's cough got worser. We come over a long hill and down beside a branch where they was a line of sycamore trees. Daddy coughed until he was red in the face, and he leaned over holding to a sapling. It was like he

159

couldn't hardly get his breath. They was a house about a hundred yards ahead.

"You run down there and get a dipper of water," Mama said to me. "Ask them for a dipper of water."

I told Katie to come with me. We hurried on, trying not to step in puddles. In some places the branch had washed right across the road, and we had to jump over the muddy water. They was a big cur dog in the yard and it come growling out at us.

"Anybody home?" I hollered from the road. "We just want a dipper of water." They was smoke over to the side of the house and I walked around the edge of the yard till I seen this old woman bent over a wash pot.

"Could we borrow a dipper of water?" I hollered. The dog growled and come toward me. But the woman looked up and called the dog to be quiet. I walked over to her.

"My daddy's took sick," I said, "and we need to borrow a cup of water."

"Where is your daddy?" the woman said. She had a snuff stick in her mouth and didn't take it out to talk.

"He's down at the road," I said.

"Why lord a mercy child," the woman said. "You bring him right to the house. I don't want nobody sick out on the muddy road."

The woman called to the cur dog, and Katie and me went back to get Daddy and the rest of them. The old woman stood in the door watching us walk across her yard. The house was a big frame house, but it looked like it had never been painted.

"You all come right in and set down," the woman said. She had us set down around this big table in the kitchen. We must have been a sight in our wrinkled clothes. "Where you all from?" she said.

"We're going back to Asheville," Mama said. "We been to Texas."

"Lord a mercy, you mean you walked all the way from Texas?"

"We rode the train to Greenville," I said. I knowed we looked awful from being rained on and sleeping in our clothes. I wished I could wash my face and comb my hair.

The woman's name was Mrs. Lindsay. She said her man had gone to mill. He always went to mill when she done her washing. That way he didn't have to help carry water from the spring. She give Daddy a drink of water, and she made a pot of fresh coffee and served us biscuits with jelly. She give Daddy a spoon of sourwood honey for his cough.

I drunk the hot coffee but I couldn't eat the biscuits. They must have been cooked for breakfast for they was cold and greasy and the jelly made them seem slimy. I must have been half sick myself. I set there trying to be polite and watching Mama and my sisters eating biscuits and jelly, and I thought my stomach was going to turn. But the coffee made me feel better. And the honey seemed to help Daddy's cough.

"The roads is terrible this time of year," Mrs. Lindsay said. "A wagon will sink almost up to its axles." I knowed she was hoping we'd tell her what we had done in Texas, and why we was out on the road with just the clothes on our backs and our little cardboard boxes. But they really wasn't no mystery to it. We was broke. Else why would a man and woman and half a dozen half-grown girls be out walking the muddy road? She was trying to be neighborly, but I could see she was curious.

After we drunk the coffee and they eat some biscuits it was time to start again. Mrs. Lindsay give us some sweet taters to take with us. Daddy was the quietest I'd ever seen him. He wheezed when he breathed, but he wasn't coughing so bad. "Much obliged," he said.

161

"It's turning off cold," Mrs. Lindsay said as we stepped out on the porch. And sure enough, the sky was bright and clear, and the wind had picked up a chill. It was coming from the north, right where we was headed.

~ · ~ · ~

Daddy used to tell us stories about way back yonder when he was a boy. He said they was a time, after the Texas war, when near about everybody wanted to go to Texas, because of all the free land. People that lived on little scratch-farms squeezing a living from rocks and trying to put in crops beside branches would just up and disappear. People left their little washed-out farms by the dozen. Sometimes they burned the barn and house down to get the nails. But most of the time they just left, took their horse and mule and wrote "GTT" on the doorpost, "Gone to Texas." Sometimes they might be going to Arkansas or even Indian Territory, but they still wrote "GTT" because Texas meant the West, which was an awful big place.

When Daddy got tired of farming his wore-out acres over in West Asheville, and after they had a big fuss and falling out at the church over who was to be the new preacher, and then when Grandma died and Mama and her sister Hettie got in this awful feud about who was to heir the silverware, Daddy just up and sold his little dab of land on the creek and we headed out for the West. "Gone to Texas" he would say to hisself and smile, like he had a secret, like he had found an answer to his troubles. I just wish it hadn't been so different from the way he planned.

~ · ~ · ~

After the coffee and Mrs. Lindsay's hot kitchen the wind felt fresh and thrilling. After about a mile we come across the top of a hill and the air hit me smack in the face. It was getting colder, and we didn't really have no winter clothes. The mountains rose ahead, black and far away.

I buttoned my little jacket tighter around my neck and we all walked closer together. The sun was still warm on our backs. If we stayed closer together those in the middle and back could keep warm. But whoever walked in front had to take the cold wind.

"You walk in front," Mama said to me. I knowed she would say that cause I was younger than her and Daddy and older than the other girls. It was my job to take the brunt of the cold air. I wished then I'd eat some of the greasy biscuits. When you're out in the cold without much clothes on, you have to think yourself warm. It's like you make extra heat with your will to push the cold back. You make your whole body tense and alert and you meet the cold air with the heat of determination.

I got out in front and walked like I was shoving the cold air ahead of me. I was breaking trail through drifts and shoals of sharp wind. The road was drying and the lips of ruts was firm enough to walk on in places. The wind was drying a crust on the clay. Daddy started coughing again.

"Don't hurry so," Mama said.

We had to slow down and stop while Daddy coughed. The honey that soothed his throat was wearing off. Daddy must have coughed for five minutes, and then throwed up the coffee and biscuits. When we started walking again he was slower. He still carried the box with the Bible and pants in it. But he let the box dangle on its string while he coughed.

"We ought to find a place to stop, where you can lay down," Mama said.

"No, I'll be alright," he said.

I didn't see no hope but to keep walking. If we didn't get to

163

Uncle Dave's soon it looked like we would all die on the road. I didn't feel no pride anymore about going back to Uncle Dave's with nothing. We was flat, and it didn't do no good to deny it.

The road was getting steeper, up and around hills. We crossed a creek on a shackly footlog. I noticed Daddy's hands was trembling as he held onto the rail. He had always been the strongest one of us, but he had lost his get up and go. Seemed like every house and cabin we passed had a woman doing her washing in the yard. Must have been raining for weeks, and the first clear day they was trying to catch up. You could smell the smoke from fires by the branch. The smoke got knocked around by wind and smelled like ashes and lye soap.

Finally the road went into a deep holler. They wasn't any more hills, and it seemed the tracks disappeared into the side of the mountain.

"This here is Chestnut Springs," Mama said. And we all knowed what she meant. Chestnut Springs was at the heart of Dark Corner, where most of the blockaders, the whiskey men, lived and carried on their business. What she meant was it was getting toward the middle of the evening and we had to climb up the mountain and cross into North Carolina before night come. We didn't want to be caught in Dark Corner after dark.

"Girls ain't safe in this country," Mama said. "Ain't nobody safe after dark."

I tried to walk as fast as I could but not get ahead of the others. Daddy was wheezing and walking with a limp. His face had red splotches on it, like people's with a fever does. He limped not like he was crippled, but like he didn't have the strength to take regular steps.

The houses we passed looked like ordinary houses, except

they was little. Every place had a dog that run out to bark and sniff at us. I knowed it was better to ignore dogs, or if one seemed mean you could reach out your hand and it would wag its tail. People come out on their porches and called their dogs back. They said "Howdy" and they watched us walk up the holler like they'd never seen such a big bunch of girls hoofing up the road. None of my sisters said nothing all evening. They was too tired, and too embarrassed.

The creek looked like it had red paint spilling into it from the patches behind the houses. It must have been raining for a long time for all the slant ground seemed full of wet weather springs bleeding muddy water.

We come to this place where the road went right up the side of the mountain, swinging back and forth. It was called the Winding Stairs and they must have been fifty switchbacks. I didn't see how a team with a wagon could make it around the sharp curves. It was more like climbing steps than a road.

Mama was helping Daddy to walk, and Katie started holding his arm too. They got on either side of him and held him up. There against the face of the mountain we was out of the worst wind. I begun to sweat a little. But Daddy was out of breath. We had to stop to let him rest. Nobody said nothing. We was all thinking the same thing, that we had to get up the mountain before nightfall.

When we finally reached the top of the Winding Stairs I seen it wasn't the top of the mountain at all, but just the lip of a valley floor. They was poplars growing along the branch and little houses set back on the sides of the ridge.

"Where is this?" I said to Mama.

"This is Chestnut Springs," she said.

They was several taverns clustered along the road at the place where spring water was piped down off the mountain into a trough. Horses was tied to rails and you could hear people laughing in all the places. In one house they was fiddle music. A woman that was only half dressed come to the door of a tavern and looked at us go by.

"Let's hurry on," Mama said. But she didn't need to say nothing. We was all afraid. I had always heard about the shooting and knife fights at Chestnut Springs. It was said somebody was killed about every week there.

A man wearing clean overalls and a fine gray hat stood on the porch of one of the houses. He tipped his hat to us and said, "How do."

I answered back, but not so as to seem too friendly. I didn't want to invite any attention to us. Just then Daddy started coughing again. He took the worst coughing fit he had yet, and Mama and Katie had to stop and hold him up. It was like every inch of his body heaved and shook with the coughs. He wasn't strong enough to take deep breaths anymore.

"Give him a drink of water," the man in overalls said. He brought a dipper from the spring. Mama waited a second, like she didn't want to have nothing to do with the strange man, and then she took the dipper. But Daddy was coughing so bad he almost choked when he took a sip from the dipper. He tried to swallow and coughed all the water out, spraying some of it on Katie's dress.

"Maybe he needs some medicine," the man said. He pulled a flat whiskey bottle from the pocket of his overalls. Other men had come to the door of the tavern and was watching us.

"He don't need none," Mama said.

"Might help him breathe," the man said. "It's the best medicine they is." The man's face was red, like he had had a lot of liquor hisself. But he didn't seem drunk. He was just calm and helpful. He held out the bottle and Daddy reached for it. Daddy took a little swallow and held it in his mouth, like he was holding his breath to keep from coughing. And then he took a longer swallow. He coughed, but only after the liquor had gone down. "Much obliged," he said, wheezing.

"You folks need to find a place to stay," the man said.

"We'll be on our way," Mama said. We started walking on up the road. It was getting late, and the valley was in shadow. The music had stopped in the tavern and everybody in Chestnut Springs seemed to be gathered on the porches watching us. The sun was still bright way up on the peaks, but it would be dark in another hour. They would be frost that night; you could feel it in the air.

"I could find you a room," the man said. "My name is Zander Gosnell. I don't believe your husband should be out in this wind."

"We'll be on our way," Mama said. "We've got to get to the top of the mountain by dark."

We started walking again. The man stood by the side of the road watching us. He had on the cleanest overalls I had ever seen. They even had a crease ironed in each leg. His hat did not have a wide brim, but it looked finer than any hat I had seen in Texas.

When we got further up the road the fiddle music started again. I didn't look but guessed the men drifted back into the tavern. I wanted to hurry, but they was no way Daddy could walk faster. They was nothing ahead but the holler in deep shadows.

"Where are we going to stay tonight?" Rita said.

"Hush up," Mama said. "We'll find a place."

"Daddy still has a dollar," Callie said.

"He has a dollar and twenty cents," Ella Mae said.

"He don't neither," Shirley said. "It's only a dollar and fifteen cents."

"Hush up," Mama said.

Daddy wasn't coughing as bad, but he seemed even weaker.

It was like the liquor made him slow and sleepy. His eyes shined with the fever. Part of the time he walked with his eyes closed. "Are we home?" he said. That was the first time I knowed he was out of his head.

"We ain't home," Mama said. "We still got to cross the mountain."

"I want to stop," he said.

"We can't stop yet," Mama said. "We've got to climb over the mountain."

The road ahead looked so dark I wondered if that was why this place was called Dark Corner, because the mountain was so black and the holler so deep. I could hear wind high up on the ridge, but by the creek they was spring peepers chirping. I shivered, and I knowed Daddy must be cold.

I took Katie's place on the other side of Daddy, but he was having trouble standing up, much less walking. They was a crackling in his throat, and his breath come in quick pants. The sun was gone now and the cove looked cold and shadowy.

We got Daddy about a mile up the road, to where they was a steep turn over a little branch. Mama said it wasn't much more than a mile to the state line. I don't know what we would have done if we had got to the state line, for we was still thirty miles from Asheville, but it seemed to us desperate to get to North Carolina and out of Dark Corner by nightfall.

But Daddy wasn't able to go no further. We was almost carrying him. He was so sick and fevered he didn't know where he was no more. And I don't reckon he much cared either. He wasn't paying no attention, and he was hot as a stove. He would have fell down in the road if we hadn't held him up.

When the worst things happen to you it's like you know how bad they are, but you don't quite feel it. So many bad things had happened since we got to Brownsville, that maybe

I couldn't feel anything anymore. I was so worried I had quit shivering, for I knowed this was the worst we had seen. But it was like the Lord was protecting me by giving me something to do. Mama was wore out, and my sisters was tired and scared.

"You help hold Daddy," I said to Callie. She took him under his arm. He was leaning over now, breathing short and hard.

It was getting dark quick. I followed the branch from where it crossed the road. Laurel bushes growed almost in the water, and they was no clear place at all. We couldn't let Daddy lay down in the muddy road. I squeezed my eyes to see in the dark, and remembered you could see most at night by looking out of the corner of your eyes.

About fifty feet up the branch they was a little open place among the laurels. It was a kind of shelf of ground above the branch. I went back to the road and we almost carried Daddy up there through the bushes. It took all of us to help. Rita and Ella Mae brought the boxes, and they was crying. Mama didn't even tell them to hush up.

After we laid Daddy down in the leaves and put what scarves and clothes we had over him I looked in his pockets for the matches. He had a little box with not more than five or six matches in it. They was a hard wind on the ridge above, but by the branch we felt only gusts. I heaped up some leaves and little sticks, and after striking four of the matches finally got a fire going. Me and Callie felt around in the dark for more sticks, bigger sticks that wasn't too damp.

When the fire got brighter we could see Daddy had took even worser. He had the kind of pneumony that chokes you up and smothers you fast. His breath come in quicker and shorter pants, like his lungs was full of water. The fire lit his face and the laurel bushes like some terrible dream. Mama set by Daddy and held his hand. She didn't say nothing.

To keep from looking at Daddy smothering I went out in the dark to gather more sticks. It was going to be a long cold night. I built the fire higher to warm us. The flames crackled and the branch splashed below us. Up on the ridge the wind roared like a train in a tunnel. I lost track of time, but sometime during the night I heard this voice and woke up. There at the edge of the laurels was Zander Gosnell. He held a blanket and jug.

"I thought you might need these," he said.

We wrapped Daddy in the blanket and give him a drink from the jug. Zander helped me gather more sticks for the fire. My sisters was still asleep, and Mama just set by Daddy and wouldn't say nothing. Zander and me bent over Daddy, giving him drinks from the jug. I watched our shadows move on the laurel bushes. They stretched like some kind of puppets in a story you couldn't make any sense of.

Sometime before daylight Daddy quit breathing. He gasped harder and shorter, harder and shorter, and then he just stopped. I don't think he knowed a thing after it got dark. I don't think he knowed where he was. He kept talking all night about farming and planting corn. He said it was time to plant the corn.

$$\approx \cdot \approx \cdot \approx$$

After Daddy was dead and turning cold in the dawn, we was all so washed out we didn't know what to do. I can't guess what would have happened if it hadn't been for Zander Gosnell. I suppose we would have buried Daddy with our own hands. But Zander got some of his friends from Chestnut Springs and they carried Daddy down to one of the taverns. They laid the body out and made a coffin for him. Mama said Daddy wanted to be buried in North Carolina.

Some of the women there at Chestnut Springs, some of the

bad women, helped us clean our clothes and even give us some new things to wear. They was bright and silky things.

Then they put the coffin in a wagon and drove us to the top of the mountain, to the Double Springs Cemetery. And the liquor people had even got a preacher to preach the funeral by the grave. I don't know what we would have done without them.

We stood there in the cold wind while they funeraled Daddy. We must have looked like beggars and vagabonds in our odd pieces of clothes. The people of the community come out to see us. That's why I'm glad nobody knows I was one of that family. I didn't dream I would marry some day and come back here. I always wanted to thank those people in Chestnut Springs, but was afraid to give myself away. I've put flowers on Daddy's grave over at Double Springs many a time, but I'm glad people never knowed I was one of that family of girls. It was hard enough to live through that time, without having to live it down.

1916 Flood

It HAD BEEN RAINING eleven days and nights. The ground was so saturated great chunks of mountainsides had broken away and slipped in mudslides down the slopes, knocking over trees and tearing out new boulders. The pasture hill ran with springs from several eyes in its soil. The fields, too wet to walk in, were festering with weeds. It was not time for laying the corn by yet, but the baulks had not been touched by a hoe or plow since the middle of June.

From where he lay Raleigh saw the river rising. First the current turned a dishwater tinge, as mud from the ditches and feeder branches began to cloud into the stream. Then the river grew reddish-brown and ugly in its spate, slapping overhanging branches, and tearing loose debris from the banks. Waves seemed to reach up and grasp at stumps, and pull everything underneath. The river moved faster, hurrying with the power of a freight train, accelerating between narrow banks. Its speed was hypnotic, as it inched up plucking away leaves and sticks, stirring saplings. From where he lay he watched the flood creep out of the banks, eating and lapping through the fringe of trees into the fields.

As it rained he lay with his cheek on the wet soil, watching the river spread toward him. The brown water took the bottom land clod by clod and furrow by furrow, pulling at the watermelon vines along the lower edge and swirling into most of the corn rows. In the dark he saw the river widen out across the field as though spreading wings, pushing little sticks and lather along its edges.

Why had he thought it would not reach the cemetery? As the river spilled into the garden, floating gourds and squash, it washed into the hogpen and poured into the pit under the outhouse. The scouring backwash reached into the spring and dirtied the pool, and had almost reached the smokehouse where the meat lay on salty shelves.

Why had he not thought it would touch the graveyard? From where he lay, cheek on the wet dirt, he watched the water invade every trail in the pasture, find the playhouse under the pines, poke a cold finger in the snake holes under the crib. Only turf could resist the rub and pull of the current.

The new dirt on Mama's grave melted like sugar when the river reached the burial ground. From where he lay he was helpless to stop the advance, though he had to watch the destruction. The water came shoaling up the road through the woods, sweeping around turns, and pushing bird nests and hornet nests off brush.

At the end of the cemetery, the front of the flood took jars of flowers, and toys off babies' graves. The red water approached mound by mound up the hill, as snakes and toads scurried before it. He cried out when the first water touched the raw soil on Mama's grave, but of course he could make no sound. The advancing water dissolved the mound and ate into the packed earth beneath.

From where he lay he watched the flood soak down and trickle through the new clods and shovelfuls of turf, sinking around pebbles and flowers thrown over the coffin. The water worked so fast it loosened all the tamped dirt around the pine box and spilled onto the casket itself. Daddy and Grandpa had ordered the rosewood coffin from town. It was the shiniest wood he had ever seen, polished and lacquered like a dark red mirror. But he refused to touch the box when it lay on two chairs in their parlor, and he refused to kiss Mama's powdered forehead as she lay in the front of the church, though Aunt Docie held him up to see her and said, "Kiss her one last time; it'll mean a lot to her in heaven."

From where he lay he wanted to cry that he would kiss her if he had the chance again, though he was still scared. But of course he could say nothing.

As water sank into the grave and the clods softened, the sealed coffin became buoyant. It rose in the pine box and pressed against the lid. As water swirled and the hill was eaten away, the mud in the mound turned to slush, and then liquid. The coffin knocked its way upward through the pebbles and mud, pushing from wall to wall in the grave. The coffin tilted, and shivered within its container like a football held under water.

From where he lay he wanted to hold the coffin down, but it was too late. The flood had dissolved the soil above and there was nothing to stop its rise. Bumping on rocks, and the pine container, it pushed like a chick trying to break from its shell. A stone lodged on the lid held the box down for a moment longer, but the rocking motion rolled the weight to one side.

One end of the box rose faster than the other, perhaps because the feet were lighter than the head. As it reached the surface the box leaped clear of the water, and when it fell back the lid tore off the pine box, and the coffin slid into the waves. The impact loosened the latches, and the coffin lid swung open. And there was rain beating down on Mama's face, melting the powder over the measles rash. The rain opened her eyes and she was looking at him.

~ · ~ · ~

When Raleigh woke screaming silently, the rain was steady on the roof and in the gutter above his window. The tin roof hummed and the pipes swallowed as they had for weeks.

He did not know why he felt guilty about the rain. True, they had not been able to work in the fields that needed hoeing so badly. But there was nothing to do, while the rain continued, except sit in the crib and shuck the last of the corn. And he had gone fishing only once, on a day when it cleared up briefly, after the first five days of rain.

The pounding on the roof was ominous, and the drumming in the gutters. It was as though the world had been abandoned to flood as it was in the Bible. The sun was gone, and there was nothing but clouds and darkness and more rain. The hills were washing away, and the fields stood rotting in water.

If his dream was true, that the graveyard had been reached by the flood and the graves opened, he was somehow responsible. Mama had been dead for four years, but in his dream her grave was fresh as though she had been buried yesterday. Was that a sign she wasn't resting peacefully, because he had not kissed her, because he did not say his prayers? He shivered under the damp quilt.

"Get up," Missy was calling from the kitchen. He reached for his overalls, relieved the night was over, but dreading another long day of rain.

"Want to go to the homecoming at Poplar Springs?" Grandpa said as he laced his shoes in the kitchen.

"They won't have it because of the rain," Missy said.

"Maybe it will stop before dinner time," Grandpa said.

"I won't go nowhere in the rain," Missy said.

"I figure it's time for it to stop," Grandpa said.

"It's never going to stop," Missy said.

"We're going to wash away like in the time of Noah," Raleigh said. "And I haven't seen no rainbows neither." But he hoped Grandpa was right. They took the milk buckets that Missy had been scalding, the handles still hot and wet. Nothing would dry in this dampness.

Daddy was grinding coffee on the back porch. The freshly ground beans smelled especially good because nothing else seemed fresh or dry. The screen door had swollen so it no longer closed, and the varnish on the wood had melted to gum that stuck to his hand. The yard was mostly puddles, and, while there was a raw earthworm smell, it was obscured by the scent of rot from the woods and barn. The rain had gone on so long everything was decaying. Mushrooms had pushed up through the grass like little snowmen, and raised through the duff under trees. Mold grew on bark and even green leaves looked blue and white with mildew. He and Grandpa splashed through the puddles as they ran to the barn.

Out of the corner of his eye Raleigh saw the water had now reached the edge of the chicken house. The bottom land was completely submerged, with corn rows standing in two or three feet of muddy backwaters.

"What will we do if there's no corn?" he said as they reached the hallway of the barn.

"We'll save some of it. You'll see."

The barn smelled stronger than ever. Water was seeping around the walls into the floor of the stalls. The manure and straw had turned into a stinking mush. They had not cleaned the stalls since the rain began.

Raleigh milked hurriedly. He wanted to get out of the barn and back to the house to wash his feet. Manure squeezed between his toes as he pulled the teats.

After milking he and Grandpa turned the cows out to pasture. But instead of cropping, the cows walked straight to the white pines and stood in their shelter. Only the horse seemed not to mind grazing in the rain. He stood right out in the downpour and cropped the tall grass, his tail free from the swishing flies.

When they put the buckets of warm milk on the porch for Missy to strain, Raleigh dashed back into the yard, and washed his feet in the biggest puddle.

"Hey, don't get the yard dirty," Missy called. "Go wash in the branch."

"The branch is in the field," he hollered back.

He washed his hands and wrists in another, cleaner puddle.

As he sat down at the table his hair was dripping and his overalls were wet. Missy made him place a towel on his chair. The oatmeal was hot and the biscuits just out of the oven.

"Let's have some sourwood honey," Grandpa said. "It's Sunday."

"Every day is just alike in the rain," Daddy said. "It must be a curse on the land. It's the year of the seventeen year locusts, and I ain't seen a one."

"It's the war in France," Missy said. She read the paper every day.

"The locusts have been kept in the ground by the rain," Grandpa said. "They'll come out when it stops. You can't stop them."

"The bridge at Saluda is washed out, and the bridge on the French Broad at Arden. Jarvis said a railroad tunnel had collapsed, but I forget where," Daddy said.

"This may be the end of time," Missy said.

"No, the world will never flood again," Grandpa said. "That's a promise; that's what the rainbow is."

A clap of thunder broke in the sky straight above them, shaking the windows and rattling dishes on the shelves. There were echoes off the mountains, and then another clap, further away.

"That means the end of the rain," Grandpa said. "Let's go to the homecoming."

The graveyard was on the road to Poplar Springs. Raleigh would see if it was flooded. He would tell no one his dream.

~ · ~ · ~

By the time they were dressed for church the rain had stopped and the sun was out. Raleigh polished his shoes and began to lace them up. But Grandpa said, "No use to wear your shoes. They'd be covered in mud in no time. You would ruin them."

Boys and girls always wore their new clothes, their best clothes, to homecomings. It was a way of showing off, where the most people would see. Missy carried her shoes as they walked up the road.

After eleven days of rain the grass in the pasture was a foot high and spotted with mushrooms. Weeds along the fences glittered with their load of drops. As the sun came out through thinning clouds the world seemed in shock, as though a light had been shown into a cave world of perpetual twilight. Everything was waking up again, blinking and stretching. The mountaintops were still covered with clouds, and strands of fog lifted out of the hollows, as steam rose off the river.

"Maybe there won't be a homecoming," Missy said, as she and Grandpa and Raleigh picked their way along the muddy tracks above the spring.

"There's always a homecoming," Grandpa said. "Especially now that it's stopped raining."

"What if the bridge is out by Garfield's?" Raleigh said.

"Then we'll take the footlog above the shoals."

"And what if the footlog is washed out?"

"There's another one further up by Bane's."

"Look there at Thunderhead," Missy said and pointed to the top of the mountain. As the fog cleared, the gash of a landslide was exposed.

"It tore away the cliff," Raleigh said.

"No, the cliff's further over."

"That big rock could have rolled down on top of us in the night," Missy said.

The big slide above them seemed to mean that the cemetery was certainly flooded, but Raleigh could not have explained the connection. He felt sure the two events were related. Still, he wouldn't mention it. It was bad luck to talk about what worried you. Just talking could make it come true.

Above the spring, runoff from the pasture had filled the ditch with trash and then cut across the road, carving out a canyon through the ruts. The dirt here was golden and mealy, and flecked with mica. In the new sun the ground sparkled and signaled. The new gully was so deep they would have to fill it with rocks and brush before a wagon could easily cross.

On the roadbank every pebble stood on a column of dirt.

"How come it rained so long, Grandpa?" Missy said.

"There's no telling about the weather," Grandpa said.

"Is it because of the war in France?" Raleigh said.

"There's no telling about the signs," Grandpa said. "Sometimes we know how to interpret them, and sometimes we never learn."

"At least the spring's still clear," Missy said.

"It might have got some runoff and then cleared up again," Grandpa said. There was a ditch above the spring to divert water; its walls appeared intact.

Where their road connected with the county road, another ditch had been washed. The erosion had undercut a white pine just at the gate and the tree had fallen across the entrance.

"We'll chop it away when we get back," Grandpa said.

"But we can't work on Sunday," Raleigh said.

"The Lord lets you get an ox out of the ditch on Sunday," Grandpa said. "I reckon this is a kind of ox in a ditch."

The whole family of the Brights were walking up the road. They were a big family from down near the cotton mill. Mrs. Bright carried a basket on her arm. Her husband carried only his walking stick.

"People ain't been living right," Mrs. Bright said. "And the Lord is sick and tired of it."

"Is the turnpike bridge intact?" Grandpa said.

"Still there, but I wouldn't cross on it," Mr. Bright said.

"The Lord has a way of reminding people of his power," Mrs. Bright said.

Raleigh fell in step with Grady Bright who was almost his age. They hadn't seen each other since the end of the school term.

"What you been doing?" Raleigh said.

"Catching frogs that come up out of the river."

"How come?"

"We burn their tails with a hot stick."

"And they come back out?"

"They have to get out of the flood."

A great cut had been washed across the road at the forks to Poplar Springs. Several wagons had stopped at the lip of the gully. It would take a day of shoveling and dragpanning to fill up the wash. Raleigh and Grady stood at the rim which was still crumbling off into the rushing water. He could see the layers of dirt under the road, the top level packed with gravel, and underneath the sand of the earlier road, and then red clay beneath it all.

Someone had thrown a couple of fence posts across the rushing ditch and they stepped singly across. The graveyard was just a little further up the road. Raleigh felt a pain in his knees as they approached.

"It's the locusts," Grandpa said.

"I don't hear nothing," Missy said.

"No, they're coming out. Listen."

But Raleigh was running on ahead. The sun was hotter now, and the mud was beginning to smell even more of rotted things, of sour roots, and decaying debris washed off the hill. The water-sickened weeds smelled as though they had been scorched and their leaves were starting to sour. He wondered if some of the stink could be coming from the graveyard above.

"Wait for me," Grady called.

But Raleigh did not slow down, and Grady ran to catch up with him.

"Hey, where you going?" Grady called.

Raleigh did not answer. He was getting too out of breath to talk.

The cows were out in Stacy's pasture cropping the wet grass. Raleigh could hear the suck and wheeze of their feet in the soft ground. When Mama died suddenly of the measles, Raleigh was seven. It had been raining, and when Grandpa said she was dead he ran down the hill to the orchard and cried with his face against an apple tree, his tears smearing on the lichen soot of the bark. The woods today smelled like that tree.

"I'm going fishing tomorrow," Grady said, as he caught up with Raleigh. "Nelse caught a seventeen-inch trout yesterday in the Johnson Hole with a grasshopper. The river's been washed out there something terrible."

The graveyard was just around the bend. Raleigh climbed the bank and cut through the woods to get there quicker. His pants got wet on the undergrowth of sassafras and sweet shrub.

"Where you going now?" Grady panted behind him. "We'll get wet."

They came to the edge of the burial clearing, and Raleigh expected to see it all under muddy water. But instead the hill was green and sparkling in the sun. Bees fizzed among the flowers on graves, and the juniper still stood beside Mama's mound. The mound had been covered with grass for three years. The graves of the family, Great-grandpa and Uncle Joe, and Grandma, stretched in a row across the crest of the rise.

Raleigh ran among the graves getting his feet soaked in the grass. He felt so light he could hardly keep his feet on the ground. He ran to the tulip poplar on the north side and shook a heavy branch so that drops showered on the grass, and he ran to the west side and climbed upon a boulder already warm in the sun.

"Hey, what's the matter?" Grady called.

But Raleigh only smiled and ran on. When they got back to the road the others had caught up.

"Wish I had that kind of energy," Grandpa said.

"These younguns have the Lord's own joy to be back in the sunshine," Mrs. Bright said. She brushed a fly away from the cloth over her basket.

"They's whole towns washed away in Virginia," Mr. Bright said. "I heard it at the store yesterday. And the railroads can't run."

"The Lord has spared us," Mrs. Bright said.

The footlog over Cabin Creek was still in place, and they walked it one at a time. Water was backed up into the brush at both ends of the footlog, and the ford was buried under four or five feet of flood. The water shone like a polished floor under the trees. It was Missy who looked through a gap in the sweet shrub bushes and gasped. Raleigh thought she must have seen a snake in the limbs.

"What is it?" Grandpa said.

All crowded to the edge of the water where sticks and bits of bark and bugs were floating. Small waves lapped at their feet. Raleigh saw a body in a gray coat lodged against a river birch. The face was turned away. Grandpa and Mr. Bright began wading out toward it, carrying sticks as though they expected trouble.

They rolled the body over in the muddy water.

"It's nobody I know," Mr. Bright said.

"The Lord help us," Mrs. Bright said.

"Raleigh," Grandpa called. "You run on up to Poplar Springs and tell them to bring a wagon down."

"I'll go with you," Grady said.

But Raleigh was already running. His feet blurred on the path and then on the road again. He couldn't hear Grady running behind him for the wind in his ears. He could not remember when he had felt such a thrill of speed. His feet appeared to be moving a foot above the ground.

For the first time he heard the locusts in the woods. They were all around him, chanting "pharaoh, pharaoh," as Grandpa said they would, remembering the plague in Egypt. The road ahead was muddy and scattered with puddles, and he jumped over some and skirted others. In the worst places he ran through the weeds on the shoulder. The stench of the flood was in his nostrils, but he felt as if he could outrun it. Though his assignment was solemn and serious, he felt he could outrun all troubles and fears.

Murals

THERE WAS A CROWD at the post office when he arrived. Gardner had never seen that many people gather at the door at opening time, except on the first of the month when Social Security checks came. There were two or three men in the crowd he recognized: Joe from the hardware store where he had bought the steel brush, and Mr. Clark the tax assessor who also sat on the board of County Commissioners. It was Mr. Clark who had written the letter to the regional office in Atlanta asking, or at least agreeing, to have the murals painted in the post office lobby.

"Hurry up in there," someone shouted, and banged on the outside door.

"The war will be over before they open the damn doors," someone else muttered, and there was laughter.

A door rattled inside and Old Joyner, the postmaster, who always wore an eyeshade and garters on his sleeves, unlocked the outer door and the crowd of men pushed past him. Gardner was afraid they would knock over his scaffold as they pressed around the window. He had to stand watching, for there was not room for him to put his ladder up.

Old Joyner unlocked the inner door and let himself into the cage where stamps were sold and the mail sorted.

"What can I do for you gentlemen?" he said.

"We want registration forms," Mr. Clark said.

"Yeah, we want to sign up," another man said.

"Which registration form?" Old Joyner said. He assumed the serious air he always did when people tried to rush him.

"Don't act so dumb," Joe said. "You know damn well what we're here for."

"Some minds I can read," Joyner said. "Some I can't."

"Are you going to give us the forms, or ain't you?" Joe said.

"You applying for the Civil Service exam?" Joyner said.

For the first time Gardner saw that Joyner really didn't know what they were talking about. He lived by himself in a big old house at the edge of town and everybody knew he didn't have a radio or telephone and didn't read newspapers. His life was spent standing in the stamp window glowering at people foolish enough to bother him about letters and packages. When he was at home he worked in his garden.

"We want to register," Mr. Clark said.

"You're dumber than you look, Joyner," Joe said.

"I only have about a dozen forms," Joyner said, "if it's the draft registration form you want."

"Welcome to the Twentieth Century, Joyner."

"Hand them over, old boy."

The papers were grabbed from Joyner's hand even before he could count or sort them. Some were torn. Several men were left without forms.

"You order some more, Joyner," they said.

"You can go over to Homer," Joyner said. "They might have some more there."

The last three men hurried out arguing about whose car to take to Homer.

"You can get gas at Leland's," one said.

"Better get gas while you can," his companion said.

~ · ~ · ~

When they were gone the post office was as deserted as it usually was in the early morning. Old Joyner stood looking through the bars as though he was still waking up. The bags of mail from the depot wouldn't arrive until eight-thirty. After that he'd have to spend an hour or two with Ralph the rural mail carrier sorting into pigeon holes and tying up bundles for the rural route. The first hour of the day was usually Joyner's time for dusting off his desk and counting stamps into the drawers. He claimed Gardner's work on the mural created more dust in the post office, and he resented Gardner's presence in general, disturbing his early quiet hour.

Gardner put down his paint box and got the ladder from the corner of the lobby.

"You here?" Joyner said.

"What do you think? It's Monday morning and time for work," Gardner said.

"Nobody else seems to think so."

"Things will quiet down," Gardner said, carrying his paint box up the ladder and pushing the canvas on the platform up against the wall under the spot where he would be working.

"You ain't going to join?" Joyner said.

"Not till I finish the job. I've got a contract."

"The Government will cancel your contract," Joyner said. The postmaster always thought of the most discouraging thing to say. He had a talent for it. He had complained about the mural from the beginning, about the dust and scaffold in the lobby.

Gardner had meant to work on the combine today. Since he was in art school in Chicago, indeed, since he started drawing in high school, he had taken pride in his human figures, huge men in overalls hurling shovels, women in plain dresses

186

that flowed over their bodies revealing attractive shapes. He was good also with animals and the curves of the landscape. But he was late developing a touch with machinery. Either his drawings looked like meticulous designs for a factory, or, if he tried to be expressive, they looked wrenched and arthritic as a child's fantasy of a machine, half tractor and half rhinoceros. Machines were much of the power of Rivera's murals. Most of Gardner's friends had no trouble executing something futuristic, or celebrating cars and cotton mills, assembly lines and bulldozers, the energy of the industrial sublime.

But Gardner had dedicated himself to the goal of learning to paint machines. He would never be a really good muralist if he couldn't do machinery. His plan was to stick with simplicity, bold direct lines like a Rockwell Kent, say. Draw machinery as if he were designing a woodcut using the fewest lines. Over the weekend he had made several drawings for the combine, each one bolder and plainer than the one before. At first he had thought of the combine as a kind of steamboat of the prairie, with its paddlewheel slapping through the wheat. Gardner was pleased with the comparison until he thought about it more, about the gamblers and ladies in fine dresses on a steamboat, and saw the parallel was only superficial. He kept drawing the combine from different angles, once with horses pulling it, once with a Caterpillar. But the version he liked best was a view of the combine almost from underneath, with the paddlewheel against the sky, turning like a windmill. The wheat reached like hands and flames through the turning blades.

Men and women would be advancing around the combine as though pulling themselves up out of the earth. "Get Up and Go," he privately called the mural. His boss from Atlanta had not seen the new designs, but Gardner was sure he would approve them. Johnson liked epic struggles in his murals, men and women fighting with, and along with, nature for a decent community, for dignity.

"Picasso turns people into flounders," Johnson liked to say. "Two eyes on one side of their face and thin as paper. Our job is to draw the future, draw people as they are and can be. There's no need for art to rub people's faces in ashes. Their faces are rubbed in crap every day anyway."

By the time the stores opened around nine Gardner was up on the scaffold trying to draw in the combine. It was harder to work from his new designs than he had thought. He had never been good at transferring designs, not as good as he should be. Any technician can transfer, he told himself. But he knew that was no excuse. He rubbed out what he had started and began again, working free hand, from memory. The top blade of the paddlewheel went almost to the ceiling. He wanted to put a cloud up there, a white bulging cloud of lightness and assurance. But the cloud would have to be put slightly to the side.

Working close to the ceiling was fine in winter. The heat collected up there and he didn't mind the smells of sweeping compound and ink and newsprint from the back of the post office. The summer was when mural work was terrible. At his last job in Kentucky the heat and humidity had gathered around the ceiling and could not be dispelled. The smell of sweaty bodies, including his own, hung there, and sweat dripped into his eyes. The electric lamp made it even hotter. He had looked forward to the winter, and to this new job, his first on his own. The post office here was small but had a long high wall above the postmaster's window.

People gathered on the street as though it was a holiday. He could not see the street from the scaffold, but he could see the sidewalk where clusters of men formed and dissolved. He could hear some of the talk, bits of the conversation.

"If they bomb here I'll get out my deer rifle and shoot at them," a man said.

"Naw, they won't bomb this far. But San Francisco or Charlotte is liable to be hit."

"I wouldn't live in California for no amount of money."

"Somebody seen a Jap down in Charlotte yesterday and they run him into a park and beat him up before the police come got him."

"I'm going to buy me a new car before the price goes up."

Many kids seemed not to have gone to school. They ran up and down the street shooting each other, their mouths sounding like machine guns.

People came in to check their mailboxes after the mail was put up by Joyner and Ralph. But they did it distractedly, their minds on other things.

"Hey Joyner, look out for saboteurs," one called.

A man backed into the scaffold as he closed his mailbox. "What is this damn thing still doing here?" he said, then looked up and saw Gardner working.

"What you doing up there buddy?" he said. "The president is going to address Congress in thirty minutes."

Gardner kept working on the combine. For the first time he thought he might be getting it right. The wheel loomed up against the sky and touched the outline of the cloud. It turned like a great ferris wheel in the carnival of work and the men were turning with it, pitching straw, lifting sacks of grain, spinning the wheels of tractors and trucks. The sky was one long curving wheel of clouds and blue implying the pageant of the seasons and the orbit of the planet around the sun. For the first time in weeks Gardner was beginning to feel good about the mural.

"Hey you up there," a woman called. He looked over the edge of the platform.

"WPA projects are being phased out. I just heard it on the radio."

People came and went all morning looking up at him on the scaffold as though surprised to see him there.

"Don't splatter none of that paint on me," a man called to him.

"He only paints with red paint," another said.

"I always said old Franklin Delano would get us in a war," a woman said.

"No, Franklin don't want waa and Eleanor don't want waa," the man with her said, and they both laughed.

A euphoria had swept through the town, through the county, an invisible gas poured in from Tennessee and making everyone high and pleased with their tipsiness. There was a kind of élan Gardner had often dreamed about, a spirit bringing people together as a bad storm will or a fire. It was a feeling of common enterprise, of community, that no amount of organizing and speeches and guitar playing had ever been able to accomplish.

Sweat dripped down on Gardner's glasses. He had almost gotten the combine drawn in. In the afternoon he would paint it bright red, with the paddles white as Don Quixote's windmills and the wheat heads leaning gold with ripeness.

"Hey four eyes," a boy shouted up at him as he wiped his glasses.

"I bet he's a spy," another boy said.

"I'm closing up for lunch," Joyner called. "You coming?" Joyner would never leave him in the post office during his ninety minute lunch break. He always chased Gardner out before he locked up.

I'd better go back to the boarding house and call Johnson, Gardner thought. Find out if this talk about the WPA is true. All he wanted was a few more days to finish the combine, even if he couldn't fill in all the space on the wall with people and highways and villages on the horizon.

~ · ~ · ~

When Gardner heard the news on Sunday afternoon he was writing a letter to his girlfriend Sheila. She was still an art student in Chicago. As soon as she finished in May they were going to get married, if he was kept on by the WPA. Johnson had the option of picking him for another mural in the region or dropping him, and Gardner felt it all depended on how well he did the machinery in the present mural.

"The future is with machines," Johnson had said to him several times. "Machines are our friends, machines are the allies of the common people. Only machines will get rid of poverty and discrimination." Johnson had worked as assistant to Rivera on the big murals at Detroit and he was always looking for a second Rivera among the artists he hired. If Gardner could do the combine as heroic helpmeet to the common man, he was sure Johnson would keep him on, and he and Sheila could marry. Maybe Johnson would hire Sheila for the projects also.

"The word combine is important," he wrote to Sheila. "Not only does the machine combine several functions different men used to do, cutting, gathering, threshing, bagging. It connects man and earth, present and future, steel and muscle. The combine ties a bond of energy...." It sounded too grand, even for a letter to Sheila. He was about to start over again when the landlady, Mrs. Chester, ran up the stairs. "Listen to that, listen to that," she was saying. "Just listen."

Gardner left his sentence unfinished and ran back down the stairs with Mrs. Chester. They stood by the big radio in the living room and listened to the frantic announcer. By then people were calling the radio station for more information.

191

"Please don't call us," the announcer said. "When we have more details we will give them to you on the air."

The other boarders gathered around the set too, those who had gone to church that morning and were still in their Sunday clothes after going out for dinner. They were returning from movies and from visits with friends.

"It's a stunt," someone said. "Like the invasion from Mars thing."

"No, this is real. That's Paul Alvin the news announcer."

"You'll see. It'll turn out to be a hoax like the thing in New Jersey that had everybody scared to death."

Gardner had to get out of the house. The street was deserted except for a few people running from house to house, or getting in their cars and driving away. He passed a man sitting in his Ford roadster, his ear to the radio on the dash. Phones were ringing in the houses up and down the street. The tinsel and the plastic Santa Clauses on the telephone poles looked somehow pathetic. Christmas lights in windows winked like lit, scattered marbles.

Gardner walked by the post office and out by the feed store near the railroad tracks. There was a farm machinery business further on at the edge of town, but only tractors and corn pickers sat in the yard.

He had spent Sunday morning sketching the combine, then after lunch sat down to write Sheila. When he got back to the boarding house Gardner slipped through the parlor without being noticed and climbed back up to his room to rewrite the letter.

~ · ~ · ~

I had better call Johnson, he thought again, after he had eaten the soup and sandwich Mrs. Chester placed before him. Was he imagining it, that everyone at the table looked at him accusingly? It was certainly his imagination, but he decided not to call from the boarding house where everybody at the lunch table could hear him. He would go down to the pay phone in the basement of the courthouse. Webster had at best a half dozen pay phones in the downtown area. The very busyness of the courthouse would ensure he would not be bothered.

An army recruiter had set up a table in the basement of the courthouse and lines of young men stretched out into the street. Gardner had to squeeze past them to get in the door.

"Hey, he's breaking in line," someone called.

"I'm not breaking in line," Gardner said.

"He wants to fight Hitler all by hisself."

It took some elbowing to work his way to the booth. But once inside he was pleased to find he had several nickels in his pocket, along with two dimes and a quarter. The operator had to ring Johnson's office three times before anyone answered. It was Johnson's secretary.

"Is Johnson there?" Gardner said.

"Who wants him?" The secretary giggled, as though someone was making faces at her as she talked.

"This is Gardner in Webster."

"Well Gardner in Webster, Mr. Johnson is here and he isn't."

"Can I talk with him?" There was laughter in the background.

"He has joined the Air Corps and they are giving him a farewell party."

"Will he come to the phone? Let me congratulate him." There was a pause and some murmuring, as Johnson came on the line.

"Gardner, old buddy," he said. From the pitch of his voice it was obvious he had been drinking.

"Is it true, Mr. Johnson, that the WPA artists program is being discontinued?"

"Course it's true. Our country needs us."

"And present projects won't be completed?"

"There's a form, H-W-5, you can fill out, asking to stay on for up to two months to complete current projects. I can have Geraldine send you a form."

"And I can't stay without applying for the special extension?"

"That's right. There's a war on you know."

"I know."

"It's been nice working with you Gardner. See you over Tokyo." The line went dead.

By the time Gardner returned to the post office at one-thirty he was more confused than before. Had his job already been closed out? Was he now painting on his own time? Without the special H-W-5 form and an official extension was he in effect already fired? A group of young men gathered in front of the post office, waiting for a bus that would carry them to the nearest induction center. One's jacket had been folded up and was being thrown like a basketball over the owner's head as he grabbed and missed. Joyner called to Gardner as he came in the door. The afternoons were the long, tedious time in the post office. The mail had been put in the boxes, the rural carrier was off on his route, and most of the town folk had already come in for the mail.

"Gardner, I want to talk to you," Joyner said. The last person Gardner wanted to talk to just now was Joyner. He needed to get back to work. He wanted to finish as much of the mural as he could before he had to leave.

"I've had a lot of complaints about that scaffold," Joyner said. "It's been in my way for two months, and your picture don't look any closer to being finished."

"It's mostly done," Gardner said. "Once I get the combine painted I can quickly fill in the blue sky." But even as he said

it he knew it sounded weak to argue with an old fart like
Joyner. Better ignore him the way everybody else did.

"I want you out of here," Joyner said.

Gardner hung his jacket on the cross braces of the scaffold.
He needed to get started if he was to fill in the outline he had
made of the combine that morning. He had to decide just
which red to use on the housing of the machine.

"The federal Government gave me a contract," Gardner
said.

"The federal Government is cancelling all WPA projects.
You heard that."

"There will be two months to finish current projects,"
Gardner said. He needn't tell Old Joyner about the H-W-5
form. He put the ladder up against the frame and began to
climb.

"I have news for you," Joyner said, raising his voice. "We
need this space here for a booth to sell war bonds. Every post
office will have a space where war bonds are sold."

"You can put it somewhere else," he shouted down to
Joyner. A door slammed in the back of the post office.

It was warm up near the ceiling, and cozy. He sat down on
the planks just under the outline of the combine and began to
mix reds. He needed to get a shade that showed the machine
had weathered some but wasn't rusty. All paint developed a
frosting and faded if it was exposed to the sun and elements.
The way he had drawn the combine it looked like a shoulder
heaving out of the earth pushing the paddlewheel.

Gardner squirted two worms of pigment together on the
board and began mixing them with his knife. One was darker
red and one had orange in it. The colors stayed separate in
streaks until he stirred them with his palette knife. The streaks
became hairs of color then melted and merged into each
other. He turned the blob of paint over, the way you might

turn an egg, to see if the colors were blended on the bottom. Never had he felt so confident of his ability to judge color, to predict what shade the dried mixture would have.

On the street a parade of some sort was going by. People were stopped on the sidewalk. When he stooped down on the platform to look Gardner saw it was a group of veterans from the World War who were marching. There was a drum and someone played snatches on a trombone. Some of the men had on old uniforms, or pieces of old uniforms, a gun belt, a jacket, an officer's cap. Some wore a sash over their civilian clothes. A few had medals and ribbons pinned to their business suits.

Old Joyner left his cage and stood by the window watching the troops go by. The veterans were followed by the high school band, with majorettes twirling along the sides of the street. Everybody's face seemed flushed with the excitement and cold air. Behind the band marched a lot of high school boys, and then older men with armbands. One here and there carried a hunting rifle over his shoulder. A group of police marched in ranks, and behind them came a fire truck with its lights flashing. In an open car rode the mayor, and the county commissioners followed in another car. There were more flags than Gardner had ever seen before in Webster, as if they had been saved from Fourth of July celebrations and taken out of closets and attics, out of storerooms and cedar chests and basements. Many people along the sidewalk carried little flags, and elementary school boys marched with flags.

When the parade had passed Joyner turned back from the window and looked up at him. "I'm going to call in some carpenters to take your mess down," he said.

"You'll be interfering with official government work," Gardner said.

"I never wanted any mural," Joyner said. "And now the war has changed all contracts. You know that."

"The post office doesn't belong to you," Gardner said. "It belongs to the public."

"The public don't want any mural either."

"The mural is about done," Gardner said. And it would be, if he just had a few more days, or even one day of uninterrupted work to finish the combine and fill in the sky.

"I'm going to let the sheriff evict you," Joyner said.

"He has no authority over a federal project."

"He can arrest you for trespassing."

Gardner needed to call Johnson again, to get a clarification of his status with the agency as of this afternoon. If he left the project unfinished he could be breaking his contract, and never be able to work again, after the war was over. But he was afraid to leave the post office even for a few minutes, for Joyner might call in somebody to dismantle his scaffold. As long as he was up there working surely they would not touch the platform.

Rather than take the chance of leaving the scaffold Gardner decided to work through the afternoon without coming down. Usually he came down in midafternoon to get some coffee and go to the bathroom.

Gardner put a touch of red paint on the wall and held the electric lamp close to the wet spot to make it dry. He wanted to be sure the color dried as he intended, with just the right amount of buffness. On top of the combine he would get the gleam of the harvest sun, but that could be painted on later.

Somebody opened the door of the post office and a draft of winter air swept in. Gardner could smell the town in that gust, not only the car exhaust and smoke from chimneys, and fumes from the bakery, but also the smell of rotting cornfields beyond the town.

When he was a boy Gardner tried to imagine the relationships between specific things out in the woods and fields, a rock, a particular tree, a spring hidden in the cedars, with the great world in general, the government, the mass of people, things in books, in history. And he wondered which was truer for him, the smell of the cow stalls where he milked, or the discussions of milk and dairy products and a proper diet in his health book.

Gardner remembered the exact date, when he was in art school, when he realized that he needed both kinds of perceptions to be who he was. He could draw and paint the isolated, tattered cornstalks, the hidden alcove in the pines, but in doing so he had to be conscious of the world in general, all kinds of people, even the course of history. He could not have one without the other.

Gardner was so busy concentrating on the combine, smoothing out the reds he had mixed, that he did not hear the voice calling him from below.

"Hey you up there," it was saying. "Hey buddy."

He leaned over the edge of the planks. A man in a dark suit and holding a briefcase stood by the stamp window.

"You talking to me?" Gardner said.

"No I'm talking to God."

"I'm busy," Gardner said.

"I'm busy too," the man said. "I'm Cyrus Downes, postal inspector. And I'm here to tell you your scaffold is coming down. We're putting up war bond exhibits in every post office in the district tomorrow."

Joyner stood behind the grille nodding as if to say I told you so.

"This painting is not finished and it's a federal project," Gardner said.

"Not anymore, not as of today," the man said.

"I haven't seen any orders from my office to stop," Gardner said.

"I'm giving you your orders now, buddy," Downes said. "This scaffold must be down by tomorrow morning, if not sooner...." He gave Gardner a long hard look, and left, banging the door.

"You see, it's out of my hands," Joyner said.

Gardner's only hope was to temporize that afternoon while he tried to finish the combine. They would never let him return to the mural. But if he got the combine right it would be there at least through the war. They would not go to the expense of re-painting post offices while the war was on.

"Let me finish this section and I'll take down the scaffold tomorrow morning," he called to Joyner.

"Take it down now," Joyner said.

"There's no need to take it down before quitting time," Gardner said. He turned back to the wall and began spreading more red on the brushed plaster. He had almost finished with the housing, and could get the paddlewheel and some heads of wheat, and maybe the cloud above and some sky if they let him work steady until five. He spread the paint, going over the largest area with a wide brush, a house painter's brush he had gotten at the hardware store. He could use a wide brush for the blue sky also.

A man with a wide brim hat and a holster on his belt called up to him. It was Sheriff McFee.

"Hey Gardner," the sheriff said.

"Yes sir." Politeness was his best tactic.

"Joyner says he has asked you to leave, and you refuse to vacate the premises."

"This is a federal project and I have no orders for cancelling it."

"All WPA work is now closing," the sheriff said. "You know that. There's a war on."

"I have to finish working today to draw my pay."

"Don't be a sap, Gardner. It's my duty to evict you."

"You have no authority to evict anybody who is working on a federal project on federal property. Joyner knows that. Only a federal marshal can evict from this property. Isn't that right, Joyner?"

"Then I'll get a federal marshal," Joyner said.

Gardner mixed his yellows and white for the paddlewheel, making the paddles look like arms swimming through the wheat.

A group of recruits came into the post office. Their bus to the induction center hadn't arrived, and they had been killing time by going from bar to bar along the street. Several times they had been given free drinks.

"Hey, 'fessor," one of the recruits shouted up at him. Gardner didn't look down or answer. He was afraid one of them would try to climb up if he acknowledged them.

"Hey, 'fessor, why ain't you in the army?"

The recruit took hold of the ladder and shook it against the platform. "There's a war on, professor."

Several of the boys gathered around the posts of the scaffold and shook the frame. They took hold of the crossbars and shook them like branches of an apple tree.

"Stop that," Gardner hollered down. He held onto the palette board and braced a hand against the ceiling. He was afraid he would touch the wet paint and smear it. He had to think of some way to appeal to the drunken boys.

"Don't shake this down," he said. "I've got to finish this job so I can join up tomorrow."

"Join up now," one said. "Yeah, join up now and have a drink," another said.

"You boys go on now," Joyner said, coming out of his cage. "Just go on now." He acted as though he were shooing chickens out of a flower bed.

200

"Hey old fart," one of the recruits said.

"Let's set Old Joyner on the scaffold," another said.

They gathered around Joyner as though to pick him up. Gardner thought he was going to have to jump down on top of them, for they were almost certain to knock down the scaffold. He gripped the paint board in his left hand.

"Stop that," a booming voice said. A man in a brown suit with a Stetson hat stood in the doorway.

"I'm Johns the U.S. Marshal," he said. "You boys are going to miss your bus."

"I don't see no bus," one of the recruits said.

"How can you see it in here? I just saw it coming down by the high school. It will leave you if you're not out there waiting for it."

The recruits let Joyner go and began edging to the door. There was a war waiting for them and they did not want to miss it.

"Better hurry up," the marshal said. When they were gone he looked at Joyner, and up at Gardner on the platform still gripping his brush and the palette. "OK, now what's the situation?" he said.

"This scaffold has got to go," Joyner said, his voice weak from the exertion of the scuffle. "We need this lobby for a war bond exhibit."

Gardner almost said he had signed a contract with the federal government and had to finish the mural. But he saw that was useless. "Just give me an hour and a half to finish this section," he said, looking at the clock. "Give me to five and after that I'll be gone. I'm going to join up myself tomorrow or the next day."

"Who's going to take this mess down?" Joyner said. "Somebody has got to clean it out."

The marshal pulled out his pocket watch and looked at it,

then looked out the window at the recruits lining up and jostling each other. "OK, you've got till five," he said.

Joyner stamped back into his cage, shaking his head.

Gardner got his tubes of blues and grays from the paint box. He held up his right hand to see if it was steady. The fingers were still enough to hold a telescope.

"In painting clouds you get the roundness, the bulges, with shadow, with gray receding back to white, the lit edges," his teacher at the Institute had said. "A cloud should seem so real the viewer feels it floating out of the wall into the room. You can only do that with highlights and shadow. You can only have shadow if you know where the light is coming from."

Never had Gardner worked so hard. He knew the light in the mural was a mid-afternoon light, in the harvest season, not an early morning light, and not a golden sundown light. The cloud drifted above the combine and the wheat and the men, as lovely and ambiguous as the future. He did not have time to glance at the clock again. All his years of practice went into his strokes. The cloud seemed almost lit from below, by the work and by the harvest, and by the viewer looking up at the wall. In two years, maybe in ten, long after the war was over, people would look up and see the combine advancing over the curve of the earth and the clouds drifting free above it.

As he worked Gardner's plans sorted themselves out in his mind. He would go back to his room and pack his things and take the bus to Chicago that night. If there wasn't a bus tonight he would go next morning. He would see Sheila and ask her to marry him, and he would enlist as soon as they would take him. Maybe they would put him in the infantry, but more likely in some special unit doing posters.

When Gardner finished filling in the blue around the cloud it was two minutes till five. He was damp with sweat, and his arm and shoulder felt trembly with exertion. He packed the tubes and brushes in the paint box and climbed down. The brushes could be washed after he got back to the boarding house. There would be plenty of time if he did not catch the night bus. Old Joyner was shuffling around the back, probably counting change and stamps, recording the day's transactions. Gardner did not call to him as he gathered up his drawings and put on his jacket.

When Gardner slipped out the post office door he saw a crowd gathered on the sidewalk where three or four army buses were being loaded. There were cheers when a bus pulled out, and girls were kissing their boyfriends good-by. Mothers and aunts were weeping, and fathers slapped their sons on the back and gave them steady, tearless looks of encouragement. No one noticed Gardner with his paint smudged hands and face as he headed toward the boarding house.

The Welcome

Dutch had promised himself he would not cry when he got off the bus in Tompkinsville. He hadn't cried when he left Lena at the bus station almost three years before. And there was no reason for tears now: he was coming home.

He had felt his eyes get moist when he saw the blue chain of mountains to the west as the bus swung through the foothills. And when he swallowed there was something stiff behind his tongue. He had been softened by the months in the camp, but he would not let that show. He set his jaw, and felt the firmness of the fillings and crowns the army dentist had given him after he was released and returned to England.

The bus station in Tompkinsville had once been a dry goods store, and its false front loomed like a building in a Western. The bus lurched into the parking lot and Dutch saw his daddy's pickup. It was a wonder Daddy had kept the truck running through the war, with tires and gasoline, spark plugs and everything else rationed. There was no one in the truck, which must mean Mama and Daddy were inside the station waiting. A crowd had gathered near the platform where the bus roared to a stop, but Dutch saw nobody he knew.

As he stood up in the aisle and took his duffel from the overhead rack Dutch's knees trembled. This was the moment he had waited for since parachuting out of the burning Liberator and finding himself somehow alive in a muddy German cabbage patch. Now that he was here he felt it was happening to someone else: he was just a spectator to his homecoming. He couldn't feel the elation, could only try to observe it.

As he stepped out into the spring sunlight, the town looked both strange and familiar. The buildings on Main Street, the dime store, the brick movie theater, the courthouse with its silver dome, looked smaller than he remembered. Compared to the churches he had seen in England and Germany, the steeple of the First Baptist Church looked like a toy.

There were hugs and clapping and yelps of joy as the boys came down the steps of the bus. A girl jumped up and down and screamed, "It's Ross, there he is! It's him!" It took a second to see Mama and Daddy. They stood near the steps at the edge of the little crowd. Daddy waved to him and sunlight glinted on the lenses of his glasses. Mama had her hand over her mouth, as she always did when she was excited. Dutch made his way to them.

Mama wore the same black dress she had worn to church before the war, and the same hat that appeared to be made of black fish scales. Her hand pressed her lips as though holding in an outburst. Dutch set his face in a smile and lunged forward to hug her. He felt the brooch on the front of her dress press through his uniform like a thick medallion.

"Oh, Dutch," Mama said and shook her head. It was all she could say.

"Where's Lena?" Dutch said.

"She's waiting for you," Daddy said. "There was no room in the truck." Daddy put a hand on Dutch's shoulder and they started walking toward the pickup. Mama took a handkerchief from her sleeve and wiped her eyes.

"You look so pale," Mama said.

"I've gained ten pounds since March," Dutch said.

"Is that all your things?" Daddy said.

"This is it," Dutch said, and heaved the duffel bag into the bed of the pickup. "I was in a prison camp, not any place to get souvenirs."

"I'm so happy," Mama said as they climbed into the cab. "I prayed every night for you."

"I knew I would make it," Dutch said.

"We Garners are tough," Daddy said. He jerked the truck into gear and swung the steering wheel toward the street. Daddy had never really learned to drive well. He had bought the pickup when he was near sixty and driven it home without any lessons.

A sign stretched across Main Street in front of the Highland Hotel: Welcome Home Our Heroes. Cars were driving up and down the street honking their horns and people leaned out of car windows and shouted. Others standing on the sidewalks clapped.

"Boys have been coming home for the past two weeks," Daddy said. "There is going to be a ceremony at the courthouse at the end of the month."

"And some have not returned," Mama said. She dabbed at her eyes and held Dutch's arm below the shoulder.

Daddy pushed the button in the middle of the steering wheel and added the oogah-oogah of the pickup horn to the random chorus of honks and blasts.

"What happened to Bumgarners?" Dutch said. There was a gap in the row of buildings on Main as if a giant tooth had been pulled.

"Burned down last year," Daddy said. "They thought somebody must have set it."

At the south end of town they passed a lot with many colored pennants strung around it. A number of structures stood in a space that had been a field of weeds the last time Dutch had seen it. "What's all that?" he said.

"That's Billy Joe Williams's new outfit," Daddy said. "He's got a hot dog stand and a miniature golf course. And he sells used cars and real estate."

"That's what he did instead of going to the army," Mama said.

"He has one leg shorter than the other," Dutch said. "Everybody knows that."

"Didn't stop him from making money," Mama said.

"Lonzo has to work today," Daddy said. "The cotton mill wouldn't let him off."

"They'll be laying off hands soon," Mama said.

"Just when returning boys need jobs," Daddy said.

"Don't worry about me," Dutch said. "I have almost two years' pay they saved for me."

"I'll fatten you up," Mama said.

They drove by the big pine trees in Flat Rock and passed Fletcher's store. Everything was just as Dutch remembered it, except it had shrunk. He had thought every day while he was in the camp of this ride back from town. Dutch knew his happiness must be so strong he could not feel it. Instead he felt little spurts and squeaks of joy that spilled from the overload of exhilaration.

They passed Ansell's garage where Dutch had worked one summer before the war.

"I talked to Roy the other day," Daddy said. "He said they would make every effort to give you your old job."

"I'm in no hurry," Dutch said.

"You need some rest," Mama said, "before you even think of going back to work."

"I'm rested," Dutch said. "I've had nothing to do but rest for six weeks."

"You need to get over what they done to you," Daddy said.

"I know they starved you," Mama said.

"They didn't feed us on T-bone steak and gravy," Dutch said.

"What did they give you?" Mama said. They drove past the brick schoolhouse. It was recess time and children were playing around the swings and slide. Children had been playing there the day he left for the army.

"They fed us potato peelings," Dutch said. "And sometimes cabbage soup."

"No wonder you lost weight," Mama said.

"It's a good thing we won the war," Daddy said.

Beyond the school they passed the cotton mill with its chain-link fence around the warehouse and front office. Steam climbed from the window of the mercerizing room, and Dutch thought he could smell the chemical dampness inside, though it was probably just his imagination. Before the war Dutch had wondered if he would ever get out of the mercerizing room. In the camp he had wondered if he would ever get back to it.

"Did they hurt you over there?" Daddy said.

"Now don't start that," Mama said. "Dutch is trying to forget all that."

"Nobody got hurt if they didn't try to escape," Dutch said.

∾ · ∾ · ∾

As they passed Leland's Lunchroom, Dutch saw Hendrix standing outside by his Ford roadster. Daddy hit the pickup horn twice and Hendrix waved and reached inside the roadster and tapped the horn. Hendrix was only three years older than Dutch, but he had been turned down by the army because of a trick knee.

"People are glad to see you," Mama said.

"Not as glad as I am to see them," Dutch said.

As they approached Davis's filling station Dutch noticed a number of cars in front. The yard looked like a used car lot. There was a sign over the gas pumps, a long sign made of cloth and fluttering in the breeze.

"Has Davis gone into the car business?" Dutch said.

"Look at the sign," Mama said.

Dutch saw the "WEL" at the left side of the banner, and knew it said "Welcome Home Dutch." His heart kicked in his chest and something turned strange in his gut, like a funny bone had been hit. He felt as if his skin was turning silver.

And then he saw there were people in each of the cars and trucks. There was Ed Jones in his old Model-A and Jack Gordon in his pickup. There was Adger Harmon in his black Chevrolet and Bill Johnson in the little Ford with the rumble seat. They all waved and horns began beeping and howling and oogah-oogahing.

"You mean they were all waiting for us?" Dutch said.

"No, they was waiting for the Fourth of July," Daddy said.

"They heard you was coming home," Mama said.

"They should all be at work," Dutch said.

"Don't you know it's Saturday?" Mama said.

Daddy pounded the horn and Dutch waved to his friends in the cars. "Ain't you going to stop?" he said.

"Why do that?" Daddy said and grinned.

Dutch looked back and saw the cars and trucks at the filling station begin to pull into the highway behind Daddy's pickup. Daddy slowed down and the vehicles formed a line behind them. Their lights were on and all the horns were sounding. Dutch swallowed. "This is like a funeral procession," he said.

"More like a victory parade," Daddy said.

Daddy turned off at Green River Road, and the train of

cars followed. The valley echoed and trees appeared to shiver with the sound of the horns, doubling and tripling and answering each other. There was no one in the yard of Lena's house. Maybe she was in one of the cars behind, though Dutch had not seen her daddy's green Dodge.

"Look at the thrift in Ophelia's yard," Mama said. Thrift in bloom cushioned the bank above the road like luminous colorful pillows. The thrift was even brighter than Dutch remembered it. Lena's mama had always grown the most impressive thrift in the valley.

The bin of the sand pump stood like a roofless barn on the river bank below the road. The structure looked awkward and ugly on its poles where trucks backed underneath to take on loads of sand.

"The sand pump looks deserted," Dutch said.

"Construction had to stop during the war," Daddy said. "They'll be pumping sand again now."

Cattle stood in the pasture above Riley's house, grazing and ignoring the racket of the line of cars. But a horse bounded across the lower pasture, spooked by the noise. A rooster sat on the fence behind Riley's barn, its neck feathers flashing in the sunlight.

"Looks like Riley has more cows than ever," Dutch said.

"The government paid him to produce milk," Daddy said. "He got a contract to sell milk to the army base in Greenville."

There were more cars parked in the church yard. Dutch saw Alvin Green's pickup there, and Robin Oakes in his strip-down. They hit their horns as Daddy's pickup passed. The church needed a coat of paint. In places the white had scaled off the steeple, showing patches of weathered wood.

"Is everybody out in their cars today?" Dutch said.

"We'll just have to see," Mama said.

Beyond the church it was less than a quarter of a mile to

their driveway. Dutch saw the weeds and broom sedge had been trimmed around the entrance. The white wagon wheel Daddy had placed by the mailbox had lost most of its paint. The tracks of the driveway were deeper, and the grass in the middle taller than he remembered.

As the pickup bounced on the ruts Dutch saw there were already several cars in the yard. One was Lena's daddy's green Dodge, and there was a Studebaker he didn't recognize.

As soon as the pickup stopped he saw Lena standing by the steps going up to the front porch. She stood with her hands in front of her, palms pressed together. She looked slimmer than he remembered. But she had always been slim, even looked frail at times. It depended on the way she stood, and how tanned her face was.

Dutch was out of the truck as soon as Daddy stopped. He skipped and then paused, stepped slowly toward Lena. This was the moment he had been waiting for for three years. Lying on the cold planks in the prison barracks he had visualized this meeting so many times it was memorized. But the event was unfolding beyond his control. He was watching it happen to another person.

"Hello, Lena," he said. She waited, as if expecting him to say more.

He took her hands, and then dropped them as he spread his arms. Dutch hugged her, knowing all those in cars stopped along the road were watching. He saw himself embracing her and heard himself say, "Long time no see."

When he pressed his cheek against Lena's he felt a warm tear crush between their skin.

"You never answered my letters," Lena said.

"What letters?" He stepped back and held her hands.

"I wrote you at least once a month," Lena said, pretending to be stern.

"I never got any letters," Dutch said. "The Germans must have throwed them away."

"I sent you a cake, too," Lena said, "at Christmas."

"I bet the Germans eat it up," Dutch said.

"Or the Red Cross eat it up theirselves," Lena's daddy said. Dutch turned and shook hands with him.

"Welcome home," Lena's dad said.

"I feel like it's somebody else coming home," Dutch said.

"Who else would it be?" Lena's daddy said.

"Somebody else with my name," Dutch said.

≈ · ≈ · ≈

Everyone who arrived brought a plate of something. Lydia Green walked up the driveway carrying a casserole dish of banana pudding, and John Coleman brought a gallon jar of iced tea. There were platters of fried chicken and creamed potatoes, sliced picnic ham and quivering bowls of jello with pieces of fruit suspended inside.

Dutch's cousin Everett, who had served in the coastal artillery, came out of the house carrying a chair in either hand.

"Let me help you," Dutch said.

"You old son of a gun," Everett said. "Did you bring me a German Luger?"

Dutch had brought gifts for Mama and Daddy and Lena, but they were in his duffel bag, and he could not bring them out until the other guests were gone. "I wasn't near any souvenir shops," he said.

Mama brought a table cloth from the house and spread it on the grass under the oak tree. The ground in the yard was swept clean of pebbles and acorns. People said Mama kept her yard neat as the kitchen table.

"I'm glad to see the end of rationing," Johnny Carlisle said as they set the dishes and bowls on the white cloth.

"Now that the war is over, the depression will come back," John Coleman said.

"Don't say that," Lena's daddy said. "This is a happy day."

"Our years of trial are not ended just because the war is over," John said.

"Don't be such a sad sack," Mrs. Coleman said. "What will Dutch think, after two years as a prisoner."

"Dutch will know he's back among his own complaining kin," John said.

"I'm just glad to see my folks," Dutch said, "and to not have a fence around me."

He looked at Lena. They had not been exactly engaged when he left, but they did have an understanding. Lena had been only sixteen then. Dutch wasn't sure what he would say to her when they were alone. It was clear everyone expected him to marry her. And it was what he had planned in the camp. But he had no idea how he would ask her.

"I think it's time to eat," Daddy said, after the plates and silverware had been placed on a bench beside the table cloth. "Let Deacon Green lead us in prayer."

The men took off their hats. Dutch removed his overseas cap. He had not heard anyone pray since MacAbee the tail-gunner used to lead in prayer in the camp. MacAbee planned to be a minister when he got home and he held services in one of the barracks every Sunday morning. MacAbee didn't really know how to preach, but he had a torn Bible he read from and a good many boys attended the services because there was nothing much to do.

"Oh Lord, we want to thank you from the bottom of our hearts for sparing Brother Dutch from the harm of war and returning him to those who love him. We know that you who see the fall of a sparrow will look after all...."

While the deacon was praying Dutch heard a car door slam

down by the road. He opened his eyes to a squint and saw Roger Jarvis get out of his pickup truck. Roger was always a practical joker. At Christmas he threw firecrackers in people's yards, and once at prayer meeting on Halloween he had dropped a cherry bomb in the stove at church.

Roger took something out of the bed of his truck that looked like an ammunition belt. Dutch saw the flare of a match.

"Go with Dutch and bless him as he takes up his life again," Deacon Green was saying. The first firecracker sounded like a bark, but then the others went off in drum rolls and machine gun bursts. The firecrackers must have been of different sizes for some yelped and others boomed. Dutch winced at the sound and shuddered. Roger lit another string and threw it on the lawn below the picnic. Everyone forgot Deacon Green's grace.

"Brother Roger has his own way of giving thanks," the deacon said, and they all laughed. Smoke from the firecrackers drifted up the hill under the oaks.

"Roger likes to enter in a cloud of glory," Steve Jeter said.

"With a hundred and twenty-one gun salute," Ed Jones said.

"I've noticed draft dodgers like to be loud," Lena's mother said.

"Shhhh," said Lena.

Mama brought a jar of lemonade from the house, and Lena handed Dutch a cup. Someone passed him a plate with fried chicken and potato salad on it. It was only when he looked at the chicken, at the crisp greasy skin, that he knew he wasn't hungry. His stomach felt like a question mark.

"You must be starved," Lena said, "after that long bus ride."

Dutch wished he was doing something else. He wasn't sure

what. He wished no one had been there when he got home. He wished he could have arrived secretly and taken off his uniform and put on work clothes. He wished he was out in the mountains fishing. He wished he could go sit on the side of the mountain and look out over the valley. In the camp he had often thought of a place where he used to rest, while hunting squirrels. It was a pit his great-grandpa had dug, looking for zircons. Under October leaves it was a kind of shelf to sit on and watch the trees. He wished he could just go up there and rest under the quiet woods.

Dutch stuck a fork into the potato salad and brought it to his mouth. He could not refuse to eat after all the work these neighbors had gone to fix the picnic. They assumed he had to be hungry, and he must not disappoint them. He chewed the cold diced potato and took a bite of the chicken leg. Lena had remembered that he preferred dark meat.

"What do you think of this Truman?" Deacon Green said to him.

"I never heard of Truman till I was brought back to England," Dutch said.

"Let the boy eat," Lena's daddy said. "He don't have no interest in politics."

"Polly who?" Dutch said, and everybody laughed.

"Bet the Germans didn't give you no fried chicken," Roger said and punched Dutch with a mock blow on the shoulder.

"No fried chicken and no Co-colas," Dutch said.

"We'll soon fatten you up," Lena's mama said.

"New potatoes will be in soon," Mama said.

Dutch was not only not hungry. He was a little sick at his stomach. He had ridden the bus all night and only slept in snatches. But he wasn't sleepy. He just wished he could be alone. He hadn't even gotten into the house since he arrived. His duffel bag lay on the ground by the path to the back porch.

He wished he could walk to the edge of the yard and stand in the woods and try to feel like he was really here.

"Did you like the looks of them fräuleins?" Mitchell Jones said.

"What a question," Roger said.

"What fräuleins?" Dutch said. "I didn't see any fräuleins in the prison camp."

"How about some coleslaw?" Mama said.

"Just a second," Dutch said. He saw what he had to do to get away for a few moments. He had not gone to the toilet since he got off the bus. He edged toward the pump house and put his plate on the pump house roof. As soon as people saw he was headed toward the outhouse they pretended to ignore him. All eyes turned back to their plates.

Daddy had mowed the backyard with the push mower, and the path was a sunken trail with bare spots where grass had not covered the flagstones. The toilet was out of sight around the edge of the smokehouse. Dutch noticed his fishing pole still resting on nails under the eave of the smokehouse where he had left it three springs ago.

When he reached the outhouse Dutch looked back to see if anyone had followed him. No one was in sight. Instead of going into the outhouse he stepped past the little weathered building toward the hogpen. He had forgotten the particular stench of the hogpen, and the smell blossomed against his face in the bright air. The scent was so foul it was almost sweet: manure and rotten mud and fungus, and putrid water.

"Ooof," the pig said behind the planks, expecting some slop poured down the chute. Three pigs had been raised and fattened and killed since he left, but this one sounded and smelled like the shoat that had been there when he was drafted. The stink of the hogpen was the most real thing Dutch had encountered since getting off the bus. Smelling it, he almost felt like his old self again.

Dutch skirted the lush, giant weeds around the hogpen and slipped into the edge of the woods. A crow heckled from the top of an oak tree. A spider web was strung between two saplings. Dutch pissed on the web until the strands looked decorated with amber beads.

After buttoning his pants Dutch stood listening to the breeze in the trees above him. He thought he heard a hawk whistle. But there were too many voices from the back yard for him to be sure. He thought he could hear the falls over on Mills Creek, but it might have been a truck on the highway a mile away.

As soon as Dutch stepped out of the woods he saw Roger and Mitchell standing by the outhouse. "There you are," Roger said. "We wondered if you had fell through the hole." He pulled a pint bottle from his hip pocket.

"We thought you might be a little dry," Mitchell said.

"After your long bus ride," Roger said.

Dutch took the bottle and unscrewed the top. The scent of the whiskey was like the fumes of very ripe fruit in a cellar. It was cheap rye and he took a long swallow with his eyes closed. The dram burned his throat so fiercely tears sprang into his eyes. But as the liquid sank into his belly he felt the world get lighter. The sunlight was a little brighter.

"Good stuff," he said, and handed the bottle back to Roger.

"We figured you might want to celebrate with something stronger than iced tea," Mitchell said.

"There is more where this come from," Roger said.

"I know where there's a whiskey spring up on Pinnacle," Mitchell said.

"A whiskey spring?" Dutch said.

217

"Sure, the liquor just flows out of the mountain clear and ninety proof."

"Like hell," Dutch said.

"Let's drive up there and we'll show you," Roger said.

~ . ~ . ~

When Dutch got back to the picnic Mama handed him a plate with banana pudding and coconut cake. They had always been his two favorite desserts. Dutch took the plate and thanked Mama. But he wasn't hungry for sweet things. The drink had made him feel lighter. He only wanted another drink.

"Would you like some coffee?" Lena said. She was holding a pot she must have brought from the kitchen. A tray of cups had been set on the bench.

"Maybe later," Dutch said. He didn't want any coffee to counteract the lift the rye had given him. He wondered if Lena could smell the drink on him. She had once said she would never marry a man who drank. Maybe she would not recognize the scent of the rye. Lena would expect him to go back to her house after the picnic, to sit on the porch and talk, or maybe go for a walk down by the river. He didn't want to be alone with her just yet. He didn't know what he would say to her.

There was an explosion nearby that washed over the crowd and out to the rim of the mountains, then returned as an echo. Dutch jerked and almost dropped the plate with pudding and cake on it. Everybody looked downhill and saw Roger standing beside his pickup holding a shotgun pointed to the sky. He fired again, and the blast jolted the air.

"This is like Christmas," Lena's mama said.

"It's better than Christmas," Lena said.

"Hey, Dutch, let's go for a ride," Roger called.

"Let's go up on Pinnacle," Mitchell said and winked.

"You don't want to go now," Daddy said and looked around at all the guests.

"I just want to see the valley," Dutch said.

"He wants to see if the old valley is still there," Lena's daddy said. "I can understand that."

"You can go later," Mama said.

Dutch set the plate down on the bench. He had to get away. He couldn't say anything more to the crowd standing around the yard. Riding with Roger and Mitchell up the valley to Pinnacle was as good an excuse as any to escape the crowd.

"We'll be back in a jiffy," Dutch said over his shoulder. He didn't really look at Lena. He didn't want to see the look of disappointment or confusion on her face. If he didn't look at her, he wouldn't have to respond.

Several boys followed him down to Roger's pickup. Roger and Mitchell and Dutch got into the cab and Adger and Hendrix and Ed Jones and Jack Gordon climbed into the bed. "Whooopeee," Adger called out and banged on the roof as they started.

"Yiiiipee!" Ed Jones yodeled. That was the way the boys acted when they won a game for the cotton mill baseball team. Mitchell reached out the window and slammed the outside of the door like a drum. "We're going to have us some fun, now old Dutch is back," he said.

The bottle was passed between those in the cab and then handed out the window to those standing in the bed. The second drink tasted even sweeter to Dutch, and he felt the extra illumination in his veins.

"Say, Dutch, did you get any over there?" Mitchell said.

"In prison camp?" Dutch said.

"We heard they had Russian girl prisoners," Roger said.

"That must have been another camp," Dutch said.

219

"You wouldn't lie to us," Mitchell said.

"Only woman I seen in all those months was the colonel's wife," Dutch said. "And she weighed about three hundred pounds."

The truck rumbled on the bridge over Cabin Creek. "How's fishing been?" Dutch said.

"The trout have been on strike, waiting for you to come back," Roger said.

"Roger don't know how to fish except with dynamite," Mitchell said.

"At least I don't use a tow sack for a seine net," Roger said.

Most of the fields along the creek had been plowed and many had been planted in corn. They passed a patch where last year's stubble and corn stalks sparkled in the sun. "Looks like Corbin ain't planted yet," Dutch said.

"Only thing Corbin is planting is the graveyard," Roger said. "He died last fall."

"And his boy Mark?"

"Mark is still in the Pacific."

The Corbin house looked deserted. Grass and weeds grew up to the level of the porch.

"Still can't believe I'm back," Dutch said.

"Maybe you ain't," Roger said. "Maybe somebody else come in your place."

The bottle was handed back into the cab, but it was empty. "Thanks a lot," Mitchell shouted and tossed the dead soldier out the window.

"Look under the seat," Roger said.

"Old Roger always goes prepared," Mitchell said, "like a good Boy Scout." He reached beneath and pulled out a quart mason jar. "Look at this, my children, look at this," he said.

When Dutch put his lips to the rim of the jar, he could tell from the oily roily look how powerful the corn liquor was.

The jolting of the truck made beads rise to the surface. "This ain't liquor, this is airplane fuel," Dutch said.

"Don't I save the best for my buddies," Roger said.

As the moonshine sank into him, Dutch felt a great weight shift within, independent of the way his body moved. It was the shift of intoxication, as if great masses were trading sides in his head.

They passed Mountain Valley Baptist Church and Dutch saw the paint on its steeple was cracked and scaling. "Has everybody forgot how to paint?" he said.

"Where could you get any paint?" Mitchell said.

"Paint all went to army barracks and ships and government hospitals," Roger said.

"I'll paint the church," Dutch said, "now that I'm home."

"Maybe they will make you a deacon," Roger said.

A blast roared in the back of the truck. One of the boys had fired Roger's shotgun. "Put that thing down," Roger yelled out the window.

"Hendrix was shooting at a bumblebee," Adger called.

Dutch heard himself laugh. It was all so funny he couldn't resist laughing. He couldn't remember what had been said, but he knew it was funny as hell. Mitchell handed him the fruit jar again.

"If I keep drinking this stuff I'm going to be drunk," he said.

"A man's got to do what a man's got to do," Mitchell said and giggled.

"A man has a right to wet his whistle," Dutch said.

"Wet his whistle and his pizzle," Roger said. Roger swung the pickup onto a smaller dirt road and they began to climb a steep ridge. The ruts were rocky and full of potholes. The truck bounced and lurched, and limbs swished on the windshield. There were yells in the back. Dutch's right shoulder crashed into Mitchell and his left shoulder hit Roger.

"Yiiipeee!" Adger called in the back.

Roger shifted into low on a switchback, and the truck spun and bucked on gravel. Sourwood limbs leaned across the road and slapped the windshield.

"Slow down," Ed Jones called. "This ain't no rodeo."

"Throw their asses off," Mitchell said and chuckled.

Dutch found he was laughing again. He must have been laughing all along.

"Maybe we will see a bear up here," Roger said.

"If we see a bear we will offer it a drink," Mitchell said.

"What if it don't drink," Dutch said.

"Any bear that don't drink ain't fit company," Mitchell said.

When they came out on top of the mountain and Roger stopped the truck, Dutch did not even notice the view until Mitchell opened the door. There were mountains rolling away to the edge of the world on every side.

"Ladies and gentlemen, the pinnacle of Pinnacle," Roger said.

Those in the back of the truck jumped off the tailgate. A great boulder stood beside the road and they scrambled to its top. Mitchell passed the jar around.

"I hear Brother Dutch is going to preach for us," Ed said.

"Only if the spirit moves me," Dutch said.

"We could take up a collection," Jack said.

"Looks like something is on fire," Hendrix said and pointed to a twisted column of smoke to the west. The valleys and ridges below them progressed in steps from brown and new green to darker green to hazy blue. The far peaks of Pisgah were almost lavender.

"Must be a house burning," Roger said.

"Or maybe just a big brush pile," Mitchell said.

"Look at the new road to Brevard," Jack said. Where he pointed Dutch saw a strand of red clay partly hidden by trees.

Directly below them a small lake sparkled like a sapphire among trees.

"Bet I can throw a rock into the lake," Adger said. He picked up a rock from the road and hurled it as hard as he could into the air beneath them. The rock disappeared into the trees on the steep ridge below.

"That's the lake the new Florida people built," Hendrix said.

"Bet I can roll a rock into the lake," Ed said.

"The hell you preach," Mitchell said.

There were dozens of rocks that had been bulldozed out of the road lying on the shoulder. Most were flat and gritty with red dirt.

"Watch this," Hendrix said. He stood a rock up on its side and gave it a push. The rough wheel wobbled and almost fell over, but as it gathered speed on the steep bank below it gained stability and stayed upright. As it accelerated the rock bounced and blurred and disappeared into the trees below. But they could hear it skipping on the leaves and banging on saplings. A hollow sound told them it had hit a tree. They listened like hunters do to their hounds far out in the woods. A crash told them the rock had hit a boulder far below.

"That ain't nothing," Adger said. He grabbed a bigger rock out of the dirt of the shoulder and rolled it to the lip as though pushing a calf. With a shove he let it go over the edge. But the rock had a flat place on one side and instead of rolling it just flopped over.

They all clapped. "You really showed us," Mitchell said.

Adger grabbed the rock again and set it upright. This time the rock took off and continued to roll until it disappeared into the brush straight below them.

Everyone rushed to seize a rock and set it rolling. Dutch found a rock that was more a triangle than a wheel, but after several tries he got it to roll away. He found a rock the size of a suitcase and made it spin and soar. He dug out a rock that was almost round as a ball and sent it down the steep slope. He was clearing off the top of the mountain. It was satisfying to get rid of all the rocks in sight, as if he was putting the world in order.

"We will bomb the lake," Ed shouted. The woods rang and shivered below them. The scattered avalanche of rocks shook trees and broke saplings far down the mountainside.

"Bombs away," Roger shouted.

Dutch dug out bigger rocks and smaller rocks. He got dusty and sweaty, and he scraped a knuckle so it bled. The whiskey made him as hot as if it was midsummer. He worked further down the road to locate better rocks. This was the best welcome yet.

Hendrix and Adger found a rock so big it took both of them to set it upright. They shoved it off and the rock lurched sideways and staggered. Hendrix gave it a big push and it rolled over Adger's foot.

"Hell!" Adger screamed, "you trying to break my leg?"

"Your damn foot's too big," Hendrix said.

Adger's face was pale and sweaty. "I didn't go to hurt *you*," he said.

Hendrix dusted his hands off and wiped them on his pants. "You should have sense enough to get your foot out of the way," he said, so calm all the friendliness had gone out of his voice.

"You should have sense enough not to push a damn rock over on me," Adger said. He limped closer to Hendrix, his hands on his hips.

"Ain't you got brains enough to see where a rock is going?" Hendrix said. He wiped his forehead with his sleeve. All the others had stopped rolling rocks.

"You been riding my ass all day," Adger said. "You been riding my ass since Dutch got home."

"Nobody is riding your skinny ass," Hendrix said.

"Are you showing out for Dutch?" Adger said. He shoved Hendrix's chest.

"I don't need to show out for Dutch!" Hendrix said.

"Are you afraid you won't be such a big boy around here, now that Dutch is back, and Lena will go out with him?" Adger said.

"That's enough of that," Roger said. All the boys gathered around the two who were facing each other.

"Man, if you had tits we could see you was a girl," Hendrix said.

Adger's fist caught him on the chin before he had finished the sentence. Hendrix staggered back, braced himself, and lunged for Adger. They went rolling and grunting down the bank into the brush. The others stood on the bank watching them clawing and kicking among the briars.

"You shit-sucking coward," Hendrix yelled as he emerged on top. He kicked at Adger in the weeds, staggered back, and kicked him again.

"Stop it!" Roger yelled. "Stop it, or I'll leave you all to walk home."

Adger stumbled to his feet and faced Hendrix. Blood ran from their noses and mouths, and from cuts on their arms. They were so exhausted they could hardly stand. Both crawled back up the bank into the road. Dutch had seen them fight many times before. The fight made him feel he had almost not been away. Now that the anger had gushed out in their fight, both looked a little embarrassed.

"Have you been dating Lena?" Dutch said to Hendrix.

"Hell no," Hendrix said. "I just drove her home from a basketball game once is all."

∾ · ∾ · ∾

Dutch dropped to the ground and wiped his forehead with his sleeve. He loosened his tie and saw his hands were dirty and there was dust and blood on his uniform. His shoes which had been polished like brown mirrors were scuffed and covered with dust.

The others flopped down on the bank of the road and Roger passed around the jar until it was empty. Now that he was sweaty and dirty Dutch felt a lot more like himself. But he was suddenly so tired he could hardly sit upright.

"Man, we can have some fun, now old Dutch is home," Hendrix said.

Dutch looked out over the long valley below. He could see as far as Asheville. A smokestack wrote a black scrawl on the horizon.

"Everything is going to be different, now the war is over," Mitchell said.

"You mean people will have three eyes and talk with their assholes?" Roger said.

"What's different about that?" Hendrix said.

"I mean it won't never be the same," Mitchell said.

"I feel the same," Adger said.

"That's because you ain't been nowhere," Jack said.

Dutch wished he could just go to sleep. The momentum had gone out of the day. He wished he did not have to go back to the house. He knew Mama and Daddy and Lena would be mad because he had left the picnic. He did not know what he wanted to say to Lena. He wished he could just be by himself.

Tailgunner

Tailgunners lose their fingers, if not their lives," Baxter had said.

Jones worked his index finger inside the glove, and wiped breath fog off the bulbous window. The P-47's were peeling away, leaning to dive beneath the bombers and head back to England.

"Boys, we're on our own now," Carver said over the radio from the cockpit. "Keep those trigger fingers warm, and don't wet your diapers. We're going up."

As the B-24 began to climb Jones had a view of the blue and gray countryside. There were lakes and rivers and straight lines that might be canals or highways. He imagined he could see a column of tanks or trucks. They were almost certainly over enemy country now, and the Messerschmitts would appear any second. The Germans always knew just where the fighter escort would use up half their gasoline and turn back.

It was a sight that always made him catch his breath, the formations of bombers behind them. The squadrons were clustered as far as he could see into the west, hundreds of ships tilting and bumping on the air currents, in waves. Those that came back would fly further apart, since pilots often nodded off on the return journey. In the ass of each of them sat some tailgunner like himself, cramped and trying to keep his fingers warm.

"Since the most effective attacks are from the rear of your craft, the life of your crew and the success of your mission will often depend on your marksmanship, on keeping your trigger finger awake," Baxter said, slapping the chart with his ruler.

Jones slapped his gloves together and scanned the sky above the formations. Since they were near the front he would be shooting up high. The turret would get those underneath and the waist gunners those on the sides. Billy in the overhead turret and Jim in the nose might be busy today. They might be under fire for hours, because the target was far to the east, beyond Leipzig.

As the plane continued to climb Jones hoped he would not throw up. Nothing like frozen puke in your compartment. Riding backwards always made him a little sick, and the rocking on updrafts didn't help. He took off his gloves and ate another pill from the can in his hip pocket. It was already below zero, and ice was forming on the edges of the window sections. Frost crystals shone on the magazines of his guns, but they would burn away as soon as he started firing.

Though he had completed fifteen missions of his twenty-five, Jones did not expect to return home. But he did not want to die today. On every mission he prayed only to survive this trip.

"All right, let's go to oxygen," Carver said on the radio. The mask was so cold it burned his face at first, but Jones felt immediately the waking up that always came with breathing pure oxygen.

"Five o'clock, five o'clock," Jim shouted. The left waist gun and maybe the overhead opened up. But he couldn't see anything. The sky was clear behind. He flexed his fingers. His hands were cold but not yet numb. The turret and nose guns on the planes behind were firing, for he saw the sparkle of their tracers.

"One o'clock, one o'clock, Jones wake up." Bending low he could just see the Messerschmitt swing over into his field of view and start diving on them. He tilted his guns as high as they would go, but the Messerschmitt was still out of his sights. It was coming in fast, its guns sparking, and he started firing even though it was out of the line of his aim. The .50 cal. belts of ammunition looked like hands with an endless number of fingers he thought as he squeezed the trigger and the guns knocked and spat out shells. The plane started rocking and smoke began to fill his compartment.

"Hang in there," Carver said. "We lost an engine."

The Messerschmitt swung by so close he could see the pilot's face.

When he looked back he could see they had dropped out of formation and were banking away to the left.

"We're going down," Carver called. "Everybody out."

Thrown by the fall of the plane, it was only with the greatest effort that Jones pulled himself back through the hatch into the bomb bay. The floor tilted so he could not walk but was flung along the wall.

He looked into the overhead turret and saw the glass was covered with blood and what looked like brains. McCall had been hit in the head and streamed blood into the cabin below.

The right door was open and Jones, after tightening his parachute straps, lunged into it. But the wind threw him back. Flames were reaching out of the front of the aircraft and he saw Jenkins the navigator clinging to a post just behind the cockpit. "Come on," he shouted to him.

But Jenkins was frozen to the post. He would not loosen his grip. Jones tried to knock him loose, knock him out and push him to the door, but a lurch sent him reeling backward. He clawed his way over bombs and bodies to the door and hurled himself outward. But the air pressure was like a brick wall.

The plane was spinning now, and he could do nothing but hold onto a gun mount. There was no up or down, and tools and bodies hit him as he turned over and over. The flames burned into his sheepskin jacket and through his gloves. His eyes were singed.

At that instant Jones knew all his life he had been waiting for this moment. His learning to swim in the creek, his training at gunnery school in Wyoming, his survival of typhoid fever in 1927, all led here.

Wind and flames rushed by him, and there was a great pop, as though a nutshell had broken. He was flying through smoke and oily mist, tumbling, his fingers working. He saw the clouds below rising up white and gray.

$$\sim \cdot \sim \cdot \sim$$

Jones looked at his watch, fifty minutes before news time. He had chosen the charcoal watch face with gold hands over a digital. He liked to buy the newest things, but in this one little thing he would be old-fashioned. There was time to go for a walk, or he could watch half a movie on the VCR. Lorna had bought him his own copy of *Twelve O'Clock High* for his birthday. He had seen it a number of times over the years, originally at a theater in Spartanburg, then on late night TV cut up for commercials. But he never tired of the opening sequence where Dean Jagger bicycles out to the abandoned airfield and looks around at the hangars and control tower, and the grass at his feet begins to ripple in wind that becomes the backwash of a B-17 warming up as the film flashes back to the war.

The pain in his chest was bad today. He should take another Advil before starting on the walk. First he would have a couple of soda crackers with margarine on them for energy. That was stretching his diet, but only by the tiniest fraction. And Lorna would not be back from her meeting until six. He munched the crackers as he stepped outside.

When they bought the house, the development was at the edge of open country. Now there were new houses with carports and wooden fences all the way down the road, and they were building more out where the fields had been bulldozed into sandy lots. He had to walk past the construction to reach the country, and he resisted the curiosity to look at the framing going up. Thirty years in construction had been enough. He had been ready to quit even if he had not had the heart attack. They did not even *build* houses anymore, but just knocked together sections already assembled at a factory. He had not held a hammer in two decades when his heart put him in early retirement.

But it was only in the last few days that he had realized, while he was walking, that he had not been happy since he quit working with his hands.

"It's your nerves, from the war," Lorna explained, when he was depressed. But he never showed anyone else his depression as he rose from carpenter to foreman to supervisor and finally to vice-president. Jones was the sunny one, always chewing gum, smiling, as he looked over blueprints and readouts. He was their best contact man, for lunches with prospective clients, soothing irate homeowners on the telephone after their wiring was found defective. It was something he had learned in the Air Corps and prison camp: at the worst moments, when everything seems to be going to hell, you just smile and act like a screw maybe needs tightening, or there is a slight mistake in the column of figures which you can go over and correct.

He wished he had not eaten the crackers, for the soreness under his ribs grew as he walked past some kids tinkering with an off-the-road three-wheeler. A kid about ten was red-faced from pulling the starter cord. They stood back as Jones bent over the engine. The scent of the flooded carburetor affected him like smelling salts. He pushed back the choke all the way and held it, telling the kid to pull again. The spark caught on the second try, and the engine fired and puffed out blue smoke. He flicked the choke down and it roared into a steady normal rhythm. Without looking back at him the boys climbed on the machine and sputtered away.

The smell of gas on his hands made him faintly nauseous. He tasted the margarine, rancid in his throat.

"The Thomas appetite will kill you," Lorna liked to say. It was an old joke in the family. His mother was a Thomas and her folks liked to brag about their relish for rich food. Grandpa Thomas was supposed to have killed himself eating molasses and butter on biscuits. They referred to "the Thomas appetite" as though it were some special talent, an inherited giftedness, a blessing of luck.

There was the scent of new lumber from the last construction site on the road, and he paused to inhale the fumes of fresh pine, hoping they would make his chest feel better. But the pain had increased, and his stomach was restless. He continued on the level road, glad there was nothing to climb, even though he still missed the broom sedge and pasture hills of the mountains. They had moved to Sumter to be closer to Alva and the grandchildren. It would never seem like home.

He turned off the road, stepping through weeds and sandspurs, and entered a stretch of pine woods half a mile from the development. In two or three years the grove would be knocked down and covered with houses. But it was one of his favorite spots. He liked to walk out there and just stand beneath the pines, listening to the sigh in their tops, like the sound of a distant ocean. In the shade of the pines he felt more himself, as though he was closer to a self he had lost in the

war and never recovered. But there was a way he felt in the
pine woods that reminded him of moments in the war, as well
as of childhood. It was as though he had forgotten something
about himself for almost forty years. He could not explain
why the peacefulness of the trees reminded him of instants
of great danger and sickness, why he felt close to some
bedrock definition, some value. It was just a little stand of
woods. He looked up at the green canopy swaying like a lake
surface. He had once stood in a similar forest in Germany,
after his release.

The roar of the three-wheeler took him by surprise, and he
jumped aside from the path as the boys blasted past. Their
laughter reverberated above the engine noise, and they disappeared down the trail, leaving fumes of burnt oil. The tires
had torn the needles loose on the trail, and he kicked at the
cleat-molded dirt. It was almost news time.

"You've been eating margarine," Lorna said as he came in.

"How do you know?"

"You left it on the table. Do you think I'm a fool?" She was
emptying the dishwasher and starting to boil things for supper.
He turned on the news and sat down in the living room. If he
sat still long enough the pain in his chest might quiet down.

"Are we going to Tampa?" Lorna called from the kitchen.

"To Tampa?"

"To the reunion. I saw the newsletter," she said, wiping her
hands as she came into the living room.

"Would you want to go? That's really for pilots and co-pilots
and navigators. There won't be any non-coms there. I was
just a tailgunner, remember."

"And you amounted to more than any of your squadron."

"The rest of the squadron was killed."

"The Ninety-second Bombardment Group should be proud
of you. You should go and see them again."

He had only begun getting the newsletter last year. It was an accident that he knew about it. An old buddy he had run into at Columbia had told him about the Memorial Association.

"Fame's Favored Few!" it said on the cover. He read the letters and looked at the snapshots of bombardiers and radiomen sent in. But he would feel embarrassed at a reunion, a tailgunner hobnobbing with officers, listening to a lot of lies and stories he had heard before.

"I want to go," Lorna said.

It amazed him to think he had been married to Lorna for forty years. Their wedding was just something that happened to him when he got back after the war, underweight and dazed. He had never planned it, or thought it would last. He had always assumed he would eventually marry someone else more suited to him. Yet in her way she was a good person. Alva had come and grown up and married, and they were still together. The years had come and most of them were gone.

～ ∙ ～ ∙ ～

As he fell into the German cabbage patch, Jones saw the woman out of the corner of his eye. He was drifting sideways fast in the wind, and she broke into a run toward where she thought he would land. And when he hit and rolled over, tangled in the chute lines, she stood over him, not with a hoe or pitchfork, but a long knife. It was October and she was cutting cabbage.

"*Achtung, achtung,*" she shouted, and held the knife over him. At the moment he didn't feel the pain of the broken collar bone more than he might have noticed a hangnail. Instead he smelled the smoke on his hair and leather flight suit, the singe of flesh and scorched oil, burned powder. In the damp air he stank like an incinerator.

His hands and clothes were smeared with the mud of the cabbage patch, a dark mud he saw was mixed with cow manure and human dung.

"*Achtung, achtung,*" the fat woman shouted and pointed toward the end of the field with the knife. He reached to unbuckle the harness, but she shook her head and tapped him on the shoulder with the blade. She assumed he was trying to reach inside the flight suit for a pistol.

Gathering the cords of the chute in one hand she chopped them with the knife and pointed to the village beyond the field. He stumbled through the wet cabbages and mud dragging the loose ends of the harness and lines, and the woman followed, pointing her knife at his back. He had lost a glove somewhere in the fall and his right hand was cold, though not frozen.

In the village the woman turned him over to what must have been a policeman, an old man in a black uniform who locked him in a cellar while he made phone calls. It was just as damp as in England, and colder. The air in the basement seemed filled with mold and the fumes of rotten grease. His shoulder was beginning to hurt. He wondered if he would be shot. Luckily this was the countryside and had not been bombed. Just at dark a van came and took him to a prison in a large house, almost a castle.

"You will wash up here," the guard said in perfect English, and showed him to a sink in a closet. After he had washed his hands and face and wiped the mud off his suit he was led upstairs into a kind of office. An officer in a red-trimmed uniform sat behind a gleaming desk.

"Good evening, and welcome to Germany," he said, and pointed to a chair. Jones sat down, and found his knees shaking.

"Don't be afraid," the officer said. "You have nothing to fear. The Reich respects all warriors."

He was questioned in exactly the way his sergeant in gunnery school told him he would be. After he gave his name, rank, and serial number the officer asked what unit he belonged to.

"Nothing to say," Jones said, his jaw trembling. His shoulder was hurting worse now.

"Don't worry; we know you're in the Ninety-second Bombardment Group, 325th Squadron, stationed at Bedfordshire. Am I right?"

Jones did not answer. The carpet on the floor was the color of a ruby, and sparkled in the lamplight. The officer referred to a stack of small file cards.

"We know you come from Henderson County, North Carolina," he said. "And we know you were born in 1924, and attended gunnery school in Caspar, Wyoming. Your father is named Cyrus Jones."

"Then why bother to ask?"

"We know a lot about American soldiers, especially fliers." The officer stood up. "Get out," he said. "You're useless to us. Someone will fix your shoulder in the camp."

~ · ~ · ~

The days in the prison camp never ran together. He arrived on October 3, 1944 and worked out a calendar in his mind that extended far into the next year. Each day was its own battle. It was cold and damp, and all they got to eat were potato peelings and a kind of soup made of old cabbage and other kinds of leaves. He could not explain why the months went easier for him than for many others. While other boys were cracking up and hanging themselves, talking disjointedly of home, or telling silly stories with bravado, he listened to the bombers going over every day and at night watched the fires on the horizon in the direction of Darmstadt. He was astonished to be alive after the fire and explosion. He hadn't expected to survive anyway. He wrote two or three letters for the Red

Cross to deliver home, but got none in return. He expected to someday panic and run for the fence and be shot, but never did. When others were weeping in their bunks or talking with strange expressions on their faces, he sat quietly or played another round with the soiled cards. When you think it's bad, he told himself, just remember it can get a *lot* worse.

The Third Army liberated them in May, and Patton himself came by in a jeep and saluted them. Jones felt less euphoria than the others. It was a peculiar day. The soldiers lined the guards up at the gate of the compound and walked each prisoner by them. The big sergeant with the New York City accent held his .45 and asked of each, "Did he treat you good? Did this one?" Jones said they all treated him well. But when a man behind him said a guard had hit him with a rifle butt the sergeant put the Colt to the German's head and shot him on the spot, blood and brains spraying over the others. The former guards never flinched, never begged for mercy, never responded to threats or questions.

$$\sim \cdot \sim \cdot \sim$$

The anchorman was talking about the position in the polls of all the presidential candidates. Jones could hardly tell the candidates apart. Then there was a report on Nicaragua, and one on the Palestinians. He wondered if there was any good news anywhere in the world. Yet he watched the news devotedly every morning and evening. Perhaps it was what people did now instead of praying. His uncle Jennings, back in the mountains, used to go out and pray in the feed room of the barn. "Jen is out there talking to the cows and corn meal," his daddy would say.

He concentrated on the soreness under his ribs, and the hunger that seemed to come from every cell and bone of his body. When he was hungry he was hungry all over.

"Did Alva call?" Lorna asked.

"Not while I was here."

Alva had been calling less in the past few weeks. They both knew it was not because of the land, that she was busy working as an aide in Jimmy's school. But they waited for her calls. They had moved to Sumter from Spartanburg when he retired, to be with her and the grandchildren.

The land was Jones's share of the homeplace back in the mountains. He should have sold it long ago.

"Daddy, we just want to build a summer place up there, a little house to use on weekends and in summer to escape the heat. You and Mamma could stay there."

He couldn't explain why he hesitated. He almost never went back there, even in summer. The pasture had grown up in blackberries and black pines. The old log barn had caved in and been swallowed by the brush and honeysuckle. The plum trees and apple trees of his granddaddy's orchard were surrounded by tall thin pines. And his cousins seemed like strangers. They represented everything he had tried to get away from and forget: the church quarrels, the ignorant disputes about theology, the suspicion of outsiders, the money grubbing of some and the embarrassing poverty of others, the beat-up pickup trucks and the dirty children. Yet at times he ached to be back there.

There was no reason for him to deny Alva and Steve a weekend house on the old place. And yet, he hesitated.

"Everything will be yours in time," he had said.

"They just want to build a little place," Lorna said.

"If you don't want us to do it, we sure won't," Alva said. She was hurt, and it hurt him to have hurt her. And there was no reason not to give the place to her now. And yet he did not do it.

"I want the kids to get to know the mountains, to love the place where you grew up and talk about so much," Alva said.

They did not quarrel any more about it, but she came over less often these days. And on Sundays she and Steve took the kids to McDonald's or somewhere instead of bringing them for dinner after church.

"You still want to go back there," Lorna had said.

"I do not."

"You fantasize going back to that awful place," she said. "I know you better than you know yourself."

"I left there, remember."

"You want to go back there and get in a boundary dispute with one of your fine cousins. Nothing else will satisfy you."

He leaned closer to the television, hoping she would go back in the kitchen.

"You want to buy a pickup truck and drive in the mud up the mountain and down along the creek. And you want two shotguns in a rack on the back window."

"And what do you want?"

The fever around his heart was spreading into his shoulder and down his left arm. He had walked too far. And the dirt vehicle had surprised him. He would have to sit still for two or three days, before he started exercising again.

"She can have the land for whatever she wants," he said. "I just want her to wait a while, until we see what interest rates are going to do."

"You want to go back and scratch in the mud. You'd still be there if I hadn't pushed you after the war."

$\sim \cdot \sim \cdot \sim$

The day his parents received the telegram from England saying he had been shot down, they called a prayer meeting at their house. Lorna and her parents had come. He had dated her a little in high school, and written her a few times from Bedfordshire, and got a cake from her at Christmas.

239

And the day he returned home after the war her parents had driven up to the house with a box of cookies she had made. "Lorna is at home waiting for you," they said.

It had happened as fast as water running downhill. The engagement, the wedding, the first carpentry job in Greenville with her father. He never worked on the farm again. He bought a new rifle but never took it hunting. Instead they drove up every year for Homecoming in a new car. When Alva was growing up they brought her along in sunsuits to play with her cousins, warning her to watch out for snakes in the weeds and mud along the branch.

The TV was too loud, and he leaned forward to turn it down. The thud underneath his ribs must have shown on his face.

"Are you OK?" Lorna said.

"I just walked too far. I'm a little tired."

"I'll get your pills."

"No, no, I'm all right."

"You don't look all right."

The blaring of the TV, and her hovering over, made him want to shout. As he used to at board meetings when he had to get his way. But that was the worst thing he could do now, get any more worked up.

"We'll call Alva and take them all out for dinner tomorrow, to the Western Steer," he said.

"You may not feel up to it. You've gone and given yourself another attack, charging out on walks, like you want to kill yourself."

Lorna had never understood the sharpness of her tongue. It was a habit she had developed as a teenager, and it had grown on her over the years. She did not realize how she sounded. He had thought of recording her on tape and then playing it back to her. She would be astonished at the harshness in her

voice, at the belittling tone of her comments. She knew how
to be polite in public, and with her friends from church. It
was only with him, and with her sisters, that side of her came
out. But she was mostly a good woman, though he had not
meant to spend his life with her. That was why he seemed so
tolerant, why he almost never quarreled. If he let himself go
who knows what he would end up saying. He might let it out
that he had never wanted to marry her, never wanted to be
with her. It would tear away whatever grace their life had
had, pull down the scaffold and show how badly fitted and
supported they really were. It would ruin her opinion and
pride in herself. His very lack of feeling for her had been the
essence of his devotion and patience, which so many friends
had praised, especially at the times when other friends had
divorced.

"I'll go get your pills," she said.

"No, it's just a little heartburn. I shouldn't have eaten the
margarine."

"I don't like your look. You'd better take something before
it gets worse."

"OK, I'll take just one."

~ · ~ · ~

By the time the news was over he had begun to feel better.

"Do you really want to go to the Ninety-second reunion?"
he asked as they sat down to eat.

"Sure, I'm tired of staying home." She served up a helping
of tuna casserole. "And we could go on down to Miami or
Key West afterward."

"I was thinking we might invite Alva and Steve and the
children to come along."

"Do you think they would be interested? I mean they
wouldn't know anybody there."

"We could stop at Disney World."

"I don't think they are interested in World War Two stuff. You know how the young are."

He had never talked much about the war to Lorna and Alva. When he first got back everyone asked and he did not want to try to describe or explain the explosion, and the months in the prison camp. And when he met the overhead gunner's mother in Washington, D.C., on the way home, he could not tell her he had seen McCall's blood and brains sprayed all over the glass dome. Instead he told her only that McCall had died instantly of a direct hit and felt no pain, which was probably true. At least he didn't know that the screams he had heard behind him were McCall's.

Twenty years later, when he decided he wanted to talk about the war, no one was interested. In 1965 nobody, at least of Alva's generation, cared about that war. And he was too busy to think about it much, except that he did relive moments when he was alone. At times he caught himself flexing his trigger finger, and visualizing the two barrels of his guns spitting tracers. The .50 caliber fingers stretched far out into the stratosphere to touch an attacker. It was the miracle that he had survived, he alone, that kept coming back to mind. There must be some purpose for which he had been spared, but he didn't know what it was. "You are sitting in the hind end of death," Baxter liked to say, "and it's cold there."

If there was any one image from the war that kept coming back to him in the last few weeks it was the mud. The base at Podington in Bedfordshire was nothing but ruts and puddles except for the paved runways and parking circles. It rained every day, and water stood in front of the mess halls, the motor pools, the Quonset barracks. Even the smell of the mud came back to him, a slightly burned, faintly rotten smell. Maybe the area had once been a dump for ashes, for charcoal.

The countryside was green, even in winter, but everywhere a jeep or truck or foot had touched was sucking, slurping mud. The base was so vast you couldn't see the end of it, except for the miles of B-17's and B-24's lined up for take-off in the early morning. It was only when they got into the air that he could look back and see the shape of the place, the huge central runway and the turnaround loops through the green fields, and the clusters of buildings. If the cloud cover was high enough he could always see the clock face on the village church as they started climbing.

The mud and the waiting were the real facts of the war. The mud in the prison compound had bits of brick and cement in it, probably rubble from bombed buildings. The mud was brown, and smelled like the latrines. It was worked and churned by hundreds of feet in the enclosed space. In the spring of 1945 they had to put down boards and sections from crates to walk on.

Since his retirement he had remembered that waiting, and felt a boredom he was ashamed of. If it were not for his heart he would go back to work.

"You'll enjoy talking to the others," Lorna was saying.

"They'll all be pilots, flight officers. I remember what buddies they were."

"There will be other gunners."

"Tailgunners don't go to reunions."

"You can take your uniform. I'll get it out of the cedar chest."

He felt a pressure building in his torso, like the push of a basketball under water trying to rise. He put his finger over his mouth and belched.

"Are you all right?" Lorna said. "I'll get another pill."

$\sim \cdot \sim \cdot \sim$

When Jones came to he was floating through a cloud of smoke

and burned oil. He heard wind, and the sound of airplane motors far away. The air underneath was pressing him. As he realized he was falling he automatically reached for the rip-cord D-ring and found it. The cord was partly burned but he yanked it and felt the jerk of the blossoming chute. The plane had exploded and thrown him free. The wind fluttered and the clouds below gave way as he plunged through. It occurred to him he might be dead and this was his journey into heaven or maybe hell. The steam and smoke coiled around him, and something fell past, a piece of wing or rudder. If this was death he was too numb with cold to feel anything. His trigger finger was stiff. He remembered the pool in the creek where he had learned to swim, and the drawing paper they used in gunnery school to describe a trajectory. There was the smell of the schoolhouse on the first day of the new year, the puke smell of glue on the new books and scent of oil on the floors. He had seen a Santa Claus once in a store window in Greenville where they had gone to the dentist. The Santa Claus had electric eyes that winked. He could remember the instant he was brought up out of the river at his baptizing, and the way light and time had started again after the shock of the cold water. There was a smell in the front room of his Grandma's house, a mixture of mothballs and mildew and flowers. The clouds opened underneath and he could see the terrain swelling closer, into focus, and the miracle was it wasn't heaven at all but a muddy German cabbage patch he was floating into.

Death Crown

I HAD NO SOONER WALKED into the room, maybe into the
house, than I saw what the truth was. It was like a smell in
the air, or a sound you can't really hear but know is there. It
was a feeling in that old house and it hit me as soon as I
stepped through the door. I didn't even pay much attention to
Myrtle or to Annie where they set by the fire. I must have
spoke to them but I don't remember it. It wasn't Myrt and
Annie I was concerned with anyway. They didn't seem to realize
what was happening though it was taking place right in their
own house. And they was just setting there hunched up by the
fire.

"Harold," I said soon as we walked in, "You might as well
go on back home. I'm staying here to the end." And I don't
know what he did after that. He must have stood around the
fire with his hat in his hands talking to Myrt and Annie as he
always did about the weather and about their cow and about
the terrible people running the government. But I didn't
notice. And I guess he eventually walked back down the hill
to that little pickup and drove home by hisself. I don't know.
I had other things on my mind.

We had come out on a drive to the old place to see how
Alice was. It was just a hunch I had, to see how she was
doing. It was one of those cold clear days in November, the

first real cold day we'd had. The leaves was finally all gone, after about a week of rain, except a yellow one hanging here and there on a branch willow. But it looked like winter and the country had been scrubbed and polished by the rain. It was cold enough so the hemlocks got that black look they have in freezing weather. The ground in the yard was beginning to freeze.

When I stepped through the door into Alice's room the first thing I saw was the ball of white light on her pillow. It looked like the sunlight from the window had poured itself into a little cloud. There was a crack in the blind and the light had found its way right to the pillow and just seemed to hover there. It looked like a puff of breath had just stayed and caught fire.

But it was just Alice's hair. She had the purest white hair you ever saw. As she got older it just got whiter, not yellow and tired the way some old people's hair gets. It had a snowy look that almost startled with its whiteness.

I couldn't see her face at first. You could smell the change in the room, but it wasn't anything you could describe. Myrt and Annie had kept her clean and it wasn't anything like a bad smell, and it wasn't just the smell of camphor and the old wood smell of the house. The house had been there so long, it had its own scent of leather and smoke and coffee mixed with must in the attic. And sometimes I thought I could still smell the smoke of Great-grandpa's pipe, though he had been dead for twenty years.

This smell was different from them all. It was something in the air like the heat of a hot electric wire, or the feeling there's just been a loud noise which disturbed the elements but wasn't heard by humans. I expected to hear a rustling, or see a curtain move, but the air was absolutely still, even when wind outside pressed the house and shook it a little.

Her hair was so bright you couldn't see Annie's face at first. But when I bent closer I saw there was a new expression there. It was not a look of pain so much as struggle. The look confirmed the feeling I'd had. I'd seen that look before on Grandma and on Aunt Mary's face before they passed away.

So I just got a chair out of the corner. It had a blanket and a hot water bottle and a pile of papers on it. But I set all that aside and brought the chair close to the bed. If I was going to stay I might as well make myself comfortable. I was wearing my Sunday clothes with my old gray coat. We'd come over after church and I had on earrings and a necklace. But it didn't matter because I wasn't thinking of myself.

I pulled the chair right up to the bed and took Alice's hand. Even though it was under the covers it was a little cold. I held her hand in both of mine and said, "Alice, you know who this is?"

Her head rolled on the pillow and she opened her eyes and looked at me. But she had that wild look, the way she sometimes did. Most of the time she had the mind of a child and was sweet as a little girl. But sometimes she'd get this look in her eyes like she was going to hurt somebody or run away, or no telling what. And then she would quiet down and be herself again. It would scare you to see that look on such a little woman with all that white hair.

She looked at me and then she closed her eyes again. I couldn't tell if she knowed me or not. When she was having a bad spell it was like she didn't know anybody.

"Alice," I said, squeezing her hand. "I've come to stay with you; I'm not going to leave you."

And I could feel her hand squeeze back. It was just a faint squeeze, but I could feel it for sure. She never opened her eyes, but I could tell she knowed who I was.

"I'll be here if you want me," I said.

The sun had moved a little bit off her hair, and I couldn't see her face well. But the shaft of light was still on the pillow, blinding me a little. My eyes would have to get adjusted to the dark.

$$\sim \cdot \sim \cdot \sim$$

Ever since I was a little girl I was Alice's favorite in the family. We just naturally enjoyed each other. They never let her go to church or to school, and most kids was afraid of her. I remember once Mama brought me over there for Sunday dinner and I took my doll. It was a new doll, a china doll, with long blonde hair, and I carried it everywhere with me. Alice seen me holding it as we stood around on the porch before dinner and she pulled me into her room and showed me her doll. It didn't even strike me as strange that this old woman, who was really Mama's aunt and whose hair was already getting white, was playing with dolls. I thought, she doesn't have any children but she has dolls instead.

Her doll was just a rag doll, and it was kind of worn out and dirty. But she held it in her arms the way I held my new doll.

"My baby," she said, and rocked it. She had a laugh I liked. We talked about the dolls till dinner time when they brought her a tray from the kitchen and I had to go set at the table.

And every time I went over to Grandma's house I'd see her and we played hopscotch or run in the meadow below the spring.

Her job was to carry water for the family. She loved to carry water, bucket after bucket, up the hill from the spring. She felt useful doing it, and would sometimes empty a bucket off the back porch just so she could go back to refill it.

"I've carried six buckets," she'd say and smile, though I don't think she could count and would just choose a number she had heard.

And when Myrt was doing the washing Alice carried buckets to fill the wash pot, and to fill the tub where the washboard was.

But soon as I come over she'd want to play, and set her buckets down on the trail and run to the meadow. We'd run and laugh so hard we'd fall down and roll in the grass. Then Myrt would find us and tell her to quit footercootering and bring the water on up to the house where they was about to boil some corn. That's the word Myrtle always used, footer-cootering. I never heard anybody else use it. And I'd help her carry a bucket, though looking back I wish I'd helped her more.

∾ · ∾ · ∾

"She's been going down since Wednesday," Myrt said, when I went back to the fire to warm my hands. "We called the doctor and he come out and listened to her heart, but he didn't know hardly what to do. He said if we brought her to the hospital he could run some tests."

"Did he give her anything?"

"He give her some pills, but I don't think they do no good. And there's no way we could get her to the hospital. I think she'd die before she'd go. She ain't left this place in seventy years."

Myrt was right about that. And besides, it was too late for the hospital to do any good.

I told Annie to start a fire in the cookstove and heat a kettle of water. I was going to wash Alice off. I thought she might feel better if she was cleaned up a little.

"No, no, I'm going to freeze," she said when I pulled back the bedcovers a little. She held onto the quilts right over her throat.

"Now Alice, I'm not gonna hurt you. I'll just wash a little bit at a time and dry you off. You'll feel better."

She had that wide wild look in her eyes again. I put my hand on her forehead to calm her down.

"You're gonna be all right," I said. "This is Ellen. You remember Ellen."

She rolled her eyes and come back to herself a little. "How's Evie?" she said.

"Evie's fine," I said.

My mama, her niece, had been dead for twenty years, but I didn't want to upset her. Time had stopped for her long ago.

"I'm going to wash you a little," I said. "And then you'll feel better."

I pulled back the bedclothes a little at a time and washed her feet and ankles and then her legs and upper body. It was pitiful to see how thin she was, just a skeleton with skin, like she hadn't eat anything in months, which she hadn't. I was careful not to drip any water on the sheets. And when I finished I tucked her in again. I was going to empty the pan off the back porch.

"I'll be back," I said, and patted her shoulder.

"I can't breathe," she said. "They ain't no air in here."

"They's plenty of air," I said. But there was terror in her eyes. She fought back at the quilts I had tucked around her.

"Open the window," she said.

"You can't open a window," I said. "It's winter outside."

She tore the quilts almost off the bed and rassled to get up.

"You can't get up, Alice," I said. "You're too weak."

"Open a window," she said.

"All right, stay in bed, and I'll open a window."

I wrapped the quilts back around her and raised the window a crack. Wind cut through even that and chilled the room. It was getting late in the afternoon by then and the sun had moved away from the window. Wind rattled the sash and stirred the papers on the night table. I closed it down to the finest crack, as the counterweights knocked in the walls.

"Open the window," Alice said. "I can't breathe."

I reopened it so she could hear the whistle in the slot. The room was already cool, but it got colder quickly with the fresh air. You could smell the air off the pasture and the sour of the new-fallen leaves in ditches. I got a blanket and put it around my shoulders, and moved my chair far as I could from the window and still be able to reach Alice.

But the wind seemed to make her feel better. She began to breathe more regular and closed her eyes. I thought she was going to sleep. But then she opened them again, to make sure I was still there.

"Alice, are you hungry?" I said because it was getting on toward supper time and I could smell cooking in the other end of the house.

"Would you like some soup?" I said. "Smells like Myrt's cooking some hog sausage."

I thought she was gonna nod her head yes, but no sooner had I asked than she closed her eyes and just seemed to go to sleep. She must have been tired from the struggle to breathe. Her breath was now regular. I eased the window down so as not to disturb her.

While Alice was sleeping I wondered what my duty was. Was she a Christian? Was she ready to die? She never had been to church since she was a little girl. Had she ever in her mind reached the age of accountability as the preachers say? Was she responsible for herself?

My daddy, who was a preacher, used to argue with the deacons about who would be saved. "Ain't nobody going to heaven that's not been baptized," one said.

"But how about the Indians that died here before the white men came and brought the Word?"

"They will die in their sins," Carl Evans said.

"And how about all the people in China that never heard of Jesus?" Daddy said.

"I've heard they will be give a second chance," another deacon said.

"You must be born again," Charles Whitby said.

"And how about the little babies that die before the age of accountability?" Daddy said.

"You must be washed in the blood," Carl Evans said.

But Daddy said later they was just ignorant. It didn't make sense to condemn people that never had a chance to believe. What kind of God would do a thing like that? All the little children that had died early would be in heaven. And Alice in her mind was still a little child.

It put my mind to rest to think about Alice as a little girl, even though her hair was white and her face wrinkled. As it got dark in the room you couldn't see nothing but her hair which seemed to glow against the pillow. It was like a shiny little cloud that just floated there.

"Do you want some supper?" Myrt said, and light shot from the opened door on Alice's face.

"She's resting now," I said.

"Poor thing, she needs some rest," Myrt said. "The last three nights she kept us awake with her raving. You'd think she had a demon in her the way she carries on."

"She's sleeping now."

"Annie's cooked up some sausage and taters," Myrt said. "You better come eat if you're going to stay with her."

"I can't leave her," I said. "Not now."

Myrt brought me a plate of sausage and potatoes and a glass of iced tea. I lit the lamp on the night table by the bed hoping it wouldn't wake Alice up. In the shadows from the lamp the room looked even bigger than it had before. The shadows pulled at the light, drawing it away from the shiny chimney.

It seemed strange to be eating in the room there with Alice, but I went ahead anyway. The belly don't know any shame or any rules except its own. Annie's sausage was hot and filling.

Alice shifted in her sleep and I wondered if she was awake and keeping her eyes closed. Maybe the smell of the sausage woke her up. But her breathing continued regular and I put the empty plate on the night table and leaned closer. The fuzz on her chin sparkled in the light. But her skin was still very fair.

Mama told me that when Alice was a teenager she was the prettiest girl in the valley. Her hair was blonde and her skin perfect and glowing. Boys would come by on Sunday after-noons just to sit by the fire and look at her. They pretended to be visiting her brother or be courting her sisters. If she was feeling good she would sit in her corner and smile. If she was upset she run off to her room and slammed the door. Nobody seemed offended by her doings.

One boy, Otho Jarvis, was struck on her more than the rest. He come every Sunday for a year, and had dinner and stayed to talk to the family. One time he took Great-grandpa aside and asked if he could marry Alice.

"She ain't no woman to marry," Great-grandpa said.

"Mr. Jackson, my intentions are honorable," Otho said.

"But you see what she is. In her mind she's just a child, less than a child."

"But she's a woman also. I'll marry her and take care of her, just like she is, and be kind to her."

But Great-grandpa wouldn't agree to it. He said it wouldn't be fair to nobody. That Alice in her childish mind wouldn't be able to take care of children and look after them and raise them. And it wouldn't even be fair to Otho when he got older, trying to look after a place, and the children, *and* Alice. So Great-grandpa put a stop to it. And one by one the other children married and left home and Alice stayed with the old people, carrying water from the spring and playing with her doll. But later Grandma took her in after she heired the old place and that's why Mama growed up with Alice in the house.

～ · ～ · ～

The wind picked up again, after it was dark, and rattled the window sash. You could feel the air seeping in through cracks of the old house. The lamp flame fluttered a little in its chimney. I pulled the blanket tight about my shoulders and wondered if it was going to snow. If the wind died down it was certainly going to come a hard freeze. I must have dozed a little.

"Open the window," Alice said. She was awake, and her eyes rolled in terror.

"I can't breathe," she said.

"It's cold out there," I said. "Hear the wind?"

She fought at the covers and was working to get up.

"I'll open the window just a crack," I said. I raised the window just enough so you could feel the cold air slicing through the room but things wasn't blowing around.

She relaxed again, and lowered her head on the pillow. Her hair had been flattened behind and stood straight up. Her eyes wandered around the room.

"Where's Mama?" she said.

"Mama's all right," I said. "She's in the next room." There didn't seem to be any point in telling her that Great-grandma had been dead thirty-five years.

"Everything's just fine," I said. I looked at my watch. It was almost ten.

"Would you like some coffee, Ellen?" It was Annie at the door. "I just made a fresh pot," she said.

"I'll have a cup," I said. "And maybe Alice will have some too."

Alice was looking toward the door. She had always loved coffee, and the smell of the fresh pot was strong through the open door.

"Bring me two cups and I'll try to feed her some," I said.

Annie returned with two steaming mugs, and took the supper plate away.

"Here's some coffee for you," I said to Alice, blowing on the cup to cool it off.

She was too low in the bed to even sip from the full mug. She seemed lost among the quilts except for the glowing hair.

"I'll have to pull you up," I said, and put my hands under her arms. It's always astonishing to find how hard it is to move someone. Leaning over her I had no way to get any leverage.

"Can you push with your feet?" I said, but she didn't seem to understand me. "Push against the end of the bed," I said.

But I don't think she even understood me. Bracing myself against the bedpost I dragged her up and put a pillow behind her back. I blowed on the coffee again and held the mug to her lips.

"It's hot," I said, but she didn't listen. She took a sip, a big sip, and then spit and shook her head.

"You scalded me," she said, and glared.

"I told you it was hot, to go slow," I said. But she shook her head like a two-year-old.

"Too hot," she said, and looked at me with that wild look.

"We'll just take it slow," I said.

She shook her head and slapped at the cup. "No," she said, and knocked half the coffee down her shoulder and on the pillow.

"Ey, ey, ey!" she screamed.

255

I put the mug down on the night table and tried to sponge up the coffee with a kleenex.

"It's OK, it's OK," I said, and put my left hand on her forehead as I tried to soak up and wipe away most of the coffee. The skin on her shoulder was not even red, so I doubt that she was burned much.

"You hate me," she said, and turned her face away.

"That's the way she treats us all the time," Myrt said from the doorway. "Here's a towel."

I lifted her head and put the dry towel on the pillow, and held her hand. Gradually the crazy look in her eyes went away, and she closed her eyelids. With my left hand I eased the chair closer and sat down.

The way her head sunk into the towel on the pillow reminded me of the old story of the death crown. Old timers used to say that when a really good person, say a preacher that's saved lots of souls or a woman that's helped her neighbors and raised a lot of kids, is sick for a long time before they die, that the feathers in the pillow will knit themselves into a crown that fits the person's head. The crown won't be found till after they are dead of course, but it's a certain sign of another crown in heaven, my daddy used to say. I've never seen one myself but the old timers say they're woven so tight they never come apart and they shine like gold even though they're so light they might just as well be a ring of light.

Alice's head sunk into the pillow like it was the heaviest part about her. Her body was so thin it hardly showed through the quilts. You could look at the bed in the lamplight and imagine there was no body in it at all, only the head at the top and the flying white hair. It looked like her body had evaporated and gone, and left her head there with the fear in her eyes. That was the opposite of what happened when she was a little girl, when her mind had gone and left her in a beautiful, healthy body.

Mama said Alice was the beautifullest little girl you ever saw. She had been told by Grandma how fair and blond Alice was, with blue eyes and a sweet smile. Until she had what the old timers called "the white swelling." I don't know what doctors these days would call it, but back then they named it the awful "white swelling."

What happened was the kids at school, or maybe it was a church on homecoming day, was playing wild horses and cowboys. And one big old boy, Mama said he was a Jones, was wearing these big brogans, and he made like he was a wild mustang and kicked Alice. He didn't mean to actually kick her, but he did, in the shin. And she was just this little girl with her skin all white and delicate. Where he kicked her it took the white swelling and the whole leg got inflamed.

The place itself swelled up white and she had a fever so high and long it ruint her mind. Her development stopped right there, in the pain of the fever, and never started again.

But the funny thing was her body seemed to get over it. Her leg was swelled up all them months, and they put hot compresses on it day and night, and soaked it in all kinds of things, and put on salves and plasters. And by grannies a piece of bone that had been broke where she was kicked worked its way out through the skin, a splinter off the leg bone. And the place, after about a year, healed up so she could walk again. She limped a little. She always did have a slight limp if you watched her. But she could get around and carry water. And they thought she would be OK, except her mind didn't grow no more. It seemed to go back after the fever to two or three years old, and it stayed there.

I remember bringing Harold over to meet my folks. I was so proud cause I was getting married and getting away from home, finally. I was tired of looking after the little kids and Mama was failing even then so most of the work had fell on me.

Harold had this old truck he used for logging. It had a rough bed and all the men he worked with cutting timber up in the Flat Woods rode on it every morning bouncing up the creek road. I don't see how their behinds stood it in the cold. But they laughed and carried on like a bunch of drunk school-boys. You could hear them banging and hollering miles away.

Anyway Harold drove me over to see the folks and I was proud he was such a big strong feller. He was kind of quiet around strangers and women, but you could see Myrt and Annie liked him. And Grandma was alive then and he give her a five dollar bill. Everybody was smiling and Harold stood by the fire with his hands in his pockets. Myrt was making coffee to go with the coconut cake. And Alice comes in with two buckets of water.

She smiled when she saw me. I always brung her some-thing, a dress for her doll, a piece of candy, a little vanity set. She set the water down and come to me smiling.

"Alice, I want you to meet Harold," I said, taking her by the arm. "Me and him is to be married."

And this look come over her face, come over gradually like a stain spreading in cloth, and her lip went crooked and she started to cry.

"Alice, Harold is a nice feller," I said. But she turned and run to her room, leaving the water buckets there on the floor. I had explained to Harold about Alice, but it embarrassed me something terrible for him to see her do that, the first time he visited them.

$$\approx \cdot \approx \cdot \approx$$

Alice seemed to be having a bad dream. She said, "No, no," and lifted her arm, knocking away the covers. I put her arm back under the quilt and told her everything was all right.

She was calm for a few seconds, then opened her eyes and

rolled them around, and she jerked back like she had seen the devil or a snake.

"What's wrong, Alice?" I said, putting my hand on her shoulder. She was small as a child, but could push with surprising force.

"Oh god, no, no," she hollered and tried to raise up. I bent over her.

"What's wrong Alice?"

"He's coming to get me," she said.

"Ain't nobody coming to get you," I said.

Her eyes looked like she had seen hell itself, but they was looking nowhere in particular.

"Alice, it's me, Ellen, and nobody's going to hurt you," I said again.

"Oh lord, he's coming. Oh lord, it hurts," she hollered. There was nothing I could do to stop her but try to hold her down on the bed. Myrt and Annie had come to the door in their nightgowns and asked if they was anything they could do.

"You got any sleeping pills?" I said.

"We ain't got a thing but aspirin," Myrt said.

"Well, bring me that," I said.

They brought me a bottle of aspirins but I couldn't turn loose her shoulder to give her any.

"Bring me a glass of water," I said.

Annie come back with water in a teacup.

"You'll have to put one in her mouth and give her a drink while I hold her," I said.

But Alice kept hollering that something was coming to get her. When Myrt tried to drop an aspirin in her mouth she spit it out, and when Annie held the cup of water to her lips a little spilled on her chin, but none got in her mouth.

"We'll have to forget it," I said. I held her down until she started to get tired. I was getting tired too, and my arms was trembling a little. When she finally quieted down Myrt and Annie went back to bed.

"I hate it you have to do this," Myrt said.

"I don't know what we'd a done without you here," Annie said.

I looked at my watch in the lamplight. It was 2:30. Almost everybody dies between midnight and six in the morning, Mama used to say. Alice had another three or four hours to go if she was to make it to another day.

She had wore herself out and was still with exhaustion. But she had that terrible look on her face, like she was anguished and scared, like she was crazy as people said she was. People will rumor anything. But she never was sick in her mind really, like they told it on her. She was just simple, child-like. People will spread around the worst things they can think of.

But because she was afflicted the family would never take her nowheres, not to school or church singings, or the Fourth of July picnics. Somebody would always have to stay with her, though she begged in her innocence to be carried along. She wanted to go places bad as a little kid does that sees everybody else dressed up and ready to leave. She cried and begged, and they still left her at the house like they was ashamed for anybody to see her. Mama had to go stay with her a lot when she was young, and Grandma before her.

That was how come Grandma and Grandpa got the place, because they agreed to take care of Alice. When Great-grandma died she left them the house and most of the land for taking care of her and Alice too. That was the way they did things back yonder, leave the place to whoever took care of the old people. Usually it was the youngest that stayed home and done it.

Grandma always hoped Alice would stay in her room when visitors come. That's why the front door was always closed since I was a little girl, cause Alice lived in the front room. I was the only one that went in to see her when we come to visit on Sundays. She'd show me her doll, and talk about play-parties she'd been to, infares and dances. But she made it all up, the way a kid will do.

I remember one time we come over at Christmas in the A-Model truck. That was before I was married. And we carried up a whole sack of presents to the house to put under Grandma's tree. That little room just seemed flooded with presents. I was afraid the house would catch fire there was so much papers scattered around when we started unwrapping. Names would be called out, and they was oo's and ah's and squeals of delight, and "You shouldn't" and "How did you know what I wanted?" I had brought a little box of candy, just a little box of peppermint sticks, for Alice. And I stood up to take it to her room. She never did eat with the family or join in much by the fireplace.

"I'm giving this to Alice," I said.

"Oh the shame," Mama said. "I forgot to bring her a thing." And I could see Mama was hurt to think she had forgot Alice at Christmas. But that was the way things turned out most of the time.

∼ · ∼ · ∼

I must have been sleeping because when I looked at my watch it was four thirty-eight. The lamp was still burning, but the room seemed different. It was real still, inside the house and out. It was like something had been there and just gone. Alice was sleeping, but there was a kind of catch in her breath, and a faint gurgling in her throat. I didn't know if it meant anything or not. Her face was relaxed, though it still showed the lines of the earlier struggle.

There was that smell in the house again, the odor I had caught

261

when I first walked in the day before. It was a peculiar old house smell, akin to the scent of coffee soaked into the wood for a hundred years, along with smoke from the fireplace, and mothballs in the big wardrobe, old wool and yellow newspapers. But I couldn't describe the scent itself; it was of age, and dust in rugs. Added to the kerosene smell of the lamp was that other smell, like some electric spark, a warm radio, though there was no radio in the house.

I looked around for Alice's doll, but couldn't see it anywhere. It must be under the bedcovers. She would never have lost it or thrown it away.

In the still every pop and creak of the house sounded like growing pains. I thought of a ship out at sea, the way they say it will groan and creak as the wood gives with the waves.

The skin on Alice's forehead gleamed almost as white as her hair. It was smoother than most old people's skin, and I thought she was lucky in a way to have never growed up, in the times she had lived through. When she was a girl the trains hadn't even come into the mountains, and she lived through the wars with never a worry about them. Now people flew everyplace, and they talked about going to the moon. She had lived through the Depression and didn't know a thing about it while she carried water every day up the hill and set under the pines above the meadow, or sipped coffee in her room. I hated it that her mind was troubled now.

There was a longer gurgle in her throat and her breath come in little jumps and then stopped. I was going to run to get Myrt and Annie, but realized there was nothing any of us could do. Alice's mouth fell open and her head turned sideways a little. Her eyes was closed and there was a long sigh of air coming out of her chest.

It was so still I kept waiting for her to breathe again. But she didn't. "Alice," I said, but she didn't respond. Her face started to relax until it was completely placid. I know people like to talk about how somebody smiles or sees angels or kinfolks that have already passed on when they die, but it was nothing like that. She was dead and her face seemed plain and untroubled. It was a beautiful death.

The Ratchet

W<small>HEN</small> F<small>RED</small> <small>TIGHTENED</small> the third chain on the load of
logs he made sure the ratchet was locked. The other two
chains would hold the load, but he meant to be safe. Shifting
logs were the most common cause of wrecks of timber trucks.
Once logs started rolling off on a curve the truck would go
out of control. He had heard on the radio only last week
about a truck in Swannanoa that slid off the highway and
rolled down the mountainside.

"Let's go!" his brother Albert hollered. Albert wanted to
get to the sawmill and unload and get their check and reach
the bank before it closed at five. There was a long holiday
weekend ahead and the bank would be closed till Monday.
Albert planned to take his family to the beach, and he couldn't
go unless he got his money.

"I'm not going to leave a chain loose," Fred said as he
climbed into the cab and threw the ratchet handle behind the
seat. "At least I want to reach the sawmill." His wife Mabel
had said he had to get paid today also, for she wanted to buy
an air conditioner for their trailer.

The air in the cab was hot as a blowtorch. Fred didn't
know how a truck cab sitting in the woods could gather so
much heat. If it was ninety outside, it felt like a hundred and

twenty in the truck. The air smelled of motor oil and sweat, gasoline and the sour of fresh oak.

"Myrtle Beach, here I come," Albert sang as he started the engine and threw the truck in gear. They were overloaded, and Fred could feel the hesitation in the big truck. Logs brushed limbs over the haulroad. The truck rocked from side to side on an uneven place, another sign of an excess load.

"Better be careful," Fred said.

"You telling me how to drive?" Albert said. He turned and stared at his brother.

"I ain't telling you nothing," Fred said.

"Good," Albert said. "Because it sounded like you was telling me how to drive this truck."

"It's just this is a mighty big load," Fred said.

"You think I don't know that?" Albert said. "Like it wasn't me that loaded the logs on."

When Albert was in a hurry he got irritable. And when he was irritable he insisted on driving the truck. "All I'm saying is we are overloaded," Fred said.

"I learned to drive this truck when you was still peeing in your britches," Albert said.

"I'll pee in them again if you drive too fast," Fred said.

Albert snorted and chuckled. The tension was broken.

The logging road wound along the ridge they had been cutting all spring and summer. Albert speeded up to get through the mud near the branch, and he slowed down where the road tilted around the hill. The truck lurched on potholes and scraped the limbs of saplings they had left standing. The timber rights had been bought from the heirs to the old Lewis place who lived in California. The bigger trees they had cut for lumber, the smaller stuff for pulpwood. The slope and the flank of the hill looked bare as a half-plucked chicken.

When Albert reached the highway, he had to stop and wait

for a break in traffic coming up from South Carolina. It was midsummer and the road was crowded with Cadillacs from Florida, holiday travelers from Georgia and South Carolina, pickup trucks loaded with pole beans, and produce trucks from Atlanta. "We'll never make it to the bank," Albert said.

"Just hold your tater," Fred said. Heat rose off the highway in fits that shimmied and rolled and burst as car after car came around the bend in the crackling mirage. Albert revved the motor and revved it again.

"Take your time," Fred said.

"Who's driving this truck?" Albert said. There was a tiny break in the line of cars and Albert eased onto the highway. But with the heavy load he couldn't accelerate. They edged across the highway into the right lane as brakes screamed and cars had to make way for them. The blast of a horn came from the left as a transfer truck hit its air brakes, then roared past.

"Don't think you made any friends there," Fred said.

"They can kiss my rusty ass," Albert said. He shifted into second and the truck picked up speed in little jerks and spurts, then smoothed out on the long grade toward the mountaintop. Fruit stands lined the highway with jugs of cider on benches and bedspreads on clotheslines. Tourist cars were parked on the shoulders around the stands. At the top of the ridge Mountain Top Baptist Church sat on the bank like a white hen surrounded by tombstone chicks.

A convertible ran out in front of them and Albert hit his horn. "Let's at least make it past the cemetery," Fred said.

"Don't ride my ass," Albert said. "You want to make it to the bank, don't ride my ass."

"Nobody is riding your ass," Fred said. The traffic was so slow there was hardly any breeze from the window. Heat came back from the engine under the dash, and the air off the highway was smothering. It was so hot Fred could feel the wetness under the hair of his temples and at the back of his head.

"Somebody up there is driving on crutches," Albert said.

"They will move faster down the other side," Fred said. He licked the sweat off his lip and wiped his forehead. Mabel was right about the air conditioner for the trailer: they had to get one.

"They better," Albert said and shifted down just as they crossed the crest. The traffic did begin to pick up speed on the downgrade. They came around a curve and could see the long descent ahead. The line of cars and trucks stretched out for more than a mile, all the way to the bend above the river. The cars looked like a chain of beads following each other in the crazy shiver of the heat.

"This time tomorrow you will be by the ocean," Fred said.

"You got that right," Albert said, and banged on the steering wheel with the heel of his palm.

Fruit stands were scattered along the road all the way down to the river. Some advertised cigarettes by the carton because they were cheaper in North Carolina. Some advertised mountain honey and handmade dulcimers. Cars were pulled off around the tables of crafts and baskets of fruit.

As the traffic began to go faster, Albert shifted up into second and then into third. A breeze freshened the window and Fred leaned into the cooler air. The big load made the truck bounce and creak when they hit a bump.

"This is more like it," Albert said. Their tires sang, keening on the hot pavement.

Brake lights went on ahead, as cars slowed for someone pulling into the lot of a fruit stand. "Damn tourists," Albert said. He hit the brakes but the truck did not slow. He pushed the brake pedal again.

"What's wrong?" Fred said.

Albert didn't answer. He pumped the brakes and the truck slowed a tiny bit. "Brakes must be hot," he said.

"Everything is hot," Fred said.

The line of cars began picking up speed again and Albert took his foot off the brake. He shifted down into second. "Have you checked the master cylinder lately?" Fred said.

"No, have you?" Albert said.

"It might be a good idea," Fred said. He had noticed something spilled on the ground where the truck had been parked, but thought it must be oil, or coolant. He had meant to look at the master cylinder, but forgot it.

"Damn!" Albert said. The brake lights ahead were shining again. He touched the brake pedal but the truck did not slow.

"What's the matter?" Fred said.

"These brakes act like they're dead," Albert said.

"Shift down," Fred said.

"I know how to drive," Albert said. He pressed the clutch and the truck moved faster. There was grinding in the transmission as he tried to shift back into second. The cars ahead were moving, but the truck was gaining on them.

"Watch out!" Fred said.

"What do you mean watch out?" Albert shouted. "This sucker won't go into second."

"Then try low," Fred said.

The grinding in the gearbox sounded like a saw on a nail as Albert threw the stick to the lower left and tried to make it catch. As the cars in front got closer Fred stamped the floorboard with his right foot as if expecting a brake pedal to be there.

In a field far below them on the right Fred saw a hay baler behind a tractor toss a block of straw into a wagon. It was Kevin Jones's field and Jones was calmly baling hay. If only he could be safe and going about everyday things himself, Fred would gladly give up the check, give up the air conditioner, give up the holiday weekend. He wouldn't even mind the hot trailer. Mabel at that very minute would be sitting down in front of the fan, after canning strawberry preserves.

They were gaining on the powder blue Cadillac convertible in front of them, at least a foot a second. The Cadillac had lots of flashy chrome and the woman in the passenger seat wore a straw hat tied with a fluttering scarf. Albert hit the horn, two short bursts.

"What good will that do?" Fred said. "They can't get out of the way."

"They could run off on the shoulder," Albert said. "Or they could speed up."

"The whole line of cars is not going to speed up," Fred said.

"What do I care what they do?" Albert said.

"You're always right," Fred said.

"I usually am," Albert snapped. Sweat dripped from his eyebrows.

"You are the older brother and you're always right," Fred said.

They were within thirty feet of the back of the Cadillac. As the truck accelerated its tires sang soprano, higher and higher.

"Try the emergency brake," Fred said.

"That would put us in a spin," Albert said.

"Try to pull it slow," Fred said. His feet were cold in his boots. It was a hundred degrees in the cab, but his feet were icy as marble.

Albert reached for the brake lever, but soon as he began to pull it the truck started to veer to the left. The weight behind them shoved, and Albert quickly released the handle. "Any more great ideas?" he said.

"Now you can kill us both to show how you're always

right," Fred said. He pushed with both hands on the dash as the fins of the Cadillac inched closer to their bumper.

Albert hit the horn again and again, and steered to the left. There was no one in the oncoming lane for about a quarter of a mile. They eased to the left, just missing the tail fin of the Cadillac. Albert pounded on the horn and out of the corner of his eye Fred saw the silver-haired driver of the Cadillac shake his fist at them. The tourist thought they were just trying to hog the road.

People in the yard of Evans's fruit stand turned to stare as they roared by. A woman with bright lipstick and sunglasses clutched her lap dog. Six hundred feet ahead a huge transfer truck was coming straight at them. Fred heard the deep honk of its horn, like a fog horn, except there was no fog. The truck was barreling at them in the bright sunlight.

"Can't he see I've lost my brakes?" Albert shouted.

"He thinks you're just trying to pass," Fred said.

Albert banged the horn as if he was pounding a stake into the ground.

"Please Lord, help us," Fred said. He had never prayed in front of Albert before. Albert didn't go to church, and they never talked about religion to each other since Fred had been saved when he was sixteen.

"I don't think *He* is going to help," Albert said.

In the heat shiver over the highway the eighteen wheeler bore down on them like a bull with its head lowered.

"He thinks you're playing chicken," Fred said.

There was no break in the line of cars and trucks in the right lane. There was no slot to pull into, and no broad shoulder to run off on. But it was better to shove into a car or pickup truck on the right than hit the transfer head-on. Better to brush a few cars sideways than crash into the eighteen wheeler.

Horns squawked and brakes squealed as Albert edged back

toward the center line. They almost slammed a pickup truck but it pulled onto the shoulder just as they shot by. Albert banged the horn and at the last instant the transfer truck swerved to the edge of the highway leaving just enough room in the middle of the road for them to slip through. There couldn't have been more than a few inches of space on either side of the logs.

Albert jerked the truck into the left lane again, just missing an emerald green Imperial. They could see all the way down the grade to the bend above the river now. The highway swung with a long sweep into the curve above the river bridge. If they could make it all the way down the hill without hitting anything coming in the left lane, they would still have to get around the sharp curve. Their only chance would be if the chains held on the load. Once logs started shifting the truck would go berserk.

On the left ran a deep ditch. It would do no good to try to run the truck into that at the speed they were moving. If only there was a field or a hillside to turn onto. Gordon's filling station stood on the left at the bottom of the hill, just before the curve. But the yard of the filling station was cluttered with cars and trucks. There was no room to pull off.

They blazed past the line of cars in the right lane, faster and faster. The wind was hot as a dirty flame licking Fred's face, sucking his breath away and blurring everything he looked at.

A car was coming at them two or three hundred yards ahead. "What are you going to do?" Fred said.

"How the hell do I know?" Albert said.

"You have always give the orders," Fred said. "Now give this one."

"Somebody has to give orders," Albert said.

"And I have had to take them," Fred said.

"And I have been stuck with you since you was a snot-nose,"

Albert shouted. He pumped the brake again, but it did no good. It was as if the pedal had been disconnected.

Their speed made everything brighter. The sun reflected from car windows was blinding. Their growing speed made the cars in the lane beside them seem to stretch out to twice their length. Speed made the world on both sides of the road appear to curve and cup around them. Speed made the sun brighter and the sky appear to hover just over their heads.

"I never never did like you," Albert shouted. "I never did like — the way you suck and slurp your coffee."

"I never did like nothing about you," Fred hollered.

"Mama always liked you better," Albert yelled.

"I don't blame her," Fred said.

"I would like to shit on the whole world!" Albert shouted.

The sound of the tires rose to a shrill chant as they got faster. Smoke rose from the front wheels and seeped into the cab. The smoke smelled of burnt chemicals, and burned metal.

"If we can get around the curve we might make it," Fred said.

"If we could spread wings we might fly," Albert said. He tried again to ram the gear into second, but the stick jumped out of his hand with a bone-sickening shudder. He couldn't even get the shift to go back into third. The truck was out of gear and coasting in free fall.

"Can't they see us coming?" Albert screamed. The oncoming cars didn't slow down. It was as if the drivers couldn't believe a log truck was plunging straight at them. Perhaps the drivers were dazed from the heat and not noticing what was ahead. Fred pounded the dash as though it was a horn.

But at the very last moment the two cars pulled to the left, throwing up gravel and dust on the shoulder. Albert roared into the opening they made. Fred heard the truck horn echo from the wall of the filling station as they flooded by. Johnny, the pump jockey, stared at them with his mouth open.

Ahead was the causeway and curve leading into the bridge. The curve was only slightly banked. The highway had been built before they knew to tilt steep curves.

"Lord, please let us make it. I'll do anything," Fred said through tight lips.

If there was a car coming at them across the bridge they would hit it. On the curve there was no way to avoid a collision. Albert kept almost to the center line, close as he could without ramming the cars in the right lane. Fred saw the face of a driver looking at them in horror. They were pulled to the left in the curve as though sucked that way by a vacuum. Fred leaned against the door as if he could tilt the truck like a motorcycle.

As they came into the guts of the curve Fred saw there was no one in the oncoming lane. There was space for them to shoot through. Without thinking he had reached into his pants and held onto himself. He pulled his hand out and smelled his crotch, his own shit. If they could get beyond the bridge they might run off into Adger Harmon's pasture.

"Please, Jesus," Fred said, gripping the door of the truck.

"Yiippee!" Albert shouted, and pounded the horn.

At that instant there was a bang and rumble behind them. The truck jolted, as if rammed by a bulldozer. They were still in the last arc of the curve and Fred thought maybe a car had hit them. Albert wrestled with the steering wheel, but the truck lurched and began to rotate sideways, as if skidding on ice.

"Damn it all," Albert shouted.

Fred knew what had happened. One of the chains had snapped and the logs were shifting and beginning to roll off. The truck swung as if on a turntable and the heavy logs flew

273

past Albert's window and rumbled on the shoulder and pavement. The worst thing that could happen had. This is the way you die, Fred thought. It would soon be over. There wasn't anything he could do.

"Albert, I love you," he shouted. He didn't know where the sentence came from; the words just shot out as the truck leaned and things rushed at him.

"Mama!" Albert screamed.

Fred saw a poplar tree flying and papers and cans on the shoulder of the road. He saw the corner of the bridge soar by in a rage of light. The brown water of the river passed in fury. Light flew at him all the way from the end of the world, and beyond.

~ · ~ · ~

When Fred woke there were voices and horns sounding. Muddy river water swirled around in the cab. He was cold and numb, and he couldn't move his neck. But he was breathing. He saw Albert pushed up over the steering wheel and pressed against the corner of the cab. Fred wanted to move his hand, but found it was lodged under a great weight. He had to reach over to Albert and find out if he was still breathing. "Help!" he shouted, but no syllable came out. He saw a log floating away on the current, and he felt how cold the river water was.

Sleepy Gap

THE THING IS," the warden said, "if there are ever a man among you that takes a drink while serving time, he will be throwed into the Outhouse." The Outhouse was the box in the prison yard where they locked somebody for solitary confinement. It was a stinking hole of a place full of spiders and ticks. On a hot day it roasted you and on a cold night you froze with one threadbare blanket to wrap around your shoulders.

"But I can't blame a man for taking a drink," the warden said and picked his nose. "Any man would want a drink while going to school for the government. This ain't supposed to be no resort." The warden spit on the grass. "But the fact is that I find the man that brought him that liquor, and sold him that liquor, I will break him. Ain't no man that can't be broke, and I will do whatever it takes to break him."

We knowed what the warden meant. There was nothing subtle about his punishments. His methods was simple and direct. He didn't practice any advanced psychology, and he didn't worry about modern theories of rehabilitation.

"Show me a man that thinks he's tough, and I will show you somebody that can be broke," the warden liked to say. "You are here at the taxpayer's expense, and I mean to see that the public gets its money's worth."

275

If somebody broke the rules they had to sit in the Outhouse for a couple of days. If they broke the rules again they got whipped. And when a man got whipped he was led out into the prison yard and stripped naked. Then he was tied across a big oak log with his hands strapped to rings at either end of the log. From the windows of the block it looked as if he was taking a swan dive.

And there was nothing fancy about the instruments the warden used for whipping either. He didn't keep bullwhips or sticks that could break bones. He had a collection of sourwood and maple limbs, lean and supple. And every time we worked along the country roads he made the trusty gather more shoots and limbs, willow and hickory, as well as maple and sourwood. In a whipping he might break half a dozen switches and he wanted to keep a generous supply on hand.

The warden did the whipping himself. "I wouldn't ask any man to do something I wouldn't do," he said. "And I want it to be clear the punishment is official, that the punishment comes from the top."

When the warden talked to us over the intercom or in the cafeteria, he usually ended up by saying, "You all don't know it, and you may never believe it, but I'm the best friend you have. The only salvation for a man incarcerated is hard work, to get his mind right so he can respect hisself. And I'm here to help do that. I can guarantee that you will work hard, and I will do my best to help you begin to respect your sorry selves. A man can't respect hisself until he pays his debts. And the only way you can pay your debt is hard work."

∾ · ∾ · ∾

The day I'm talking about was a cool summer day. You know the kind of day we have in the mountains. It had rained the day before and cleared off during the night. Puddles stood muddy as coffee in the road, but the air was so clear it bit your eyes, and every leaf on every tree looked waxed and polished. Shining white clouds drifted over the mountains, and the mountains was so blue their tops whispered to the blue sky.

My friend Mike was in the prison for making liquor. A lot of people in the county made liquor back in the 1920s and 1930s. It was the only way to wring a few dollars from the steep mountain acres. Mike had made blockade since he was a boy. And I guess his daddy had made it before him, in a spring hollow on the back of their place. But Mike got caught because he sold a quart to a tourist that was arrested for drunk driving. They promised the tourist they would let him off light if he told where he got the booze.

Mike liked to tell about the trial. When he saw they was going to send him to the pen, he told the judge, "I've been stilling corn for spirits since I was a shirt-tail boy, and my pappy stilled it before me. And long as the sun shines or grass grows green in spring I will be making it, judge, reckon on it."

"We'll see," the judge said, and rapped his hammer. Mike got two to five, and they took his cow and horse to pay the fine. The sheriff even took his wife's chickens.

"The thing is, don't never sell to a stranger," Mike said.

∾ · ∾ · ∾

We climbed into the truck early that morning, and they drove us way up the valley toward Sleepy Gap. The bouncing truck made me belch the watery oatmeal we had for breakfast. It tasted better the second time. "This is my end of the county," Mike said, looking out the back of the truck. "When we get out one day I'll give a party for you all."

They put us to clearing brush off the high bank of the road

near the gap. Every man had an axe or a brush hook. It was going to be a long hard day. The only comfort was the air was dry and the breeze cool.

"Watch out for poison oak in this brush," Freeman, the guard, said.

"Hell, poison oak will die when it touches me," I said.

"Look who's bragging," Mike said.

"And there's poison ash along the ditch," Freeman said.

"Maybe we can find something sweeter in these weeds," Mike said.

"Like a rattlesnake," Gosnell said. Gosnell was a glue sniffer. He saved every nickel he made to buy airplane glue. During the night you could hear him snuff up and giggle. He would laugh to hisself in the dark for hours.

"Maybe the tooth fairy will leave something under a bush for us," Mike said. Mike had lost an eyetooth and if he laughed you seen the gap. He looked ten years older when he opened his mouth.

"Maybe the angel Gabriel will step out of a cloud and call us to glory," Gosnell said.

"That would be one hell of an escape," Coggins said.

"Except you would be called to hell," Gosnell said.

"The hell you preach," Coggins said.

"That's exactly what I preach," Gosnell said.

"Stay out of the trees!" Freeman called. He held his shotgun pointed at the sky. It was loaded with buckshot. "Just work in the brush where I can see you." Freeman had a high-powered rifle in the truck cab, and he carried a .44 magnum on his hip. But the 12 gauge was his primary weapon. "Buckshot will cripple but it won't kill," he liked to say.

~ . ~ . ~

To this day I don't know exactly how Mike done it. I mean I

know in general what happened. But none of us saw a thing. And I know Freeman didn't see a thing. We were scattered out along the bank chopping bastard pines and slashing locust sprouts, poplar bushes and whips of sourwood. The bank was tangled up with blackberry briars and honeysuckle vines. Some of Mike's kin must have followed the chain gang truck up the road toward Sleepy Gap. They couldn't have knowed beforehand that's where we'd be working. They must have slipped along the edge of the woods and somehow signalled to Mike, and put a jug behind a stump or under a pine bush. None of us seen a thing until about mid-morning. We was beginning to sweat and Mike whispered as he swung his hook, "You want something to wet your whistle?" He pointed to a jug in the broom sedge at his feet.

"What is that?" I whispered back.

"What do you think it is?" Mike said.

I edged closer to see the jug. It sparkled in the weeds.

"Don't you all stop working," Freeman called out.

Mike stooped behind a poplar bush and took a swig and then moved on. News of the jug was passed along the bank quick. I swung my hook near to it and leaned over and took a drink, holding the jug with my left hand, still swinging the hook. The whiskey burned like ether, and seethed like soda water.

One by one the men worked their way near to the poplar bush and took a drink. Some took two and got hissed at by the man closest to them. We worked and sweated in the sun, our faces red. When every man had had a drink we started working our way back again. Everybody moved slower and my arms felt so light they seemed to float. We had a party there on the steep bank. Men chuckled and joked as they worked.

"Old Sneaky Pete," Coggins said and giggled.

"No, that's white mule," Gosnell said. "You can tell by the kick."

"You all owe me fifty cents," Mike said.

"Send us a bill," Gondan said.

I think we would have got away with it. We would have drunk the blockade and sweated it out in the sun before dinner, feeling free and crazy in the work. Except that Coggins stood up too high to drink from the jug the second time. It was nearly empty and he stood straight up to get the last drops. I guess he was pretty happy by then and had lost his caution. Freeman must have seen the glint of the jug in the sun.

"Wait a minute," the guard shouted. He fired a shot into the air. "Everybody freeze!" he called. "I have five more shells in this gun and I can kill every one of you."

Freeman made Coggins bring him the jug. The guard sniffed it and said, "Having yourselves a good old time, boys? Now where did you get this?"

Nobody said a thing, and Freeman looked at each of us on the bank. But somehow he guessed it was Mike who had got the liquor. Maybe it was obvious since Sleepy Gap was so near Mike's place, and Mike was serving time for making liquor.

"Go call the warden," Freeman said to the trusty. "Tell him what has happened." There was a radio in the guard truck like a police radio. We all stood there in the bright sun. I felt a little dizzy with the liquor buzzing in my ears. I was happy to have the drink inside me, and then I felt sick that we had been caught. A day in the Outhouse was a high price to pay for a slug of liquor.

"Damn that Freeman," Coggins muttered.

"You all get back to chopping brush," Freeman shouted. "The government has not retired you yet to rocking chairs."

"It ain't Freeman you have to worry about," Gosnell said.

Mike did not seem as concerned as the rest of us. He had drunk more from the jug than we had and he was proud to be the host and benefactor to the whole gang. Also he had not been inside as long as the rest of us and had not witnessed a whipping. "I need me another drink," he said.

"Ain't you got another jug?" Gosnell said. Gosnell was in for hanging paper, and he had another year to go.

"Wish I did, boys, wish I did," Mike said. He almost sung it, he was so pleased with hisself. It was said that Mike was the song leader at the Sleepy Gap Baptist Church. I knowed he had a fine voice for he sung sometimes when he worked, and when the chaplain come to the prison and conducted services. And it was hymns Mike preferred, more even than songs from the radio.

"One drink just whetted my thirst," Filson the mother beater said. Filson had held his mother down while his wife beat her to make her sign the home place over to them.

"Boys, when you all get out you can gather at my place for a barbecue," Mike said. "And we can drink all we want."

~ · ~ · ~

The warden drove up in his car. It was a state car with the seal of North Carolina printed on the door. The warden set in the car a full minute before getting out. We tried to pretend we was working, but the truth is none of us could take our eyes off the car. When the warden finally got out he hitched up his pants and looked at us scattered on the bank above him. I expected him to call us down to the road to gather in front of him. But instead he motioned for Freeman to follow him and they begun to climb the bank. "Come on up here, boys," he said to us.

The warden made us line up at the top of the bank, at the

281

edge of the woods. He made us stand back at least ten feet from the trees so Freeman could watch us all. At first I didn't see what he was doing. And then I understood that he was getting out of sight of the road below.

There was a sourwood that had been pushed over by a sleet storm. It leaned about a yard off the ground just inside the woods. The warden took two pieces of rope from his pocket and had the trusty tie Mike's wrists to the sourwood so his ear was pressed against the tree.

"You have picked the wrong man," Mike said to the warden.

"Is that so?" the warden said.

"I had a drink," Mike said. "I won't deny that."

"You certainly did," the warden said. He had the trusty cut four long switches of maple and sourwood. The warden slid the withes between his pinched fingers to strip off the leaves.

The warden turned to the line of us. "You men know I play by the rules," he said. "You learn your lessons and behave like men here and you graduate. I'm interested in only one thing: your obligations to society. But for some people extra methods is called for. They can't abide by the ordinary discipline, and they can't be educated by ordinary means." He slapped one of the hickories on his pants leg.

"Do you know where Mike got his liquor?" he said. We stood like we had not heard his question. I looked at an oak tree, and then at the white cloud above the oak tree. A jarfly broke out in whirring song. "None of you don't know nothing?" he said. "Am I right?" He turned to Mike.

"I will give you a chance to help yourself," he said to Mike. "Tell me where you got the liquor and you'll feel a lot better."

"Found it under a stump," Mike said out of the side of his mouth. There was snickering.

"The same place your mama found you," the warden said. There was more snickering.

"You all may think this is funny," the warden said. "But I don't think it's funny. It's never funny to break a man. I hate to do it. But some men has to be broke."

The warden slapped a hickory on the sourwood log beside Mike's hand. "What I'm going to do is for your own good," he said to Mike.

"Much obliged," Mike said.

"You will sing a different song in a few minutes," the warden said.

"Your mama is a slut," Mike said. It was like he had just woke up and realized the situation he was in. The surprise made him angry, and fear made him jerk at his bonds. He flung his hips around and kicked at the leaves, but he couldn't tear free.

"Mike, you have a lot of learning to do," the warden said in a gentle voice.

"Ain't you the great professor," Mike said.

The warden spit his tobacco into the brush. He had the trusty pull Mike's shirt up over his head and slide his pants down around his ankles. Mike's back and buttocks was white as an invalid's skin. Mike twisted around and farted at the warden.

"I never whip a man in anger," the warden said. "I only do it because it's my duty." He dropped three of the switches on the ground and stepped to the side of Mike. The first lick was so soft it was hardly a blow, more a flick or tickle. He switched Mike on the middle of his back, and then he switched him on his shoulders. He struck a little harder on the small of his back. My Uncle Calvin used to say you could kill a snake by switching it up and down its length. The light blows stimulated the snake's nervous system until it died of seizures. The snake writhed in frenzy and trembled in convulsions and died faster than if it had been beaten with a stick.

I could see by the set of his jaw that Mike had braced hisself for the worst pain. But the warden teased him with a dozen light flicks and stings. Then suddenly he swung with all his might and hit Mike just above his tail bone. Mike screamed with the surprise of the pain.

"Now do you want to tell me who give you the jug?" the warden said.

"To hell," Mike spat out.

The warden beat him across his legs and backside. Mike stiffened and then trembled with the cut of the licks. His skin got red, as if it had been raked by claws. The warden beat him across the back until the hickory broke, and then he took up a second switch. All the men was quiet. We couldn't take our eyes off Mike's back.

"This is a lesson for you all," the warden said. "This is advanced civics." The warden was sweating, and he wiped his forehead with the back of his wrist. As he begun hitting Mike again Mike moved first one knee and then another, like he was trying to crawl away from the bite of the switch.

"Are you ready to talk?" the warden said.

Mike only howled in reply.

The warden broke the second hickory on Mike's back and picked up the third. He begun hitting Mike on the buttocks again. He swung as though trying to put out a fire. "What did you say?" the warden shouted.

But Mike was only sobbing. He gritted his teeth to keep from crying as long as he could, but now he couldn't help hisself. His body heaved as he sobbed. His buttocks was crossed by welts big as bloodworms and nightcrawlers.

"What did you say?" the warden asked.

But Mike didn't answer. He tried to choke back his sobs and swallow. Mike clenched his fists and unclenched them.

When the warden begun hitting Mike with the fourth switch

we saw Mike start to foul hisself. Blood run off his back and mixed with sweat and shit on his legs. And when the warden hit him, blood and shit and sweat flung off. We stepped back to avoid the spray.

"Look at you," the warden said. "You've soiled yourself and humiliated yourself. You should be ashamed."

Mike sobbed against the sourwood log, and bark stuck to his cheek, to the tears and sweat. It was the crapping on hisself that broke him.

"What did you say, boy?" the warden said.

"I'm s-s-s-sorry," Mike hiccupped.

"What did you say?" the warden said.

"I'm s-s-s-sorry," Mike shouted.

The warden looked at us. His face was red, and his forehead was dripping with sweat. "Who give you the liquor?" he said.

"My cousin Johnny," Mike said.

"How did he get it to you?" the warden said.

"He left it by a poplar bush," Mike said. Mike sobbed against the sourwood like a baby.

"Are you going to do it again?" the warden said.

"No sir," Mike said and tried to clear his nose. "No sir, I won't never do it again."

"Are you broke?" the warden said.

"Yes sir," Mike said almost in a whisper. "I'm broke."

I glanced at the row of men. They was looking away from Mike. Some looked at the ground and some looked into the trees beyond. But none was watching Mike where he hung from the sourwood.

"That's better," the warden said. "That's much better."

$\approx \cdot \approx \cdot \approx$

I seen Mike once more, years later, after we was out of the pen. I thought he would be ashamed to see me, because of what I had witnessed done to him. But Mike acted perfectly glad to see an old acquaintance from the prison days. He wore clean overalls and held his granddaughter on his lap, sitting on a bench in the park near the courthouse on a Saturday afternoon.

"You know, I owe a lot to that warden," he said.

"I know you do," I said.

"No, I mean it," Mike said. "He changed my life. He taught me a lesson that I ain't forgot. I never went back to my old habits."

Mike chuckled and bounced his granddaughter on his knee.

"If that's the way you see it," I said.

"There ain't no other way I see it," he said, like he had convinced hisself the warden had done him a favor.

It was a late summer afternoon and I glanced up at the courthouse dome that glittered in the bright sun like a helmet. And above the dome a cloud hung in the sky white as sugar frosting. I thought how the world is always stranger than we think it is.

"There ain't no other way to see it," Mike said again.

I watched him bounce the granddaughter on his knee. Her cheeks got red with excitement and she screamed with delight. Mike grinned at her and held her hands as though they was dancing.

The Bullnoser

HE THINKS HE'S SHIT ON A STICK, but he's really just a
fart on a splinter," Carlie said. It was a cotton mill saying she
had been repeating for years. She especially liked to say it
about T.J.

T.J. was walking back down the hill to his pickup. He had
brought her another case of Budweiser, a bottle of pills, and
a carton of Winstons.

"He's hoping I will drink myself to death and then he won't
never have to pay me," Carlie said as she tore open the carton.

"Whyn't you get the law after him in the first place?" I
said.

Carlie lit a cigarette, and pulled a can out of the box of beer.

"Give me one of them," I said.

"Get your own beer you lazy pup."

I helped myself to a can and popped the top. The beer tasted
a little bit like aluminum, but it was cold, and mighty good
on a humid day. It was a taste I craved when we didn't have
no money.

"Whyn't you get the law after T.J. in the first place?" I said
again. This was a conversation we had at least once a week.
I knew all the answers already, but we couldn't resist going
through the motions, especially when we had beer. When Carlie

was on her pills she liked to listen to rock and roll on the radio and laugh and sometimes dance. She danced by herself in the dark room with a cigarette in her mouth. She circled round and inhaled and laughed. And she didn't want the light on. She didn't want to see the mess on the floor and on all the chairs. She just wanted to turn in circles and smoke and think about when she was a girl working in the cotton mill and had a boyfriend named Grover. That was way before she met Daddy and moved up here to the farm.

"On Saturday nights we'd go dancing at the Teenage Canteen," she'd say. "That was just before he went overseas." Sometimes she'd say Grover was killed in the war and never did come back, and sometimes she'd say he returned and married somebody else. It was hard to know what the truth was in her stories because she made up so much. In fact, I don't think there ever was a Grover. I think that was just a fig leaf of her imagination.

But when Carlie drank beer she liked most to talk about how terrible T.J. had done us, and was still doing her.

"Why'd you agree to sell him the place in the first place?" I said.

"Cause your Daddy, bless his poor little dried up soul in hell, borrowed five thousand dollars from T.J. and I couldn't afford to pay it back."

I noticed a speck of dirt on top of my can. "I wonder where T.J. gets such dirty cans," I said.

"Probably at the Salvation Army," Carlie said, and laughed. She laughed so hard she bent over in her chair and the ash from her cigarette fell on the floor.

"The world is my ashtray," she said in falsetto.

"This floor ought to be swept," I said.

"You're a big strong feller, sweep it yourself," Carlie said. "Stead of sitting around on your fat ass drinking my beer."

"T.J.'s beer."

"It's payment on what he still owes me."

I wiped the top of the can with my sleeve. For some reason I like the top of a can to be dry when I'm drinking from it.

"Why'd Daddy owe him five thousand dollars?" I said.

"Cause your daddy didn't have a mite of sense and he had cancer and couldn't work. The truth was he never did work much. And I was too sick after you was born to go back to the cotton mill."

"So he just borrowed?"

"He borrowed against the place. He was going to inherit this big place. Everybody said Riley's place was the finest place on the creek."

"Give me a cigarette," I said.

She pulled the carton out of my reach. "Get your own cigarettes," she said. "Besides, smoking is bad for you."

"And it's not bad for you?"

"Don't do as I do, do as I say do." She laughed, but the laugh turned into a cough. I took a cigarette from the pack and lit it.

"Next time T.J. comes tell him you'll sue him," I said.

"And he'll say we got to move out."

"We can move out if he'll pay us the rest of the mortgage."

T.J. had built a trailer park on the pasture hill, cutting out level places almost to the top of the ridge. The ridge was called Riley's Knob after my grandpa who kept it clear and grazed cattle on the very top.

"How much does he still owe us?" I said.

"He claims he don't owe us nothing, that we done used it all up in rent for this old house and in the beer and little bits of groceries he brings."

"People say he paid you years ago and you drunk it all up."

"That's a damn lie."

"He tells people he lets you live here out of the goodness of his heart."

"People are dog puke," Carlie said, and opened another can.

"Ain't it about lunch time?" I said.

"No, it's almost time for *Tucson Days*." That was a soap opera that comes on in the middle of the day which she had been watching for several months. It was all about people in a retirement community and their families and people who work at the center. There was always somebody dying of cancer, or some old guy who turned out to have a second younger family in Phoenix. And then there was somebody with AIDS, and somebody impotent, and a young nurse who was trying to marry an old guy for his money, except the young nurse is really a lesbian.

"Maybe I'll get my gun and go talk to T.J.," I said.

"You ain't gone talk to nobody," Carlie said. "You want to talk to somebody go talk to somebody about a job."

It was a point that always came up in our conversations, that I had lost my job. And she knew as well as I did it was impossible to get another one. When I worked in the cotton mill they put me to lifting boxes in the stockroom and I hurt my side. Their crooked doctor wouldn't give me disability and when I stayed out a few days for my side to heal they fired me. Because they fired me no other company would give me a job. All these plants work together against poor people.

Carlie turned the TV on and sat about a yard away from the screen. She kept her lighter in her right hand and a can in the left.

"Ain't you going to fix no lunch?" I said.

"Get out of here," she said below her breath.

$\approx$ · $\approx$ · $\approx$

You always feel stuffy when you've been drinking in the daytime and go out into the sun. It's like the light presses against you and pushes you around. And you don't feel like doing anything either. Even while the beer makes you feel lighter it pulls you down inside. That's why Carlie likes her pills in the morning, and sometimes even when she's drinking.

I'd grabbed a pack of cigarettes on my way out of the dark house and I lit one, bending over to get out of the bright light and the breeze. The smoke tasted good. It was the only thing interesting out there in the yard.

The pickup still sat where I had jacked it up the week before. "I'll let you have my old pickup," T.J. said. But he'd just use it as another excuse not to pay us the rest of the mortgage. You don't get nothing from T.J. for nothing. The bearings were gone in the left front wheel, but I couldn't afford another set. I could squirt some grease in and drive it to the store if I had to, but the front end shimmied like sixty and I was afraid it would ruin something else. I had to wait till I got some money from T.J. or from working for the rich people down on the lake. They'd come after me sometimes to help fix a railing on a deck, or dig out a ditch along their driveway. But my back had been killing me again, ever since I wrenched it crawling under the truck to get the bearings out.

"You get that damn truck fixed so we can go to town," Carlie said.

There wasn't a thing to do but walk down to the mailbox to see if a letter had come from the unemployment office. I applied for compensation but they said I couldn't draw anything unless I could prove I was laid off in good standing. They said I'd have to contest the mill's claim I was fired. I filled out another form for them. I said I was as hard a worker as the next man, except when my back was acting up. It was their crooked doctor that wouldn't give me disability.

So they said they would have a hearing about it, and I've

been waiting ever since, and not drawed a cent from the government.

Used to Grandpa kept the yard mowed clean in front of the house. But after the lawn mower broke down and wouldn't start I couldn't keep up with all the weeds. And then Carlie threw out her old washing machine in the side yard, and the rusty barbeque grill and about five hundred cans, and it was such a mess you couldn't hardly walk out of the house without stepping on glass or a snake. And the weeds had already grown up around the truck like it had been parked there all summer.

When I was a kid Grandpa kept the driveway neat as a golf course. But T.J. had covered up the old drive and made a road to his trailer park. He was always bringing in trucks and building more spaces for trailers. I could hear a bullnoser somewhere up there grading, way on back of the Knob.

I took T.J.'s road across the little creek and up the hill to the mailbox. Grandpa had a little bridge there, and it was the perfect place for a kid to play, where the mowed grass came right down to the water and you could watch minnows shoot around the pools. I waded there and made little dams, and fished with a stalk of grass. I could slip through the edge of the pasture when the bull was penned up. Grandpa would take me over to the orchard on the bank below the road and peel an apple or pear with his knife and let me eat it. It looked like a little park in there, the way he kept the place, the gate and apple trees, the little bridge over the branch, the boxwoods along the driveway. Carlie sold all the boxwoods right after Daddy died to help pay for the funeral, she said. If she had known what T.J. was going to do she would have sold off everything else too.

One time I went by the barn and pulled all the railings out of the gap. I liked to slide the poles back and forth in their slots and drop the ends on the ground. But they were too heavy for me to lift back into their holders and I left them down when I saw the mailman stop and I ran to the mailbox.

When the bull got back to that end of the pasture he walked out, just stepped right through the bars. And he was a mean bull too. Everybody was afraid of him. Grandpa kept him to breed people's cows, and he made some money for he charged three dollars a time. People were always driving their heifers down when they were spreeing, and bawling along the road. And the bull would hear them and bawl back, and then come running from whatever part of the pasture he was in. People usually brought their cows down late in the day, after they had stopped work in the fields and when they knew Grandpa would be around the barn, milking or watering the stock.

But when the bull got out it took half the people in the valley half the night to find him. I knew I'd done something bad, but Grandpa said nothing. He lit his old barn lantern and went out looking. Carlie smacked me across the mouth with the flat of her hand so my lip cracked.

"You'll get somebody killed with that bull and we'll all go to jail," she said.

I followed Grandpa and didn't go back to the house. The men hollered and ran along the fence at Fairfield's place, where the bull had run trying to get in with the cows. Grandpa couldn't hear too well and the men talked about him like he wasn't there.

"Riley's too old to keep a bull," they said.

"And Riley's boy has fouled his nest," they said.

"Now he's got cotton mill trash in on him," another said.

"Got to keep your breeding stock up, otherwise a family will run to ruin in two generations."

Grandpa walked along with his lantern not saying a thing.

They followed the bull along the fence up into the holler and cornered him among the poplars. Grandpa snapped a chain to the ring in his nose and they put a halter over his head.

"You want us to lead him back?" they said.

"Much obliged," Grandpa said. "I can handle him."

I walked in front of Grandpa carrying the lantern.

∽ · ∽ · ∽

Where the old driveway wound through the apple trees up to the mailbox, T.J. had bullnosed a new road for the trailer park and put in a culvert over the branch. It was all raw dirt. Grass wouldn't seem to grow on anything T.J. made.

"This place is all clay," he said. "I don't see how Riley ever growed a weed on it."

But T.J. knew how to grow trailer sites. They were all over the old pasture, all over Riley's Knob to the very top.

There wasn't no mail except a circular and three bills. I threw the circular in the ditch and stuffed the bills in my pocket. Carlie won't hardly ever pay bills until they cut the electricity off, and then she has to ask T.J. for the money. Of course, if T.J. owns the house like he says he does the bills should come to him.

I saw I was going to have to have it out with T.J. I couldn't count on what Carlie said. She got mixed up, and she'd stretch anything to suit her, depending on who she was talking to.

I tried to remember if T.J.'s truck had gone up the hill after he left the beer, or if he had turned back toward the road. If he was up on the Knob I could catch him and have some things out. But I couldn't recall. I had been too busy arguing with Carlie about the beer to notice where T.J. went.

You could hear the bullnoser up there, working somewhere on the Knob. And there was always trucks going up there, pulling new trailers and carrying loads of this and that. You would have thought he was building a shopping mall up there for all the stuff they hauled up the mountain.

I hadn't been up on the Knob in years. It was a steep climb, and T.J. had cut down all the trees so there was no place to squirrel hunt. And they were always working up there. You could hear the bullnoser going almost every day, and the clank of a well driller, and the shower of gravel being dumped on the road.

I'd just go up there and have a little talk with T.J. There wasn't anything else to do, except go back and watch TV with Carlie. The beer was wearing off and I was starting to sweat.

The old house sat on the only spot of ground that hadn't been bullnosed by T.J. Where the barn and shed stood he had covered up the old boards with dirt and filled in over the culvert. The whole hill behind the barn had been skinned off, with rocks and dirt showing. Where T.J. sowed grass around the trailers it mostly didn't take, and the little bits of shrubbery died. But them people living up there didn't care. They came and went, some working at the cotton mill and some with construction crews. Several trailers had Mexicans in them. They worked in the shrubbery business as diggers and weed cutters. But you almost never saw them. They left before daylight and didn't get back in the rattly pickup until after dark. One time I heard they bought a goat and roasted it for a celebration. But I don't think it was anything voodoo. They just like goat.

My feet kept slipping on the gravel of T.J.'s drive and I was out of breath before I got halfway up the hill. Too many smokes, I thought, and too much beer. Most of the trailers I passed were deserted. Sometimes you could hear the sound of a TV from one, or the buzz of an air conditioner. Pretty little wives sitting around in shorts watching television, I thought. That's what you could have if you worked: a pretty little wife in shorts sitting cool at home when you get off from work. The oil tanks on their stands stood like steel cows behind every trailer, and off on the side of each one a satellite dish tilted like a big white flower. I glanced through a window or two but I couldn't see anybody inside.

Up ahead a little kid was peddling his plastic racer around. It was a low tricycle that was meant to look like a motorcycle. The plastic wheels crunched hollow on the gravel.

"Ruddunn, ruddunn," the kid said, revving his engine. The kid was making so much noise with his throat and with the sound of the wheels on gravel, he couldn't hear a truck coming round the switchback above. It was one of those trucks with sideboards, the kind they use to deliver building supplies. The kid kept peddling out into the road, and the truck didn't slow down, but seemed to be gaining speed.

"Hey," I hollered, and tried to run up the hill. I tried to flag the truck driver, but he just kept coming, like he didn't see the tricycle. The kid was peddling right out into the middle of the road, and at the last second the truck swerved and missed him and then passed me in a cloud of dust. I didn't even get a look at the driver. The name on the truck door said something about "Division" but I didn't have a chance to read it.

"Does your Mama know where you are?" I said to the kid. He didn't seem worried by what had almost happened. I felt like I had been electrocuted, and needed to stand still. The dirty little kid had nothing on but a pair of shorts.

"I'll race you down there," he said, and pointed down the road.

"You better get back in your yard," I said. There was no woman in sight around the trailer, and no car neither.

"Better get out of the road," I said.

"You ain't my daddy," the little boy said, and peddled on down hill. It wasn't clear which trailer he belonged to.

Grandpa used to take me for sled rides on the pasture hill. He'd hitch up the stone boat to get wood around the Knob and let me stand on the sled while the horse pulled it up the pasture hill.

"Why don't you use the wagon?" I said to him.

"Because it's too steep here," he said. "A wagon would tip over or run away."

From the Knob you could see all the way down to the river valley, and the lake and cotton mill town. Today all I could see was the superhighway they cut through above the cotton mill. The traffic on it was a steady roar. It was too hazy to see much further.

I heard the bullnoser going around the back of the Knob, and thought that's where T.J. must be working. He must be clearing more woods and cutting out more places for trailers. I'd just go over there and see what he was doing.

The Knob used to be a grassy top where you could sit and look all over the valley. But it had grown up in bushes and briars, right at the summit. The new road T.J. had cut went around to the back, into a kind of holler between Grandpa's land and the Casey ridge. What could T.J. be doing back there? It wasn't even part of the place.

Whatever it was, they had been busy, for the road was packed down and dusty. A few ragweeds drooped in the middle, but they didn't have much of a chance against the traffic and dust. Dead roots stuck out of the bank of the road.

The new road went further into the holler, into the trees. I could hear the bullnoser rev up and then quiet down, screech into reverse, lurching and grinding like a tank. That seemed strange. Why would T.J. be making another trailer place further in the woods when he still had space in the pasture?

You could smell the diesel exhaust in the holler. Kudzu had climbed up the oak trees right to the top and then hung over.

I don't know how the kudzu got started because it wasn't there in Grandpa's time. The Caseys brought their bottles and cans and dumped them in the holler. Maybe they had brought a sprig of kudzu or a seed of the stuff with their trash.

T.J.'s pickup was parked right in the road, and then there was another big truck beyond it. Republic Industries: Carrier Division was painted on the big truck. It was the kind of truck that had an elevator at the rear, but the bed was empty.

T.J. stood at the edge of the clearing watching the bullnoser work. The whole place had the smell of opened dirt, which always reminds me of mothballs and camphor, and the smoke of hammered rock. There must be some kind of fumes that come up out of the ground. Far above the clearing the kudzu hung from the oak trees in a mournful way.

I couldn't tell what the bullnoser was doing, except there was oil drums and big paint cans on the ground, where they had rolled them off the truck.

You should have seen the look on T.J.'s face when he saw me. Maybe he knew what I'd come to talk to him about.

"You ain't got no business up here," he said. "This is no trespassing land."

"It ain't even your land, yet," I said, sounding madder than I felt because of the heat and being out of breath.

"Don't start that again," he said. "This wasn't never your Grandpa's land. This was Casey land and I bought it from them."

"Just like you bought Grandpa's?" I said.

"Let's go talk in the truck," he said. "It's air conditioned."

He practically pushed me toward the truck.

"It's time to settle this," I said, feeling bolder than I ever had before.

"Let's get out of the heat," he said.

T.J.'s pickup was practically new, but the cab was already

dusty and piled with bills and invoices, candy wrappers, old coffee cups, a crowbar, and a basketball goal.

"I'm going to put that up for Jerry," he said, pushing the goal to the floor. "When I get time. Just push everything out of the way."

When he started the motor and turned on the air conditioning it was hotter at first, and then the breeze got cold. The sweat made me shiver, and I could see he was hoping to dampen the anger I'd worked up. It's harder to be mad sitting beside somebody than standing up and facing them. I expected him to start in telling me how Carlie had already drunk up half the price of the place, and smoked and borrowed the rest, like he always did. But he didn't.

"Are you hurting for money?" he said. "I knowed you got laid off."

"I'm always hurting for money," I said.

"I could let you have some," he said.

"T.J., it ain't dibs and dabs I'm talking about. This was a big place."

"It's just a rocky mountainside."

"Not when Grandpa had it."

"Your Grandpa killed hisself to make something out of this brush and hardpan."

"You're going to have to pay up," I said.

"Or you'll what?"

"Or I'll go to law."

"If you need a few dollars I can let you have it."

From the cold inside of the truck I could just barely see the bullnoser. But for the first time it occurred to me what the bullnoser was doing. Those oil drums weren't full of fuel. He was covering them up. He was burying the paint cans and barrels.

"What you putting in the ground there, T.J.?" I said.

"Just some trash from the Republic plant." He offered me a cigarette, then put the truck in gear and started backing away. "We can talk better down at the house," he said. "Or better still, we could go down to the highway and get some dinner. How'd you like a hot dog and a Pepsi?"

Nothing T.J. said was what I expected him to say. He didn't get mad and cuss like he usually did. His face was red but he didn't seem mad. He hadn't even claimed the place was paid for a long time ago.

We bounced down the ruts and washes of the road, and the truck whined on the switchbacks as he geared it down. He had a real good air conditioner. It was a funny feeling, looking down on the valley through summer haze from Grandpa's Knob, from a box of chilly air, and winding among the trailers and scraggly bits of shrubbery T.J. had set out.

And then it struck me what the bullnoser was covering up back there, and why T.J. was being so friendly.

"You're burying poisons and chemicals up there," I said. Carlie and me had seen on TV about how it was illegal to put chemicals in the ground. You could be sent to jail for poisoning the water system.

"What you mean?" T.J. said. "I give them permission to put trash from the factory there."

"Them barrels are full of poison," I said. "Now I see."

"You don't see nothing," T.J. said, all his friendliness gone.

"You could be sued."

T.J. was driving faster, banging on the washouts.

"You cotton mill trash will have to get off my land," he said. "Tell Carlie she's got to move."

"We ain't moving," I said. "Not after I tell the law what you're putting up there."

T.J. kept going faster on the switchbacks, sliding on gravel and throwing rocks every which way. I was glad to see the kid on the plastic bike was off the road and waving from the shade of a trailer.

"You tell the law a thing and you're out in the road with your old TV and stinking couch," he said. "And they'll lock Carlie up in the asylum for crazy people and drug addicts."

"And they'll lock you up for poisoning the ground," I said. "Then the place will come back to us."

"Get out," he hollered, and slid to a stop in front of the house.

"You're in trouble," I said and slammed the door. He spun off throwing rocks fifty or sixty feet. The heat felt good after the cold cab.

≈ · ≈ · ≈

The screen door scraped on the back porch when I opened it. The bottom of the screen had scratched a curve on the floor boards. I'd meant to fix it for months, but a door is harder to repair than it looks. We'd probably have to replace the whole thing one of these days, because if you unscrew the hinges and put them on again slightly different the door will rub in other places, and the latch won't click, or one of the corners won't fit into the frame. It has to be a complete job or nothing.

Carlie had tied a piece of cloth over the hole in the screen to keep the flies out. It looked like something put there for a charm to keep the bad spirits away.

"Where the hell you been?" she said.

"I've been around," I said, and pulled the bills out of my back pocket to hand to her. She'd had two or three more beers since I'd left, and maybe another pill from the jar.

It was so dark in the house I could only see her face reflected in the TV light. The air was filled with smoke. She was so wrecked she couldn't tear open the envelopes, and gave it up and threw them on the table.

"You'll have to pay them," she said. "I'm just an old woman."

"You got years left in you," I said.

"Trifling lard ass," she said, and tossed her head, as she does when drunk, like she was a debutante on TV.

"I seen T.J.," I said. I wouldn't tell her about the chemical dump for a while. It was my little secret.

"You get any money from him?"

"I told him he'd have to pay up."

"You lazy-assed chicken," she said. "I'd rather eat shit with a splinter than beg for money." That was another of the cotton mill sayings she liked to bring out when she was drunk. She lit another cigarette, not touching the flame to the tip until the third try.

I decided I wouldn't tell her at all. The oil drums buried across the Knob would be a secret between T.J. and me. He would keep me in beer and cigs and maybe get the pickup fixed. There was no way he could throw us out, and I didn't need to tell Carlie a thing about it.

"Give me one of them beers," I said.

"Get your own beer."

There was a game show on the TV with a laugh track. I hated game shows much as Carlie loved them. I popped a beer and headed back outside. I hadn't felt so good since I found a twenty dollar bill in the parking lot of the plant before I was laid off. I sat on the porch looking down at the driveway T.J. had put in where the barn was. The cold beer tasted like both hope and confidence. I'd have the pickup running again by next week.

When Grandpa was old and couldn't really work anymore he piddled around the barn, mowing a few weeds, watering the horse, sharpening his hoes, and talking to hisself. When I was home on leave from the army he took me down to the shed adjoining the barn where he kept his tools. There was an old table with sacks piled on it, and he showed me one by one where he hid his mowing blade and pliers, his hammer and wire cutters, whetrock and file. He said people stole so bad nowadays you had to keep things hid. He wanted me to know where they were in case he died. The tater digger and ax leaned behind some boards in the corner. The good harness for the horse was behind the table with some sacks piled on it.

A Taxpayer & A Citizen

REVENGE IS THE BEST FORM of living well," my friend Charlane said as I was leaving. She was always saying something funny, especially when we talked about men. Charlane had this bottle of sweet Portuguese wine which we had finished, and everything she said was hilarious. We had been discussing my suit against Larry, my up-to-this-summer husband.

"All men want is a virgin with the skills of a whore," Charlane said, and we laughed again. Talking to Charlane always made me feel better. And believe me, I needed to feel better that day. My lawyer had finally drawn up the papers and they had been served on Larry that very morning in Brevard where he lived with this thing that called herself a country singer, Lurleen Stamey. I've heard Lurleen sing, and she's no more country than an alley cat, and no more musical than a can opener. But Larry always was crazy about music. That's one of the reasons he fell for me, because I could sing. I always could sing, since I was a little girl up on Briar Fork and played the dulcimer.

"Might as well have one for the road," Charlane said, and poured me a shot of JD. "You've got a long night ahead."

"A long night alone," I almost said. But I was feeling too mellow to be morbid. And I wanted to laugh some more.

"I've got all the groceries in the trunk," I said. "And Jamie's liable to burn the house down making popcorn if I don't get back." Jamie was my oldest girl, and she looked after the two younger kids when I got home late, or if I went out with Charlane or one of my other friends. After Larry left for that thing in Brevard I had had to make a new life for myself.

"Jamie is as responsible as you," Charlane said.

"That's what I'm worried about," I said, and we laughed again.

It was the week before Halloween and Charlane had a carved pumpkin on the porch. There was no candle in the jack-o'-lantern, but its gap teeth showed in the porch light and made me giggle again. "That pumpkin looks like my late husband," I said.

"Not late enough," Charlane said. And we laughed again. I never left Charlane but what I was feeling better. She had that effect on me.

≈ · ≈ · ≈

Now I've always been able to drive after I've had a drink. In fact, sometimes a drink or two improves my driving, makes me looser, more in control. After I've had a drink with Charlane or the other girls from work, I'll have a cup of coffee, just to make sure, as a kind of insurance that I'll be okay.

But that night I wasn't too worried. I was relieved to have had the papers served on Larry. I laughed to myself as I backed out of Charlane's driveway. Charlane lived in a trailer about six miles out in the country toward Bat Cave. I imagined Larry getting the papers I had filed and having to explain to his little songbird Lurleen that he was being sued for everything he had, including his pickup truck which he used in his roofing business. My lawyer said we didn't want to harm

Larry's livelihood, since we needed him to pay maximum alimony. We just wanted him to think he was about to lose the business and would be walking and carrying shingles on his shoulder.

As I backed into the road a horn sounded and lights flashed by in the twilight. Where had that car come from? I had looked both ways before I backed. The car must have been driving without its lights until it saw me. Steady, old girl, I said to myself. You know you are in control. Nobody can hurt you but yourself. It's what I always said when I knew I had to get through a tight spot.

As I headed down the highway, I switched on the radio, and there was this country song, "You Cheated, But You're Still a Loser." I turned it off. I didn't need any country music just then. Instead I started singing to myself an old song Daddy used to sing, "I'm Just a Poor Wayfaring Stranger." It was a sad song, and I needed a slow sad song to calm me down until I could get home with my groceries.

All along the road people had put cornstalks and pumpkins around their mailboxes. There was a witch riding a broom over one mailbox. A big black cat sat on a pumpkin at a driveway a little further on, its eyes brighter than flashlights.

I came around a curve just before I got to Highway 64, and this thing stepped out in front of me. It looked like a white cow browsing on the shoulder, or maybe a person in a waitress or nurse uniform. I hit the brakes and the car skidded sideways and slid to the shoulder. When I looked up over the steering wheel I saw this stuff flapping against the windshield. It was a sheet somebody had cut and hung from a limb to look like a ghost. Two eye holes had been cut, and a smile drawn on the face with a marker.

"I'm just a poor wayfaring stranger," I said to the ghost, and laughed at myself. A car shot out of nowhere and passed, its horn blaring. I saw brake lights come on ahead as it reached the highway.

Just get yourself home, I said to myself. Just get yourself home and see what Jamie and the other two are doing.

∾ · ∾ · ∾

Traffic was not heavy on Highway 64, but I tried to avoid looking at the lights of oncoming cars. The bright lights blurred in my eyes and made them sting. Maybe it was time I got new glasses. It was nearly dark now, and I drove by watching the white line along the edge of the pavement, the way I do in fog or heavy rain or when it's snowing. With bad visibility that white line is about all you have to go by.

As I drove I thought, every second I'm getting closer to home. I wished Charlane lived in town, or I wished she could stay over with me. But my children made Charlane nervous. And she was never as funny when Jamie and Curt and Susie were with me, maybe because so many of Charlane's jokes were about men and sex.

I noticed this car behind me, following steady at about the same distance. It wouldn't pass and it wouldn't fall behind. Maybe it's Larry, I thought. Larry has got the papers and now he's following me. It was hard to tell in the dark if it was a car or pickup truck. I tried to guess by the height of the lights, but couldn't. I speeded up a little, and the lights behind me speeded up too. I slowed down, and the vehicle behind me slowed.

You are being stalked, I said, and drove faster, holding to the white line. A red sign flashed by, and an intersection, and I realized I had driven through a stop sign. I slowed down again, and the car behind me stayed the same distance. I was about three miles out of town when I drove under a bright light at the lumber yard and saw the police bar on the car behind. It was a patrol car that looked like it was wearing epaulets. Oh shit, I hissed, and fumbled in my purse for a breath mint.

With my heart punching like a fist in my chest, I slowed down again. Control yourself, I said, it may be nothing. The road appeared to veer off to the right, and I swung the wheel to stay alongside the white line. My hands trembled as they held the wheel.

I drove with painstaking care about a minute, and then I saw the blue and red lights flash on. And the headlights on the police car flashed back and forth like a ball being passed. "Shit-damn," I said. "Shit-damn."

I was supposed to pull off the road, but where was there to pull off? The shoulder looked like weeds in a ditch. I didn't want to wreck just to pull off the highway. And I couldn't just stop in the middle of the pavement.

A siren screamed out a burst, and a voice on a bullhorn shouted, "Pull over."

"Where the hell am I supposed to pull over?" I said, and pounded the steering wheel with the heels of my palms. Sweat was forming on my forehead.

I drove on for what seemed like hours until I saw the place this old Esso filling station had stood. Nothing was left but kudzu vines over the yard. I drove into the space where the pump islands had been, sat up straight and turned off the engine, holding the breath mint on my tongue. Were the car registration and insurance card in the glove compartment? I knew my driver's license was in my wallet.

The trooper came around with a flashlight and pecked on the window. Remember you are a citizen and a taxpayer, I said to myself. I rolled down the window.

"Ma'am," the trooper said, leaning closer and playing the flashlight around the interior of the car. "What time of day would you say this is?"

"About seven-thirty," I said.

"Why do you think other people have their lights on?" the cop said. It hit me like an electric shock that I had never turned my lights on. That's why he had been following me.

"I just forgot, officer," I said. I almost breathed out a sigh of relief. But I didn't want him to smell the mint and get suspicious.

"Let me see your driver's license," he said.

I fished in my purse for my wallet, and held the billfold up to him. He played the flashlight on my face.

"Take it out of the wallet," he said. My fingers shook as I pulled the card out of the plastic envelope. I wondered what Charlane would say to the trooper, if she was in my place. Something funny, probably, like "Officer I have lost my contacts and was driving home to get them." I snickered a little.

"What's funny?" the trooper said.

"I lost my contacts," I said.

"You're wearing glasses," the officer said.

"These are my old glasses," I said.

He swept the flashlight over the inside of the car again. I was so glad I had not brought anything to drink with me. He held the light on my face.

"I'm sorry I forgot to turn on my lights," I said.

"Have you been drinking?" he said.

"Just a glass of wine with a friend," I said.

"Just one glass?" he said.

"We were celebrating my separation papers," I said.

He stepped back and played the light over the car. A transfer truck plunged by and wind shoved through the window. I thought of Jamie back at the house and wished more than anything else I could be there with my younguns.

"Will you step out of the car?" the officer said.

"Is something wrong?" I said.

"Just step out of the vehicle," he said.

I grabbed my purse and opened the car door. Suddenly I felt dizzy, and had to steady myself on the side of the car as I stood up. Calm yourself, I whispered. The car wobbled a little, and another big truck roared by. The patrol car behind me flashed like some giant Christmas decoration.

"Hold your arms out straight and walk along the white line," the cop said.

"Certainly," I said.

But my knees were shaking and my legs almost buckled. I stepped up on the pavement, but leaned off it. I climbed back on. "I'm fine," I said. But I moved slow, stepping off the pavement again. The white line appeared to shift to the side as I took a step.

"Would you step back to my car and take a Breathalyzer test?" the patrolman said.

"That's not necessary," I said. My heart leapt into my throat. "I just had one little glass of wine."

"Will you please do as I say?" the cop said. He was showing me how cool and professional he was. He couldn't have been more than twenty-six or twenty-seven. But he was a big hunk, at least six-four.

"I thought this was a free country," I said, and let more irritation into my voice than I meant to show.

"I can't force you to take the test," the trooper said. "But your refusal will become part of the record."

"Oh, I'll take the damned test," I said. "I have children waiting at home, and my groceries in the trunk."

He led me to the flashing cruiser and opened the back door. Another car hissed past, and I hoped it was nobody who recognized me. I slipped into the backseat and the patrolman unwrapped a plastic thing that looked like a toy, something between a party noisemaker and a diver's inhaler. "Breathe into the tube," he said. "Breathe as long and hard as you can."

I put the tube to my mouth and started blowing into it. The plastic tasted like it had soot or powder on it. I gagged and coughed, and held the thing away. "I can't do this," I said.

"Just breathe into the tube, Ma'am," he said.

Tears grew in my eyes and blurred everything. I knew I could not breathe into the dirty little device. The air in the car swirled in a close smothering way. "I don't have to do what you say," I said. I thought of Jamie and Curt and Susie at home and how they were probably watching MTV.

"Breathe into the tube," the officer said, "or I will go ahead and read you your rights."

"You don't need to do that," I said.

The radio in the front seat crackled and a voice said, "Number 74, are you there? Come in, Number 74."

The trooper opened the front door and took the mike from its holder. "This is Number 74," he said. "I have an eight-o-four out on Highway 64."

"Do you need back-up?" the woman's voice said.

"No back-up required," the officer said. He hung up the mike and turned to me in the back seat. "Miss, will you please complete the test?" he said.

"I only had one glass of wine," I said.

"Then you have nothing to worry about," he said.

"Have I broke the law?" I said. "Have I hurt anybody?"

"You ran through a stop sign, and you were driving after dark without your lights on," he said.

"But nobody was hurt," I said. "I need to get home to cook supper."

"Complete the test," he said, "or I will go ahead and read you your rights."

"You just sure as hell do that," I said. Suddenly I saw how

perfectly things had turned out for Larry. If I was arrested for DWI my lawsuit against him might collapse. A judge or jury could rule in his favor and he would get everything. He would have that trashy country singer with her skinny hips, and custody of the children and maybe the house too. And I would have probation and a suspended sentence. Or maybe a real sentence. And I wouldn't have my license for driving to work. Mama always said I had a nose for bad luck. "If there was one disaster in a barrel of choices, you would pick it," she said.

As the officer reached into the front passenger seat for something, I knew I had to get out of there. I didn't have time to think. I just knew I had to go before he made me breathe into that stinky little machine. I hurled myself through the door and jumped onto the shoulder. Another truck shot by and hot wind off the pavement stunned my face. I tasted grit on my lips. If I could make it back to my car I might get away, might get off on a dirt road and disappear into the woods.

But I had started running in the wrong direction behind the police car. I had gotten turned around, and the cop was behind me. He shouted, "Stop right there."

It was completely dark off the road. I would have to get away from the highway if I was to escape the cop. The headlights of an oncoming car appeared, and I jumped off the shoulder into the ditch.

"Stop, or you'll be guilty of resisting arrest," the young trooper shouted. His flashlight shot past my head into the brush. My feet rattled and tinkled on bottles and cans in the ditch. The ditch was full of litter.

I jumped up the bank and brush slapped my face. I elbowed away scrub pines and briars and some kind of vine. Luckily I had put on my sneakers when I left work. I tried to remember what was along the highway here. I'd driven by a hundred times. Was it open fields or pine woods behind the old filling station? I hoped it was pine woods, for then I could lose myself. When I was a girl I sometimes ran in the woods. I could out-run anybody. And when we played hide and seek I'd disappear into the brush and nobody could find me.

But beyond the scrub and briars which tore my dress and stockings I hit a stalk of some kind, and then another. Something heavy and hard hit my hip. I was in a cornfield that hadn't been picked yet. It was hard to run through cornstalks without being heard. My only hope was to get far enough ahead of the officer to stop and hide. But the ground was uneven and stalks slapped me in the chest and in the face. My feet were getting caked with the wet dirt.

Once I had tried to get away from Larry, and he had caught me at the edge of the yard and grabbed me by the waist and carried me kicking and clawing back to the house and into the bedroom. This trooper was much bigger than Larry, and much younger.

"Stop right there," the officer shouted.

I wondered if he had his gun out. Would he shoot me if I didn't stop? I wished he would shoot me. It would be such a quick, sweet solution to my mess. If I couldn't make it to the pine woods I would just as soon he shot me in the head. Except that if I was shot, then Larry would get the children forever, and remind them I was killed while drunk, trying to escape the law.

I stopped in my tracks and let the patrolman catch up with me. He was out of breath and so was I. "You shouldn't have done that," he said. "It will go into the record that you tried to escape."

"And then I gave myself up," I said. My feet were wet and mud caked on my shoes made me feel crippled as we stumbled back across the field dodging cornstalks. He held me by my upper left arm, in a grip tight as a blood pressure cuff.

"I'm afraid for my children," I said. But he didn't answer.

I guess he had been trained not to get personal with those he stopped. I tore my clothes and scratched my legs even more on briars as we climbed down into the ditch. When we got to the patrol car he told me to get into the back seat again.

"But I'm all wet and muddy," I said. I wanted to show him how considerate I was.

"Doesn't matter," he said.

"We can get in my car," I said.

"Just do as I say," he said. He almost clenched his teeth as he talked, to show how in control he was.

I have usually been able to get along with men by showing how sympathetic I am. But this young policeman resisted all notes of intimacy I put in my voice.

"Do you refuse the test?" he said, and held the instrument out to me once I was seated in the back of the cruiser. My feet ground mud into the carpeted floor.

"I'll take your damned test," I said. I reached for the Breath-alyzer and blew long and hard into the mouthpiece. When I ran out of air I gulped and blew again, like I was playing a trumpet. I bulged out my cheeks to make it look like I was exploding, but the officer didn't laugh. When I handed the toy back to him he examined it under a light on the dash and wrote something down on his clipboard.

"Well, how did I do?" I said.

"You have a blood alcohol content of .013," he said.

"Is that good or bad?" I said, and added a giggle.

"You are over the legal limit," he said.

"But just a teensy bit," I said.

"You have the right to remain silent," he said, reciting the words the way they do on television. "Anything you say may be...."

"Okay, okay," I said. I pushed my back against the seat to show how pissed I was.

"I'm going to leave you here for a moment," he said, "while I get some information off your car."

"I have my groceries in the trunk," I said.

He closed the door but the lights stayed on inside the car. I watched him in the glare of the headlights walk up to my car and start going through the trunk and backseat. Did he think I was carrying drugs or concealing weapons? Larry usually carried a pistol and some pills in his glove compartment. But I didn't even have any aspirin.

It occurred to me the cop was looking for drugs or money he could seize and sell. He could be a rogue cop, or maybe not a cop at all but someone posing as a state trooper to rob or kidnap people. That was why he had not asked for back-up. He had stolen both the car and the uniform. He had thought I was carrying a load of marijuana or heroin, and he was hoping to confiscate it. Maybe he was planning to kidnap me and ask for a ransom. Maybe he wanted to hold me in some remote place as a sex slave, someone to torture in kinky ways.

The air in the car spun around, and I thought I was going to faint. The air washed against my face like it was coming in an avalanche. I reached out to steady myself in the blast from the car's heater.

Get hold of your silly self, I said.

My best hope was to use the radio to call the real highway patrol. It was my duty to let them know what was going on. It would make me look good in my lawsuit with Larry if I did a citizen's duty and helped them catch the outlaw.

I jumped out of the car and opened the front door. As soon as I was in the passenger seat I reached for the mike on its holder, grasped the device and pulled it to me, stretching the spiral cord. "I want to report a kidnapping," I said. There was no answer. "I want to report a kidnapping," I said.

And then I saw the button on the mike. I pressed the button and there was the crackle of static. "I want to report a kidnapping," I shouted.

"What car is this?" a voice said.

"This is —" I tried to remember the number the cop had used. "This is car Number 74," I said.

"Who is speaking, please?" the dispatcher said.

"This is Sallie Evans," I shouted into the mike, "and I'm being held prisoner in car Number 74."

There was a pause on the other end. Then a man's voice came on. "Lt. Williams speaking," he said. "Can you tell me what you are doing in car 74? Over."

"I was stopped for nothing by this guy who claimed to be a state trooper," I said, out of breath.

"What were you arrested for?" the lieutenant said.

"I had forgot to turn my lights on," I said.

"You stay right there," the man said.

"I have three children waiting at home, and my groceries are in my trunk," I said.

"You just stay there, Ma'am," the lieutenant said.

"How can I go anywhere? I'm locked in this car," I yelled.

"Someone will be there shortly," the man said.

"They damned well better be," I said. "I'm a taxpayer and a single mother, and you can't treat me this way."

"What way is that?" the man said.

Just then the driver's side door opened and the patrolman tried to grab the mike out of my hand. I jerked away and shouted into the receiver, "He's assaulting me!"

The cop wrenched the mike out of my hand and said into it, "Please send some back-up."

I hit him on the side of the head with my fist. It felt like my hand was broke his head was so hard.

"I will have to handcuff you," he said.

"The hell you will," I screamed.

He backed out of the front seat and stood in the open door. He reached for a pair of handcuffs on his belt. I knew it would take him a few seconds to go around to the passenger side. If he got the cuffs on me I was finished.

Just as he rounded the front of the car I started to open the passenger door. I clawed at the handle and got it open and rolled out into the weeds on the shoulder and down into the ditch. And then I stumbled to my feet and began running.

This time I knew better than to try escaping through the field. The trooper had proved he was so much bigger than me he could run me down. I climbed out of the ditch and started down the highway.

"Come back," the trooper called. "You will get hit."

Headlights were approaching on the highway, and I ran toward them waving my arms. "Help!" I shouted in the blinding glare. The beams were so bright they bleached the air.

I stepped on the edge of the pavement and a horn sounded a sour, stretched note as the vehicle swerved around me.

"You stop right there," the patrolman shouted.

I looked back and saw another car coming from the other direction. I would just have time to make it into the far lane before it reached us. I spun around and crossed the highway and stood in the oncoming lane. The blast of the headlights scalded my face and the brightness scorched my eyes. My legs were trembling as I waved my arms. "Help me!" I screamed. "Help me, this man is a kidnapper!"

There was a scream of brakes as the lights got closer and closer, as if in slow motion. As the lights almost washed over me I turned away and looked in the other direction. Headlights soared at me in that lane also. If I jumped out of the left lane into the right I would be hit by an oncoming car from town.

I wheeled around and saw the first set of headlights almost on top of me. Brakes hissed and a truck horn blared. I put my arm up to block out the searing lights. I felt like I was going to fall, and stumbled sideways.

Someone took me by the arm, and I saw it was the young trooper. I tried to pull away, but he held me in a powerful grip. Cars and trucks were stopped in both directions, with motors revving and people shouting. I was dizzy and sick at my stomach. When we got to the shoulder traffic started moving again, very slowly. The air stank of exhaust.

"What are you doing, officer?" someone shouted from a car window.

"Keep moving," the policeman hollered. He held my arm with both his hands.

What rammed up into my throat was driven like a jolt of lightning. It came with no warning, and I tasted the sour wine and crumbs of cheese and crackers in the back of my mouth and in my nose. I tried to lean over as the vomit sprayed from my mouth, but the officer thought I was trying to escape and jerked me around so the puke went right onto the front of his shirt and down onto his crotch.

I heaved again. I wanted to heave out all the poison and pain I had taken in. I wanted to throw up the confusion and frustration, the humiliation Larry had given me. I needed to empty myself of the horror of nausea, of the terror the patrolman had made me feel. I vomited again and again, and the trooper held me over the ditch so I wouldn't get any more on his fine pants and shoes. But his shoes were already muddy from the run through the cornfield. As I threw up I wished somebody would hold my forehead.

～ · ～ · ～

When I finally stopped heaving and stood up, my face was

streaming with sweat and tears filled my eyes. The roots of my hair were damp. I tried to wipe my mouth with my sleeve, but the trooper was holding my arm too tight.

Cars passed us slowly, as people tried to see what was going on. "Are you finished?" the cop said.

I guess vomiting is a kind of shock treatment. I felt like I was waking from a nightmare. I was so weak my knees wobbled and my teeth chattered. But getting all the wine out of my belly made my head clearer. My eyes were wet and my nose snuffed up. I must have gotten a little vomit up my nose. But the sickness had scrubbed the world and made it firm again.

"I need to sit down," I said, almost too weak to talk.

The trooper led me slowly to his car and helped me into the back seat. He put the handcuffs on me and locked the back doors. Then he got into the driver's seat and picked up the mike.

"All I had was a glass of wine with a friend," I said. "Have you never had a glass of wine?"

"Tell your story to a jury," he said. He wiped the front of his shirt with a handkerchief.

"I have children waiting at home," I said.

"I'm sympathetic," the patrolman said, "but the fact is you were driving drunk."

"Don't you have any conscience?" I said. "I didn't hurt anybody."

"But you might have," he said, holding the mike ready to push the button.

"What is your name?" I said.

"Officer Stallworthy," he said.

"Don't you have a first name, Officer Stallworthy?" I was getting some strength back into my voice.

"My name is Jerold," he said. He rubbed down the crotch of his pants with the handkerchief.

"Have you never done anything, Jerold?" I said. "Have you never made any little mistake?"

"You will have the opportunity to tell your story to the court," Officer Stallworthy said.

"Have you never been in trouble?" I said.

A tractor trailer passed so fast its wind rocked the police car.

"That truck is speeding," I said. "He's doing something more dangerous than I was. Yet that driver will get home free tonight and sleep in his own bed."

"I'm sorry," the trooper said.

"My husband left me for a slut that sings country music," I said. "I have three children to support."

The patrolman got a box of kleenex out of the glove compartment and wiped the insides of his pants legs and the tops of his shoes. As he finished with each kleenex he stuffed the soiled tissue in a plastic bag. The mike lay on the seat beside him.

"Can't you be human for once and just let me go home to my children," I said. "I didn't hurt anybody."

"You're under arrest," he said.

"I have a week's groceries in the trunk," I said. "My children don't even have any groceries."

"You should have gone on home," he said, "instead of drinking wine with your friend."

"Don't you think I know that?" I said. "Don't you think I have said that to myself a thousand times?"

A Greyhound bus roared by, lit up like a ship at sea. I wished I was on it, with a ticket as long as a jump-rope.

Officer Stallworthy picked up the microphone and said, "This is car Number 74."

"Where are you, car 74?" the lieutenant said.

"I'm still on Highway 64," the patrolman said. "I have made an arrest for DWI and I'm bringing her in."

"What is the individual's name?" the lieutenant said.

"Don't tell him," I said.

"Sallie Evans of 347 River Road," the trooper said.

"Now I'm finished," I said. "If I lose my license I can't get to work."

"Is the individual in custody?" the lieutenant said.

"The subject is under arrest," Officer Stallworthy said.

"Another car is on the way," the lieutenant said.

"Send it back," Stallworthy said. "I have everything here under control. We'll be in shortly." He hung up the mike.

"Are you proud of yourself?" I said.

"I'm just a public employee doing his job," he said and started the engine.

"Did you have a mother?" I said. There were tears in my eyes again.

"Yes, I had a mother," he said.

"What if your mother was arrested on the way home with groceries?" I said.

"My mother worked in a cotton mill," he said. "She worked in a cotton mill to raise four children."

There was a matter-of-factness about his statement that was unanswerable. I tried to think of something else to say. I had no influence over him. He had already given headquarters my name. It was too late to change anything. I belched up bile into the back of my mouth. There was just the faintest taste of the Portuguese wine in the brash.

"Will you at least let me take the groceries to my children?" I said.

"Where do you live?" he said.

"You have the address," I said, "347 River Road."

"I'll take the groceries to them," he said.

I leaned back on the seat and rested my head on the cushion. That at least was something. Jamie would have something to cook, until I could get home, until I could arrange bail. I might as well relax for the moment. I was under arrest and there was nothing else I could do.

The Balm of Gilead Tree

I WOULDN'T SAY I NOTICED a thing unusual at first. There were airplanes coming in and taking off most of the day, and the new road was right under their path. It was the height of tourist season, and the sun was so bright you didn't want to glance up at the sky anyway. I wanted to look into the shade of the trees beyond the highway construction, and forget about the awful heat, and the headache I'd had all day.

"Hey look at that," Roy hollered. He was pulling up the surveyor's markers and throwing them into the foreman's pickup. "He's going to hit."

I looked to where he pointed. The airliner was coming in from the south, probably the flight from Atlanta. It was a DC-9 with its flaps down, slowing for landing. I knew what kind of plane it was because I had flown on them when I was in the service. With the sun high in the sky you couldn't see much else about the plane. It was near two o'clock and I still had that heavy feeling from eating my bologna sandwiches too fast. And the headache wouldn't go away. I wished I had some aspirin.

"He's going to do it," Brad said. Brad stopped with a load of dirt in his shovel raised about a foot off the ground. My eyes stung with sweat and the bright light, but I saw it too. It was one of those little private planes—bigger than a Piper

323

Cub, a Cessna—coming from the west and headed directly toward where the airliner was going.

"My God," Joey the foreman said. He was tinkering with his transit beside the pickup. "I don't believe it," he said. I guess everybody on the job was looking up there, except maybe the earthmover and bulldozer drivers who couldn't hear anything and had to keep their eyes on the grading markers.

"Aye God," I said, sounding like my Uncle Albert without meaning to. It just came out.

"He *ain't* going to do it," Roy said.

It felt like electric shock jolted through me as the little plane came on. It stretched on and on toward the airliner, seeming to rip the sky in front of it.

"The Lord have mercy," Joey said.

It didn't seem possible. I expected the big plane to turn aside, or the little plane to bank and dive, or suddenly climb. But both pilots must have been blind. It all happened in a second or two, but it seemed to take hours. I couldn't watch. I had flown in planes in the army, all the way to Vietnam and back, and I thought of those people up there, in the clean air conditioning, just having finished lunch and thinking they were about to arrive in the mountains. Women in their fine clothes and perfume and men in business suits and double-knits in the middle of August, and kids with toys in their laps.

"Aye God," I said, and raised my shovel like I was trying to push the little plane away. Dirt slid off the blade onto my sweaty arms and chest just as the two planes touched and turned into a fireball bigger than the sun. I don't remember if there was any noise or not. Maybe the sound of the motors continued even after the collision.

The fire just hung there in the sky for a second, and then the two planes pulled apart. The little Cessna went down like somebody had dropped it. It fluttered into pieces that wobbled. I didn't see it hit except out of the corner of my eye because I was watching the DC-9 as it swung away from the impact in a steep curve, carrying the fire on its back, but not spiraling.

"They's people falling," Roy said. And sure enough, we saw the dots and little figures thrown from the burning plane. At first it looked like debris from the explosion, but you could see the tiny arms and legs.

"God-damn," Brad said.

Suddenly the tail of the plane broke off and more people spilled like seeds out of a pod. And the two main sections of the aircraft dropped like somebody had pitched them. They fell among scraps and burning pieces all the way down the sky. I thought at first they were falling right on top of us, but as they descended it was clear they were going to the south, further down the new road-way. As they fell the pieces seemed to get further and further away, and by the time they hit in showers of fire, they looked about two miles down the road, down the river of red clay and machinery.

"God-damn," Brad said again.

"Let's go," Roy said. He jumped into the cab of the foreman's pickup and started the engine. Brad and me threw down our shovels and climbed into the back.

"Hey," Joey called. But Roy ignored him. Roy and Joey had been playing a game of chicken all summer. Roy would see how much he could get away with without being fired. Joey would see if he could act superior to Roy by not losing his temper and not cussing. We had all gone to high school together and played football together. But Joey had stayed out of the draft by taking a course in engineering at the community college, and when we got out of the service he was foreman on the new highway job.

The roadbed was graded dirt, and Roy had to swing the pickup around bulldozers and fuel tanks and piles of crushed rock. Some of the earthmovers were still working and we almost hit one as it lurched across the bed with its belly full of dirt and both front and back engines blasting diesel smoke.

"Watch out," Brad hollered, and beat on the cab with his fist. But what we had to worry about most was other vehicles racing down the soft roadbed. Dozens of people on the job site headed just where we were. And people from town and from the shopping centers had seen the crash and were driving in the same direction.

"People is going crazy," Brad said.

We had to hold on because Roy was hitting rocks and bumps and piles of dirt that hadn't been smoothed. The new road looked like bomb craters in places, a shelled zone. Roy hit a caterpillar track that had been left rusting in the dirt, but he kept going. It was further to the crash than we had thought.

The first body we came to Roy slammed on the brakes. A farm truck loaded with hampers of pole beans roared past us raising the orange dust. "Damn buzzards," Brad called after it. Nobody but those building the road were supposed to be on the site. The headache pulsed like a strobe light under my hardhat.

Roy got to the body first. It was an elderly woman with blue looking hair. She was lying on her side with a shoulder drove into the ground. Her glasses lay in the dirt nearby, looking like they had been tossed there. Her dress was thrown up over her thighs and you could see the straps of her garter belt.

Roy rolled her over and felt for her pulse. Her eyes were open and a thin line of blood ran from the corner of her mouth. "She's dead," he said.

"No shit," Brad said. "She just fell a mile out of the sky."

I bent down to look at her, and when I straightened up I felt dizzy from my headache and the blinding sun. Cars and pickups, jeeps and tractors, whined over the rough dirt toward the black smoke of the wreck. I saw another body about a hundred yards ahead, right at the edge of the highway cut, half in the weeds. "Can't do her any good," I said, and started running. I tried to think of what first aid I could remember from the army, in case any of the bodies was still alive. I glanced back at Roy and Brad and they had started going through the old woman's pockets and purse. For the first time it came to me why so many people were running to the crash. We all wanted to get there first, before any authorities arrived and secured the area. I ran up the bank to the edge of the construction.

It was the body of a businessman that lay half in the weeds and half in the graded dirt. There's a sad dry look to dirt and weeds in late summer, and the body had fell right against some blackberry briars. The berries were ripe and splattered and I couldn't tell at first what was berry juice and what was blood. The man was laying face down in the weeds and I rolled him over. The face was mashed in a little, nose flattened, and the eyes popping out with dirt and trash stuck to them. He was dead as a door bolt. There wasn't a thing I could do for him. A bad smell rose from the body, like it had just farted. His suit coat had been ripped at the arms, maybe by the explosion or by the wind when he was falling. I lifted his wrist to feel the pulse and his watch was cold as if it had been in a refrigerator. It was still cool from the air conditioning in the plane.

I was really sweating from the heat and running, and from the headache. I reached into his coat pocket to get his wallet. I knew businessmen did not keep wallets in their hip pockets, but in their breast pockets. I thought, I'll just see what his name is. He had this fancy wallet made of madras cloth and rimmed with gold on the corners. I opened it and there was his driver's license and a bunch of credit cards and pictures of kids. The license said "Jeremy Kincaid," and the address was in Aiken, South Carolina. I looked in the bill compartment and there was a sheaf of twenties, and behind them a couple of fifties and a single hundred. I thought, I'll just leave this here for his wife and kids. And then I thought, somebody else will go and take it. Might as well be me.

The whole road was crawling with people far as I could see. More were arriving in trucks and cars, on motorcycles. In the distance I could hear a siren, and then the donkey horn of a fire truck. The bills felt cool and new. Cold cash I thought. A cool million, as they say. It amazes me sometimes how people have already thought of everything. I took out the bills and put the wallet back in the coat. His family will get all the insurance money, I thought. And none of this would ever get back to them anyway. I folded the bills like pages of a little book and slid them in the pocket of my sweaty jeans. Then I thought of the credit cards and reached back into the wallet for the shiny plastic. But I saw they were useless. I'd have to forge Mr. Kincaid's signature on any charges, and I didn't want any of that.

"Hot damn," I said and stood up. The headache crashed down on me. I'd had headaches ever since I got back from the army. I wished I had some cool headache powders, some Stanback or aspirin. People swarmed over every inch of the highway, among the earthmovers and bulldozers, backhoes, between piles of dirt and holes dug for culverts. Somebody had left a tractor running.

I saw there was no way to look further in the highway site. The smoke of the wreck seemed to come from a field or apple orchard to the left, toward the Dana Road. I ran out through the weeds in that direction. The blackberry briars reached out and clawed as I passed. I had to stomp down catbriars and hogweeds, big ironweeds and the first goldenrods. I could see people ahead running out through the brush and into the trees, like they were racing each other.

Cold cash, I kept saying to myself in the terrible heat. I thought of cool sharp-edged bills that would slice a finger and I thought of a whole plateful of fifty dollar bills served like a feast, and the filling station I would buy to get out of construction work, and the mechanics courses I would take at the community college. Ever since I got out of the army I'd had to work so hard I couldn't make use of the GI Bill. I thought of my girlfriend Diane in her cool lavender shorts and how we could get married and build a beauty shop next to the filling station and she could get out of the hot basement at Woolworth's. Diane was the prettiest woman I'd ever seen, and we had been engaged since last year. I thought of us under the cool sheets at night. She deserved a beauty shop and I deserved a filling station. Enough for a down payment, and the bank would loan us the rest.

Suddenly I saw somebody bent over in the weeds ahead of me. It looked like an animal pawing carrion, a big dog or a bear. But it was a man's back rising and falling. I was going to run around him. I didn't care what he was doing. But he had already heard me and looked around. He was a big red-faced fellow that was almost bald, and he was wearing the brown uniform of a delivery man. I think it was a bread company. He was one of those men who drive bread trucks.

"Hot dog," he said. He was going through the pockets of a boy and had found a wallet. He had the boy's watch already and he was fumbling with bills in the fold of the wallet. "Hot dog," he said. "What a way to get a case of chiggers."

I run around him still headed toward the smoke, and he looked at me like he wanted to stop me, like he didn't want anybody to get ahead of him. "Hey boy," he hollered. "You ain't trying to hog it all for yourself are you?" I ignored him and ran on.

There was a fence with a hedgerow in front of me. I was looking for an easy way through the barbed wire when I saw the body in a post-oak tree. The body was caught in the limbs about twelve feet off the ground. Some of the branches had broke but the body was stuck there. I thought of climbing the tree. I grabbed the ends of a limb and tried to shake it loose. But the body had lodged between the branches and would not slide off.

I looked around for a stick or pole to push it loose. The bald-headed man in the brown uniform was running toward me and I figured if I could just get the body down before he reached the fence it was mine. There was a dead poplar sapling leaning in the hedgerow and I jumped on it with both feet. But it didn't break; it was still rooted in the dirt.

"Hey hog," the bread truck driver hollered. "You can't claim all of them." He had a look in his eyes, like he didn't hardly care what he was doing.

"You stay away," I said.

"*You* stay away," he said. He reached up for the oak limb and tried to shake the body loose. He shook the tree like he was trying to make acorns fall.

The second time I jumped on the poplar it broke. I snapped off the tip and had a pole about ten feet long. "You stand back, bastard," the bald-headed man said. He took a hawk-bill knife out of his back pocket, the kind of knife you use to cut cardboard or linoleum.

"I'll cut your balls off," he said, holding the knife with one hand and jerking the oak limb with the other. I swung the pole

330

and hit him on the back of the head. He went down like a sandbag in the weeds. "Bastard yourself," I said, but he was out cold.

With the pole I knocked the body in the tree loose and it fell almost beside the bread truck driver. The arms and legs were turned wrong, where they had been broke when they hit the post-oak. The man looked about seventy and was wearing a Hawaiian shirt. There wasn't more than forty dollars in his billfold, but he had a book of traveler's checks in his pocket. I tried to think if you could spend traveler's checks, but they were already signed in one corner and I threw them in the weeds. I was about to run on when I noticed the great bulge in the bald man's uniform pocket. I reached in and pulled out what must have been a wad of a hundred twenty dollar bills. I would leave him his wallet and whatever he had that was his. But I would take the wad because he had threatened me with the knife.

On the other side of the hedgerow was a bunch-bean field. It had been standing in water earlier in the summer and most of the vines had turned yellow. The ground looked painted with baked silt, like the bottom of a dried puddle. There were suitcases and overnight bags fallen among the vines, most of them busted open. I looked through some of them, but they were mostly just shirts and blouses, hair brushes, women's shoes. I didn't even see any jewelry.

There was a piece of blackened airplane lying in the row, still smoking. It smelled of burnt fuel. It looked like a piece of the DC-9 with a shattered window.

There was a whole lot of sirens now, coming from all directions. And there were voices, and horns honking. I knew the police would arrive any second. I heard a helicopter coming from somewhere. That really reminded me of the army. But at no time in Nam had I seen this many bodies.

331

There was a woman on her knees in the bean rows near the creek, and I thought she must be picking over a body or a suitcase. I saw her out of the corner of my eye and avoided going in that direction. But after I went through ten or fifteen pieces of luggage and found only one purse with seventy dollars in it I looked her way again. She hadn't moved, and she was leaning in a peculiar way. Her back was twisted.

I ran over there and saw the strangest thing I'd seen all day. She was sunk in the soft dirt by the creek up to her knees. She had fell out of the sky standing up and drove into the ground like a stake. Her face was stretched from the impact. Her necklace had broke off and was lying in the dirt. It looked like diamonds. I didn't see a pocketbook. It spooked me to look at her face with the eyes pushing out. My headache thundered louder. I grabbed up the necklace and ran on.

To go toward the smoke of the wreck I had to cross the creek. The stream was low from the late summer drought and almost hid by weeds. Mud from the highway construction lined the banks, and the creek itself seemed one long pool through the level bottom land. It was green stagnant water, a dead pool, like a coma of water poisoned by bean spray and weed killer. There was no easy way to cross. A snake slid down a limb and plopped into the water. A scum like green hair and paint floated on the top.

I didn't see any way to cross except walk right into the creek, so I splashed in. I was halfway across and the water up to my chest when I bumped into something. The body must have been floating just under the surface for when I touched it it turned over and the face shot right up in my face. It was a man whose head had been burned and his brains had busted out. I pushed the body away and crossed the creek quick as I could.

I climbed up the other bank brushing moss and green scum off my jeans. The water smelled sour but I didn't pay it any

mind. When I broke through the tall weeds I was at the edge
of a field of apple trees. The wreck was burning still further
on, beyond another hedgerow. I could hear people hollering
and sirens in that direction. I figured I would stay away from
where the crowd was. The orchard seemed to be full of bodies
and pieces of the wreck.

It was a young orchard which meant there were wide spaces
around trees and you could see a long way between rows.
There were dozens of people picking through the rows. I figured
if I moved quick through the trees I wouldn't be any more
noticeable than the rest. I hoped I didn't see anybody I knew.
I hoped I didn't see Roy and Brad again.

The orchard had been plowed once that summer, which
meant there was an open break of red dirt around each of the
trees. The ground had baked hard and rough. Weeds rose right
out of the unplowed ground into the limbs. The trees were
loaded with green apples. The spray looked white and silver
on the fruit. I had been raised in an apple orchard down near
Saluda and it sickened me to think of the sweat that had gone
into that grove. You grafted and fertilized, pruned and waited,
sprayed and plowed, and still a late frost or early frost, a bee-
tle or fungus, drought or wet summer, could ruin you. A hail-
storm, a flood, a plane crash, a drop in the market price, could
wipe you out. You have to fight, I said to myself. I thought of
the filling station and the beauty shop I would build.

∾ · ∾ · ∾

The sirens were getting closer, and growing in number. It
sounded like all the fire trucks and patrol cars and ambu-
lances in the world were screaming and wailing. I was glad I
had got off the road, but I had to work fast. The fire truck
horns were blasting toward the column of smoke and car horns
answered the sirens.

"Clear the area, clear the area," a voice thundered out of the sky. I looked up and saw the chopper. It was the sheriff's chopper, the one they used to look for marijuana fields in the mountain coves.

"Clear the area, clear the area," the voice boomed again, rattled by static on the loudspeaker. I could feel the wind off the blades washing over the apple trees, fluttering leaves and shaking green apples. For a second I thought they were going to land and try to arrest me. I kept my head down in case they were taking pictures. The heat of the wind and the pulse of my headache made me feel I had slipped through a time warp. If they landed I could try to run for the woods at the other end of the orchard. Then I realized they couldn't land among the apple trees. They were trying to scare people away from the wreck.

The helicopter tilted and swung away ahead of me. I gave it the finger; but there wasn't much time. I ran around a tree and there was this old couple in Bermuda shorts bent over a body. Their straw hats and sunglasses told me they were tourists from Miami. The mountains had been overrun by retirees from south Florida ever since I was a kid. They filled up the streets and highways with their long Cadillacs, driving in the middle of the road. "They come up here with a dollar and one shirt and don't change either," my Uncle Albert liked to say. Aye God.

They were crouching over the body and the old woman jumped when she heard me coming. She had on thick red lipstick and make-up. "We were just trying to see if we could help," she said.

"You go right ahead," I said.

"Is there nothing anybody can do?" the man said. He was holding his right hand behind his back. He must have taken the wallet from the body and hadn't had time to slip out the bills.

"We're just trying to help," the woman said.

"You all go right ahead," I said. I ran past them and they watched me like they expected to be mugged.

There was a piece of the private plane laying up against an apple tree. It was a part of the cockpit. The fuselage had been sheared like it was cut with a torch. The metal was blackened but not burning. I thought I saw a face behind the window and I ran closer. It was a face, and I lifted the torn section of the plane to free the body. But I instantly wished I had left it alone. It was a little boy about eight years old. The half of his face I had seen through the window was unmarked, but the other half had been sliced off by the impact. The kid never saw what hit him. Nothing I had glimpsed in the infantry was more sickening. I dropped the section of the Cessna and ran.

"You will clear the area," a voice said over a bullhorn. It was from a police car cruising around the perimeter of the orchard. "Looters will be arrested." I crouched down behind an apple tree until the flashing lights were past. It made me think of those preachers' cars with loudspeakers, one horn pointing forward and one backward on top of the car.

Got to fight, I said to myself. You've got to fight. It's what I said to myself for a whole year in the army. It's what I said to myself as a boy working in the orchard, in the heat and mud and stinging spray.

"We're sweeping the area and arresting looters," the loudspeaker crackled.

There were bodies and pieces of bodies all over the orchard. I ran quick as I could from one to the other, avoiding the people like it was a game of hide and seek. Flies were finding the torn limbs in the weeds.

There was a beautiful stewardess still in pieces of her uniform, but she didn't have either jewelry or a billfold on her. She had fallen into the lower limbs of a spreading apple tree and looked like she had gone to sleep there.

Some bodies were naked, but I avoided those, not only because I knew there wouldn't be any money on them but because it was embarrassing to get close. I didn't want to be seen looking at naked corpses, and I didn't want to see myself doing it either.

My pockets were stuffed with cash, some of it slightly burned, some of it bloody, some of it dirty. Some of the money had been soaked in diesel fuel. I found more and more businessmen, but most of them had credit cards and little money. The women carried more cash in their purses. I threw away a lot of traveler's checks. I found bodies that had already been searched.

I was nearing the edge of the orchard and getting closer to the smoke and the gathering sirens. There was another hedgerow, and then a field where the main part of the wreck seemed to have come down.

"Clear the area immediately," the bullhorn blasted. "All looters will be arrested. It is a federal offense to tamper with an airplane crash."

I dashed out of the orchard and across the haulroad. A pink lady's purse lay in the brush against the hedgerow. I was about to reach for the handle when a black bullet shot in front of my face. And then I saw the hornets' nest about the size of a peck bucket behind the purse. The falling pocketbook had knocked off a section of the nest and the hornets boiled out of the hole. They hummed and shocked the air like ten thousand volts.

The purse was made of soft pink leather. I just knew it was full of money. But it was dangerous to get near a nest that big, especially if they were all riled up. Ten hornet stings can kill you, can put you to sleep forever. There must have been a thousand in that nest.

"Everybody clear the area," the loudspeaker said. "Only

members of the volunteer fire department should be in the area. They will be wearing red armbands. All others will be arrested."

I thought I might have ten minutes before they got to me. The cruiser with flashing lights was circling back on the haulroad. I wiped the sweat out of my eyes and watched the hornets circle. The handbag lay among the weeds and baked late summer dirt.

As I broke a twig off the tree above my head and brought it to my lips I smelled the aroma. It was Balm of Gilead. The bright spicy smell woke me up from the heat and reminded me of the tree by the old house down at Saluda. The twig smelled like both medicine and candy.

Somebody was coming. There were voices and it sounded like the volunteer firemen were already sweeping the area. Of course they would take everything they could find for themselves, same as the cops would. Wasn't any reason to leave the money for them, money that would never get to heaven or hell with the owners, or to the rightful heirs.

I had heard boys brag about breaking off a limb with a hornets' nest on it and running down the mountainside so fast the hornets couldn't sting them. But I never believed them. A hornet can fly faster than the eye can see, and these were already boiling. I didn't have any smoke to blow on them, and I couldn't wait till dark. And I didn't have a cloth to throw over them either.

I took the red bandanna off my neck and wrapped it around my left hand and wrist. The hardhat would protect part of my head. I grabbed the handle of the purse and jerked away, but the first hornet popped me on the shoulder and another got me on the elbow. I ran hard as I could through the weeds. A hornet sting always hits you in two stages. First the prick of the stinger, and then the real jolt of the poison squirting home. A hornet must release its venom with powerful pressure because it always feels like you've stopped a bullet or had a bone broke and your flesh rings with the pain. I got hit twice more.

I ran along the haulroad like a scalded dog until I didn't hear the hornets circling anymore. There were voices on the other side of the ditch and I dropped down behind a sumac bush. The heat was terrible. It magnified the pain of the stings and speeded the ache of the poison through me. A hornet sting makes your bones and joints feel sick. It makes you feel old with rheumatism.

But my headache didn't seem as bad. I had heard people say you could cure a headache with a bee sting, but I never believed it. Most likely the hurt of the sting makes you forget the headache. But there was no doubt the throb in my head was fading. I thought of the cool frosty powders of aspirin, and looked up at the snowy edge of a cloud far above me.

The voices on the other side of the hedgerow got closer and I hunkered deeper under the sumacs and the Balm of Gilead trees. There must have been a whole row of the trees, which is real unusual. I tried to quiet my breathing by chewing a twig. In the shade I could smell myself, the sweat from work in the sun and running, and the raw smell of fear and pain from the stings. My sweat dripped all over the soft leather handbag. It was the most expensive leatherwork I had ever seen. Every seam was rounded and the stitching was concealed. It was leather made for royalty.

At first I didn't see anything inside but a compact and lipstick, some keys to a Mercedes and a bottle of perfume. There was a wallet with credit cards in the slots but I didn't find but thirty dollars in the bill compartment. I started to throw them all out in the weeds, but that seemed disrespectful, though I couldn't explain why. The woman was dead and wouldn't need her purse again. There was a driver's license that identified her as a resident of Coral Gables, Florida. I pushed aside the little bottle of mouthwash, the cellophane wrapped peppermint candies, a couple of unmailed letters, and was about to give up when I saw the zipper almost concealed under a flap of shiny lining. I unzipped the pocket and felt inside. I touched edges that seemed stiff and sharp as razor blades. I got my finger around the packet and pulled it out. There was a wad of folded bills, brand-new bills, some twenties, some fifties, and some hundreds. It was the old woman's stash for her vacation in the mountains. The bills were starched with newness, the green and black inks printed in biting freshness, with some serial numbers and seals in blue. What fine cloth money is, I thought. There must have been over three thousand dollars in the folded pages. They were like a new printed book, every page crisp. I stuffed them in my pocket, deep so they wouldn't fall out.

All my pockets were full of bills and jewelry. If I found anything else I'd have to stuff it in my underwear, though that was dangerous for it might fall out. Better to stuff money in my boots. I took the red bandanna off my hand and tied it around my right arm. It probably wouldn't work, but if anybody stopped me I could claim I was a volunteer fireman.

There were shouts from the direction of the crash. The fire trucks wailed and somebody was on the bullhorn again. I could see lights flashing through the hedgerow. "Clear the area, the area must be cleared," the voice echoed across the fields and back from barns. A patrol passed on the other side of the ditch not more than fifteen feet away. They could see me if they looked close. "Whatever we get we will divide up," one of the men was saying.

I had to think fast. If I was stopped by the firemen they would just take everything I had found. There were too many of them, and they would claim I was looting, or resisted arrest or something. If I was caught by the sheriff or one of the troopers they would either take what I had or beat me up with their clubs, or both.

I chewed on the spicy twig in my nervousness. I used to do that when I was crouched down hiding from my brother, or waiting for the enemy to move or fire. It seemed to help. The medicine smell of the Balm of Gilead woke me up a little from my worry. There was something about the smell of the bark that reminded me of soft drinks like root beer or Dr. Pepper. I wished I had a cold drink. If I ever got out of there with my money I would celebrate with a case of cold Pepsi.

"This is the U.S. Marshal," a voice said over a loudspeaker. "All who don't leave the site will be arrested. It is a federal offense to loot an airplane crash."

There were shouts and more sirens arriving. A truck horn blasted for a full ten seconds. I waited until the firemen had gone on fifty or seventy-five feet on the other side of the ditch, and then I laid the purse down and stood up. The blood must have drained out of my head because it felt like a shadow had passed over everything. I waited for a few seconds to focus my mind. The stings ached worse than ever, but the headache had gone.

There was nobody in sight and I started walking to the east toward the Dana Road. I figured it was safer if I stayed away from the new highway where all the trucks and cars had converged. I would try to get back to the place we had been working before anybody else did. If I got back soon enough I could put my money in my lunchbox and nobody would ever see it. That's what Bishop the bulldozer driver did when he uncovered a mason jar of money on the pasture hill down at the south end of the county. When they first started building the highway, he had cut into a bank and a fruit jar rolled out, a quart stuffed full of twenties. He got off the dozer and emptied the jar inside his shirt, then threw the jar away. Wouldn't anybody know he got the money except one of the Ward boys saw him. But when the Ward boy told the foreman and they asked Bishop he said he hadn't seen any money, and he showed them his empty shirt. He had already moved the money to his lunchbox and thermos. Wasn't long after that, maybe three months, till he bought a store and fruit stand over near the line and quit driving the bulldozer.

I walked fast as I could without seeming to hurry. A hurry will draw suspicion. I was about a quarter of a mile from the end of the orchard when I saw the red and tan sheriff's car coming down the middle of the grove with all its lights flashing. At the same time I heard the chopper again. I don't know who spotted me first, the patrol car or the helicopter, but the next thing I heard was the bullhorn in the sky, "Hey you there, in the hardhat, stop."

I kept going for a few steps and the bullhorn blasted again, "Stop there, or I'll shoot." I could hear the patrol car whining through the apple trees toward me. The chopper came in closer and its wind hit me like a slap. "Halt there," the voice in the sky said. "You're under arrest."

I wondered if they had seen my bulging pockets. I had to think quick. The haulroad was too narrow for the chopper to land in, but the sheriff's car would run me down in a few seconds. I had to do something or lose everything. The chopper wind smacked at my face.

I dove into the brush and rolled under some sumac bushes. Then I crawled on my elbows through the blackberry briars. The grit cut into my skin. I hadn't crawled like that in years. A moccasin snake plunged into the ditch ahead of me. The water was cloudy with chemicals and moss. I threw down my hardhat and slid in after the snake, and was going to head east, the way I had been running. But I changed my mind and started back the other way, toward the creek. I crawled as fast as I could until the sheriff's car stopped, and then I backed in under some honeysuckle vines and listened.

"Right in front of you," the loudspeaker from the chopper said.

The deputy who got out of the car looked like he had never been out of air conditioning. His shirt was starched and ironed to his back and shoulders. He walked to the brush, peered into the hedgerow. "He went right in there," the voice from the helicopter said.

I wished I had something to darken my face. There was a good chance my skin would shine right through the honey-suckle bushes. I sunk low as I could, almost to my nose in the water. There was green paste thick as pancake batter floating on the surface. I squeezed my lips to keep water out.

"Look right there," the loudspeaker boomed. The wind from the blades shook the leaves of the Balm of Gilead trees and trembled the surface of the water. If the chopper came in lower it might blow the vines aside and expose me.

The deputy parted the sumac bushes and looked into the ditch. He looked like he was afraid ticks and chiggers and snakes and spiders would attack him. He never took his sun-glasses off, otherwise he would have seen me for sure. He looked at the water and paused, and I was certain he had seen me. I could feel the ditch water soaking into my pockets among the wadded bills. Luckily money won't melt. The ditch water was warm as a mud puddle. But the money still felt cool.

"Look to the left," the voice on the bullhorn said.

The deputy peered past the sumac bushes and took out his gun. He must have seen my hardhat. "Come out or I shoot," he said. I pushed back under the vines far as I could. He fired twice and sent the hat skipping into the ditch.

"Look to the left," the voice from the chopper said again. They had seen me running that way and guessed I would continue in that direction. I waited until he had gone forty or fifty feet, and then I slid out of the honeysuckle vines and began crawling on my side through the ditch scum. I didn't have to worry about noise because of the chopper, but if I came out in an open place they would spot me. The chopper hovered just above the deputy.

Another snake slid off a limb, winding like a corkscrew, and disappeared into the cloudy water. I'd heard snakes have trouble biting in water because they can't brace themselves to coil and strike. I hoped that was right. The ditch was full of bottles and cans and all kinds of trash. Everything was covered with a slimy coat of silt. Everything felt like mucus. I could have made it out of sight except there was this burlap erosion dam across the ditch, the kind we're required by law to put around construction sites. They don't do any good, but they're supposed to catch the dirt washing into ditches. The burlap was almost rotten and covered with leaves and dried mud. But it wouldn't tear. I had no choice but to climb over it.

If I stood up they could see me through the hedgerow. The deputy was about a hundred feet away, and the chopper right above him. I hesitated for a moment, but realized I didn't have much time. If they didn't find me in that direction they would come back looking in the other.

I stood up slowly and bent across the dam, and just as I was swinging over the voice from the chopper blasted, "Look over there, look over there." I had took my chance and failed. I was going to have to run for it as best I could and hope they didn't shoot. I wheeled myself over the burlap and started running, but out of the corner of my eye I saw these two boys come out of an orchard row lugging a big suitcase between them. They looked like farm boys, maybe fourteen or fifteen,

343

barefoot and without shirts. They started running back into the orchard and the deputy took after them. "No use to run, boys, no use to run," the voice from the chopper said.

I knew that was the best chance I would have, so I dropped back into the ditch water and crawled on my hands and knees for another hundred feet. There were sirens and horns and screams and loudspeakers from the site of the crash to my left. It sounded like hundreds of people had gathered there now. I couldn't go in that direction, and I couldn't go east to the Dana Road. I had no choice but to head toward the creek, and then to the highway construction.

After crawling another hundred yards I climbed out on the bank and started running. I crossed the haulroad dripping on the scorched weeds and darted into the apple trees. My pants were heavy with wetness and the wet bills weighed in my pockets, but I dashed from tree to tree. I didn't know if the helicopter could see me, but I couldn't pause to find out. I ran like I used to as a kid through the orchard, throwing myself forward into every stride, thrusting my chest out and pushing the edge of the world ahead of me.

As I ran I thought how cool my wet pants were in the wind, and how cool the money in my pockets was even where the wet cloth pinched. I passed a sprayer covered with white chemical frost and swung around it.

It was about a mile to the new road, but I could make it in a few minutes. Another half mile and I would be home free.

This book has been set in Sabon,
designed by Jan Tschichold,
the first and last 'harmonized' typeface,
designed for hand-composition
foundry type, as well as setting by
Linotype and Monotype machines.
In this digital age this book has been
set on a Macintosh G3 using
QuarkXPress 4.04. Printing
by Thomson-Shore, Inc.